Don't Go Baking My Heart

ISLAND BITES

N.G. PELTIER

PIATKUS

PIATKUS

First published in the US in 2022 by N.G. Peltier
First published in Great Britain in 2022 by Piatkus

1 3 5 7 9 10 8 6 4 2

Copyright © 2022 by N.G. Peltier

Cover design: Leni Kauffman
Editing: A.K Edits

A CIP catalogue record for this book
is available from the British Library.

ISBN 978-0-349-42976-2

Printed and bound in Great Britain by Clays Ltd, Elcograf S.p.A.

Papers used by Piatkus are from well-managed forests
and other responsible sources.

Piatkus
An imprint of
Little, Brown Book Group
Carmelite House
50 Victoria Embankment
London EC4Y 0DZ

An Hachette UK Company
www.hachette.co.uk

www.littlebrown.co.uk

N.G. Peltier is an anime watching, book reading, video-game playing, story writing kinda girl.

A devourer of words and books from a young age, she enjoys writing romance and creeping people out with the Caribbean folklore stories she grew up hearing.

A Trinidadian born and raised, she currently lives in Trinidad with her mountain of ideas and characters battling each other for whose story get told next.

Read more at ngpeltier.com

You can also find her on Twitter @trinielf

ALSO BY N.G. PELTIER

Island Bites series

Sweethand

To mummy. We love you and miss you. I know you would've been proud to see me put out my second book ❤

Don't Go Baking My Heart

CHAPTER ONE

AUGUST

DEVON

Devon King didn't like anything that derailed his daily plans. He knew, of course, that in business, it paid to be prepared for the unplanned. Be proactive rather than reactive—but there was nothing that could've prepared him for this meeting so early on a Monday morning.

He stared around the crowded conference room, the excited chatter the equivalent to the screech of nails on a chalkboard. It wouldn't bother him so much if everyone was this hyped up about something work-related—hell, there were enough projects in the pipeline for that—but the block letters on the whiteboard made him frown harder.

FIRST ANNUAL COMPANY BAKE-OFF COMPETITION!!

Dax Jenkins, the CEO of their architectural design firm, tapped the board. "Alright, everyone, I know we're all excited, but simmer for a sec."

Devon glared at the board. There was even a lopsided cake drawn next to the words. *This* was the reason for the buzz? Devon wanted to storm out and go lock himself in his office to get some actual work done. They had shit to do, and his boss had called everyone together to talk about some bake-off. How ludicrous.

If everyone was in this room, then who was manning the phones? The thought of potential clients getting irate because they couldn't reach anyone didn't sit right with him. No one else seemed to give a damn, though. Everyone's attention was on Dax and the words on the board. The incessant buzzing was enough to make Devon want to scream, but then the focus would shift to him. He didn't need that.

He crossed his arms over his chest, waiting for Dax to explain what the hell all of this was about.

When he entered the building this morning, he was greeted by several choruses of "Happy Monday!" sung loudly by his co-workers. He hadn't appreciated their attempts to add some cheer to the start of the week and had, in fact, ignored the exuberant thumbs up and the multitude of clichéd motivational quotes they tried to send his way. He didn't need shouts of "Carpe Diem!" to actually seize his day. He did that on a daily basis instead of ambushing his co-workers with nonsense.

Devon had barely settled down to get started on work when this alert from Dax had gone out with no prior notice of a planned meeting. Not that he could have refused his boss's request; he simply wished there had been some heads-up. He would have shifted his schedule around to suit. So now everything was being thrown off. He could have been sifting through important emails right now.

He had already suffered through everyone being way too laid-back last week due to the country's Emancipation holiday. No matter that August 1st had fallen on a Wednesday, his co-workers had kept their laissez-faire attitudes right through Friday, acting as if they had an extended long weekend, using the fact that schools were closed for the vacation period as an excuse. There were a few people on vacation right now so they could be with their children, and yet, there had been those who didn't have children rolling into the office late on Thursday morning, as if that was okay. And now this.

Who had time to waste on some bake-off when real work had to be done? Obviously, he couldn't simply leave. Not when everyone was here on Dax's orders. He tried to look less like he'd rather be anywhere else and forced his hands into a relaxed drape across his lap. Hopefully, he succeeded in schooling his scowl to something that resembled casual indifference.

Dax had a knack for sniffing out people's true feelings. He didn't know how the man did it, but Devon couldn't afford to be called out for being less than enthusiastic about all this. Not that anyone expected him to be, but it didn't hurt to look like he was paying attention. It certainly wouldn't work in his favour if he pulled out his phone and proceeded to check his emails from there.

If his intern—well, former intern, now—Kim was still here, she'd poke him in the side and tell him to fix his face. But Kim was back in London for school, and there wasn't anyone to keep his expressions in check. He actually missed the kid. Kim had been an exceptional intern who was irreplaceable in his estimation. Dax had been hinting that Devon needed to choose a replacement soon, but Devon wasn't sold on the idea; he had been stalling on shortlisting candidates based on the applications received. He would have to buckle down and do it before Dax got on his ass again.

Kim had set the bar so high, he couldn't envision

anyone else working to his standards. Devon knew he could be a bit of a hardass and that his ornery ways, as Kim had put it, could scare anyone off. He didn't have time to placate some new person's hurt feelings. Whoever he eventually chose would just have to adapt to his persona.

In spite of wanting to be back at his desk, getting some real work done, he remained seated and quiet. Dax was always a jovial man, quick to smile, but underneath all that was a sharp mind, always cooking up some new scheme to motivate his employees. It was great that their leader took the time to care about all that, but Devon couldn't see how this was going to help any of them. Trying to look less annoyed by this entire disturbance of his morning was getting harder by the second.

"So, as I mentioned a bit ago, we've decided to do a bake-off this year. We'll still have the sports day next year, but after the success of the Building An Appetite initiative spearheaded by Devon and his intern, Kim, I got to thinking. And well, you all know I love my belly, so it was a no-brainer that we come up with something a little different this year."

Dammit. This ridiculous idea had sprung from that?

"And we'd like everyone to participate, if possible," Dax continued, gaze fixed on Devon for a few seconds before he moved onto someone else. Had that been a coincidence? Or was Dax sending him a not-so-subtle message?

Devon was infamous for not taking part in company extracurricular activities. If it was work-related, he was there one hundred percent. Sometimes Dax joked about Devon's anti-social behaviour, but had Dax been noting every time Devon refused to join some waste-of-time event?

He didn't hang out with his co-workers after work or

get heavily involved in the annual events like the sports day. He didn't see the point. He was here to work, not make friendship bracelets and bond.

The bracelets had been an actual venture suggested by one of his colleagues. Devon could still recall Evan's excited yapping about it. What self-respecting grown ass adult walked around with embroidered bracelets? In Devon's estimation, there were way better ideas to boost morale than sporting a bracelet with supposed motivational words and phrases. Evan had never forgiven Devon's very vocal shutdown of the ridiculous idea, or so he assumed since Evan didn't try to be friendly with Devon so much anymore, which was exactly what Devon wanted.

Sure, organizational health was important—the damn survey that HR had started sending out last year showed that employees wanted more company extracurricular activities—but Devon didn't need to personally involve himself in any of them.

He spied Evan one row over from him, eyes riveted to the board. Of course, he'd be all for something like this. Evan was a champion of upping employee engagement; he was constantly trying to outdo HR and whatever ideas they came up with. There was too much work to be done to stop for cake and ice cream in the lunchroom, after-work karaoke, or whatever other shit he concocted in that mind of his.

As head of the staff club, there was always an email from him about some new and exciting thing he wanted employees to be a part of. Devon had created a separate folder for emails from Evan, and he barely looked at them. He didn't need his inbox cluttered with Evan's ideas. His inbox wasn't an out-of-control dumpster fire, and he was proud of that.

Belting out a song on the office rooftop that they shared with the other companies in the building wasn't going to get his work done faster. No, it would most likely give his co-workers a good laugh at his expense. His voice wasn't anything to swoon over, and while he could carry a tune better than his brother Keiran, performing wasn't something Devon would ever be up for. His father lamented all the time on how Devon should do something with his voice, considering his father was well-known in the music industry, and his brother was becoming more sought-after every day as a producer in his own right.

Devon didn't give a single damn about any of that. He was right where he wanted to be. Well, in general, not currently. He *definitely* didn't want to be in this room right now. The number of emails he had to address, the details of the big project he needed to nail down the proposal for, were way too much. Maybe he should get back to looking at those applications. He truly did need someone to help him. He was a champion at organization, but even he could admit Kim had made a real impact while she was here. He needed an actual full-time assistant. He didn't think anyone could measure up to Kim, but if he could find a candidate who could take direction well, maybe he could shape them into someone good enough that he might keep them around on a permanent basis.

How did Dax even think they had time for any of this?

"Since the idea's inspired by that, Devon should sign up first, no?" Evan's annoying voice rang out, and all eyes turned to Devon.

Devon ignored the stares, cutting his eyes over to Evan, who wore one of his shit-eating grins. "I don't have the time." Simple. A factual statement. He couldn't be taken to task for that, could he?

Getting work done that could add to the company's bottom line should take priority.

"I mean, we're all busy, but we're willing to make the time, aren't we? Showing we're all in at Dax Designs isn't just about the technical work but camaraderie, too."

Evan was laying it all on a little thick, but Devon could see others nodding. He turned to look at Dax, who was watching them, amusement dancing in his eyes. Dax would never force any of them to participate, but this sort of thing was something their boss loved.

A sheet of paper slid in front of him, and Devon glanced towards the woman who held her pen out to him. "He's not wrong, you know," she said, voice lowered, so her words remained between them. "I'd suggest being the first to sign up. It would look good and make Dax and the board see you're committed to being a team player."

Devon blinked at Dax's Executive Assistant, Amanda. She didn't seem to be joking, but he couldn't usually tell. Amanda always had a look of concentration on her face from holding Dax's entire schedule in her head and her devices, so Devon wasn't surprised. The woman was a miracle worker and could sweet-talk anyone into anything when it came to getting stuff done for their boss. But she couldn't be serious about this.

"I'm a team player."

She nodded. "Of course, but trust me, Devon. Your definition of team player and Dax's are vastly different. Dax prides himself on his work *and* play balance. I know you're angling for a Principal position and being more involved in things like this will go a long way. I've worked closely with Dax for years; you know I know the man."

Shit. Had Dax mentioned something to Amanda in passing? Devon had been working his ass off to achieve his career goals. He'd thought he'd been on the right track with his plans. He was determined to earn a coveted spot as a partner of the firm before he turned forty. He had an entire spreadsheet dedicated to keeping track of his goals. He was serious about charting his progression, but could participating in this bake-off really give him a leg up with a promotion?

As a Senior Project Manager, he was so close to the next phase of his plan, and he didn't want anything to jeopardise that. Something as frivolous as this couldn't actually ruin that, could it? He also didn't want to do it because of Evan's annoying words.

But he couldn't risk it. Couldn't allow a single thing to hinder his detailed life goals. He had an exact vision of where he expected to be in the next five years. Making Partner. Getting married. Having two children, which was sufficient on his current trajectory. He was frugal about his finances. According to his calculations, he could afford to raise two children with his spouse's combined income.

None of that involved baking.

Amanda placed the pen across the blank sign-up sheet as Dax went on about the rules of the competition.

"People are encouraged to team up, but if you'd rather be brave and go it alone, that's fine, too. Depending on the interest we get, we'll have team and individual prizes. The most important thing, apart from having fun, is documenting your thoughts leading up to the bake-off. This includes any trial goodies you decide to make," Dax's expression turned serious, "which *must* be made by you or your team members. No store-bought treats, no trying to pass off someone else's as your own."

"But how exactly will we know if someone actually

made it?" a voice asked from somewhere in the back. It sounded like one of the junior designers, Terry.

Dax grinned. "This is where the video diaries will come in handy. Throw in some discussion on how you decide to match your creation to the theme without giving away too much. Make it interesting! The trial diaries will give you bonus points and will count towards the overall score. An email will be sent outlining the rules, theme, judging categories, and the link to where the vid diaries must be uploaded. Just so we're clear on everything." He winked, and Devon suppressed a groan.

This sounded more annoying by the minute.

"You can get someone from outside the company to assist you or guide you, but the creations *must* be your own. You'll be the one making them on the bake-off day, anyhow, so I suggest those who aren't the best bakers to get those lessons going! This is why we're telling you two months ahead of the event. The bake-off also takes place after my big birthday bash, so we're making it a weekend of treats."

"Isn't putting a bake-off after your epic party just cruel?" Terry joked.

Devon hadn't attended last year, but from what he'd seen previously, Dax's birthday events were usually over the top and tended to get a little wild. It was as if the staff was too excited to get into the free liquor to think about the consequences of their behaviour on Monday morning. Devon had seen some things the one time he had attended and would prefer to strike it from his memory forever.

Dax shrugged. "Well, we couldn't make it too easy for you all. If you can attend the party and function enough the next day to whip up some goodies, then you deserve to win."

Devon sighed. Dax was speaking in his easy, friendly tone, but the man was serious about these types of events. He would disqualify anyone who tried to cheat. It wouldn't get them fired or anything like that, but Dax wouldn't forget it. He always remembered a slight against him, and he would take this personally.

Mention of the party also meant that Devon would need to show up for that too. Dammit. The party was usually open to employees and their partners, though it wasn't a big deal if someone came with a family member or friend in lieu of having a romantic partner. He hated small talk and mingling with inebriated people, especially co-workers who couldn't determine a boundary once they were tipsy. Hell, some of them didn't know the meaning of personal space while they were sober. That shit would get messy as hell.

But he didn't think he could get away another year without at least popping in for a bit. He would need to be on his A-game for the competition the next day, so late-night partying wasn't his plan. Perhaps the timing would work in his favour after all. He could slip out early and get some rest while those who decided to party late into the morning would do themselves a disservice. He knew Evan never left the party early—he had heard enough stories on the Monday after—so it was possible he would be off his game for the contest, Devon hoped. Evan's overachieving ass was sure to go all out on his idea.

He signed his name on the first line and slid the sheet back at Amanda. She patted his shoulder. "Too bad your intern isn't around."

Banging his head against the desk sounded really good right now. Kim not being here wasn't ideal—this entire venture was right up her alley. The Building An Appetite event had been her baby. He'd used his Senior Manager pull to help her get it approved and off the ground. Had crafted an extensive proposal complete with benefits to the company for agreement to be given. Kim was interested in culinary arts and architectural design and had meshed the two to conceptualise the idea for the Building event. The event was a hit and a bright spot on Kim's résumé and Devon's file.

Devon hadn't doubted the success for a second. He excelled at spotting profitable ventures and had been thorough in his presentation.

Garnering lots of media buzz, it had put the company in a positive light of fostering young talent on their island. Guests had gone gaga for Kim's creations that were delicious geometric concoctions. The showstopper piece had made some people question whether the 3D design was even edible. Kim was that good.

Devon had been damn proud of her and hoped, after her studies, she would return home to work here. She was already guaranteed a job, but there would be so many other firms courting Kim, it was no certainty she'd want to come back to the island to work with them.

But damn if he didn't wish she was still here. With her help, he would be sure to win the ridiculous bake-off. Now, what was he supposed to do? He had put his name down, which meant he had to somehow come up with a plan for this. No way in hell was he going to look like he couldn't hack it at some pointless extracurricular venture. He didn't do failure—even if it was at something he had no idea how to do.

Devon took great pride in his planning and organizational skills. His mother and siblings usually rolled their eyes at his carefully curated lists and spreadsheets. But what was life without some structure? They might be okay just winging shit, not him.

After the meeting, Dax clasped his shoulder. "Good to see your name on there. I look forward to your creations. Hopefully, some of Kim's talent rubbed off on you, eh?"

Dax chuckled like that was the funniest thing in the world. Devon gave his best estimation of a smile back, but he was already trying to strategise. How the hell was he going to pull this off? One option could be to team up with Evan. Devon had no clue whether the man had any baking skills to speak of, but he was such a kiss-ass Devon was sure Evan would find a way.

No. He would find some other option. Working with Evan would end in disaster. He could picture himself wanting to strangle the man the entire duration of this ridiculous venture. Going it alone was the right choice.

Dax's comment meant Amanda had been right. Shit. He couldn't back out now, but he needed help. He couldn't bake for shit. YouTube videos could be helpful, but Devon wasn't leaving his fate to that. He needed in-person help.

His mother might be all too willing, but he nixed that idea immediately. If he had to work with her, she might drive him up a wall before they even made it a week into this. She wasn't as terrible as Evan, but she would definitely use all that forced time together to get all up in his business. He loved his mother, but it wasn't worth all the prying.

He moved to make his way back to his office when Evan stepped in front of him. "I saw your name on there. May the best man win." Evan stuck out his hand, and Devon considered not shaking it, but Dax was still lingering, chatting with some other employees.

"Hope you're prepared to bring your A-game," Evan went on.

"I always do."

"Maybe at work-related stuff, but this is a little off your usual path, isn't it?" Evan's smirk made Devon want to walk away, but he kept his cool, shaking Evan's hand briefly, outwardly ignoring his statement.

"I welcome the challenge."

He might not know a damn thing about baking, but he wasn't letting Evan have him running scared. The man was clearly looking for some sort of reaction from him.

After he had shot down the bracelets idea, it seemed as if all the ideas Evan came up with were specifically designed to annoy Devon in some way. He had no hard proof that was actually true, but he didn't trust anyone who was always so damn cheerful. It was odd. He watched as Evan walked away. He needed to ponder his course of action. Evan thought he had this one in the bag, but there was no way in hell Devon was going to be shown up by that guy. He didn't *want* to do any of this, but he couldn't lose to Evan, either. That felt wrong on all levels.

Obviously, there was only one person he could safely ask who wouldn't judge him for this. He might actually have to swear her to secrecy, too, which might be harder than getting her to agree to his plan. His brother dating a pastry chef was about to be useful to him. Cherisse seemed like the helpful sort. But thanks to the unplanned morning meeting, he was now behind on catching up on emails, which threw off his daily schedule. Emails were usually his first task on a morning.

Replying to the ones at the top of his priority list was his first order of business. He squinted at an email from his mother and sighed. He'd told her countless times not to email him at his work address, that calling would suffice. But his mother had figured out his strategy after a while. She knew he checked his work emails before anything else. He felt a little guilty about ignoring her phone calls until after work, but seriously, ever since he'd moved into his own house two months ago, she'd been calling and messaging him for ridiculous things. Random bits of advice as if Devon hadn't done all his research prior to getting the keys for his new place.

He shook his head at the subject of her latest email. Housewarming ideas. Another thing she kept insisting on. Why did he need to invite a bunch of people to his new place? None of that sounded fun. His family claimed it was a thing he needed to do *and* that he also needed to get the house blessed. When his mother got like this, it was usually easier to give in, but he was ignoring it for now.

Devon simply wanted to enjoy his new space without an invasion of people coming in to critique his design choices. If he decided to invite guests over, it would be a small, intimate affair that involved a simple meal, maybe some wine. Not the backyard bashment his family seemed to expect.

His office line rang, pulling him away from his emails. He didn't recognise the number shown on the little screen.

"Devon King."

"Boss man! You really signed up for a baking competition?" Kim's squeal of laughter was so loud he had to pull his phone away from his ear.

"How in the hell did you hear that already?" He'd been checking and replying to emails for about an hour. Could news have gotten to Kim so fast?

"I got my sources. Everyone in your office loved me, so I have my informers."

He didn't doubt that. Kim had been a great first-year intern. She was smart, eager to learn, and plied everyone with her delicious creations, which he'd realised, belatedly, was her way of placating his co-workers after his grumpy ass had passed through.

"So, you really doing this? Wilfully entering an office activity?"

He sighed. "Yes."

"You'll need help. You can't bake for shit."

Another reason why he'd liked Kim. She was straightforward. "I'll get help."

He would definitely talk to Cherisse. She was a busy woman, but he'd pay. Just because she was dating Keiran didn't mean he'd expect lessons for free. She could tutor him in her baking ways, and while it wasn't a guarantee he'd win—even though he wanted to now more than ever after that run-in with Evan—participation points had to count for something. At least Dax would be happy.

"Why are you even doing this? You hate these things."

"I don't *hate* them."

"You refused to do the karaoke. Or make greeting cards that one time. You didn't eat any of the Christmas cookies. You almost snarled at Evan when he asked you to choose one of the fun headgear to wear for that Halloween thing. Should I go on?" Kim asked sweetly.

"I just refuse to waste time that could be spent on work. Besides, the key denominator in all of that is Evan," he admitted because Kim knew he couldn't stand the man for his unnatural constant office cheer.

His cell phone chimed as Kim continued to tease him. He briefly glanced at the notification on his screen, rolling his eyes as he saw the familiar name. Another meme from Reba Johnson.

There's another option.

No. Absolutely not.

That was the worst idea. Possibly more so than Evan.

Reba Johnson gave off too much chaos vibes.

He'd met her at Cherisse's sister's wedding in June, where Cherisse had been the maid of honour and Keiran the best man. The wedding reception had been the first and last time he'd been face-to-face with Reba. She had inundated him with chatter while he'd listened, sort of. She'd also enlisted Keiran's help with putting her number in his phone while he had gone to the bathroom. He definitely hadn't saved anyone in his phone under the name Pretty in Pink. The tiny profile picture at the top only showed the back of someone's cotton candy pink hair, but Devon just knew it was Reba. She was the only person he had ever met with hair that colour.

Keiran had also shared Devon's number with Reba— apparently because his brother found the entire thing hilarious. Devon mostly ignored the ridiculous memes from the first moment the messages had started popping up.

"Anyhoo, don't burn your house down trying to butter up to Dax with this."

Devon shook his head as Kim rang off. He didn't have to worry about this. Cherisse would help him, and he would just have to swear Keiran to secrecy since he expected her to inform him. Their relationship was new, so asking her to lie wasn't ideal. Reba wasn't an option he should entertain when Cherisse was available. From their short meeting, it was clear that he and Reba would get on like oil and water —so, not at all.

He realised he didn't actually have Cherisse's number, but a quick call to his brother would fix that oversight.

"Yeah?"

Devon frowned at Keiran's rude greeting. "Is that how you answer your phone?"

"I know it's you, D. The days of rotary phones and guessing who's calling are over."

"Still, you should always give a proper greeting regardless. Just in case."

Keiran sighed. "Is there a point to this? I'm busy."

Of course. Keiran was a bit of a workaholic like Devon, although he knew for a fact his brother made time for his girlfriend. Unfortunately, their mother gushed about how cute the two were to Devon all the time as if that was something he cared about. He was happy for Keiran, but Devon didn't delve into his sibling's private life. It wasn't his business, and his mother's updates every time they spoke were too much.

It also led to questioning him about when he was going to settle down. His reply had been the same since his last relationship had ended: he was working on it.

He was being careful about it since everything he'd thought he was going to have with Monica hadn't quite panned out. She'd accused him of seeing her as just another thing to check off on his life goals list.

That hadn't been true. He'd cared for Monica, and they were compatible. He'd even been shopping around for rings. Her getting upset over finding his risk analysis of their relationship had been irrational at best, which had been so unlike her. Monica was calm, usually, until she'd found that list and freaked out.

Perhaps it had been for the best. They weren't meant to be. So, he'd had to uncheck that box. He didn't need or want drama in his life.

"I need Cherisse's number, please. I'd like to hire her for something."

"Hmm, what something?"

Devon rolled his eyes. He didn't have time for Keiran to suddenly adopt the role of jealous boyfriend, and he also didn't want to admit right away why he needed Cherisse's help. Knowing Keiran, he'd just laugh his ass off and annoy Devon further. "I'm not trying to steal your girlfriend or anything like that."

Keiran busted out laughing. "Devon, buddy, I'm in no way worried about that. You are *definitely* not Cherisse's type."

"Why not?" It was ridiculous to even ask, but Keiran was practically choking with laughter. Devon didn't appreciate it.

He was a good-looking man—he got told that enough—had a good job with room to go further up the organisation, a home that was all his own. He would be considered a catch.

"You'd bore her to tears. You're too stoic, and, I don't know, you're not me."

"Well, I'm glad to see your confidence is at an all-time high, but can you just give me her number? It's an important work thing."

"I'll text it to you. Bye, D."

Keiran hung up, but true to his word, he sent Devon the number. He drummed his fingers against his desk as the phone rang and rang. He preferred to get this out of the way now. He hated things lingering on his to-do list. Nothing was more satisfying than completing a task and crossing it off the list. Old-school, perhaps, when there were apps for that, but it worked for him. He used technology for other things.

Cherisse wasn't answering, but Devon didn't let frustration get the best of him. If you couldn't reach someone directly, and they had an assistant, chances were you could reach them that way.

Against his better judgement, he opened his WhatsApp, and sure enough, there was a new video from Reba of cats doing something strange. As Cherisse's assistant, she could help him. But would she want to? He'd never responded to any of her videos, effectively leaving her on read for months —not that his lack of reply had stopped her from sending them—so he couldn't be sure she wouldn't take offence to him reaching out now that he needed her to get to Cherisse. Reba was an unpredictable factor that he had been ignoring until now. He didn't have much data to discern a pattern of how she could react. But he had to try.

He typed:

Devon: *hello.*

Stared at it a few minutes. Deleted. Tried again. Went with something a bit less abrupt.

Devon: *What are these cats even doing?*

Hit send before he could reconsider.
And waited.

CHAPTER TWO
REBA

REBA PRIDED HERSELF ON BEING PROFESSIONAL. MOST DAYS. Well, she made an attempt simply because she liked her current boss. Her varying hair colour choices weren't seen as professional by some. Before she started working with Cherisse, she had ventured into the corporate world. Big mistake, and *so* not for her, but the need to ensure her independence, even while living with her parents, did add a level of desperation at times.

Plus, all her fun clothes and wigs weren't going to suddenly appear without money.

Those corporate jobs had placed so many restrictions on the staff that had her itching to leave many times until she had finally decided enough was enough. Besides, most of the execs had acted as if being an assistant meant they could treat her like shit. She had grown tired of the disrespect, emailed her resignation, and never returned.

She hadn't minded burning that entire bridge down because she didn't plan to go back ever. Leaving that place had been her best decision to date. She didn't have to give a damn what those people thought anymore. Cherisse didn't have an issue. Reba could wear a damn rainbow on her head for all her boss cared.

But she lost herself for a moment when the text came in and blurted out, "Oh, shit."

Reba fumbled her phone, nearly sending it skating across the floor towards the pool. She caught it before it went anywhere near the ground or water, heart pounding. That phone was her life and how she kept track of everything for her job. The death by watery grave would have had her in tears. She would have had to slash her makeup and hair budgets to buy a new one. A sobering thought.

Cherisse glanced over at her. Boss lady was walking around the other side of the pool with their latest client, who was busy gushing about how she wanted the dessert set-up to look. The client had a massive thirtieth birthday party planned for this weekend, and they were finalising everything.

This bougie ass woman wanted some next-level triple-tiered cake that defied gravity or some shit. Cherisse had been trying to tell her for the past fifteen minutes that maybe she should try some less "accident waiting to happen" options, especially since this woman had children who would be running around at the party. But she wasn't hearing it.

Rich people were weird like that. Reba supposed a cake that would cost a cool couple thousand dollars wasn't a big deal for this lady. Ah, to be rich and wanting what you wanted, regardless of knowing there was potential destruction in the item's future. Must be nice.

Either way, Reba was lucky the client didn't hear her curse or was ignoring it. Hell, the woman probably didn't even remember Reba was there. She was used to these types ignoring the assistant because, of course, Reba didn't matter to them. Cherisse was the focus.

Reba grinned at Cherisse and mouthed a 'sorry' before looking back down at the text she'd gotten from Devon King.

He'd actually replied. After two months of sending him memes and videos just because she could without any reply, she didn't know what to make of this.

> **Reba:** *they're being cats obviously.*
> **Devon:** *I don't know what that means.*
> **Reba:** *cats gonna cat, Devon. don't you see how they're just casually pushing stuff off the desk? it's such a cat thing to do.*
> **Devon:** *And this is funny why?*

Reba rolled her eyes. Of course, Mr. Super Serious wouldn't get it. The ringtone she'd set for Devon blared from her phone, and she almost dropped the damn thing again. He was actually calling her? What the hell? Who did that? Actually called a person on the phone?

Devon King, obviously. Reba shouldn't be surprised. He didn't seem like much of a texter, and in the meagre interaction they'd had at the wedding, he had behaved like a crotchety old man. A shame, really, because Devon King was way too fine to be acting like he was ready to settle into a rocking chair and shake his fist at children who dared venture onto his lawn.

She hadn't seen the man since Ava's wedding, but Reba wasn't about to forget that tall, lovely drink of water. That perfectly coiffed beard that looked like her next favourite seat was the stuff of dreams. She remembered how it framed his lush lips perfectly. Mmm, she wondered if he still sported it?

Focus, woman, he's actually calling you after leaving you on read all this time. This is a damn miracle.

She wasn't too keen on phone calls. She loved interacting with people, but face-to-face was where she shone. Reba preferred texting otherwise. Gifs and memes were life. Of course, she had to speak on her phone for work, but Devon King wasn't a client.

"What the hell are you doing?" she demanded, glancing over at Cherisse. She was still too focused on the client to notice Reba on the phone.

"Hello, Reba."

She felt that deep baritone all the way to her soul and other more inconvenient parts of her body. Like between her legs. How dare his voice be this deep and sexy? Shit, were her nipples hard? She was actually wearing a bra, so it wouldn't be too obvious, but one could never be too careful because damn, that voice could make even the strongest padded bra useless.

"Hello, are you there?"

Right, Serious and Sexy had called her for some unknown reason. "I'm busy. To what do I owe this stunning event of you actually calling me after acting like I didn't exist all this time?"

"I'm in a bit of a predicament and need your help."

Reba checked the date on her phone. Okay, still August 2018. She looked up—nothing seemed off. So, she hadn't been catapulted into some weird dimension where Devon needed her for anything to the point where he was willingly calling her. What could he possibly want from her? Devon had made it clear he had no desire to communicate with her beyond them being stuck at the same table at the wedding. Not that Reba cared. She excelled at filling silence. His frown the entire time hadn't deterred her.

Reba loved challenges, and Devon certainly fell into that category. The way his eyes had swept her pastel pink hair and tight silver dress had immediately sent the message that he disapproved. Nothing Reba hadn't experienced before. It had only been more satisfying when she'd gotten his number from his brother. Keiran had been amused by Reba's antics, so she had, with his blessing, been sending Devon random videos ever since. He hadn't blocked her yet, so she supposed he wasn't too bothered by her randomly messaging him.

"What could you possibly want from me?"

"I need you to put Cherisse on, please. I tried calling her, but no response."

"She's busy with a client. I can take a message."

"There's no way she can talk now?"

"Listen, I don't know if you're used to people being at your beck and call, but Cherisse's time is precious. Especially since that sexy man of hers finally convinced her to go with him to St. Lucia. Have a lil' vacation while he's on his work trip. So she's trying to wrap up our pending stuff."

"Vacation?" Devon asked as if the word was a foreign concept. Perhaps it was. Devon struck her as the type of person who was allergic to fun and didn't know the meaning of relaxation. "They haven't even been dating that long. When are they leaving?"

"This Sunday. How do you not know this? Keiran's going to work with a St. Lucian artiste, and he asked her to go with him."

"I don't get into my siblings' business. Besides, I don't live at the house anymore."

Well, that was news to her. As far as Reba knew, all the King siblings lived with their mom. "You moved out?"

"Yes, right after the wedding. Not important. I need Cherisse to help me win a bake-off."

Reba pulled the phone away from her ear and stared down at the screen, then pinched herself hard. Okay, she felt that. She wasn't dreaming.

"I'm going to need you to repeat that. Slowly."

He sighed. "It's a work thing. I need her to teach me to bake. I'll pay her for her time, of course."

"She can't do it. Didn't I just tell you she's leaving Sunday?"

"Yes, I got that, but it's only Monday. That still leaves some days. An entire week, to be precise. Surely she can make time."

The nerve of this man. "No, she can't. We're busy all week."

"You didn't even ask her..."

"Listen, I know her schedule like the back of my ass."

"That's not how the saying goes," he said, tone as dry as ever.

"I've inspected my ass in countless mirrors long enough to know what it looks good in. Everything, but that's not my point. When I say she's booked, she's *booked*. But, I could totally help you because with C on vacation for the next two weeks, I'll have some time."

"You?"

Reba considered hanging up because Devon's tone suggested he'd rather do anything else than accept her help. But his desperation had come through loud and clear, and Reba wasn't above taking advantage of this situation. "Yes, me. What other choice do you have? It's a bake-off. I bet you're planning something easy. I can handle you."

"I don't need to be handled. I just need assistance."

Oh, he was so wrong about that. Devon King needed a firm hand, someone to drag him into the light and get some fun into his life. Put a smile on that too serious, too handsome face. Reba wasn't being vocal about that for the simple reason that Devon wouldn't go for it. Too set in his ways. Too rigid. He might frustrate even her carefree ways with his no-fun-having self.

Although recalling the yummy picture he had made at the wedding in that suit, Reba wondered if she wouldn't want to handle him after all. No, she was absolutely getting ahead of herself. Devon would be fun to play with and unravel, but she should stick to business, not potential pleasure.

"Well, I'm offering my help, especially since you'll definitely not win this thing on your own." Devon paused for so long, Reba wondered if he'd hung up, but the call was still going. "Take it or leave it. Oh, and to be clear, I'm not doing it for free."

She was all for doing favours, but she had too many friends and family members who thought she was obligated to do things for them sans payment.

Silence greeted her. He still hadn't hung up—the call was still connected. "Hello?"

"Still here. Why do you think I can't do this on my own?"

Reba laughed. "You wouldn't be calling otherwise. I have no doubt you're good at a lot, but the scent of desperation is strong here. Have you ever baked a thing in your life?"

"No."

"Well, there you go. Let me be your fairy bakemother."

Silence greeted her again. He was probably rethinking

ever calling her. Reba wasn't offended. The entire situation was amusing.

"Fine. It's a deal. We can hash everything out in detail. Later. Perhaps this weekend?"

"Awesome! But this weekend is a no-go. I'll be frolicking at the beach with some girlfriends."

She'd been looking forward to this little staycation beach house getaway. She had earned that. She and Cherisse had been going non-stop, making those money moves. Laying out on the beach in a brightly coloured bikini, sipping on some homemade cocktails, and catching up with friends was some much-needed therapy.

The weather forecast called for sun, so Reba was hoping that would hold true. It was never a guarantee around this rainy season.

She could discuss everything with Devon after that. Like why was he taking part in a bake-off in the first place? It sounded really out there for him. From all she gathered about Devon during their time at the wedding, nothing seemed to bother the man, but the desperation in his voice had been too clear. Was he doing this to impress someone? A woman? Doing something showy like this didn't seem like his thing, but Reba had seen some guys do some questionable stuff to show off for someone they were interested in.

Considering how much he gave off the "this is a no-fun zone" vibe, she would surely need to milk her weekend getaway before having to deal with him.

"Frolicking. On the beach." He repeated her words like they made no sense.

Reba rolled her eyes. "Yes. The beach. You know, where people go to relax? Have fun. Chill out. You might want to try it sometime."

"Too busy."

"Well, if you want me to help you with this, you'll need to make some time. I'll leave you to figure out your schedule. I gotta go. You have my number, so send me the details."

She ended the call. No matter how curious she was about all this, she had to refocus on her job.

Devon King could wait.

CHAPTER THREE
DEVON

THE VIBRATION OF HIS CELL WAS DRIVING DEVON UP A WALL. HE should have known better than to actually text Reba. He should have said he would email or something. The woman didn't understand that she didn't need to start up an entire conversation in response to the schedule he had sent. He didn't have time to indulge her on this remarkably busy Friday morning.

Besides, didn't she say she was busy planning for her weekend getaway? Not that he'd asked for details. She had offered up all the inane bits of information on her own.

> **Reba:** *next weekend to begin operation bake-off is fine with me*
> **Reba:** *hmm, come ready with your proposal. If it's trash I'll tell you so*
> **Reba:** *wait...do you have baking equipment? Would I need to bring stuff? Have you even used the kitchen in your new place? Send me a pic so I know what we're working with*
> **Devon:** *I'm at work.*

Reba: so you don't have random pics of your house. Got it. Ooh I need your opinion on something. I'm packing for my beach trip. I feel like you'd be brutally honest. What do you think of this??

She had sent him a photo of a scrap of fabric with gift boxes printed on it. He didn't know what the hell he was looking at. He shouldn't reply. He didn't need to at this point. He had done his part and sent her the schedule he had worked out for them.

They would meet up from next week Saturday. He had already rearranged his schedule to fit her in early. There was no need to continue this pointless discussion. She was already cutting into his weekend time which he also used to work on some projects. He didn't need to devote a single minute more to Reba Johnson.

And yet, he was curious.

Devon: What am I looking at?
Reba: it's a bathing suit obviously.
Devon: Is it?
Reba: yes. Hang on.

She didn't respond for a few minutes, which gave him some time to read an email Amanda had sent about the Bake-Off. It reiterated everything Dax had said at the meeting on Monday. The theme was Game On. The rules were outlined, and the judging criteria were clearly laid out. Staff who were taking part were encouraged to upload their in-progress video diaries to the specified folder.

Now, of course, there were numerous staff members responding to Amanda by hitting reply all because he had emails coming in fast and furious. He was going to have to create a separate folder for this as well. How did they not know they didn't have to reply all? Was he going to have to ask HR to conduct a session on email etiquette? This was ridiculous.

His phone dinged, and Devon checked Reba's latest message. Fucking hell, had she really...

> **Reba:** *here, this should clear up any confusion. Bathing suit. See??* 😒

He saw indeed. Too much. Skin. So much smooth, rich brown skin in that scrap of almost non-existent fabric. Her body was turned slightly to the side, which gave Devon a glimpse of the curve of her ass cheek. This bathing suit didn't have much in the way of ass coverage. He blinked at the pink hibiscus tattoo that was a splash of vibrant colour on her hip.

> **Reba:** *well? Too much? Would the beach ppl be scandalised you think?*
> **Devon:** *Yes*
> **Reba:** *excellent. My ass is the gift that keeps on giving so...into the bag it goes!*

Reba *was* absolutely too much. Of course, she would want to strut up and down the beach with her ass out for the world to see. Why she even needed his opinion, to begin with, he didn't know. Maybe she hadn't really cared about what he had to say but more about the shock value.

It would be just like her to send him this on a Friday morning while he was at work just because she could. Just to disrupt him. Because here he, was still staring at that curve instead of chucking his phone in his drawer and ignoring her.

His work phone rang, and Devon almost knocked the receiver off his desk, fumbling to answer. No one would know he was staring at a scantily clad woman on his phone, and yet his heart rate immediately escalated before he told himself to get his shit together.

"Hi, Mr. King. I have your mother here to see you," the receptionist chirped.

"What?" Why in the world was his mother here? He wasn't expecting any visitors today, least of all his mother. Not during the day like this. She should be at her dental practice.

This day was going off the rails, one unexpected thing at a time. He glanced at his cell phone, shook his head, and replied to Corinne.

"Send her in."

Sheryl King breezed in looking fresh and radiant in one of her usual pantsuits. Her birthday was this Saturday, and she had been enjoying herself all week in preparation. They were planning to do a family dinner tonight as Cherisse had to cater a party on Saturday, and she and Keiran were flying out Sunday morning.

"Hi, sweetie." She slipped into the chair opposite him, a huge smile on her face. It made him nervous.

"Everything okay? Why didn't you call me?"

"I know you're busy, but we have a small change in my birthday plans."

"Oh?" He hated last-minute deviations from an agreed-upon plan.

"Your sneaky brother booked a beach house this weekend so we can celebrate. He felt guilty that he wouldn't be here for my entire birthday. So, surprise! We leave tonight, so there's enough time to pack some stuff before we head up. I spoke to Dax already, and he's definitely okay with you taking off a little earlier today so you can get everything packed up. Keiran and Cherisse will stay until Saturday morning, then head back, but we have the entire weekend."

Devon stared at his mother. There was no way he was hearing correctly.

"Before you say anything, Dax all but insisted you leave early and get some rest. He agrees you've been working so hard and need a break. When was the last time you even took a vacation? It would also mean so much to me, honey, to have all my kids there tonight."

He could try to fight this down, insist he didn't have time, but his mother had laid on the guilt trip a little thickly at the end there. He would look like an asshole if he was the only one of his siblings who didn't go.

It was true he hadn't had a proper vacation in a while, and it was just for the weekend, but he had so much work. Even though he had agreed to work with Reba, their schedule wasn't taking up his entire weekend, just part of it. This was an entire 48 hours he'd be at the beach.

"Taking one weekend off won't derail your life plans, sweetie," his mother said as if she had read his mind. "I promise. The practice doesn't crumble when I go on vacation now, does it? It's all about delegating. Think of it this way—it'll refresh you to keep going."

Devon sighed. "Fine."

Dax had already given his blessing, and he would look like a terrible son for refusing. One thing Dax prioritised was his family.

"Yes! Now don't leave work too late, please. We really

want to be heading up by four." His mother got to her feet and blew him a kiss. "Love you! See you later."

Devon rubbed his forehead and glanced down at his cell again. Was it coincidence that this was happening now? Or had Reba put the idea in Keiran's head? He didn't go back to the chat. Now that he was being forced into leaving work early, he had to push through to get most of his stuff done in less time.

He didn't need to add gawking at Reba to that list. He would take his laptop with him and still get some work done at the beach house. It was a simple enough plan.

DEVON WAS DEFINITELY GETTING NO WORK DONE THIS WEEKEND. His entire plan was already in shambles.

They had made it up to the beach house just as the sun was setting. He had been bombarded with calls from his mother, Keiran, and Maxi, reminding him to get his ass to his mother's house by four. Otherwise, they were storming his office to physically drag him out. Even Dax had peeped in to tell him he should be on his way.

He had arrived at the house at the stipulated time, ignoring all the excited chatter to pack their bags in the car. The faster they got a move on, the quicker they could get to the house, and he could possibly lock himself in a room to finish up a bit of work before the festivities began.

Except, they had barely settled into the beach house when Keiran had cranked up some music, and they were already talking about getting the BBQ pit going. He was getting no work done in this noise.

He wandered out to the balcony to peer down at the sand and water below, contemplating whether he could quickly check his email without being noticed. His phone was barely in his hand when it was snatched away.

"Seriously?" He whipped around to glare at his sister.

Maxi waved the phone around. "Don't even start. It's mummy's weekend, and it won't kill you to put these emails on Do Not Disturb for the duration." She lifted her brow as if daring him to challenge her.

He could easily take his phone back, but knowing both his siblings, they would team up against him and possibly hide it somewhere. Younger siblings were truly annoying.

He sighed. "Fine. I promise. Now please, can I have my phone back?"

"Sure. Now lemme put those hands to work, so you don't have time to check emails."

Devon rolled his eyes but followed Maxi to help with the mini party prep. Keiran shoved a beer in his hand as he fired up the grill that was stashed away in the corner of the balcony. With the cool sea breeze blowing in, the laughter and constant chatter, this was a far cry from how Devon liked to spend his weekends, but Maxi was right. His mother deserved some downtime and to be doted on by her children. He wouldn't argue with that. She had earned it.

His phone chimed in his pocket, and like a predator scenting its prey, Maxi's head turned in his direction.

"That's not my email tone. It's a WhatsApp message. Am I allowed to check that, at least?"

"Who would even message you at this hour if it's not work-related?" Maxi asked, brow raised again.

"I talk to people," he said unconvincingly.

The only people he regularly spoke to on his phone were work colleagues, and he rarely texted, preferring to get on a phone call with Dax and the rest of the team. He couldn't fathom casually texting Dax for anything, even work-related.

Otherwise, he had sort of alienated the handful of friends he'd managed to keep over the years—declining their numerous invitations, saying he was too busy—so they had eventually stopped asking him to anything. Or speaking to him on the regular. It wasn't ideal, but he was trying to make partner, and that meant showing the team he was willing to put in the work. He had hoped his friends would understand, but that hadn't quite happened.

Maxi folded her arms. "Right. When was the last time you spoke to Jeremy? You two even still friends?"

He wasn't sure how to respond to that. He hadn't spoken to Jeremy in almost a year. They weren't the sort of friends who needed to be in constant daily communication, but now there was just nothing. Devon kept thinking he should reach out, but then he'd get busy with work, and all of that fell to the wayside.

He swiped to unlock his phone, ignoring Maxi, not at all surprised to see Reba had sent him another message. He didn't click on it. Her last message with that damn photo had left him reeling. He didn't need any more surprises. Two in one day was more than he could handle.

"So, who was it?"

He looked up to find Maxi right in front of him, drink in hand. "Jesus, Maxi."

"Leave him alone. Maybe he has a lil' girlfriend he doesn't want to tell us about," Keiran joked, moving to put the marinated meat on the grill.

Cherisse looked up from where she had been arranging a table to lay out some snacks. "Oh, really?"

Great, just what he needed—for everyone to go into interrogation mode over nothing. There was no girlfriend.

He could have easily said it was Reba, but then he'd have to explain why they were exchanging texts. He didn't want to let them in on his bake-off mission. He had sworn Reba to secrecy. The jokes would fly all weekend if they knew.

"It's no one of importance. Just work," he lied. It was easier than listening to his family speculate and be totally wrong if he told them who had messaged him. "So I'm putting away my phone now, okay?"

He did just that, trying his best to be present when all he wanted to do was check his phone, not work emails but to see what else Reba had sent him. She had him curious, and he hated that. He didn't want to be distracted by her or any more random bathing suit shots. Who sent someone they barely knew a photo like that?

As his family laughed and ate around him, he suddenly wondered if *he* was reading too much into it. Is that what people did with mere acquaintances these days? Ask for clothing advice? He'd never done such a thing. When he was still living at his mother's place, his family would offer up unsolicited fashion advice constantly, the twins deploying good-natured ribbing of his staid clothing choices. Nothing malicious, really, but he was glad he didn't have to deal with any of that now.

Peace and quiet was what he had in his new home. None of this raucousness that was currently happening. It occurred to him like a bolt of lightning shocking his entire system that soon he would have Reba in his space. Good Lord, what had he done?

"Shit," he muttered under his breath as he realised the whirlwind he was about to allow into his house come next weekend.

"Uncle said a bad word," Leah sing-songed because apparently, she had supersonic hearing.

"Sorry."

"What're you thinking so hard about over there?" his mother asked.

"Nothing."

"It's always nothing," Keiran piped up. He had a lap full of his girlfriend, and all eyes were trained his way. "You know you can talk to us. We won't judge."

That was an absolute lie. "You all judge me all the time."

Keiran shrugged. "Okay, true, but you make it so easy, Mr. Broody. We're all having fun over here, and you're off probably thinking about how many storeys some building needs to be. C'mon, man. It can wait until Monday." His brother slid another beer over to Devon's side.

He wrapped his hand around the cold can. He didn't overindulge, knew his limits quite well. Two beers wouldn't have him doing anything over the top to make him a mess. Even when he was with his family, he was a moderate drinker. Especially after that one time with some school friends when he had made a total ass of himself. It still haunted him. Being that out of control? Never again.

"I'm here," he insisted, popping the tab on the can and taking a sip.

He needed to pay attention, not think about Reba in any capacity until he absolutely had to. God help him.

CHAPTER FOUR
REBA

Devon had left her on read again. Reba wasn't about to let that slide. He had opened the lines of communication, and if he thought she was just going back to being ignored, he definitely had another thing coming. Especially since they were about to come face-to-face at some point this weekend, whether he knew that or not.

She and her girls, Trina and Ayo, had arrived at the beach house at the crack of dawn on Saturday morning. Reba had put her bathing suit on from home, so once she removed her shorts, she was ready to hit some waves. She'd let Cherisse know she was here and would come check in on them in a few.

Reba hadn't planned to be in the beach house next to the Kings and Cherisse, but as fate would have it, that's exactly what went down not long after she had told Devon where she would be this weekend. Keiran had gotten this last-minute surprise in his head, and Reba, being the ever-helpful assistant to his girlfriend, had offered to hook him up. And voilà, here they were.

She hadn't told Devon anything because she wanted a

grand reveal, especially since he had read her message last night and not responded. How rude!

Well, she'd be dealing with his fine ass soon enough.

She strutted down the steps and dug her toes into the sand before throwing her hands up and inhaling a lungful of the sea scent. Ah, bliss. Just what she needed this weekend. Cherisse and Keiran would be leaving soon, so she was making it her goal to ensure Ms. King kept having fun for the duration of their time. She had appointed herself the Fun Ambassador for this weekend, and she took her role seriously.

Tossing her towel onto the railing of the stairs, she made her way over to the shoreline and let the water rush over her feet. By the time Trina and Ayo joined her with some beach mats and breakfast, she had already gotten some good salt and sea in.

She turned to survey the beach house next door, wondering if anyone was up yet when she spied a man on the balcony squinting down at her. The scowl was familiar, even from this distance. Well, well, now was the time for her perfect entrance. She towelled off, still facing him before turning to her friends.

"Be right back. I see movement over there. The Kings have risen."

She strutted up the stairs enjoying the way Devon's eyes narrowed with each step that brought her closer.

"Well, good morning, neighbour."

He blinked at her, his casual lean against the railing turning tense, his grip tightening on his mug. "What are you doing here?"

She pointed at the house next door. "I told you my plans, didn't I? Surprise!" She cocked her hip, giving him the exact same pose she had in the photo she'd sent him yesterday.

His eyes dipped right to the curve before swiftly swinging up to meet her gaze. "That can't be right."

"Imagine my utter delight when I told Keiran I would hook him and his moms up this weekend, and Trina's mom had a house right next door to us. She rents out beach houses up this side, and here we are."

"*You're* the reason I'm forced to change my weekend plans?"

"You act as if spending time with your mother on her birthday is a chore." She spread her arms wide. "Besides, aren't you glad you get to see the bathing suit in person? Perfect choice, no?"

He didn't answer, just kept scowling at her. Even in his casual beach shorts and t-shirt, Devon didn't look the slightest bit relaxed. How someone could be this tense with a gorgeous blue sky and waves crashing right there was beyond her. Someone needed to help him loosen up, and Reba was rethinking her earlier stance on volunteering to do just that. Devon would never go for something like that, but that didn't mean she couldn't try.

"I guess Mission: Scandalise The Beachgoers has been unlocked if nothing else," he finally muttered.

Reba laughed. She hadn't actually done that yet, considering there weren't many people out and about at this hour, but she'd get to it. Her ass was a work of art that needed to be shown off. If Devon wasn't going to appreciate it, someone else would. With schools closed for the holiday period, the beach tended to get crowded on the weekends, especially after lunch. She would have multiple eyes on her eventually.

"Hmm. On that note, it's pretty rude to read someone's message and not reply, no?"

"I didn't read your message, what are you talking about?" His brow furrowed even more. The man would prematurely give himself wrinkles with all this unnecessary workout his forehead was getting.

"It said you did." She had seen the little checkmarks last night as she had been tossing too many bathing suit options into her cute bag.

They were only here for the weekend, but Reba needed choices. Her mood could call for a sexy colourful bikini or an equally hot monokini, cut high on the leg with no back to speak of at all—like what she was currently wearing. She needed to be prepared.

"Must have accidentally done that," he mumbled.

"Wow, so you had no intention of replying to my very serious message? Shame on you. That was a quality meme right there."

Devon took another sip from his mug, closing his eyes for a second as if to savour the taste—or gather his strength to continue engaging in conversation. Reba assumed the latter. He didn't seem to enjoy conversing just for fun. Or good ass memes, either.

"I was trying to reply to a work message this morning. Must have clicked you by mistake."

"You really don't know the meaning of rest and relax-ation, do you?" Reba shook her head, her pink plait swishing around her shoulders. She was quite fond of the pastel colour. It reminded her of cotton candy, which was apt, really. She could definitely melt in some mouths once pressure was applied just right.

She giggled at her silly thoughts. Devon wouldn't appreciate the image *that* invoked, so she kept it to herself.

His loss, really. Instead, she decided to continue chatting him up because he was so clearly annoyed by her presence. Poor man. Didn't he know this was practice for when they had to meet up for his baking lessons?

"So, are you coming down?" She jerked a thumb at the water. "I'm sure my friends would love to meet you."

"I'm good."

"Are you really not going to take a dip?" she asked. She wondered how he would look if he actually smiled more. Devastatingly handsome, probably.

"Not right now." He continued sipping from his mug, not looking at her.

She didn't know if he didn't want to be distracted by her bathing suit or what, but Reba was fine with carrying this entire conversation herself.

"You know, we could have totally gotten started on our baking classes this weekend since we're both in the same space after all."

He cut his eyes her way, and Reba almost took a step back as she was blasted with the barely banked annoyance there, except she would have gone tumbling down the steps had she moved too far back. She stepped away from the stairs, which put her closer to where Devon was standing. He didn't seem to appreciate that at all, scowl growing deeper.

"I told you. Not a word to my family about this."

She folded her arms, leaning back against the railing. "Yeah, you said, but why?"

"I don't need them up in my business."

"Am *I* your business now?" she purred.

"Don't say it like that. You know what I mean."

She leaned forward. "Do I?"

He scrubbed a hand down his face over that soft-looking beard. "Why am I even here?" he asked quietly, definitely more to himself than her. "Just please keep this between us."

She saluted. "Sure thing. You're paying, after all."

"Hey, you're here."

They both turned as Cherisse strolled out, bag over her shoulder.

"Aww, boss lady, you're leaving already?"

"Yeah. Need to get the desserts to that party, then make sure I have everything for my flight tomorrow."

Since they had prepped the ridiculous cake during the day on Friday, Cherisse just had to get it to the client in one piece.

"Well, no worries. I promise a fun time for Mama King tonight." She lowered her voice. "I got the cake all stashed up in our fridge. We'll bring her over when the sun goes down. Then the fun can begin."

"More partying?" Devon asked, the crease deepening between his brows.

"Party Central over there tonight. Be there or be square." Reba looked him up and down, lingering slightly on the fit of the t-shirt over his chest. The man was truly a work of art. Tall, built, with a frown Reba wanted to turn upside down.

She would get a smile out of Devon yet before this weekend was over. She had just decided. She loved a good challenge, after all.

"Too bad you can't be there," she said to Cherisse. "But go do what you do, then have all that sexy fun with your man." She winked, and Devon fully drained his mug and walked inside without a word.

Reba pursed her lips at his rude exit. "That brother-in-law of yours is quite the character."

"Whoa, slow all that down. It's too soon for that. Marriage is *not* on the horizon." Cherisse looked ready to panic, and Reba grinned. These two were too cute.

"But someday."

"Let's survive not killing each other for a few years first, at least. Well, let me get that man of mine and head out. Don't bruk out too much tonight, okay?"

"No promises. I got the cutest outfit picked out for later. The 'gram is gonna be on fire."

"Please don't have K's mom on there doing body shots or something."

"I can't make any promises. Ms. King is a grown, sexy woman. She can drink and thirst trap if she wants to."

Cherisse laughed and gave Reba a hug before heading inside to get Keiran. Damn, Reba envied her boss in that moment. She would have loved to be frolicking in St. Lucia for the next two weeks, dipping in some sulphur springs too with a sexy somebody. Her last dalliance had ended because Mr. Man had started acting up, trying to dictate her ways and change her into someone she wasn't. All that "maybe you need to tone it down a bit" noise wasn't it. Why he had to ruin their casual sex with all that foolishness was beyond her.

It had reminded her too much of the one serious relationship she had attempted. She had brought up wanting to meet his family since they'd been dating for nine months. He hadn't felt it was the right time because they were quite conservative and wanted to ease them into meeting her. Maybe she could do something about her hair and clothes in the meanwhile? Fuck all that noise. He hadn't been singing that tune when she had been breaking his back with her sexy moves.

That had soured her on relationships for a while, so she

had been sticking to casual. She didn't need a fling to get all up on a high horse with her too. No, thank you. Just make her come and shut up with all that.

Her motto was always and forever *take me as I am or leave me where you found me.* People who wanted the fun Reba for a time but quickly began to act as if she was too much would not be in her orbit for long.

It wouldn't hurt to find a sexy diversion, but right now, this weekend was about recharging. Her vibrator could more than do the job until she was inclined to seduce someone into having a good casual time with her again.

They all bid Cherisse and Keiran goodbye and a safe trip. Leah, who had given Cherisse and Keiran big hugs before they left, looked up at Devon with her adorable face and asked, "Are we going down to the beach now?"

Devon sighed and nodded. "Sure thing, sweetie."

Reba bit her lip to keep her laugh in. So even Mr. Grumpy wasn't immune to Leah's cuteness. Good to know.

When they all trooped down to the water, Trina's brow nearly lifted off her forehead when she saw Devon.

"Well, *who* is this?"

"Devon King, these are my friends, Trina and Ayo. Devon is Cherisse's boyfriend's brother."

"Oh, I see the *fine* gene runs in that family. Sweet like a Julie mango, mmm-hmm." Trina did an over-the-top lick of her bottom lip, and Devon looked completely unaffected by her perusal.

"Hi there," Ayo said.

"Nice to meet you both," he replied before leaving them to join his family. Leah and Maxi were setting up their beach mats and chairs not too far away from them.

"Oh shit, that voice." Ayo was practically melting on

that blanket, and Reba couldn't blame her. Devon's voice conjured up impure thoughts.

"Keep it in your pants, ladies, there's a child present."

"You can't tell me your vag isn't on fire after hearing that man speak."

Reba plucked some watermelon from the fruit bowl Trina had prepared. "You might want to get that checked out or something."

Trina rolled her eyes. "Let me lust, woman, damn!"

"Like you forget you have a boyfriend?" Reba reminded her.

"I'm just looking. Nothing wrong with that," Trina insisted.

Reba hadn't yet told them she would be spending her next few weekends with Devon, teaching him some baking tips, and the way he had made it a big issue upstairs, she'd leave that for after this weekend. Trina and Ayo couldn't be trusted with secrets when high. They might bring that up while tipsy tonight, and Reba didn't want to ruin the mood because Devon definitely wouldn't approve.

Not that she would have cared, usually. Devon's gruffness wasn't a turn-off per se. She was going to get him to unwind and have fun somehow. Tonight's cake party would bring the entertainment for both Ms. King and everyone else. They would need to wait until Leah went to bed to indulge in some of her other planned activities, but it would be worth the wait.

She could be patient when it suited her.

They spent most of the morning soaking up the sun that graced them with its warm presence. Reba sent up a silent thanks to the weather gods for being cool and allowing her to bask in their glow. It was the perfect lighting for cute and sexy selfies.

Being friends with Trina and Ayo meant she didn't have to beg either of them to take photos of her, either.

"Yes, gyal, cock yuh hip just so," Trina instructed as Reba did just that, popping her booty to get the right angle and show off her tattoo.

She caught Devon watching them as if he just couldn't fathom why they were doing any of this. She blew him a kiss when his mother and sister was otherwise occupied with Leah, enjoying how he hastily looked away. Oh yeah, she knew how she looked in this bathing suit, and even if Devon would never come out and say anything, he was *looking*.

Having a mini photoshoot was always fun, but Reba definitely enjoyed laying on her blanket when she was done, sunglasses shading her eyes, allowing her to properly gape at Devon when he tossed off his shirt because *okay, yes.*

"Fuck," Trina said.

"Seconding that." Ayo, who was usually a little less vocal than Trina, pulled down her sunglasses to overtly stare at Devon's chest.

Reba didn't know when Devon found time to work out —he must have fit it in his busy schedule somehow— because his chest was a thing of beauty. She sipped the cocktail Trina had so graciously poured her from the bottle she had stashed in her basket of goodies, eyes drinking in the smattering of hair on his chest, that treasure trail, the abs that weren't too overly defined but looked positively lickable.

He swung Leah around in the water, her delighted squeals warming Reba's heart the way seeing his arms bunched warmed her pussy. Reba crossed her legs because it was damn inconvenient for her body to do this to her now when she didn't have an outlet to ease some of this pressure.

"Can you imagine him throwing you around in bed with those arms? Because I sure can." Trina fanned her face. "So, what's his deal, anyways?"

Reba shrugged. Why did they think she would know? She assumed he was single but had no way of knowing anything further than that unless she asked.

She had the basics from Cherisse. Thirty-five, which made him eight years older than her. Worked at an architectural firm. And now she knew he lived on his own. Everything else she had gathered about his personality had been from their brief interactions.

"He's the serious sort," Reba said, draining her drink.

"Yeah, that mouth looks like it could be real serious with my p—"

"Ma'am, you have a man," Ayo pointed out.

Trina shrugged. "We're not on speaking terms right now, so it's not clear if I do."

Reba rolled her eyes. Trina and her boyfriend were always going through something. She should just cut him loose and be done with it. Who needed all that stress in their life? Reba didn't care how much Trina gushed about the makeup sex. It didn't seem worth it to her. She loved a good makeup sex session herself, but once things kept going to shit, she was out. And doing this song and dance thing for ten years? No way.

"Maybe if he saw me talking to Devon, he'd get his shit together and make an honest woman of me."

Trina and Aaron had been on-again, off-again since secondary school. As far as Reba saw it, that was too long to be messing around with someone with no clear plans to mesh your futures together. And the likelihood of Devon posing for a photo with them was exactly zero, but she wished Trina luck if she tried to do that to make Aaron jealous.

Devon came jogging over to his sister and mother, Leah's hand clasped in his, water dripping off his body. He glanced their way, and Reba called out, "We got cocktails if anyone wants!"

Devon draped his towel over his broad shoulders. Reba could feel Trina vibrating next to her. She got it, truly she did. The way his hands gripped the ends of the towel...damn.

"We're good, thanks," he called back.

"Speak for yourself." Ms. King got to her feet and wandered over.

Reba laughed and prepared a drink for her. Ms. King knew how to have a good time. Maybe she would rub off on her son, persuade him to indulge a little tonight. She doubted it, but if no one else was going to, Reba would try her best to get him to engage in a little fun at least.

They packed up their stuff a little after two and went back to their respective beach houses. Reba was feeling super relaxed from the water and her drinks, but she realised she needed to let Ms. King know what was going on in case she decided to turn in early tonight. Reba couldn't have that at all. She'd missed her opportunity while they had been down at the beach, and even though she felt kind of drowsy right now, she had promised Keiran and Cherisse.

After showering off the sand and seawater, changing into one of her casual rompers, and taking her plait down so her hair could dry, she trekked back over to the Kings' beach house. Devon was sitting in one of the chairs, glaring down at his phone.

"You know, Maxi's going to be on your ass if she sees you out here checking work emails," she said by way of a greeting.

Devon looked up at her, expression not changing one bit. Damn, if she wasn't as confident as she was, he could give her a complex. Most people were happy to see her. Was Devon ever happy about anything?

"You're going to tell on me?"

"Hell yes. You need to be present. It's a beach weekend getaway. Forget work."

"You say it like it's that easy. I can't just turn off that part of my brain."

"Well, at least try for your mom."

He pursed his lips but tucked his phone away in the pocket of his board shorts. "Fine."

"Good."

"So why are you here? Isn't this cake party tonight?"

"Yeah, but I want to let your mom know upfront so she doesn't fall asleep or something. And give her time to get cute."

"Is this a fancy party?" Devon frowned. "I didn't bring anything except shorts and t-shirts."

"That's acceptable. The party's about her, so it doesn't matter what you wear." She rubbed her hands together. "Besides, when the afterparty hits, no one's going to care what anyone is wearing."

"Afterparty?" his eyes narrowed. "What exactly is going to happen at this afterparty?"

Reba waved off his question. No need to give him a reason not to show up. "Don't worry about it."

"It's you. I might need to worry."

Reba snorted. "What does that mean? It's me? You think

I'm going to do something scandalous?" She winked. "Seriously, don't sweat it."

She waved at him and made her way inside to find his mother. Her plans weren't that over-the-top. Although they may seem like that to him, Reba didn't care. She was on a mission. Get Ms. King in the know, decorate their beach house. Have fun. And possibly get Devon to at least have a moderately good time.

Nothing else mattered.

CHAPTER FIVE
DEVON

DEVON SHOULD HAVE KNOWN THAT THE FIRST HALF OF THE PARTY was set up to lull him into a false sense of security. Make him think that it was a simple affair with cake, food, and drinks. He should have realised when Leah went reaching for brownies from one of the platters that was tucked away from the rest of the food, and Reba swooped in with, "Not these ones, sweetie. These are for the adults," that this supposed afterparty was something he should avoid.

Reba had basically told him so with her winking and coy replies this afternoon. But when they walked over to the beach house, he saw some twinkly lights set up on their balcony, a spread with the cake and food, and drinks in the cooler. Music was playing from someone's Bluetooth speakers. There were even some games set up. Seemed normal enough.

A couple of Uno and Scattergories games later had everyone riled up over some friendly competition but didn't lead to anything too serious, and Devon wondered if Reba had made him think she was going to do something over the top when it was just this. The moment his mother said she was heading over to put Leah to bed and that the youngsters should stay and have fun, though, the atmosphere changed, and he knew he was in for trouble.

"Aww, Ms. King, leaving already?" Reba pouted.

"You all stay back and have fun. I saw those brownies. I know what's about to go down here, but thanks for making my day special, sweetie. Make good choices, kids!"

He had offered to go with her, but she'd insisted he stay and have fun for once in his life. Reba's friends had giggled at that. He hadn't found it quite as hilarious. He was a grown man; he didn't need his mother's scolding about having a good time.

Reba barely waited for his mother to leave before coming over to him with those suspicious brownies, a big smile stretching her deep, purple-coloured lips wide. Her pink hair flowed in waves around her bare shoulders, obscuring part of her yellow tube top, and because he was sitting, her bare stomach with that piercing in her navel was practically in his face.

He had done his best throughout the day not to let his gaze linger on Reba while she had been in that ridiculous gift box-patterned bathing suit. The sun had worshipped her as she strutted around and laid out on her blanket. On this balcony at night, with its muted lighting and the glow of the twinkle lights, she was less in the glaring spotlight, and yet he found himself wanting to make an excuse to leave so he didn't have this internal fight not to look directly at her.

"Brownie?" she asked.

The sharp smell of weed wafted over to him, and he glanced across to where her friend Trina was taking a drag of what was obviously a blunt. So this was how this after-party was going to go. Get high and eat some brownies. The questionable brownies, which definitely had weed in them too, he suspected.

"These aren't regular brownies, are they?"

"Nope. Baked with love just for the occasion."

"You know that's not what I meant."

Reba leaned in, her hair almost brushing his lap. She was close enough that he could smell her faint vanilla scent, even with the weed trying to overpower everything. "Are you asking me if these are weed brownies, Mr. King? Because they obviously are. Ever tried an edible before?"

Maxi swooped by and grabbed one up. He raised a brow as his sister took a huge bite. "What?" she challenged. "Mama needs a break too, you know."

"Well?" Reba pushed the tray closer to him.

"No, thanks."

Everyone was getting baked out here, and he didn't need any photographic evidence of him doing the same. Eating a brownie wouldn't clue anyone into the type of brownie it was, but still. He preferred to be careful. They had been taking pictures all night, and Devon had to keep a clear head, had to stay focused even during this supposed weekend of fun. He couldn't go off the rails and get high, do something he would regret, and jeopardise his chances of making partner.

Reba took a seat next to him, placing the tray on a side table someone had set up. "I'm not trying to pressure you, but just know this is a safe space if you wanted to try it."

"Not my thing. Although the way your friend is going at it over there, I could get high by secondhand contact alone."

Reba gasped dramatically. "Was that a joke?"

"No."

She shook her head. "No fun at all. Whatever, more for

me." She took a big bite of one of the brownies and groaned. "Damn, I'm good."

"You do this a lot?" He tried not to sound like he was passing judgement, not that Reba seemed inclined to give a damn. She kept eating the brownie and crossed her legs, which made the hem of her tiny black shorts ride up even more.

He couldn't see it since it was covered by her shorts, but her hibiscus tattoo flashed in his mind. Why had she chosen the flower to brand on her skin? Why that location? Most people wouldn't see it unless she was in a bathing suit like today, or, well...if she was undressing for whatever reason. He tore his gaze away from her legs, meeting Reba's amused smirk.

"You mean consuming edibles or smoking?" she asked, not calling him on getting caught staring. "The latter's a no. The former is more a social thing for me.

"Hmm."

"You like being in control, don't you?" She licked crumbs from her fingers, and Devon was convinced the weed was getting to him because he lingered way too long on the way her lips wrapped around each fingertip.

He looked away. "Yes. There's nothing wrong with that."

"Hmm," she mimicked his earlier sound. "You can't control everything, though. Some things you just need to ride that wave. You can't plan out *every* aspect of your life."

"*A* plan is better than no plan."

"Spontaneity, though. Have you ever tried it? Feels *so* damn good."

That sounded like the worst thing ever. Never having a plan for anything? Just going with the flow? Not something he was into. Also, he didn't want to know anything about the things that made Reba feel good.

The way her voice had dropped like that, almost to a whisper, made it seem like she was talking about something best left for the confines of a bedroom.

Seriously, how potent was this weed?

"Coming up with a work proposal feels good to me," he said, risking a glance her way.

Reba's nose wrinkled. "Work proposal? Bleh. I love my job, okay, but what do you do for fun outside of work? There's got to be something. What do you and your friends do together?"

"I don't have any friends because I work too much and don't have time for fun." He had definitely *not* meant to say that shit. What was wrong with him? He didn't overshare like this.

Reba didn't need to know a small part of him felt inadequate because he had failed at juggling work and friends. Although, that analysis he had run did prove he had more time for work-related things now that he didn't have friends to hang out with. So should he really feel guilty about any of it? He had never kicked up a fuss when those same friends couldn't attend something he had suggested because they were busy with their children or spouses. For all he knew, they had made up the whole thing because his hobbies bored them.

Whatever. None of that mattered now. He didn't usually lament on that stuff. He was quite content with being focused on his career goals.

Why should he feel bad because he had chosen to work instead of attending some baby shower or child's birthday party? A two-year-old wasn't going to know whether he had attended or not, and he wasn't always free to go see some movie his friends were into at that particular time.

"Oh, well, that's just sad." Reba pointed between them. "We can be friends. I'll show you how to have fun along with helping you with this bake-off."

"Shh," he hissed out, looking over to see if Maxi heard. His sister was busy looking at something on Trina's phone while she munched on a brownie.

Maxi looked too relaxed and engrossed in that phone to give a damn about him.

"Oh, right, shit, sorry." Reba giggled, clapping her hand over her mouth.

"You're definitely high."

"Yup, but my offer still stands. Let me be your fun coordinatorrrr." She dragged out the word for so long that Devon thought she'd go until she was out of breath.

"That won't be necessary."

"I'll do it for free. We can do it for free. I'm gonna love doing it with you."

"Just, please..." He rubbed his forehead. Jesus, he should really get out of here before he inhaled any more of this stuff. "Stop saying that."

Reba's eyes twinkled. "Saying what? 'Doing it?' Are you twelve? If I was talking about sex, I'd just say the word. Sexxxxx."

"I don't want to discuss any of that with you."

She threw up her hands. "Fine. I'll respect your wishes for now because I'm cool like that. It's okay." She patted his arm. "Wow, okay, damn, where do you find time to shape these guns?"

"Reba."

"Okay, yes. Boundaries. Respecting them. Sorry." She

removed her hands and placed them in her lap. "I do know how to be a *very* good girl."

Devon got to his feet. It was definitely time to get back to the house. "I'm going to go now."

She looked up at him. "Hey, wait. I'm sorry. You don't have to leave. I *will* behave. See?" She wiggled her hands. "These shall remain over here."

"It's not you."

Except, it absolutely was. Reba combined with the weed was a terrible idea. Devon was good at staying in control of a situation, but this was exactly why he'd wanted to bail when his mother left. Anything that made him feel like he was losing his grip on something was a problem.

Reba was...a lot to take in at a time.

Especially this flirty, clearly tipsy version of her. He felt himself wanting to lean in, too, respond to that *'I do know how to be a very good girl'* with something ill-advised.

Get back to the house. Drink some water. That's what he needed to do, his mother's proclamation be damned. She had probably already gone to bed. She wouldn't know he hadn't stayed for too long. He would also need a shower. He didn't want to smell like *he* had smoked anything. His mother obviously wouldn't care, but he did.

He walked over to the others. "Maxi, I'm leaving."

She looked up at him, confused. "Already? It's not even midnight yet."

"Well, I'm going. You're staying?"

He would prefer she leave with him. He didn't like the idea of her stumbling down some stairs and over to the house by herself late at night, but one thing he knew for sure was Maxi hated for anyone to tell her what to do.

She waved him off. "Yeah, I'm staying. I'll sober up before I decide to leave."

"You can sleep here if you'd like," Reba offered. She'd come over to stand next to him. "You can borrow something of mine."

"Well, there yah go. Bye, D."

"Okay, call me if anything."

Maxi had gone back to her conversation. As he turned to go, someone cranked up the music that had been playing at a decent volume before. Reba started up some dance moves that made her roll her waist like a snake.

The others were clapping and encouraging her along.

Devon left before he got even more entranced by those sensuous movements.

CHAPTER SIX
DEVON

REBA ARRIVED AT HIS HOUSE ON SATURDAY MORNING WITH HER pastel pink hair up in two buns, a crop top that proclaimed "Time to Bake, Bitches!" and tight jeans. She strolled in like she owned his place, laptop tucked under her arm.

He hadn't seen her since last weekend when the image of her slow hip movements had been burned into his brain. A distraction that kept popping up randomly throughout the week, which wasn't ideal when he was trying to finish up his presentation. Dax Designs had been one of the companies offered to bid on construction of a new adults-only resort and spa. He couldn't lose sight of his weekly to-do list, which didn't include daydreaming about Reba's legs, hips, or that damn tattoo.

It had been very unlike him to lose focus like that. He couldn't blame any of it on the weed anymore. Something was happening to him, and he didn't like it.

"Well, this is not at all colourful. Just what I expected from you. You decorate it yourself?" She plopped herself down onto his couch as she looked around. Her fingers stroked the arm of the black couch she currently occupied, her rainbow manicure a bright splash against the dark fabric.

"Yes." He followed the slow movement of her fingers as they danced over that arm.

"Man of a few words, as usual. We'll work on that," she announced.

He tore his gaze away from her hand. "Why?" She wasn't here to work on him. This was about the bake-off.

Reba crossed her legs, making herself more comfortable. He hadn't been thrilled about allowing Reba into his home, but to get this done, he had no choice. He was protective of his space, even from his family members. He hadn't had his family over for any long periods of time yet, so to have Reba here made him a little bit wary.

She was a colourful explosion in his otherwise subdued space. He didn't do wild colours and was pleased with his end result. Subtle. Minimalistic was what he had been going for. His walls boasted some tasteful art prints—which were the only splashes of true colour to be found—and designs from architects he admired. His mother had visited and found the entire black and grey aesthetic to be cold. She'd tried to get him to add some pops of colour via throw pillows she had sewn. He had tucked them away in his bedroom and the guest room. They didn't belong in his living room, and neither did Reba.

"From what you've told me about this company bake-off, there's actually two parts to my master plan. The baking and the people skills. Clearly, you need help with both. And this can bring in the 'get Devon to have some fun' bonus round perfectly."

Devon frowned as Reba reached into her overly colourful case and pulled out her laptop. Not surprisingly, the front was covered with random stickers. So much clutter. Devon shuddered as she booted it up. He didn't have a single sticker on his that hadn't already come with the laptop.

"What *is* all that stuff on there?" he couldn't help but ask.

Reba tapped the top of the laptop. "Different sayings I like. Sailor Moon stuff. Fun things. Plain laptops are *so* boring." She waved at his perfectly clear laptop and wrinkled her nose. "Case in point."

"Clutter-free. Just like I like it."

"Bor-*ring*," she repeated. She tapped a nail against her cheek, drawing his eye to the curve of her cheekbone, which glinted with some bit of makeup he didn't know the name for. Reba had a full face going on there. "We'll work on that too."

"You know, you didn't have to get this dressed up for baking."

"Dressed up? This is my casual day look." She chuckled. "Dressed up, he says." She shook her head, clearly amused.

"But your face is shiny right here." He pointed to his own cheekbones. "That means you have on that, uh, thing that does that."

"The word you're looking for is 'highlighter.' I barely have a full look going on. There's a smidge of foundation, the highlighter, my winged eyeliner. Some mascara. A swish of gloss because leave the house with a bare lip? Never." She shuddered. "And a dash of powder. That barely took me ten minutes."

"Okay." Devon didn't have anything else to add to that.

It sounded like a lot, but what did he know? He remembered being over at Monica's one time when she was doing one of her no-makeup looks, but she had taken quite a bit of time in the bathroom. Putting on makeup to look like you had none on was a strange concept, but he hadn't probed further.

Reba's makeup routine didn't concern him. What was concerning was her desire to tweak *him*.

"Anyways, I hired you to help with baking, not a personality makeover."

"Wrong. Didn't you say your boss's assistant basically told you that you needed to be more involved in work things?"

Devon regretted sharing that bit of information. When Reba had asked why he was doing this, he didn't think it would be an issue to mention that. He should have known he couldn't begin to predict what Reba would do.

"From what you've explained," she went on, "your boss is looking for more from you. He wants to know you're taking this seriously and willing to be a part of the team. Not just work-wise."

"You don't even know him." Sure, he had explained the meeting, what Amanda had said, and what the bake-off entailed, but Reba suddenly thinking she had some insight into Dax was farfetched. How could Reba possibly think she knew anything about him without having met the man? "And I have people skills. I don't need your help with that."

Her laugh was loud enough that Devon was certain his neighbours could hear her through the walls. He didn't usually have company over on a weekend. Reba's appearance was sure to be noticed. They had decided to get an early start—seven weeks seemed like a lot, but time went by quickly—so Reba had arrived at eight so they could go over their game plan. At least she was punctual.

But now, instead of actually discussing baking plans, she was talking about people skills and helping him have fun? None of that mattered, at least where Reba was concerned. He didn't need her for that. He just needed to get to the baking part.

"I told you about this fun plan of yours. I actually thought that was just you being high and talking nonsense."

"I remember everything we discussed. The fun coordinator plan is still on the table, and just so you know, I did my research on your boss. Some light social media stalking proves that man loves people and loves interacting with them. So if you think this is just about baking, I think you're wrong. Real participation is going to be important here." She stuck up two fingers. "Secondly, not to bust your bubble, but you aren't even close to being a people person. You barely acted like I existed at that wedding, and you ran away from our party last weekend."

Devon frowned. Reba wasn't entirely wrong. He could make more of an effort where mingling at work was concerned, and he planned to, in his own way. But Reba's cursory research of Dax had revealed what was a fact. The man did love people. He was an extrovert who walked around each morning, greeting employees. He wasn't like the other executives that most of them barely even saw. He liked interacting with his staff.

That didn't mean Devon wanted to acknowledge that Reba was spot-on. The thought of her teaching him to "people" or have fun? He could only imagine what she would expect him to do.

Reba was obviously fearless when it came to that. He had seen her walk up to guests at Ava's wedding and strike up a conversation as if she'd known them for years. But she was too much of a wildcard to entrust with those sort of lessons. She might try to get him to wander around in a rainbow-coloured wig to get out of his comfort zone, for all he knew.

They had to stay on track. He could work on his supposed shortcomings himself.

"I didn't run from the party," he said because that was a ridiculous assumption.

"What would you call your hasty exit, then?"

"It just wasn't my scene."

"Okay, so what's your scene, then?"

Before he'd given up on making an effort with his friends, he had met up with them for the occasional dinner, or they would go around the island checking out the old buildings. They'd even had a longstanding meet-up for the Scrabble tournaments that took place sometimes. He didn't tell Reba any of that because she would definitely repeat her mantra of "Boring." He couldn't imagine her finding any of that interesting.

"It doesn't matter. We're here to bake. This is wasting time." He turned his laptop to face her. "So, here's my idea."

After last weekend with all its distractions, he had finally decided on what he wanted to do and worked on a proposal of sorts.

Reba's eyes darted back and forth as she read his concept and looked at the photos he'd included. One well-shaped brow went up, and she shook her head. "Well, I'm a bit disappointed in you, Devon," she said.

What? He definitely hadn't expected that. "What do you mean?"

"A Pac-Man cake? Seriously? That's your grand plan for winning this thing? This entire concept is weak as hell, and frankly, I expected more from you."

"I don't understand. What's wrong with this? Pac-Man is a classic."

It was fool-proof. The nostalgia of the game coupled with the cake was sure to be a hit, wasn't it? He had calculated the difficulty level against the timeframe they had leading up to the bake-off and determined this idea was acceptable for his skill level. He could easily learn to do this.

"This is weak," Reba repeated. "It's so basic. You're not going to win with this." She shook her head, a few loose strands of pink hair waving around her face. "I thought you were the kind of man that loves a challenge?"

"You're not wrong. I want to win. Who doesn't love classic games on a cake?"

He had thought long and hard about this. He could win over the judges with a cutesy-looking treat, which would surprise them since everyone thought he wouldn't even try.

"You're not winning with this pathetic display of the mundane. It's an okay idea, I suppose, but..." Her wide grin made him a little wary. He couldn't guess what she was about to throw his way. She turned her laptop around. "You can more than win with this."

He blinked at the photos of the familiar-coloured cube. "This? Why this?" he asked.

"It's perfect for you."

"A Rubik's Cube-shaped cake is perfect for me? How?" He knew exactly how perfect it would be, but he was curious about her thought process because, frankly, it was genius. Not that he wanted to tell her that since she had shot down his idea without any consideration, and especially because he hadn't thought of this himself.

"I figured the difficulty level would appeal to you." Reba clapped her hands. "Ooh, I got it! We do a total fake-out. The video progression will show you making cookies or, better yet, cupcakes because it's what people will expect, and then bam! Show you levelling up with this amazing cake. We can call it 'Started from the Bottom, Now We Here!' It's perfect!" She pumped her fists in the air. "I considered that your math brain would love this since it requires precision. I think your judges will eat up this concept."

Devon stared at the screen. He hadn't anticipated that not only would Reba veto his idea, but she would suggest something that was so *him*. He frowned at the magnificent cake on the screen just because—not giving away how the perfectly crafted cube got him way more excited than the Pac-Man idea. The fact that he had chosen his plan because it was easy and Reba had done the exact opposite didn't sit well with him. He should have come with a better proposal. This would definitely catch the judges' eyes *if* he could pull it off. Reba choosing it because it worked with his specific skill set was commendable. It would be interesting to consider how to put the entire thing together, so it actually looked like the real deal.

Still slightly annoyed over the fact that Reba had pinpointed the one idea that would get him revved up, he asked, "Can *you* teach me how to make this?"

"I'll admit I've never made something like this before, but challenges are fun." She grinned, and while Devon agreed a good challenge got him going like nothing else, he definitely didn't think now was the time for Reba to be trying out something she had never attempted before.

He was paying her for guidance. What if it turned out horribly?

"We should stick to something you've already mastered," he suggested, even as he couldn't take his eyes off the screen. God, whoever had crafted this had done so with effortless precision. The damn cube was perfect.

"That sounds safe. I don't do safe." She turned her

laptop back around to face her. "Don't fight it, Devon. You look like you're ready to propose to whoever made this cake. This is what we're going with. Feel free to ask someone else for help if you're having second thoughts."

She shrugged, leaning back on the couch as she shot him a challenging stare. They both knew she had him. There was no one else he could ask for help. He either did what she asked, or he winged it and checked out those YouTube DIY videos, which was a no. He didn't have time to figure this out on his own. At least with Reba on board, he had some guidance. He didn't ponder too much on the bit of excitement that bloomed in his chest. A fucking Rubik's Cube cake.

Devon made a big production of sighing. He couldn't let on that his mind was racing over this cake. "Fine, we do it your way. I got ingredients for cookies and cupcakes for this morning. We can start on those."

"We'll get to that," Reba said, dismissing his efforts to get up from the couch so they could head to the kitchen. "Get comfy. I need to know some things first."

What more information could she possibly need? This baking session wasn't going as he'd expected. There was more talking than actual baking. He should have known this would be a mistake.

Being seated next to Reba at the wedding had shown him she was a talker. Her efforts to try to draw him into conversation had been thwarted by him not responding, but that hadn't stopped her one bit. She had kept on, carrying the conversation without his participation.

He wondered if it was too late to take his name off that cursed list. It definitely was. Dax would be disappointed, and that was the last thing he needed.

"What do you need to know that doesn't involve my lack of baking skills?"

Reba smiled, twirling a pink strand of her hair around one finger. "When last did you actively mingle with your co-workers that wasn't some forced work event?"

"Not this again. I don't hang with them outside of work, really." Why would he? He liked to keep his work and personal life separate. The few times he and Monica had attended Dax's birthday bash and the office Christmas party, he had gotten way too many people all up in his business.

The flip side was also true. When they realised he had come solo to the last party he attended, they easily deduced he and Monica had broken up, which then led to a host of questions. He certainly hadn't answered. It was why he had made excuses for not attending last year's.

"A couple of them actually invited me to some outing tonight. It's a monthly karaoke night thing, but..." He shrugged.

His only plans had been completing his latest proposal for their next project. Not what anyone would call fun, but visualising what any new building would look like for their clients was therapeutic for him.

He didn't need some wild night out. A quiet night in suited him just fine.

"Okay, next question. Who's your major competition for the bake-off?"

He didn't see what one question had to do with the other but trying to understand Reba in any capacity was futile. From what he had gathered, she didn't follow rules or patterns. "Everyone participating is."

"Nope." She wagged a finger at him. "Wrong. There's

always that one eager beaver in every workplace. Who is it?"

"Evan Charles," he said. The man wasn't a threat to his promotion directly, but his overeager personality hadn't gone unnoticed by Dax, who always appreciated that sort of thing.

"He's the one to beat. Is he going to be at karaoke tonight?"

"He's the one who always organises these things, so I assume yes." He'd never attended, but it was a safe deduction.

"And your boss will be there?"

"I don't know for sure." Anytime Evan tried to talk to him about anything outside of work, Devon usually gave him the brush-off.

Dax had to have something better to do on his weekend than hang with his staff, didn't he? For larger company events, he'd more than be there, but karaoke? He might show up a few times to make Evan feel like he cared, but Devon couldn't see him attending every night.

"Do you follow Evan on Instagram?"

Devon blinked. "No, I don't do Instagram."

Reba looked at him as if he'd told her he'd just committed murder. "Good Lord, you're hopeless. Okay, no worries. I got this."

She produced a phone from her laptop bag. The back of the phone looked like an entire bag of glitter had been spilled on it. He watched as her fingers flew over the screen before she started scrolling and making humming noises.

"Well, then. Here's your answer. I suggest you get your ass to tonight's karaoke." She flipped her phone around and showed him an Instagram account.

It didn't take long for him to deduce it belonged to

Evan. The man's face next to the board that announced the company bake-off was the first thing he saw. The caption boldly proclaimed:

In it to win it! Let's do this! #bakeoff #teamworkmakesthedreamwork #ilovemyjob

"How the hell did you find him on there? His name is pretty common."

Reba gave him a lopsided smile. "It's not that hard to find people online as you may think. A guy like Evan would definitely put his workplace in his social accounts and strikes me as the type to use his actual name on there, so Googling him was easy."

Reba kept scrolling until she came to a photo of Evan and Dax, drinks in hand as they posed in front of a stage. Devon noticed the other people around them were some of his co-workers.

"Dammit," he muttered.

Evan's caption for this one loudly declared:

Boss man passed through. Always grateful for his support! #karaokenight #ilovemyjob #getyouabosslikethis

"So," Reba placed her phone down next to her laptop case. "Ready to get started in the kitchen? You can think about what you want to wear tonight."

"No."

Reba sighed. "Just trust me. Here's how this is gonna go. We go to the karaoke. I scope out your competition because he's not going to be comfy spilling his guts to you, but me?" She grinned. "I can be *very* persuasive. Plus, you show your face. Your boss is happy. Points for attending."

"I don't do karaoke."

"You won't have to. I will." She got to her feet. "You just need to be present and look like you're sort of vibing and having fun, okay? Just bobbing your head to the music a few times should do the trick. Now, let's go bake."

He followed her into the kitchen, totally unsure about this karaoke business. They'd decided to start with the cupcakes as, according to Reba's plan, he needed to lull the participants into thinking he was hopelessly going with some mediocre idea for the bake-off. The cookies would be worked on at some other session, with them progressing to the grand finale cake. He got out the ingredients as Reba fiddled around with her laptop until "Honey" started blaring from the speakers.

He whirled around. "What the hell are you doing?"

"Getting a good vibe going. Don't tell me you don't like Mariah?" She set up her phone, which she explained she was going to use to film his behind-the-scenes clips for submission.

"How can you work in this noise?"

"Excuse you, Mariah is not *noise*." She washed her hands in the sink then turned back to him. "I even got your brother's riddim on here because soca always gets me in the mood to bake. The one he put out for Carnival was vibes."

"Carnival is over."

"Soca isn't just for Carnival," she countered. "Are you saying you don't listen to it outside of that?"

Devon didn't have anything against soca music. He simply didn't feel the need to listen to it constantly. Keiran rarely asked for Devon's opinion when he was working on something, but he had heard the riddim Reba was talking about. He liked it fine enough. Didn't mean he was going to have it on repeat throughout the year just because his brother produced it. His tastes lay in more old-school styles. His mother liked to comment that he had an old soul, and he was fine with that.

"I don't see the need to," he admitted.

Reba shook her head. "So, what *do* you like?"

"I never said I didn't like soca."

Reba tapped her chin. "My brain is trying to conjure up an image of you wining low in a fete to soca, and it's glitching a bit. I can't even picture it. It's giving me waltzing to some vintage stuff in a back-in-times party instead."

She wasn't entirely wrong. Devon had gone to Carnival fetes before, when he and Monica had been together, where they danced along like everyone else. Except he had kept a level of decorum that ensured he didn't end up on the front of a newspaper grinding on his girlfriend like they were exposing the world to a private moment. Not his thing. A little slow wine he didn't mind, but getting down to the point where they were basically dry humping on the floor? No way.

"Not my style."

"Maybe you haven't met the one person to make that style go out the window." Reba leaned in, smirk firmly in place. "Sometimes, when the music hits, I surprise even myself with how I let loose. Feeding off your dance partner's vibe helps too."

Devon didn't let loose on the dancefloor, which meant he had a reputation for being stush, or so his siblings said. He didn't care. He could easily picture Reba going wild. He had gotten a tiny glimpse of her moves at the beach house, and thinking back now, at Ava's wedding too.

He remembered her in that silver dress that drew the eye like a beacon, bouncing her ass in time to the music, hands on the hem of her dress, which rode up her thighs the lower she got to the floor.

"I know," he said before he could think better of it. "I saw you at the wedding."

"Hmm." She pressed her chin into her hands. "Did you now? That dress wasn't conducive to getting that low, but I managed."

She sure had, but again, they weren't here for this. "Look, can we focus on what we're here to do?"

She rolled her eyes and looked around at the ingredients he had laid out to make simple chocolate cupcakes with frosting so he could get some piping practice. He had gotten various tip sizes for the bag after doing some research online.

The plan was for her to give him a quick tutorial on cupcakes in general, then they would both make theirs separately while the phone was set up to capture everything. Seemed simple enough.

Except, Reba was going on about techniques he could use to make his cupcakes moister while his mind meandered to the finer details of his work presentation. He still had a few finishing touches before he ran it by Dax and the team. Then they would be good to go for the real deal with the client.

"Hey, you got that? Does it make sense?"

Devon focused on Reba, who was looking at him expectantly while she poured out her portion of flour. He had no clue what she was talking about, but they were following a recipe—how hard could this be?

"Yeah, sure. Got it."

"Okay, well, measure out your flour. You can follow the recipe precisely. I just tend to wing it at this point."

"Wing it? But why? There's a recipe for a reason."

Reba rolled her eyes at him again as if *he* was the one being unreasonable.

Devon measured out his flour as the recipe instructed while Reba continued on with her chaos measuring system —which was to say she didn't have one because she didn't even glance at the laptop where the recipe was up on the screen.

"It's cupcakes. I've made way too many of those in my lifetime to need exact measurements anymore."

The thought of just winging something like this made Devon nervous, but Reba's words did have some truth to them. As much as he refused to follow her chaotic ways, he had to admit this wasn't his area of expertise. He might raise a brow at her questionable methods, but he had to trust that the end result would be as she expected. He, however, didn't have that luxury of doing whatever he pleased because he didn't want to destroy his kitchen in some freak baking accident.

They continued on, with Reba's chattering competing against her music while they mixed the wet and dry ingredients together. He looked over at her batter, which didn't look any different from his. He seemed to be on the right track. The main difference in appearance would come when they got to the piping of the icing. It didn't seem like rocket science, and yet he wasn't totally confident in what he would produce—a foreign emotion since he didn't tend to venture outside of his usual skill set. Give him the challenge of coming up with the perfect design proposal, and he was excited about it. Baking was outside his normal activities.

"Not too full," Reba instructed as he poured his batter into the cupcake-lined tin. "Fill it halfway, or you'll have overflow."

"Alright, makes sense."

By the time the cakes were in the oven, Reba looked as well put together as she had when she'd rolled in this morning. Devon noticed some flour on his t-shirt, and the counter looked like an explosion of messy bowls and utensils. Flour was also sprinkled on a portion of the island where his sifting method hadn't been quite so neat.

"Let me wash up some things before we move to the next phase."

Reba came to stand next to him at the sink, putting her elbow-to-elbow with him. He had a double sink, and yet her presence felt too overwhelming.

"I don't need help, it's fine."

"It's only fair I help too. I can stack after you soap up and rinse."

He had a precise stacking routine, and he could imagine Reba just fitting in stuff on the drying rack anywhere she felt like. An image of the entire precarious mess toppling over was enough for him to grit out, "Not necessary. I like doing this."

Reba folded her arms, turning so her back was propped against the rack as she watched him. "Of course, you do. Have it your way then. Time to change the music to more local offerings."

Devon ignored the burst of Spanish and English lyrics on a song he recognised as one Keiran had worked on. He vaguely recalled his brother mentioning working with the singer, who had Trini and Venezuelan heritage. The song had an upbeat pop vibe that Devon usually avoided, preferring more mellow sounds. Finished with the wares, he turned around to find Reba shimmying her shoulders and swaying her hips in time to the beat.

He had easily avoided her dancing at the beach house by leaving. He couldn't just walk out of his own house because he found her movements distracting. She lifted her hands above her head as she kept grooving along to the track, her crop top rising with the motion. He refused to allow Reba to affect him in any way.

You are better than this. You will not allow Reba Johnson to be a threat to your peace of mind.

"Ready for the fun part?" she asked.

He wasn't. He anticipated a mess of icing covering his counter when they were done, but he had signed up for this.

"Sure," he replied because he was Mr. Cool. A pair of hips and a bare stomach didn't faze him in the slightest. "Let's do it."

CHAPTER SEVEN
REBA

Zooming in on Devon's scrunched-up face as he sampled his own cupcake almost made Reba drop her phone. She really had to get a better grip on the thing when she was around Devon. She was laughing so hard.

"Why is it so dry? It doesn't taste like yours at all. And the icing looks like a shitty blob. Why does mine not look like yours?"

"Can you curse in these diaries?"

Devon looked over at her, the ever-present crease between his brows growing deeper. "I didn't even know you were filming still."

"I'll bleep it out, don't worry."

He had tried his best at the icing stage, but Reba had to agree, his looked an entire lopsided mess. To be honest, she hadn't expected much in the appearance of the cupcakes, but she'd hoped at least the cake itself would be tasty. Then again, Devon had that perfectionist personality. The cupcake couldn't be that terrible.

"Let me be the judge." She reached to pick up one of his

cupcakes and took a bite. Oh, dear. He was right on the dry front. "Did you put the oil like I said? To make it moist?

"Oil? I thought the recipe said butter?"

"Yeah, it did, but I told you subbing oil would make it moister." She narrowed her eyes at him. "Were you even listening to me at all?"

He picked at one of the cupcake liners, not meeting her gaze. "Well, yes, mostly."

"Mostly? Well, *mostly* got you dry ass cupcakes."

Devon pushed the cupcake away like it personally offended him. She supposed it had. Reba didn't do a lot of baking tutorials—although it was something she was considering on a larger scale as an additional source of income—but it didn't take a genius to see that Devon had thought all this would be easy-peasy.

"I was a little distracted," he admitted. "I have a big work thing coming up, and..."

Reba cut him off with a raise of her hand. "You can't be distracted while baking. That's how messes happen. That's rule number one."

Devon picked up his half-eaten cupcake, placing it back on the tray with its other sorry-looking siblings. "Didn't take you for rules."

"Yeah, I'm not much for them in general, but when heat and ovens are involved? I don't mess around. When you're practicing without me here, you're gonna daydream about work and forget you have stuff in the oven? Not a good idea."

Devon stared at her, a muscle jumping in his jaw. "Okay, you're right. It won't happen again." He looked down at the cupcakes. "What do I do with these?"

"Well, I'll take some of mine. You can give away the rest to your family or co-workers. Or eat them. Baker's choice."

"I don't think mine are fit for anyone else to consume."

"Don't you dare throw them away. That's another rule. Unless something is truly inedible, you don't waste. Eat them, or give them to your fam. You don't have to say *you* made them."

"That might be a little cruel, considering."

Alright, he was being too harsh. The cupcakes wouldn't be winning any awards, but they weren't that terrible. "And I thought *I* was dramatic."

"I don't do drama."

Of course, he didn't think so. Men always got this notion that only women were given to what they like to call "hysterics." Devon didn't quite look like he was about to dissolve into tears or anything—she wondered if his tear ducts even worked—and the expression on his face wasn't complete dejection either, but he didn't look pleased. For someone like him, he would consider this failure. He had obviously expected to get it right on the first try.

"Hey, look. I burnt my first attempt at cookies. The next set spread together and looked like blobs. You can only get better from here."

"How can I do a Rubik's Cube-shaped cake if I can't even make a proper cupcake?"

"You listen to your teacher. On all fronts," she added. "Which means pack away the cupcakes and figure out your outfit for tonight. Pick me up at seven. I'll WhatsApp my address."

Devon went over to his cupboard to pull down a plastic container. "It's easier to meet me here and leave your car, so we'll take mine, considering the location of the karaoke place."

"You already don't want to do this. I'm not driving all this way to have you refuse to come out your house. I've got many talents but breaking and entering isn't one of them. So, you're picking me up. I'll be ready at seven."

He sighed, probably realising that arguing with her was futile. "Fine."

"Excellent. Well, see you tonight then."

Devon's scowl deepened as he packed up her cupcakes then showed her to the door. At least he didn't protest anymore. Reba called that progress.

She turned, smile firmly in place. "I promise you, this is the start of a beautiful friendship."

"Highly doubt it. This is a working relationship only. I don't have friends, remember?"

Reba cocked her head. "Is that so?" She laughed because he had no idea the charm she was capable of. Devon was a little tougher with that grumpy attitude of his, but Reba was a pro at this, and he was the ultimate challenge. "You're going to learn one thing about me if you learn nothing else. I'm irresistible, and you *will* fall under my spell. Toodles." She wiggled her fingers.

A noise escaped his mouth. It wasn't quite a laugh but sounded close enough.

"See, already getting half-laughs out of you."

"That was a scoff because you are unbelievably delusional."

"Okay, friend," she said, sashaying away. She would leave him to his denial, but he was going to learn real soon.

∼

"AND WHERE EXACTLY YOU GOIN' DRESSED LIKE THAT?"

Reba checked her wig in the living room mirror and barely stopped herself from rolling her eyes. She didn't have time for a lecture about rudeness and respecting her elders while also defending her style choices. Instead, she turned to her father and gave him a big smile. She hadn't lied to Devon. Reba knew how to use her God-given assets to charm her way through life, and her father was definitely not immune to it.

He always came in hot when he thought she was doing something questionable. That didn't last long because her smile had always gotten her out of trouble.

Turning up the wattage on her smile and throwing in some wide eyes because why the hell not, she said, "Just going out with a friend. Karaoke."

His frown softened a fraction. "Is a costume party or what?"

"Nope."

"So you just going like this to regular karaoke?"

She'd been rocking her pastel pink shade for far longer than any other hair colour, but tonight she had decided to shake up her look a bit with the wig she had in a deeper shade of pink. "Yes. Cute, right?" She struck a pose.

Her father hmphed, but she saw a little twitch to his lips. He would go on about her wild style and those wigs, but he couldn't tell her anything, really. She might still be living under their roof, but she was an adult, *and* she contributed to the bills, so he just shook his head when she strutted out the house in one of her "get-ups," as he liked to call it.

Her parents swore she was living in a dream world where she played someone she wasn't every day, which, okay, sometimes Reba liked to channel a specific look—like her Sailor Moon buns from this morning at Devon's—but her style choices were all her, too. Why her parents couldn't see this was just how she liked to express herself and wasn't trying to be someone else was beyond her.

But could she really blame them for not understanding her? Her parents and sister were laid-back and didn't wear colours that were eye-searingly bright. To them, Reba was this walking anomaly they just couldn't pin down. She had hoped after years that they would simply accept it. It was all still a work in progress.

Her phone buzzed with an incoming call because, of course, Devon couldn't just text that he was outside like a normal person.

"I'm walking out in a sec."

"Do people not give proper greetings on phone calls anymore?" he groused.

"Okay, Grandpa, but I know it's you because I don't have anyone else saved as D. King Grump."

He sighed. "This generation is absolutely lost. Anyways, I'm outside your door."

What? Now, why would he do that? She was quite fine walking to the car to get away from any questions her parents might have.

She turned her back on her father's questioning gaze. "Why are you at the door? You didn't have to do that."

Her mother walked into the room, and alright, she had to roll out before they started tuning that parental antenna that was always on for potential prospects for their children. If they saw Devon King, though, they would realise the man was a catch—good job, had his own house, probably had a ten-year plan for his life—which would mean stability in their eyes. Something they didn't think Reba gave a damn about.

Reba was just trying to inject some fun into Devon's life. She didn't want her parents trying to get him to rub off on her and be a good influence or whatever. The only rubbing off she would agree to was in a sexy way.

"It's the right thing to do," Devon said into her ear, and she rolled her eyes.

"Okay, parents, I'm off."

"You not going to introduce your friend?" her father asked because, of course, he would. Her mother's eyebrow went up.

"Friend? Not Trina and Ayoluwa you going out with?"

"No, it's not…"

"Is a man friend, I bet. I hope is not one of them lil' pipers from up the street. Or some other one you always seem to hang out with."

Her mother thought all the guys in the area that she was friendly with were unemployed and bad influences just because they usually hung outside their houses in the afternoon, doing nothing productive, in her eyes. Her mother didn't want to hear that even though the guys always flirted with her, they looked out for her too. They weren't as bad as her mother was making them out to be.

"Mummy, I don't want to keep my *friend* waiting. I gotta go. Meet me in the car, please," she told Devon, hoping he would listen, but of course, the man was standing outside the door when she slipped out, looking tall and delicious as usual. She closed the door firmly behind her before her parents could get so much as a peek.

"Go, *go!*" She hustled down the walkway towards his car, not waiting for him. "C'mon, open the door, man." She slid into the passenger seat as soon as the alarm beeped.

Devon came around the front and got in the driver's side. She expected him to start the damn car and go, but he sat there, staring at her, taking in her short pink wig, her clingy red dress, and fishnets that went into her black boots, then back up to her hair.

"You cut your hair? And you got bangs?"

Reba snorted. "Oh, you clueless man. This is a wig. Devon, meet the Pink Lady. She only comes out on special occasions."

Devon stared as if she had lost her mind. It was the usual reaction she got when she spoke like this about her hair. "You name your wigs?"

"Yup. Karaoke is all about the fun, so the Pink Lady was appropriate." She shook her head from side to side, enjoying the swish of the pink ends against her jaw. "Maybe someday, you'll meet Cassandra. My red wig that comes down past my shoulders in these lovely waves. Very old Hollywood glam look."

"None of this makes sense." He started up the car finally. "Why didn't you want me to meet your parents?"

"Because, to them, you're the perfect package, and they would just want to eat you up. Now, *I'm* not averse to eating anything you want to feed me." She wiggled her brows even though he was totally focused on the road. "But they'd hope you would calm me down some, so no, you don't get to meet them."

His fingers dug into the steering wheel. He still didn't look at her. "You can't just say shit like that, *Jesus.*"

"It's the wig. She brings out more of my fun, flirty side. You haven't even seen the best part yet." She rooted around in her bag for the last piece of her outfit. She slipped the cat ears headband over her hair, waiting for his reaction.

Devon didn't disappoint. The red light he was forced to stop at gave him ample time to take in the glittery headband. "Seriously?"

"Yes, isn't it cute?" She cocked her head at him. "You'd look pretty adorable in one of these. Like a big, scowly cat."

"Pass. There's not a chance in hell I'm wearing that."

"Well, I didn't bring you any, so chill. Baby steps. Let's

get you comfy talking to your co-workers first. At least you look nice." She purposefully gave him a full head-to-thigh look. "One suggestion...while I'm digging the sexy CEO look, roll up your sleeves. You'll look more relaxed."

Devon had decided to come out tonight in a snug shirt and well-tailored pants that moulded to his legs as he sat in the car. Reba had been getting her fill at the way those thighs flexed as he drove. He was bulkier than his brother, and Reba was all about it. He was too busy looking at the road, so he hadn't caught her ogling him yet, but now she did nothing to hide her frank appraisal. She could make a nice seat of those thighs if he was ever so inclined.

"I'm good."

"Come on. A little sexy forearm action goes a long way."

"It's not going to happen."

"Never say never around me. Everyone falls under my spell eventually." It sounded like a ludicrous thing to say, but Reba knew her strengths.

Devon might be a little more resistant than most who came into contact with her, but Reba didn't shy away from a little competition. He didn't know it yet, but Mission: Make Devon King Fall Under My Spell was already underway.

He looked away just as the light changed and muttered, "Thank God," as if having to focus on the road again meant a reprieve from her flirting.

Ah, poor clueless man. Silhouettes was probably about another fifteen minutes away, enough time to keep annoying him *and* give Devon a pep talk since he was so not vibing with her good mood.

"So, what're your expectations for tonight?"

"Make it to the end without wanting to strangle Evan."

"Oh, I'll deal with him. You don't have to worry about it."

He glanced over at her quickly before looking back at the road. "What does that mean exactly?"

"You *have* seen me in this dress, right? I'll turn up the charm, and boom. All you have to do is be nice to your co-workers. Less of a grouch."

"You mean actually talk to them?"

"Yes, I know, the horror, right?" she joked. "You have to make small talk."

"My least favourite thing."

"You hate small talk? What a surprise."

He shot her another one of his stormy looks as he pulled into the Valpark Shopping Plaza where Silhouettes was located. "Your sarcasm isn't appreciated."

She stretched her arms wide as she exited the car, noting that Devon's gaze slid over to her before he focused on locking the car. *Keep fighting it, buddy. Makes it all that much sweeter when you give in.*

Out loud, she said, "I thought I was speaking your language with my sarcasm?"

He took a deep breath. "You really think you have me figured out, don't you?"

"No more than you do me, but we're going to become friends, remember? Friends share things eventually."

She started walking, and Devon fell in beside her. His gaze was a heavy weight on the side of her face, and Reba smiled. She didn't have to turn to him to figure he had his default expression on. Honestly, if his frowning gave her this much pleasure, what would a genuine smile from Devon do to her? Probably wet her damn panties.

They walked up the steps to the club, and Reba was

delighted when the guy at the door gave her a once-over before breaking into a huge smile. "Very nice!" he said.

She gave him a wink before turning to Devon, who was busy looking like he wanted to turn around and walk back to the car. Well, too bad. Reba wasn't missing Saucy Saturdays at Silhouettes for anything. She was dressed to impress and needed to be seen. Devon was just going to have to suck up his sour vibes for tonight and make an attempt at conversation.

It was free entry for the karaoke—a cover charge would apply around nine when the singing ended and the lounge turned into a club vibe—so Reba waltzed in with Devon keeping pace at her side. The inside was moderately packed as they moved into the main area where the karaoke screen was set up. A few couches were already occupied with patrons chatting with their colleagues while they munched on some finger foods.

Reba looked around. She wasn't certain she would definitely recognise Devon's boss or his co-worker, Evan, in the dimly lit space, but she hoped a familiar face would jump out at her. Devon stood still, saying nothing.

"You see them?" she asked because the man was tall enough to do a wide sweep of the place and pinpoint where his co-workers would be.

"Yes." He made no move to enlighten Reba. His stony expression remained unchanged.

"Well? Where are they?"

He jutted his chin off to the side where the group was laughing while huddled together.

"So we going to let them know we're here or what?"

"I..." Devon shook his head like he wasn't certain what to say. Reba took a good look at his face. His brow was furrowed, nothing unusual there, but his teeth digging into his bottom lip was something else entirely.

Devon didn't seem like the type of man who was given to overt displays of emotion unless it was his grumpiness.

"What is it?"

"I don't..." He scrubbed a hand over the top of his head. "I don't know if I can do this. Or want to do this." Jaw tight, that muscle was getting a workout again.

"Oh." It all became crystal clear in an instant. Devon was nervous about actually mingling with these people outside of work.

Reba had chalked up his unwillingness to do so in the past as a simple desire not to engage with the people he saw every day at work outside of that environment, which she supposed was fair. She didn't know how his co-workers were in the office. She hadn't considered this may be an actual source of anxiety for him.

"Hey." She placed a hand on his arm. "You don't have to be a pro at small talk, okay, but at least try? They'll appreciate the effort. I'm going to wow them, so you don't have to do much heavy lifting. They'll just be so surprised you showed up at all. I love chatting up new people."

"They're going to expect me to get up there. Sing."

"I'm sure you have a keen understanding of how to say no to something."

"I suppose." He shrugged, and Reba could imagine clinging to those shoulders as she settled into his lap. Oh, that was a delightful image. His eyes narrowed. "What's that look about?"

"Trust me on this. You don't want to know what I'm thinking right now. I don't want to scandalise you." She gestured to the group. "Shall we?"

The first person to notice them was a tall, slim guy with

short curly hair that glinted in the lounge's lighting. He looked exactly the same from his Instagram account. So this was Evan, huh? He nudged the woman next to him, making a big show of it.

"Are my eyes deceiving me?"

The woman wore a clingy black dress that Reba approved of. She was showing off some enviably thick thighs and a leg tattoo. She looked interesting, and Reba couldn't wait to chat her up. She did a full double-take as they approached.

"I may have had too many screwdrivers because I think I'm hallucinating."

Oh, Devon was going to hate this good-natured ribbing. Reba glanced at him, and sure enough, he was frowning.

"Hannah," he said. His eyes dipped to her leg. "Nice, uh, tattoo."

Reba supressed the laugh that was threatening to break free. He was *so* bad at this. Of all the things to focus on. Granted, this woman's rose tattoo with the vines climbing all the way up to disappear under the hem of her dress was spectacular, but Reba would have instructed Devon to go a different route. This was his co-worker, after all.

Hannah didn't look perturbed by any of it. In fact, her lips curled into a little smile as she sipped her drink before responding, "Thanks."

Evan looked between Reba and Devon, a speculative gleam in his eyes. "*So*, you came. With a friend."

They were obviously curious about her, so Reba figured this was her moment. She stuck out her hand. "Hi there!"

"Love your hair and dress," Hannah said, shaking Reba's hand before Evan could get to her. She shot Devon a sly look. "You have such interesting friends. Who knew?"

"I'm Evan."

Reba reached to shake his hand when Evan bowed and planted a kiss on the back of hers. The look of utter disgust on Devon's face was hilarious. She would have to talk to him about his facial expressions later. Now was for charming these people.

"Dax!" Evan suddenly shouted, her hand still clasped in his. "Your golden boy is here!"

Reba disengaged their hands and smiled over at the older man she recognised from her internet search. Dax was solidly built with that salt and pepper thing going on. His face lit up with a huge smile when he saw Devon.

"This is indeed a momentous night." They exchanged back slaps, and Devon gestured to her.

"Dax, this is Reba."

"Well, hello, young lady. I'm assuming you're responsible for convincing him to come out?"

Reba bowed because it had been a feat getting Devon to do this, and she was definitely taking all the credit for it. "I'm known to work a little magic now and then."

"Excellent! Now, if we can get him up there..."

Reba busted out laughing. "I'm good, but even *I* can't work miracles."

"Don't be so sure." Dax winked, turning to Devon. "So you won't be gracing us with a song tonight? Even if this lovely lady asks you nicely?"

"Absolutely not."

Dax didn't appear the least bit put off by Devon's response, but before they tried to pressure him into it, Reba piped up.

"Oh, I'm excited to sing, though. I have a whole Rihanna song picked out and everything."

The group focused on her and started talking about

what songs they wanted to do. While Evan went to give the DJ everyone's selections, Reba checked in with Devon.

"All good?"

"How do you do that?"

"What?"

"Just talk to them as if you've known them forever. They like you already." He pursed his lips, the crease between his brows one of confusion. As if he couldn't fathom such a thing. Reba wasn't offended. Devon just didn't know what she was capable of. Yet.

She placed a hand on her hip. "I'm likeable. Is that so hard to believe?"

"You're..." He waved his hand over her body. "A lot."

Nothing she hadn't heard before. At times, it stung— the idea that she was too much for people to handle, which wasn't entirely a lie. They usually didn't know what to do with her colourful energy. In her mind, it was their loss if they didn't want to deal with any of that.

But tonight, she refused to let Devon sour her mood. He didn't get her, and that was just fine. It wouldn't stop her from trying to get him to loosen up.

"You say it like it's a bad thing," she joked. "Stick with me, kid, you'll appreciate all of this soon enough." She did a little wiggle, drinking in the way his eyes settled right where she wanted them.

That's right, Mr. King. You watch those hips.

Oh yes, Reba was going to enjoy the next few weeks immensely.

CHAPTER EIGHT
DEVON

IF HE HAD TO HEAR ANOTHER TERRIBLE RENDITION OF "DON'T
Stop Believing," Devon was going to walk out. He didn't
care if Dax or any of the others considered it rude. It wasn't
worth this torture. As the woman finished the song, her
wobbly off-key notes lingering around the lounge, Devon
looked over to where Reba was laughing it up with Evan
and Hannah.

Reba had secured a black feather boa from somewhere
and was shimmying her shoulders, causing Evan to laugh
loudly. Even over the music, Devon could hear the man's
annoying braying. Reba had stayed true to her word—Evan
was eating out of her hand. He was watching Reba's every
move, and Devon couldn't tell if it was because Evan was
trying to pump her for information about her relationship
to Devon or he had fallen under her spell.

The shock on everyone's faces had been clear. They
hadn't tried to hide that. He'd expected that reaction. This
was his first time coming to one of the many after-work
limes Evan organised, and he hadn't shown up alone.

But he hadn't been prepared for this fawning over Reba.

She looked like some sort of sexy fae in that outfit, working her magic over the unsuspecting humans. He sipped his rum and coke as she cheered on Hannah, who was about to go up and sing something with another of their co-workers, Maria.

When she had first opened the door at her house, Devon's reaction had been visceral, to the point where he had forced himself to have no reaction whatsoever. The wig. The dress. The fucking fishnets. Who the hell wore fishnets casually like that? He shouldn't have been surprised. Everything he had learned about Reba to date made that seem like a normal choice for her, and yet...

Devon took another sip of his drink, throat suddenly dry as fuck. Reba in casual wear or a swimsuit was a lot to take in. Dressed up like this, Devon had wanted to call the entire outing off. He didn't know if Reba was trying to get a rise out of him with her flirty comments or whether it was just how she communicated. What he did know was that he needed to be alert. Letting his guard down around Reba would be a foolish move.

"She fits in so seamlessly, doesn't she?"

Dax's voice startled Devon out of his staring. "I don't think Reba fits in anywhere. She tends to stick out," he replied without thinking.

"You make it sound like a bad thing." Dax's brows were raised, and too late, Devon realised how his comment sounded—like he disapproved, which would be odd since they were working this friends angle.

He didn't disapprove per se; he just didn't know how to deal with someone like Reba. She was a too-bright light that made it hard to look directly at her sometimes for fear that he would be dazzled. She was too distracting, and Devon didn't need any of that in his carefully planned life.

"I didn't mean it like that."

"Good, because I think that's just the kind of impact you need in your life."

Devon gaped at his boss. He couldn't be serious. The only reason Reba was even allowed in his bubble right now was because of desperation, and well, the fact that Cherisse wasn't available. He wouldn't have willingly invited her in otherwise.

"I don't..." He cleared his throat. "What do you mean?"

Dax chuckled. "Devon, I love how structured you are. You get shit done, but son, I want you to enjoy your life too. Successes are great. Trust me, I know."

Obviously he did. Dax had built this company into what it was today. He was Devon's inspiration and mentor. His accomplishments spoke for themselves, and while Dax was humble and didn't go about bragging, Devon never forgot how he had worked himself up from nothing. Dax had had a plan, a vision, and he'd executed it.

Devon saw so clearly where he wanted to go, and Dax was his blueprint for that.

"I was making time for everything except myself and family, and the burnout was real. Work hard, yes, but..." He gestured to where Reba was holding court. "Make sure you bring a little light in, too."

"Oh, no, she and I aren't like that. We're friends." It felt weird to say that, even if that's what they were portraying for everyone. He and Reba were definitely not friends.

Dax sipped his drink, giving Devon a knowing look. "Uh-huh."

"No, really. We're not like *that*." The idea was ludicrous. "Us together would be—"

A disaster. A mistake. The worst idea to ever be conceived. It would be like willingly plunging headlong into the sun.

He knew the exact type of woman he wanted in his life, and Reba Johnson was so far outside the scope of that.

"Alright. I don't pry into my employees' romantic lives, but keep her around. She's a good influence."

The so-called good influence was walking over to them, that boa still draped over her shoulders.

"I'm up. Kiss for luck?" She batted her lashes at him. She didn't actually expect him to...? Reba snickered, patting his chest before winking at Dax. "Relax. I'm playing, but I at least expect you to bask in my brilliance." She bounced up to the stage, microphone in hand.

Before the song started, she reached up to her head-band, and suddenly, the entire thing lit up. She grinned as Evan and Hannah whooped.

Dax turned to him. "How *did* you meet this woman?"

Devon was beginning to wonder if this entire thing was a fever dream, just as Reba began singing Rihanna's "Diamonds." She should look ridiculous up there with that pink hair and the glowing cat ears headband, but she somehow managed to look ethereal, like some mysterious creature come to trick them into following her to their doom.

Reba shone bright against the dim stage. She didn't have the best singing voice, but no one gave a shit; her performance captivated. She was working that boa like it could actually reel in her unsuspecting victims. Shit, he needed another drink. Or not—he should keep his head as clear as possible tonight.

She continued crooning into the mic, and Devon's flight instincts kicked into high gear when she started walking down the stage towards him, a mischievous glint in her eyes. She stopped in front of him, continuing to sing, which made the crowd go wild. This definitely wasn't going to help his co-workers thinking they weren't dating. What the hell was she doing?

Eventually, she moved on to serenade the others standing in front of him. Thank God. She had just been playing up the crowd, not actually singing to just him. He willed his heart rate to settle to its usual pace.

When she ended her song, there was a thunderous applause. Reba took a bow and strutted back over to him.

"You were amazing. Next round of drinks is on me," Dax said, moving to take everyone's orders.

Reba grinned up at Devon. "Well, I love your boss already."

"How did you do that?"

"Be amazing?" She shimmied her shoulders. "It's a gift."

Definitely. Devon could command a room when he had to give a presentation, but this was another level. He didn't know how to charm people like *that*, based on the force of his personality alone. He was aware of his limitations in that regard but hadn't considered it a problem when he excelled at getting shit done. Could he actually be passed over for the partner position because he wasn't a people person like Dax? Dax and Reba exuded different energies, but there was no denying they were both good at this.

Shit. He would need to think about this. Letting Reba convince him to show up for these after-work events was one thing but actually making a conscious effort to engage in real conversation with his co-workers? He couldn't drag Reba around and just throw her at people to distract from the fact that he wasn't saying much. That wouldn't be feasible.

Reba fanned her face and announced she was heading to the bathroom. The urge to cling to her and ask her not to leave him alone with these people was strong, but obviously, he wouldn't do anything so pathetic. He was a grown ass man. It couldn't be that hard to talk to people he saw every day at the office without Reba as a buffer.

"So..." Evan came up to him. The way he didn't even wait a few seconds before Reba left to approach Devon meant he had been waiting to get him alone. "You and Reba are just friends? How did you two even meet?"

Devon didn't have patience for this. He was so close to growling that it was none of Evan's fucking business, but that seemed like poor etiquette. They might not be confined to the rules of the office, but this was still his co-worker. He couldn't cuss him out.

This entire farce was to help him move closer to his goal. No matter how annoying Evan was, he couldn't lose sight of that.

"Mutual acquaintance of my brother." Not exactly accurate, but Devon didn't need to get into the intricacies of Reba being Keiran's girlfriend's assistant.

Evan was always hanging on someone's desk gossiping about something. Devon refused to give the man more fodder, although he had done exactly that by coming here with Reba. He shouldn't have allowed her to persuade him to do this. Sure, it would help his image a bit, but was it worth the additional fallout? He had basically opened the door to prying questions. This entire situation was annoying, mainly because he felt his thoughts ping-ponging around in his head. He wasn't used to second-guessing himself like this.

"Hmm, you got surprises up your sleeves. Didn't think you would even know someone like that."

"Shows how much you know." Fuck, that was not polite. He forced out a little chuckle, but Evan didn't look convinced. He probably thought Devon was laughing at him rather than signalling he had been joking.

How the hell did people manoeuvre these types of situations? This was a far cry from the occasional business lunches and dinners he had to attend when they were wooing clients. Devon was never tasked with being the social butterfly who would butter up the client. He was the facts guy.

"Guess you're not as by-the-book as you make it seem," Evan went on. "A woman like that seems too...what's the word I'm looking for?" Evan tapped his cheek, smiling. "Fun. Yeah, way too fun to be someone you'd be friends with. No offense, of course."

No offense, his ass; Evan meant full fucking offense. Devon bit the inside of his cheek hard. It was either that or throttle Evan for continuing to speak. He wanted to slap that annoying ass smirk off his face. No matter how right he was—Reba wasn't someone Devon would hang out with, given the choice—it didn't matter. Devon wanted Evan to shut the fuck up.

"You know, tacking on 'no offense' to whatever you say doesn't actually make it any less of a shit statement. No offense," he added because fuck this guy, seriously.

"Oh my God, the bathroom is so cute." Reba appeared at his side, and Devon never thought he would be this thrilled to see her. She looked between them before settling her gaze on Evan. "What song you doing?"

Evan's slight frown morphed into a wide smile. "I'm thinking a classic. Journey, but *only* if you sing it with me."

"Please, not another rendition of 'Don't Stop Believing,'" Devon grumbled before he could stop himself.

Evan's frown returned, and he opened his mouth to

reply, but Reba giggled, hand playfully swatting Evan's arm, effectively distracting him.

"Let's do something outside of the norm." Reba rubbed her hands together. "How do you feel about Destiny's Child? No one's going to expect that."

"Hmm, I suppose I could pull that off. You'll be Beyoncé, of course?"

Reba grinned. "Deal. Just holla when you're ready. Get Hannah in on this too."

"Now that's a plan."

Evan went off to rope Hannah into their group, and Reba wagged her finger at Devon. "What did you say to him? I saw his face. I leave you for one minute. It looked like you two were about to throw down over here."

Devon looked into the remnants of his drink, turning the glass round and round in his hand. "He's annoying as fuck."

"Agreed, but a brawl with your co-worker isn't going to work in your favour."

His head snapped up. "You agree with me?"

Everyone in the office loved Evan because he championed so many ideas for fun, or so he kept hearing, but the man had rubbed him the wrong way from day one. They couldn't be more different, and Devon supposed it was just his serious nature that clashed with Evan's always cheerful exuberance.

"Oh, I clocked him as a kiss-ass from the minute he opened his mouth. We're going to take him down. I tried to pick his mouth about the bake-off, but he's too good to spill to the competition's friend. But I'll wear him down."

It was the oddest feeling to have Reba in his corner. She was here because he was paying her, but that wasn't supposed to extend beyond the baking tutorial. He didn't know what she was getting out of this. Maybe she simply enjoyed flitting about and having everyone fall under her spell.

Not him, though. He was immune. Had to be. Reba didn't factor into his life plans in any way, and that's how it had to stay. Once this bake-off was over, he could go back to ignoring her *and* her meme messages.

"Everyone loves him. I'm the bad guy for thinking otherwise," he muttered. He hadn't needed them to like him. Once the work got done, he didn't care, but now he had to re-evaluate everything.

And after Evan had annoyed him tonight, he was more than ready to beat his ass in this bake-off. Which meant trusting that Reba would be able to help him win.

Reba tossed the ends of the boa over her shoulder so it fell like a scarf. "That's why I'm here. We'll revamp your image just a tad. Bring out your fun side. Maybe one day, you'll get up there and sing."

"No."

She pouted, which made her look cute, and alright, this was his last drink. Puppies were cute and could be disciplined. Reba wasn't the type to do anything unless she wanted to.

"You don't need to be able to sing. You saw me up there. I dazzled with my performance, so they all didn't realise without all the smoke and mirrors, I'm more wailing cat than lounge singer." She reached for the straw in her cocktail.

"I never said I couldn't sing. I said I'm not going to."

Reba sputtered around the mouthful of her drink. "Excuse me, *what*?" Eyes wide, she tilted her head to the side, the movement causing the ends of her wig to brush her shoulder. He still couldn't get over that she'd named the thing. "Are you telling me you can actually sing?"

"I can carry a note. I just choose not to." Yeah, he was done with alcohol for the night. His lips were a little too loose tonight.

He'd been caught singing along to his father's old records a couple of times as a child, and since then, his father had been behind him to make something of the smidge of musical talent he had. Devon had been more interested in putting his blocks together in unique shapes. His love for architecture outweighed any desire for a music career.

"I can't believe this. Has Keiran ever tried to get you to sing on a track?" She shook her head. "Wait, what am I saying? He knows better than to ask because you would never. Although..." She tapped her nail against her jaw. "He did convince Cherisse. Perhaps he could work another miracle."

"Reba."

"Yes?" Her wide eyes didn't make her look the least bit innocent. It just reinforced his earlier thought that she was some out-of-this-world creature who would gladly devour his entire soul after she had corrupted it completely.

"It's not happening."

"Of course, yes. I know. A girl can dream, though." A small sigh escaped as she pursed her lips. "I'll just add it to the rest of my fantasies."

Devon drained the rest of his drink, refusing to ask what other fantasies she might be referring to. That was obviously a trap, and Devon was no fool to open that Pandora's box. He looked over to where the team was currently trying to hype up Dax, who was doing his best impersonation of Frank Sinatra.

"I promise you're not missing anything. I'm no Nat King Cole." He did sing along to his favourite songs when he was home alone, though. Another thing he wasn't revealing.

Her nose scrunched up. "Who?"

Devon blinked at the confusion apparent on her face. She couldn't be serious. "You don't know who Nat King Cole is?"

Reba shrugged. "I'm assuming someone vintage since you listen to him."

"Are you joking? You really don't know?"

She spread her arms before digging into her purse to pull out her phone. "I'll Google him, but it's not ringing any bells."

She tapped her screen before bringing the phone up to her ear. "Hmm, okay, this "Unforgettable" one is sort of familiar, but like I said, vintage." She pressed the side of her phone, and the screen went dark. "I'd listen to it if I wanted to sleep or something."

The curve of her mouth said she was teasing him, but Devon shook his head.

"Hey, you tried to diss Mariah! At least I'm not shitting on your guy."

He supposed she had a point—not that he had dissed Mariah; it just wasn't what he would choose to listen to.

"I'll check him out. If I like it, it'll go on our baking practice playlist so you can stop grouching about my song choices."

Right, that. He had a breakfast date in the morning with his family, but later in the day, they had decided to meet up for round two. Which meant they should head out soon. He wasn't used to being out late or at all. His weekends consisted of work and the rare family moment when he allowed them to convince him to come over. They had taken to using Leah to draw him out because both his mother and Maxi knew he adored his niece. It was more difficult to say no when Leah asked for him to come over. He didn't call them out on the manipulation because he enjoyed spending time with her.

As far as he was concerned, Leah deserved some stable adults in her life. It had to be difficult with her father in Atlanta, and he and Maxi sharing custody. Leah seemed to be adjusting just fine, but none of that meant she wasn't affected by the divorce in some way.

"No need, I have my own collection we can play. We should leave after your next song. I have a date with my niece in the morning."

"Aww!" Reba pressed her hands together, tilting her head, so they cradled the side of her jaw. "That's the cutest thing ever. Don't forget to take the cupcakes, Uncle Devon."

Ugh, why did she have to remind him of his failure? He had planned to do just that, but he wasn't looking forward to their feedback. Children tended to be brutally honest, and he expected his cupcakes to be judged harshly.

But if he couldn't survive criticism from a six-year-old, he may as well give up on trying to further his career goals.

"Okay, only because you don't want to disappoint that sweet girl, we can leave early."

"*This* is considered early?" It was almost ten.

Reba patted his arm. "This is when the party just gets started. After karaoke, this place turns into a club vibe."

Then it was definitely time to get out of here. Reba laughed at what was surely a horrified look on his face. Thank God he had Leah as an excuse—otherwise, Reba would want to stay back. Devon couldn't think of anything else he would like to do less. Karaoke was one thing. Actually party with these people? No, thanks. Loud clubs with sweaty bodies pushing against him wasn't something he enjoyed.

After Reba and team finished up with their performance, Devon told Dax they were heading out.

"Well, thanks for coming and letting us meet Reba. It's been an absolute pleasure. Bring her to the next thing."

"Uh..." Devon didn't have a clue what the next outing was, and he didn't care to know. "We'll see. I'll be busy baking, and Reba's helping me with that."

"Oh?" Dax's gaze turned curious.

Reba pressed her hands to her chest. "Did I not mention I'm an assistant pastry chef? Silly me." She winked at Dax.

"Ah, well, it all makes sense now. I'll be looking forward to your video diaries. I know Reba will keep you on track, but don't use that as an excuse to be a stranger."

"Sure." That was non-committal enough. He hadn't promised to attend any specific events, and Dax would at least see he was serious about this bake-off.

"Oh, man, that was great!" Reba exclaimed once they gave their farewells and walked outside. "I feel so energised."

Devon couldn't relate. He was ready to get some sleep since it was too late to think about working more on his presentation. He would get too engrossed and end up going to bed late. He needed to preserve his energy for Leah.

"You made it through and didn't murder anyone with your sarcasm. The Evan moment was a close call, but I'd say it was a win." Reba raised her hand, and Devon stared at it. "You gonna leave me hanging here?" She wiggled her fingers. "Come on, I don't have cooties or anything. Although, you know, I never actually know what people mean when they say that. What are cooties supposed to be? I should Google that."

He rolled his eyes but slapped her hand in a quick high five. He didn't do high fives either, but there was no one around to see.

"There, was that so bad?"

It wasn't terrible, which made him realise that Reba was already making him do things he didn't usually engage in. He needed to get away from her and back to the safe, familiar comfort of his house.

Somehow, he was going to have to survive Reba Johnson, and he already felt himself struggling.

God dammit.

CHAPTER NINE
REBA

"So, you get him to fuck you yet?"

Reba almost tipped over her mimosa, which would have been a damn shame because it was always the highlight of brunch. Food was great, but Reba liked to get a good buzz going every so often. She enjoyed that light, fizzy feeling where everything was a bright ray of sunshine that washed away her woes, not that she was overdoing it today since she was meeting up with Devon later. Drunk baking was not a good idea.

Brunch with her girls wasn't a regular Sunday tradition —which made it even more special because they usually did it for specific occasions—but since Cherisse was off on vacation, Reba had a bit more time for "just cuz we feel like it" boozy brunch. Ayo and Trina had suggested they utilise Trina's back yard since she already had a nice table set up and space where they could be as loud as they wished. Too many times, they had done brunch at some café or restaurant and had to deal with judgy stares because she and Trina didn't possess inside voices. Not that Reba cared. She was paying her money like everyone else, and if she wanted to get her loud giggle on during some overpriced meal, she was going to do it.

Trina shared the house with her siblings, who were both out for the day. Reba got along fine with Trina's younger sister, but the eldest tended to go into parent mode a bit too much for her liking.

They had decided on simple dishes of eggs, bacon, and pancakes with some fruit on the side. Champagne was too expensive to just have for a random brunch, so their mimosas were actually made with some cheaper box wine Trina had among her liquor stashes. Worked just as well. Reba had been on her second glass when Trina had come out of nowhere with her comment.

She raised an eyebrow at Trina, who was snorting at her across the table. "Where the hell you come out with that?"

"My bad, is that not what you all are doing on these weekend meet-ups?"

"You damn well know it's not." She hadn't gone into detail but had mentioned to them she was assisting Devon with baking-related activities. She couldn't quite blame Trina for making that assumption. Reba wouldn't mind heating up some sheets with Devon instead of just the oven.

Ayo shook her head. "Damn shame. What a waste of a weekend."

Trina turned her phone around, the screen showing a selfie Reba had posted on her Instagram. "You looked cute as hell last night. He should be panting after you. Those fishnets alone are sexy as hell. You even brought out the Pink Lady. You know she gets you all the ass."

"That's not what last night was about. Besides, Devon requires a different touch. Sex isn't on the table, but I may have a little side mission going on." She winked at them, saying nothing else. Reba was a master at riling her friends up because why not make them work for it?

Trina leaned back in her chair. "Uh-oh. You got that look in your eyes. What you got for tall, sexy, and frowny?"

Reba's smile widened as her friends pegged her as being up to no good. They knew her well, but she was going to have a little fun at their expense simply because she could. "I'm going to make Devon King fall in love with me."

Ayo choked on her drink. "I'm sorry, *what*?"

Trina appeared less surprised. No matter what wild idea Reba came up with, Trina was ready to roll with it. "To what end?"

Reba shrugged. This was too good; they were really buying this. "He very clearly thinks I'm not the kind of woman he would go for, and I just want to prove him wrong, on principle."

Ayo reached across the table to squeeze Reba's arm. "Look, I know you have baggage about men, but..."

Wait, hold up? Ayo looked completely serious, her amused grin from earlier totally gone. Okay then, had Reba done too good of a job at this joke? "Baggage? Are you playing with me?" What was Ayo going on about?

"How the hell do you plan to achieve this?" Trina piped up.

"Wear him down. Men like Devon never see me coming."

"Okay, but what if you really hurt him?" Ayo asked, coming out of left field with that question.

"What? Where are you coming from with all this?" Reba shook her head. She had to bring this back on track. "I see this is going off the rails, so I was actually joking. You really thought I was gonna do this? My real mission is to make him fall under my spell, so he'll let me help bring a little more fun to his life. That's it. And seriously, what was that baggage comment about?"

"Uh..." Ayo took a huge sip of her mimosa, eyes flicking over to Trina as if to ask for help.

Trina waved a finger in the air. "Nope, don't even look at me. You on your own with that one."

Reba looked between her friends. "Do you really think I have baggage? Like, for real?"

Ayo threw back the rest of her mimosa like she needed the added fortification. "Alright, let's be real here. Your last serious relationship? He fucked you up because he was fine having you in his bed, and in the car, in the people dem cinema, and wherever else you two decided to go wild and sexy."

Reba rolled her eyes. So she didn't limit herself to an appropriate place and time when she was feeling frisky. She hadn't gotten caught yet. "Get to the point."

"But he didn't want you to meet his family as you. He wanted you to tone it down. And I know you act like that shit doesn't bother you, but we know it does, and I don't know...we just don't want you to go all revenge-y on some guy by getting him to fall for you then leave his ass or whatever."

"Wow, I..." Reba took a sip of her mimosa, unsure what to say to that.

Yes, she had a *slight* hang-up about dealing with men who saw her as this fun time girl but didn't think she was the girl they would wife up unless she literally became someone else. But she wasn't about to go on some revenge kick. With Devon no less? The man didn't even want her in his space, far less for sex.

"Sorry," Ayo said.

"Nah, it's fine." Reba drained the rest of her drink like a

shot. "But you're wrong. I'm not going to go off the rails or anything. Plus, Devon doesn't have to worry about me, at least not in that regard. He doesn't even want me around. This is an act of desperation on his part, and I'm just using it to inject some fun into his life."

Trina bit into a piece of bacon. "But why? Why do you care what he does or doesn't do?"

It was a sensible question. There was just something about Devon that made her want to push his buttons. From the moment he had ignored her at the wedding—or tried to —she had been making it her mission to get a reaction out of him, and she wasn't entirely sure why.

Could be because his stoicism offended her fun-loving nature. Either way, he had opened the door for her to get him over to the light side, where there were good times.

Reba shrugged. "He's a challenge, but I'm not gonna go overboard. Promise."

"Just seduce him while you're at it," Trina suggested. "Or maybe you don't think you can, since he's such a challenge and all."

"Is that a dare?" Trina had to be joking. Why was her friend acting as if she didn't know how Reba did?

Devon may be different than the guys she was used to dealing with, but Reba was good at getting what she wanted. If Devon wanted to be seduced, she was on board for that. He wasn't totally immune to her, whether he wanted to admit that to himself or not. He had reacted to her in her dress last night. He hadn't been quick enough to hide that minute movement of his jaw. Even if nothing came of it, flirting with Devon was amusing, and Reba was just getting started.

Trina smirked. "Sure, why not?"

Ayo looked between them. "Uh-oh. Don't throw out bets all willy-nilly like that. You know how she gets."

Reba reached out and shook Trina's hand, ignoring Ayo's concerned look. "Deal."

"Wait, so you seduce him, then what?" Ayo asked. "And what exactly does 'seduce' mean here? Just getting him to admit he wants you? Or full-on sex?"

Reba shrugged. "I think the falling under my spell and him admitting it out loud is enough. If sex happens, well... extra bonus. As for after, I dunno. I keep enjoying the fruits of my labour if he wants to. It's a go with the flow kinda situation, yeah?"

Ayo shook her head. "How do you even prove you won?"

"We can trust her word, can't we? Reba isn't a liar." Trina finished off her bacon. "You get him to admit he wants you, and dinner's on me at any place of your choosing."

"And if I lose?" Reba asked, even though she was confident she was getting that free dinner.

Trina rubbed her chin. "Spa day treat, at that place Cherisse and they were gifted by Ava and her rich ass husband."

"Okay." She didn't have a member's pass to the spa, and even a day pass would probably cost a lot, but she was so sure she was winning this.

"This is gonna bite you in the ass," Ayo mumbled.

"All this negativity isn't needed." Reba pushed the wine over to Ayo. "Shush and have another mimosa."

Ayo pursed her lips but twisted the nozzle on the bag that was in the box, adding some of the liquid goodness to her juice.

Reba's phone started playing, "You're A Mean One, Mr.

Grinch," and she couldn't help her laugh. She waved her phone at Ayo and Trina. "His ears must have been burning." She swiped to take the call. "Hello, you've reached the desk of the one and only sexy Reba Johnson, how may I help you?"

"So phone etiquette has just completely gone out the window, I suppose?"

"I'm in the middle of day drinking. Is there a reason for this call? I have enough time to sober up before we meet later so you can save whatever lecture you've got planned."

She could picture him rolling his eyes, and he graced her with one of his signature sighs. "I'm calling to say we'll have to push it to much later than we agreed on. My mother has suddenly seen it fit to *just* let me know that one of my aunts from abroad who we haven't seen in ages is here. She's coming over to see us, and it would be rude if I didn't stick around to say hello."

"Oh. You didn't tell your fam you had plans already?"

"No. I haven't mentioned *that* at all."

Clearly, he was still inclined not to. Reba didn't see the big deal about letting his family know what he was up to, but she supposed that was his business.

"Alright, well, let me know what time. Anything works for me."

"It shouldn't be too late, don't worry."

"Late nights don't worry me, Devon. It's the best time for fun."

Ayo and Trina both raised their brows, and Reba grinned.

"Oh, this man doesn't know what he's getting into," Ayo tried to whisper unsuccessfully.

"What was that?" Devon asked.

"Nothing to concern yourself over. Just be ready for me later, that's all."

"Reba. You need to stop saying everything like that." He sounded slightly exasperated. Oh yeah, she was getting to him. She had this bet in the bag.

"Like what? This is my voice."

"You know what I mean."

"Hmm, I don't think I do. Please enlighten me."

"I'll let you know what time later."

Of course, he wasn't going to call her out on it. Then he would have to admit he was affected in some way.

"Bye-bye." She hung up, reaching for some fruit while Trina and Ayo continued to look at her, amused.

"*Giiirl*, just do him, for me. You like giving your friends presents, right?"

Reba almost choked on an orange slice. Ayo wasn't usually this expressive. "If Devon and I happen to get up to anything, it will be for me, myself, and I only. Sorry."

Ayo pouted. "A real friend would give me this one thing."

Reba shook her head. "I think it's time to cut her off. She's talking mess."

Trina topped up Ayo's glass. "You've both come to the wrong place if you think I'm going to discourage any of you."

Of course, Reba knew that. Trina would enable any of her wild plans because that's just how they rolled. While Reba kept telling them any sexy plans with Devon wasn't on her agenda, if something were to go down, well, she wasn't going to run the other way.

Devon was so controlled. It made her naughty mind wonder just what she could do to get him to unravel. The possibilities were endless.

CHAPTER TEN
DEVON

MAKING GOOD ON HIS PROMISES WAS IMPORTANT TO DEVON, BUT this was one night he wanted to go back on his word. Although he had left his mother's place later than he would like, the sun just setting as he pulled into his driveway, he had told Reba they would still do this.

He had spent most of the morning entertaining Leah with her toys and paint set. He wasn't good with paint, more used to plain sketches, but she didn't seem to mind when he painted a bit outside the lines. In fact, she found it incredibly funny and kept saying, "Not like that, Uncle Devon. I'll show you!" which was unbearably cute.

Devon didn't like engaging with other adults more than necessary, but small children were okay. He liked that they told it to you straight, no façade involved. It did, however, feel like a tiny dagger to the heart when Leah disparaged his cupcakes by claiming the others looked prettier. He shouldn't have brought any of Reba's. She was simply stating a fact, but damn if that didn't bruise his ego.

It didn't help that Maxi had also taken one bite of his and lamented the dryness. "You said your neighbour brought these over?" she asked as she chewed. "They were trying to get rid of their meh batch or what?"

Obviously, Devon hadn't let on that he had made those. Instead, he had offered them some of Reba's, trying to keep his feelings in check when Leah gobbled it down. He knew he couldn't compete with someone who had been doing this for far longer than he had, and yet it irked. He had to get better at this. If he couldn't conquer a simple cupcake, he sure as hell wasn't going to succeed at a complicated Rubik's Cube cake.

How had he allowed Reba to convince him this was a good idea? They didn't have much time, and while the concept of the cake appealed to his love for design and structural specifications, it still felt like a huge task.

Reba seemed to think it was fine to wing it, having never attempted something like this, but from the videos Devon had looked up online, this wasn't something you just did on a whim. Preparation was important. He didn't want his cake to look like one of those failed Pinterest projects.

"It's not *that* bad. A little dry, yeah, but edible still." He tried to make a plug for his cakes, even knowing it was a lost cause.

"You were duped into taking these is all I'm saying. The frosting is even all wonky. Did they let their child make this?"

Devon shrugged. "It was a kind gesture."

"Yeah, nah. You been scammed, brother dearest."

He had dropped his defence of the cupcakes there. Maxi would become suspicious if he kept trying to preserve the cakes' honour. He barely interacted with his neighbours, to begin with, so even admitting he had accepted baked goods from them was unusual.

After the cupcake bashing, he had become immersed in listening to Leah's stories about school and everything she was doing on her vacation so far. When his aunt—who he wasn't actually certain was related to them in any way—arrived, that was another couple of hours of food, talking, and her wanting an update on all their lives. She wasn't shy about trying to get the details of Maxi's divorce out of her or wanting to know why Devon wasn't married with a few children yet.

Keiran had definitely chosen the perfect time to be off-island.

Devon's reply had been that he was working on the spouse part. He then tried to distract her by offering the questionable cupcakes, which had brought another round of teasing from his mother and Maxi.

"Whichever neighbour brought these for you really don't like you, boy," his mother had joked again.

His aunt had either lost all her taste buds over the years or she didn't care because she ate two without comment. It didn't make him feel any better, just wonder when he could make his escape.

He had finally made his exit, letting Reba know he was on the way. They didn't have much time and during the week wasn't ideal for any of this. And yet, right now, he wasn't sure if this was a wise decision.

Night-time Reba had an entirely different energy. She hadn't rolled up in fishnets or worn shorts like at the beach house or anything, but he couldn't decide if the soft-looking grey leggings and pink top that barely covered her stomach was far worse. It didn't make sense. Leggings weren't on the same level as fishnets, for fuck's sake, and yet he wanted to call this entire baking venture off.

Whatever that grey material was made of, it fit snugly

over her ass and shapely legs. Devon's body was enjoying all of it. What the hell was wrong with him?

"You look like you don't want me here?"

He looked away from the swinging heart that was attached to her navel ring. Shit, he hadn't even realised he'd been fixated on that and met her amused gaze. "That's not what..." He cleared his throat. "It's late."

Reba shrugged. "It's not even seven yet, but if you want me to go, that's your call."

"No, it's fine." It would be fine, *dammit*. He wasn't about to be defeated by leggings and a swingy top. He had survived last night's outfit—some soft-looking fabric wasn't going to be his undoing. "Is this what you wore to brunch?"

Why the hell was he asking about that? They needed to get in the kitchen and get going. He didn't give a damn what she wore at some day drinking event. In fact, talking about anything other than baking was prolonging her being here.

"Nope. Wanna see?" She reached for her phone before he could decline, and he ended up with a face full of Reba in a short purple dress, legs draped across a chair, long pink hair falling straight over her shoulder. "Trina took this one. She's good at making me look sexy."

Devon didn't believe that for one second. She definitely had sexiness covered on her own, even in her casual wear.

She pointed at her navel ring. "You seem to like this one. I changed it when I went home." She pressed her finger against the heart to make it swing. "Cute, right?"

"Hmm."

"You don't like it?" She looked down at her legs, tugging at the grey material. Devon took a deep breath then released it slowly.

"I didn't say that."

"Well, you're not saying much of anything. Just making sounds. No worries, I know I look good. I don't need your validation." She patted her thigh before looking up at him.

"Then why did you send me that bathing suit photo?"

Reba's grin was absolutely smug. "Aww, you're cute. That was a thirst trap. Plain and simple. C'mon, let's get to the kitchen. You have work in the morning."

He regretted following her as she sauntered to the kitchen. It gave him the perfect view of her ass cupped by that thin grey fabric. He couldn't discern any panty line, which wasn't saying much. He at least knew about seamless underwear. Although she could be wearing a thong— or nothing.

Okay, fuck no, we are not doing this. Get your shit together. Her underwear is not the focus.

The voice in his head sounded strong, confident. Devon took another deep breath to get himself under control. This shouldn't be hard. He didn't usually go around staring at women's asses. Sure, he appreciated a beautiful woman when he saw her, but this level of distraction was annoying. He frowned at Reba, who was busy queuing up her playlist again. Some dance track with techno beats started playing, and Devon reached up to rub his forehead. He preferred music that was softer with a slower beat at this time of night. The perfect background sounds for relaxation with a glass of wine, but he didn't bother to hassle her about it. The faster they got through this, the quicker Reba and her leggings could leave.

"How was your time with your niece?" she asked as he focused on mixing the batter. He had decided he was trying the cupcakes again, following her instructions on how to make them less dry.

"Leah's great."

"And did you give your family the cupcakes?"

Devon pursed his lips. "The cupcakes were not a hit."

"Aww, don't pout. Even though you look super cute doing that."

"I do *not* pout."

She pushed her lips out. "From here, this is all I see. What would you call it then?"

"Pursed lips aren't the same as pouting." He waved at her mouth. "I didn't do that."

Reba leaned against the counter, chin in her hands. "Oh, really? Please enlighten me."

This entire conversation was ridiculous, but he could easily make a case for this silly notion, couldn't he?

"The difference lies in the shape of the mouth and the intention. With a pout, your lips are pushed out a bit more. That's not what I was doing. It was a slight protrusion."

"Uh-huh." Reba looked amused, although she didn't seem to be buying his logic at all. "You know, if you put this much focus into your baking, you wouldn't have dry ass cupcakes, just saying."

"Wow, shot right to the heart," he deadpanned, hopefully not letting on that he cared about his inability to get it perfect on the first try.

Reba swiped a finger through the batter and brought it to her lips. "Do you even have a heart, Mr. Grouch?" she teased, sucking her finger clean, and Devon definitely didn't follow that movement.

Devon poured the batter into the cupcake liners. "You really think I'm some heartless SOB?"

"Nah." Reba's eyes dropped to his chest. "I think you just prefer not to show your soft, gooey centre, but it's there. You seem the type of person who shows that through the little things you do for people rather than overt affection."

He stared at her, brow raised. She wasn't looking at him, eyes still fixed on his chest, smirk growing wider. Devon *was* picky about who he let into his space, and he certainly didn't lavish his attention on just anyone. PDA wasn't something he engaged in, really. He was private about his affections.

He cleared his throat when Reba still didn't stop staring at his chest. "My eyes are up here."

Reba took her sweet time meeting his gaze. "Oh, are they? My, what pretty brown eyes you have," she said, batting her eyelashes in the most ridiculous way.

He walked over to the oven, ignoring her, and bent down so he could slide the cupcake tin in. Next, he had to get the frosting done. This time, he was going to focus and succeed at piping it properly. When he turned around, Reba's eyes rose to meet his.

"Yes, I was looking at your ass," she said as if it was totally normal to admit that.

He shook his head. "Why do you do that?" he asked, looking down at her. She had turned to face him when he'd moved towards the oven, so her back was pressed to the counter now, leaving limited space between them.

"What do you mean? Speak the truth?"

"Say things like that," he clarified. "You don't always have to say what pops into your head."

Her eyes slowly tracked down his front, then back up to his face. "Trust me, I've been holding back. I haven't said everything that's in my head because I don't want to scandalise you."

"I'm a grown man. I think I can handle it." *No, no, no,*

what was he doing? He wasn't supposed to be encouraging her.

He was tired, needed sleep. That had to be the only reason he was losing his goddamn mind and entertaining whatever the fuck was happening between them in his kitchen.

Reba sucked in her bottom lip before she released it with a pop. "I don't think you could," she countered. "I see you're grown, Devon. Trust, I noticed, but that doesn't equate being able to handle me."

"Who said anything about handling you? I know you have this master plan to charm my co-workers, but *I'm* not that easy."

Reba laughed. "I've never considered you easy. But you're telling me if I did this, you wouldn't care?"

Devon reached deep for all his willpower when Reba lifted the bottom of his t-shirt and pressed her hand to his stomach. Control. While he forced himself not to react outwardly to the feel of her nails lightly caressing him, he felt his grip on the situation slipping.

"Do you want me to stop?"

"You seem to have something to prove, so have at it."

Reba's grin was pure mischief, and Devon didn't know why he was doing this. Yes, he didn't back down from challenges, and he refused to let Reba unravel him, but why he felt he needed to prove anything to her, he wasn't quite sure.

She gripped his waist and tried to move him. "I want you against the counter. Cooperate, please."

He planted his feet, not budging. Reba wasn't going to be able to move him, and he could be stubborn when he wanted to. She pushed her lips all the way out, clutched his waist harder.

Devon chuckled in spite of telling himself he wasn't going to react to her in any way. "Definitely a pout."

Her mouth curved up into a toothy grin. "Ha! I win."

"What. How?"

Reba removed her hands from his body, dragging her nails over his skin before stepping away from the counter. "Made you laugh. A real one, too." She buffed her nails on her shoulder. "Damn, I'm good."

"Hold the fuck on, that wasn't the game. You were trying to..." Seduce me. Which, as he said it in his head, sounded truly ridiculous.

"Wasn't it? Remember I said I was going to help you have more fun, and look at you. Laughing and shit."

"Reba." He said her name with all the exasperation he felt. He couldn't keep up with her all-over-the-place actions. She didn't fit with his need to have a pattern for everything.

She smiled at him. "Yes?"

"Can we please just get back to the mission at hand?"

"Hey, I'm not the one that took us down this path, as fun as it was." She wiggled her hands. "Thanks for warming me up."

Devon pressed a hand to his forehead. He honestly felt like he was losing his damn mind. How had they gotten here? Taking control of the situation was the only thing that mattered. He didn't like being played with like this, and yet he couldn't yell at Reba because he had opened the entire can of worms with his question. He should know by now to simply ignore her outrageous statements. If he didn't give her the attention she craved, they would move on.

He moved back to his earlier position to prep the frosting. The cupcakes wouldn't take that long, and he needed to be ready. Forget the feel of Reba's hand on his skin. Bury the memory of how his entire body had become one big nerve ending that Reba had set off with just her touch. It had been some time since he had allowed anyone in his personal space like that. He tended to his needs himself, didn't seek out casual dalliances. That wasn't in his plans. He wanted something serious, which meant he hadn't been intimate with anyone since he and Monica had ended their relationship.

Two years could seem like a long time, for some, to go without sex, but Devon didn't allow his urges to overwhelm. He was quite fine dealing with that on his own until he found someone he actually wanted to build something with.

He thought about his spreadsheets, specifically the one he'd used to calculate the risks of any given situation. If he plugged in everything he knew about Reba, it would surely just show him a ton of things highlighted in red.

Allowing Reba to breach his carefully crafted space was dangerous.

"Are you upset with me?" Her question floated over to him. He hadn't looked at her once since he had decided to get back to baking. He didn't *want* to look at her now, but he lifted his head, and there she was, swaying side to side to whatever song was playing now.

"No. It's on me. I know better."

Reba's brow went up. "Because I'm a loose cannon and can't be trusted to keep us on track? Which, okay, fair, but don't beat yourself up because you enjoyed it."

"We need to stick to the basic plan and not play these games. They're pointless."

"Full offense, but fuck your basic ass plan."

Devon sighed. "Reba."

"Okay, fine, sorry. That was a bit much. Look, I just..." She stopped swaying but didn't move from her side of the room, thank God. "Is it so bad if you have a little teeny bit of fun in my presence? You won't die."

"I don't want to have fun with you. I just want you to help me win this damn thing, so Dax can see I'm making an effort, and I get the promotion I deserve. Quite frankly, it's bullshit that I even have to do any of this because being good at my job isn't enough, apparently. Making partner would mean I have even less time for these foolish after-work activities, so none of this makes sense, but here we fucking are."

Reba folded her arms. "You done?"

He hadn't meant to unload any of that on her, but the entire situation was frustrating. Which wasn't her fault. "Sorry, yes. I'm done."

"Now that you got that off your chest. You're free to sever this partnership if you wish, but I guarantee you won't win."

"You're so sure you can get me this win?"

Reba nodded. "Yup."

"And if I lose, then what?"

"Then you lose, but you made an effort, and your boss will notice. You just have to keep making little efforts here and there."

"Because you're so well-versed in the corporate world?"

Reba's smile slipped. "Don't *ever* fucking imply I'm not smart enough to understand a corporate environment."

Shit, he hadn't meant to do that at all. "Wait, hold on. I didn't mean..."

She waved at the oven. "Check your damn cupcakes."

The cupcakes seemed fine, but Devon was a little concerned as Reba watched him place them on the counter to cool. He had upset her, which, regardless of it not being his intention, had happened. Her warm flirty demeanour had been replaced by silence. She was looking at her phone without saying anything.

"Reba, can you look at me, please?"

She looked up, expression unchanging. "How can I help you?"

"I never meant to make it sound like I was questioning your intelligence. I'm sorry."

"You know, I've been an assistant for men who don't see me as a person because of my title. To them, my opinions didn't matter cuz I don't have some fancy degree. Corporate life isn't for me. Doesn't mean I don't have a clue how it works. I know *all* too well and wouldn't want to put myself there again for any reason. That's it." She gestured to the piping bag and nozzles. "Get started."

She was done with him and this discussion, which he should be grateful for. Although, he didn't want to continue feeling like he'd kicked a puppy that was just trying to be friendly with him.

He gave her one last look and considered trying to talk to her again, but she had gone back to her phone.

Okay, so maybe he shouldn't dwell on this, just enjoy the fact that she wasn't distracting him with flirty banter. He looked away from her lips—that were definitely pursed this time—and got back to the mission at hand.

CHAPTER ELEVEN
REBA

IT HAD BEEN THREE DAYS SINCE HER SUNDAY BAKING SESSION WITH Devon, and Reba was still annoyed. She was going to do something reckless; she felt it in her bones. Devon King didn't get to act as if she couldn't possibly understand a corporate setting.

His careless statement had made her flashback to the douchebags she had worked with previously, and her anger was bubbling, even all these days later.

Why? It didn't make sense. Those men had never been worth her getting worked up over, and she was tossing Devon into that category for the moment. What bugged her the most was that she hadn't anticipated such a reply from him. He claimed he hadn't meant it like that, and while she believed him, the fact that he had gone there riled her up.

Fuck him.

She felt like texting him those exact words. *Fuck. You.* But common sense prevailed a bit. She could continue to be annoyed and still take his money. Yeah, that would serve his ass right.

Her phone rang, and like he knew she was plotting

some unreasonable revenge, his handsome face popped up. She ignored it only for their chat to pling. He had actually messaged her first.

> **Devon:** *Are you just going to ignore me forever?*
> **Devon:** *Ok that wasn't...I'm sorry, ignore that message. You can be as upset as you want. That's fair.*
> **Devon:** *Does this mean our working relationship is over too?*

Reba rolled her eyes. This man, seriously. Another notification popped up on her phone, and Reba smiled, brain whirring. If he wanted to make it up to her, she definitely knew a way. He would hate it. Reba smiled wider. She didn't care what resistance he would put up.

After a quick shower and using Google Maps for directions to Dax Designs, Reba felt much better—couldn't help humming all the way to his office. She waited until she had strolled into the building, told the ground floor receptionist who she was here to see, and entered the elevator before she replied to his message.

> **Reba:** *oh you're not getting rid of me that easily just FYI.*
> **Devon:** *Thank you.*
> **Reba:** *you can say that and grovel to my face.*
> **Devon:** *Fine. I'll grovel all you want on Saturday.*

Reba grinned as she typed.

> **Reba:** *sooner than that.*

She tucked her phone away, not reading whatever reply he sent back. Let him wonder what she meant.

As if everything was falling into place for her little plan, the first person she saw when she exited the elevator was the boss himself.

Dax's grin was wide and friendly when he looked up from his phone and spotted her. "Reba! What a surprise."

"It is! I came to whisk your best worker away for lunch."

"Really?" Reba had definitely read Devon's workaholic ass right; Dax's reaction spoke volumes. "That's good. He barely takes his lunch sometimes."

"Ah, so I have your blessing to steal away with him for an hour or two?"

"Most definitely! He won't like it, though."

Reba grinned. Oh, she really liked this guy. "I'm good at convincing people to do what I want."

Dax chuckled. "I bet."

"This is actually my first time here, so if you can tell me where his office is?"

"I'll take you."

Reba tried to dial down her smile to less triumphant, but she didn't quite succeed. Everything lining up perfectly in this moment was making her too happy to suppress. She had been ready to use all her charm to get Devon to follow her out of here, but with Dax in her corner, he would definitely do it. He obviously respected his boss.

Dax knocked, and when Devon's gloriously deep voice told him to enter, Reba bit her lip to keep her laugh in. She couldn't wait to see his face.

"Well, look what lovely surprise I found in our lobby," Dax said.

Devon looked up as Reba stepped from behind Dax. He blinked once, twice, three times, and Reba bit her lip harder. This was going to be so much fun. She generally tried to enjoy her day no matter what she was doing, but there was just something about shaking up Devon's day that gave her immense pleasure. Perhaps she was wrong for that. Not that she cared one bit.

His brow furrowed. "What's going on?"

"This young lady has come to take you to lunch, so I wouldn't keep her waiting if I were you."

"Lunch? I wasn't planning to..."

Dax waved him off. "I know you skip it sometimes then eat at ridiculous hours, and I'm usually not here to tell a grown man what to do, but now I'm making an exception. She came all this way to surprise you. Go eat. Enjoy the time away from your desk. Come check me after."

Devon gaped as Dax left, closing the door behind him.

"What the hell are you doing?"

Reba pointed at herself. "This is how you can make it up to me. By taking me to lunch."

"He said *you* came to take *me* to lunch."

"I had to say something. I didn't think telling him that you needed to apologise was the way to go, so..." She pulled out the chair opposite him and made herself comfortable. She would stay here all day if she needed to.

"I..." He scrubbed his hand over his face. "What about dinner instead? There's so much I need to do. Lunch isn't really feasible at the moment."

Devon would learn just how stubborn Reba could be when she wanted something. "Nope. It has to be lunch." She tugged at the clingy material of her dress. "I wore this to be seen in the bright light of day. Besides, Dax already said it's fine." She snapped her fingers. "Come on, let's get going. I'm hungry."

He pursed his lips, and Reba couldn't hold back her laughter anymore. "Pouting again? How cute."

He gave her a hard stare before sighing and rising to his feet. She kept her eyes on him as he walked around the desk to stand next to her. She didn't move from the seat, enjoying the way he couldn't contain his frustration as he looked down at her.

Devon in his work suit was a delicious sight. She had seen him in a suit at Ava's wedding, and yet him dressed like this in his perfectly organised office was giving her ideas. Reba wanted to tug on that tie and bring his face oh so close to hers just to see his reaction. Instead, she decided to let him squirm.

Not that she could ever imagine Devon squirming about anything. He would frown just like he was doing now.

"Whatever you're thinking of doing, *don't*."

She turned to him, propping her elbows on the arm of the chair and clasping her hands together. "What do you think I'm thinking?"

"Nothing that bodes well for me."

"Not true. It would end *very* well for you, I promise."

Devon shook his head, patted at his pockets, and moved away from her. "I'm getting my wallet. Let's just go. Do you have somewhere in mind?"

"It's a little unknown place that's not too far away from here."

He paused at his desk. "What's the name?"

"You definitely don't know it." Few people did. Since it was a far cry from the type of scene Devon would be into, telling him the name wouldn't make a difference. She also enjoyed frustrating him, especially since she wasn't totally pleased with him at the moment.

His brow winged up, and just as she expected, his eyes reflected wariness.

"Where are we going, Reba?"

She wagged her finger. "It's a surprise. Just trust me, okay?"

"So I'm just supposed to allow you to get some kind of revenge on me?"

"It's not revenge. Not really. Yes, I fully admit I'm making you take me to lunch because you pissed me off, but how about you don't disparage people's intelligence, and you won't find yourself here, hmm?"

He made a noise that sounded like a grunt, and Reba got to her feet and smoothed down the front of her dress. The ribbed material tended to have a mind of its own. "I'll drive since I know where we're going."

He turned to her, ready to protest but shook his head again. "Fine."

The receptionist looked like she couldn't believe her eyes when Devon told her he'd be back in two hours, at the latest—he stressed the time as if sending her a silent signal to send out a search party if he wasn't back by then —and if anyone asked for him, he was out on a business lunch. The woman's eyes slid over to Reba and then back to Devon.

"Business lunch. Okay, yes, got it."

Reba laughed as they made their way to the elevator. "Her group chat is going to be jumping about this."

Devon looked out the window, watching the scenery as they descended to the ground floor. "You're enjoying this way too much."

"Hey, this is actually working in your favour. Your co-workers get to see a different side of you. And how can you function without proper nutrition? I'm helping you here."

"I function just fine. Your idea of helping is vastly different from mine."

"We're very different people, Devon, I'm aware. That's the fun of the whole thing."

"Fun is overrated," he grumbled. "We agreed the weekends would be your time. For baking. Now you're disrupting my work during the week?"

They exited the elevator, and Devon followed Reba to the visitor parking in the back of the building. "Yup, just call me The Disruptor," she said proudly as she pointed to where her car was parked.

"This feels weird," Devon said as soon as he slid into the passenger seat. "Not used to being driven."

"Well, sit back and enjoy the whole ten minutes it's going to take to get there. I'm an excellent driver, and you get to look at all of this instead of the boring scenery outside."

He followed her hand as she swept it from her waist to her hip, but he didn't say a thing. She could see his brain working overtime to figure out where she was taking him. Didn't matter, he was never guessing the location. She was positive Devon had never set foot into this place, nor did he know it existed.

He was silent the entire time it took them to get to the nondescript car park. Reba didn't bother him because she was too hyped to see his reaction. He followed her across the street and looked totally confused when they were in front of one of those old colonial-style houses.

"Not here." Reba pointed to the little side gate. "Down there." She pushed it open and smiled to herself as Devon followed silently behind. Usually, it was jarring when people stepped from the bright daylight into the more subdued lighting of the JamBoree Bistro.

"What in the hell is this place?"

Reba stepped aside so Devon could get the full impact of her favourite lunch spot. The music was at a decent level, but there were still people jamming out to it at their tables as they either waited for their lunch orders or chowed down on their food.

"Welcome to my best-kept secret."

Devon remained glued to the bottom of the stairs like he didn't want to move any further into the room. Fair, Reba supposed. To him, this entire place would look like chaos. She wondered how he would take it when she told him they didn't have a daily set menu.

A tall, burly guy came over to them. "Darling, I didn't expect you today!" he shouted, grabbing Reba up into a big hug and spinning her around before allowing her feet to touch the ground.

"You know I like keeping you on your toes. Well, I'm introducing someone to your amazingness today." She pointed at Devon. "JB, this is Devon. My chaos-averse comrade."

JB gave Devon the once-over. "I love a challenge, so come on. I have your usual table for you right over here."

Reba's favourite table allowed them to see the entire place. She loved people-watching. It was so easy to spot when someone was entering JamBoree for the first time. Their facial expressions were always so amusing.

Like Devon's right now. He didn't know what to make of this place. His brow furrowed even more when JB asked, "So, any allergies to anything? Anything you don't particularly like?"

"Isn't there a menu?" Devon asked, clearly confused.

"Nope," JB said cheerfully.

"That's..."

"Genius, right?" Reba butted in.

Devon stared at JB. "And what if you bring me something I turn out not to like?"

"Hasn't happened yet," JB said confidently.

"How does a concept like this even work? This sounds like a total disaster."

"Oh, it's not a new concept. I actually got the idea while I was in Paris some years ago. Decided to bring it home here. I've been open for a few years now, so guess it's not so much of a disaster, huh?"

"Come on, roll with the experience," Reba urged. "I know you want to get back to the office in the stipulated time."

Devon rubbed at his nose bridge. "Okay, just...nothing with the consistency of risotto, please."

"Got it. Reebs?"

"I'm in the mood for an explosion of flavours today. Light on the spicy, but make my tongue happy."

"I'll have Dina bring over some water and the drinks list, which should ease your friend's mind a bit."

Devon watched JB walk away before looking back to her. "I don't like surprises," he announced.

Reba placed her hands in her lap. Obviously, she knew he wasn't the type to go along with this. It was the whole reason why she had brought him here. Well, that and the slight revenge she wanted to exact. He should consider himself lucky that this was all she had decided on. In fact, it was barely a punishment at all.

"Do you want to go? Or do you, for once in your life, want to do something spontaneous that I promise won't kill you?"

"I get it, I hurt you with my careless comment, but this..." He gestured to where a couple was literally grooving to the music, in their own little world as if there wasn't a full midday sun shining brightly outside. "Just seems like you want to make me uncomfortable just because you can."

"Is it really making you feel uncomfortable? Real talk. It's not my intention at all. Yes, I was upset and wanted to frustrate you a bit, but if you genuinely feel itchy about it, we can go somewhere less exciting."

Reba liked to push Devon's buttons but causing anxiety to flare up wasn't her deal. Just because he didn't outwardly express his emotions most times didn't mean he didn't feel things.

"It's not my usual scene, obviously, but I'll live."

"Once you're sure." She leaned forward. "There's that pretty pout again."

"You live to torment me, don't you?"

"Why do you think I wore this dress today?"

The sleeveless salmon-coloured dress stopped way above her knees, which meant it kept riding up whenever she sat. Reba liked to show off her legs, so she didn't mind that an entire portion of her thigh was showing. The table didn't provide much cover either. If anyone was so inclined to drink it all in, they were free to do so.

Reba expected Devon to give his usual response of either rolling his eyes or ignoring her flirting entirely. She was in no way prepared for him to also lean across the table, gaze intense, and ask, "For me to wonder what, if anything, you're wearing under it?"

CHAPTER TWELVE

DEVON

"Oh."

The small exhalation from Reba should have slapped some sense into Devon. He should be apologising for saying something so fucking out of line, and yet the way her mouth was hanging open slightly left him feeling smug.

He had managed to leave her somewhat speechless for a few seconds. It wouldn't last long. Reba was quick on her feet and a master flirt. She would recover soon, and Devon would ultimately regret his decision to lose his entire mind and ask such a question.

He had to be hungrier than he thought. What other reason could there be for this?

For me to wonder what, if anything, you're wearing under it?

Fuck, had he actually said that? Out loud, too?

It had been an honest thought that he should have kept buried in a specific corner of his mind where he tried to stuff any Reba-related items that didn't have anything to do with baking.

When she walked out from behind Dax at his office,

Devon hadn't been sure how to deal with that. She had invaded his personal space at his home already—which was entirely his doing—and now here she was at his office, uninvited, invading his work space. In a dress that just screamed for someone to bend her over a table and...

Fuck, fuck, fuck.

He shifted in his chair, reached for his legendary control, and wiped all wayward thoughts from his mind. "I'm sorry, that was uncalled for."

He took a sip of the water he had just noticed was on the table. When had that gotten here? Jesus. He hoped JB or whoever hadn't quietly walked in on him saying that shit. He had truly had an out-of-body experience, hadn't he? Devon didn't let people walk up on him without noticing. That shit just didn't happen. But with Reba—just as he'd feared—things that were second nature for him were glitching. Until he got this person he didn't recognise.

None of that meshed with his carefully organised plans.

He shouldn't be here—in this ridiculous place that flouted a basic rule such as providing menus for its patrons —with her. He should be in his office finishing up his important presentation. Devon didn't have time to be out wasting time at lunch with Reba.

Yes, he needed to apologise, but he could have easily said no to this and left it at that. The only thing was Reba wouldn't have accepted that and might have just lounged around his office the entire day out of spite. Then what? He'd definitely get nothing done. This had been the easier and more logical choice, and yet... Nothing about this was turning out to be simple.

"Oh no, no, no, there's no way in hell we're acting like that didn't just happen." The shiny gloss on Reba's lips was even more of a distraction when her mouth curved up into that grin. The one he had come to learn meant mischief was on the horizon.

"Can we please just do that? I'm hungry. I don't know what I'm saying."

"So, you get flirty when you're hungry? Interesting." Reba poked the top of her dress with her nail. "To put you out of your misery and answer your question, I'm wearing a bra today. As for underwear, well..." She paused. "There isn't much of it, but it's there."

Devon's fingers dug into his thigh. This was his own fault. He couldn't expect Reba to ignore the easy means of teasing him he had thrown her way.

"This is you putting me out of my misery? Underwear isn't appropriate lunch discussion. Let's just talk about something else. *Please.*"

Reba took a sip of her water. "You ask so nicely, but I just don't feel like moving on yet. You opened the door." She braced her elbows on the table and leaned forward, chin on top of her clasped hands. "So, what's your preference? Boxers? Briefs? Boxer briefs? Or do you like the feel of the material against your bare skin? Quite frankly, going commando is really freeing."

"No." There was no way in hell they were doing this. He could haul ass out of here and take a taxi back to the office, but then he would seem like he couldn't handle Reba. She would be more than satisfied if he literally chose to run than face this head-on.

"No, as in you're not wearing anything under those well-fitting pants or...?"

"No, as in I will not be discussing my underwear with you here."

A throat clearing above them made Devon want to sigh at the obviously bad timing the server had. He looked up, and the woman standing there with their food didn't seem the least bit shocked. She placed a plate in front of Reba then the other for Devon.

"Interesting company you always keeping."

Reba smiled up at her. "Oh yeah. Always."

"Enjoy your meal." She shot Devon a look before adding, "And conversation."

Reba clapped her hands, picking up her fork. "Bon appétit!"

If the ground could swallow him whole at this very moment, he would welcome it. Devon wasn't easily embarrassed because he didn't find himself in such situations, usually. It wasn't that he was currently feeling that emotion, but conversations like these weren't meant for just anyone to be privy to. Another anomaly because he didn't generally *have* discussions like this in public.

Reba obviously didn't care. She began chowing down on her meal without a second glance at Devon. He couldn't stop himself from staring at her. She wasn't a quiet eater. Her sounds of pleasure and enjoyment would have irked him on a normal occasion, but he was fascinated for some reason.

He was a silent eater himself. Didn't mean he wasn't enjoying his food; he simply saw no reason to be this noisy about it.

Another moan and hum of delight from Reba was enough for him to decide he needed to get to his dish. Focus on that and not the sounds coming from across the table. Sounds that seemed way too intimate for their current setting.

The first hit of flavour burst onto his tongue, and Devon was pleasantly surprised. He couldn't name the dish, but JB had created something aromatic and colourful that included perfectly cooked slivers of steak. How the man had gotten it so right, he couldn't guess. He almost asked Reba if she had orchestrated this entire lunch to push at his buttons—had somehow known exactly what Devon's taste would be and alerted JB beforehand. That all seemed farfetched, even for her. Reba was guileless in her own way, preferring to be too honest and open as far as he was concerned.

"God, this is so good," Reba sighed. "I would seriously let JB hit this if he wasn't already married. If I could convince them to let me be their third, I'd be living my best food life!"

Devon choked on a vegetable, and Jesus Christ, if this was how he died, he would be pissed. He looked up at Reba, who had paused with her fork to her lips.

"Whoops, sorry. You okay over there?"

Devon wiped his mouth and nodded. "Yes. Perfectly fine. This is good."

"It's more than good, isn't it, but your set-in-your-ways ass won't admit I was right to bring you here. Come on, you can say it. I was right. I won't gloat too much." She licked the back of her fork, and Devon's gaze returned to his food.

"I highly doubt that," he muttered.

"Just say 'thank you, Reba.'"

"For what? I'm paying."

"But you've gained so much from this experience."

All he had gained from this was knowledge he didn't want about Reba's underwear choices.

Let's not forget she sometimes doesn't wear any.

He stabbed at a piece of steak, shoving it into his mouth. Fucking traitorous subconscious.

"I want to try cookies on Saturday." He needed to move

this lunch conversation to a path that made sense. Thinking about Reba's bare ass under her clothes wasn't it.

She shrugged. "Whatever you want."

"Oh, all of a sudden, it's whatever *I* want?" He eyed her suspiciously. Why was she being so amenable now? He didn't trust this.

"Cookies are fun and ups the difficulty level a bit. Come prepared on Saturday to show me cupcakes you made yourself, though. If I'm satisfied, we move on to the cookies. No ulterior motive." She held up her pinkie finger. "Girl Guide's honour and all."

"Were you ever actually a Girl Guide?"

"Well, I didn't quite make it past the Brownies, so technically no."

"Hmm."

"I was a Brownie until I rebelled at eight, tried to make my own patches to make the uniform less boring. The official patches and that brown dress and yellow tie just weren't it. My Guide leader didn't appreciate that, so they kindly told my parents that I should consider other pursuits more suited to my energetic personality."

Devon shook his head. "Of course."

Reba waved away his comment. "Organised institutions will never appreciate my creativity. I literally rescued a cat from a tree, so why shouldn't I have a cute patch for that? They told me my cute Hello Kitty badge wasn't an official patch, so I couldn't put it on my uniform. The audacity. A Brownie is supposed to be helpful. I was being helpful by letting them know their uniform was trash."

"So you were a hellraiser at eight? My condolences to your parents."

"Oh, he got jokes? Just finish your food and hush."

Devon couldn't help his chuckle. He could definitely

picture it, Reba telling off a bunch of adults because a uniform was a basic brown instead of something more colourful.

"Collecting those laughs like Pokémon, babyyyy!" Reba pumped her fists in the air triumphantly.

Devon rolled his eyes. "Let's finish up here so I can get back. You must have something to do as well?"

Reba checked her phone. "Okay, I actually do. Because as much as it seems like it, I don't just spend all my time thinking up ways to frustrate you. I actually have a shoot in an hour. Gotta get my mind right to get my nude on. The things I do for friends."

Devon finished off his food without somehow choking again. He planned to leave a generous tip for JB. He could admit he had been wrong about what he could expect of a place like this. JB's choice for him had been perfect.

"What do you mean, get your nude on?" he asked because trying to follow Reba's thought process was like trying to solve the world's most difficult puzzle. Usually, he enjoyed puzzles, did a few in his rare downtimes. But this woman—as open as she seemed about most things—was still such an enigma. He could truly say he had never met anyone like her.

Reba grinned. "Scott needed a model last minute for some body glow cosmetics campaign thing, so he asked me. I mean, I'll be strategically covered by the other models, and my face won't even really be seen, but yeah, can't have clothes obstructing the glow effect of the product now, can we?"

Devon pressed his palms together like he could call down some deity to save him from this moment. *Don't ask any questions. Don't ask any questions. Don't...*

"You're being serious?"

Reba's brown skin already had this glow that he assumed was her being well-moisturised; he couldn't picture how luminous it would become with some product made specifically for that. He didn't want to picture any of it because it would be weird to be sitting here, thinking of her with nothing on.

She smirked instead of answering him. "Let's get the bill, shall we? We're both very busy people."

She called JB over, and Devon settled the payment. He didn't want to ask Reba about this with others around. Why did he even care? She was an adult woman who could participate in a nude shoot if she wanted to. The only reason he was even giving this a thought was because he couldn't fathom how she could be so comfortable with this. Obviously, people did this all the time; it wasn't some novel idea. He'd just not met anyone who had done it, so his brain was trying to force him to ask questions to make sense of why anyone would agree to this. Helping out a friend didn't seem logical enough to him.

"Well, it's been a wonderful time. Thanks for taking me to lunch."

"I was basically forced, but you're welcome," he said dryly. "Enjoy your, uh, shoot."

"Oh, I plan to." She tilted her head. "You want to ask me more about it so badly, don't you?" She pointed at his face. "Your nose is all scrunchy."

"It just...you're helping Scott out? It doesn't make sense why."

"I'm pretty comfy in my skin, plus," she shrugged, "he promised me product freebies. Everybody wins."

"I..." He paused. He didn't have time to go down this path. "You know what? Just be safe, okay?"

Reba reached up and pinched his cheek. What the hell? "Aww, you're sweet."

"If you accidentally have some nude photos leaked and have to go into hiding until the scandal blows over, who'll help me with this bake-off?"

"Your mind is really something, huh? It'll be fine."

She tried to poke him in the side when they crossed the street to enter the car park. He caught her finger before she could unknowingly find his tickle spot. He wouldn't live that down, and he definitely didn't need to give Reba any more ammo against him.

"Anyway, Devon, enjoy your boring workday. And you're still holding my finger."

He dropped said finger. What was he doing? If someone he knew just happened to pass by and see him like this, there would be questions. Holding a woman's finger wasn't exactly a scandalous action, but as Reba had pointed out, Corinne had looked like she was prepping for some gossip when he'd told her he was stepping out for lunch.

As small as this action was, he didn't want to add more fuel to the fire. Showing up at karaoke with Reba had to already have the office maco-meter buzzing.

"We're not even in the car yet. Planning to drive off and leave me here?"

She walked around to the driver's side. "I contemplated it for half a sec, not gonna lie."

He looked at her over the top of her car. "Well, enjoy your thing."

Reba's laugh was so loud the car park attendant looked over at them. "You said that already. Just get in."

He did, trying to settle his mind to get back into work mode. There would be no more Reba-shaped distractions once he got back to his office.

Reba Johnson did not exist until Saturday.

Except he found himself curious about this shoot business. Not that it was *his* business because what Reba chose to do with her time wasn't his concern.

He didn't care. Not a single bit. Not at all.

He was merely curious about the logistics of the entire thing.

Snap out of it, he scolded himself. There was too much going on to spend time musing about Reba engaging in nude activities of any kind.

CHAPTER THIRTEEN
REBA

[Wednesday 3:24 p.m.]

Devon: *Just checking you got to your shoot safe and sound*

Reba: *Yes, would you like proof of life? This one isn't too racy *photo attached**

Devon: *Your reply would have sufficed. The photo wasn't necessary. You're in a robe.*

Reba: *I said it wasn't racy. Nothing on under it tho :P how do I look?*

Devon: *You look fine.*

Reba: *whoa whoa whoa easy on the compliments there buddy. A girl can get a big head from all of that. Look closer. I'm wearing the glow product, can you tell?*

Devon: *You do look a lot more glowy, yes. So it does what it's supposed to.*

Reba: *sure does. the entire effect is stunning 🌚 Anyhoo they're calling me. Time to shimmy outta this. Bye*

[Thursday, 10:33 p.m.]

Devon: *Do you have a preference on the cupcakes?*
Reba: *do you know what time it is??*
Devon: *Sorry. I'm up working. Didn't realise it was so late.*
Reba: *of course you're working. Go to sleep!*
Devon: *In an hour maybe*
Reba: *so...what you wearing?*
Devon: *Goodbye Reba*
Reba: **pouts* you messaged me at this ungodly hour. I need my beauty rest you know. I almost thought it was an earlyish booty call for a sec there.*
Devon: *It's not that late. How was the shoot?*
Reba: *you're really invested in this huh? tell ya Saturday :P goodnight*

[Friday 6:15 p.m.]

Devon: *I hope these are to your liking*
Reba: *oooh not bad. The frosting looks on point too. And it's pink! Ttyl later tho. My girlies and I are up to no good right now.*

[Saturday 6:54 a.m.]

Cherisse: *You went to JB's? and whose hand is that across from you ma'am???*
Reba: *oh I didn't realise it was in the shot. No one to be concerned about*
Cherisse: *hmm*
Reba: *just go love off on your man and don't study it*
Cherisse: *you sent me this pic*

*Reba: to show you my food cuz I know you love JB's. the
hand is irrelevant. You know how I do I gotta go. Tell
your sexy man I said heyyy*

~

THE SULTRY CROONING VOICE THAT GREETED REBA ON SATURDAY
morning would have given her ideas if it was anyone but
Devon. She couldn't name the singer, but she was definitely
bringing the sexy with that voice. The jazz song echoing
around his living room was giving her seduction vibes, but
of course, that wouldn't be Devon's intent. What a waste of
a perfectly sexy song.

Although, if she had her way, it would be the perfect
backdrop for her plans. Trina was counting on her to fail at
getting under Devon's skin. She loved being underesti-
mated—it gave her so much satisfaction when she proved
people wrong.

Ms. Sexy kept on singing, and Reba couldn't stop her
brain from going down a fun path, wondering how he
usually went about seducing someone.

Did he even employ such tactics? Devon was good-
looking and had his shit together; it wouldn't take much to
draw someone to him. What he did after that was anyone's
guess. He probably just used that sexy deep voice of his to
captivate. Panties would be dropping in no time if he truly
turned on the charm of that voice.

The actual truth was probably far less interesting. He
was so strait-laced and hyper-organised about his life, Reba
could picture him making notes on how he would approach
such a thing. She laughed to herself, thinking about it as he
closed the door behind her.

"Well, good morning," she sang as she took in the fit of

his t-shirt, which emphasised his broad chest. Reba slipped off her sunglasses to get a better look. "How *do* you find time to work out?"

"If it's important to me, I make time. I like keeping fit. Good stress reliever, too."

"There are more fun ways to relieve stress, you know," she said because who would she be if she didn't run with the perfect segue he'd so kindly dropped for her?

His face gave nothing away. He stood there watching her as she didn't do a thing to hide the fact that she was allowing her gaze to linger down his shorts to his calves and back up his chest until he rolled his eyes and walked over to his laptop. "I'm not touching that one. Give me a minute. I was replying to an email."

Smart man. He realised if he gave her even an inch, she was taking that mile and taking a trip down to Tease Town. Reba sat across from him. "Do you ever just relax at all?"

"You and Cherisse work on a weekend. Why is this any different?" he asked as his fingers flew across the keyboard.

He had her there, but Reba and Cherisse also made time for fun outside of work. She couldn't say the same for Devon. The man's life seemed to only revolve around work. Reba wasn't trying to live that life.

Working with Cherisse was great and opened opportunities for her, too—although she was quite content where she was at the moment—but even she had to remind Cherisse that rest was important. Boss lady hadn't even wanted to go on that trip with her sexy mixer king, too worried about work. As if everyone would forget Sweethand existed with her gone for a few weeks. Not on Reba's watch. She was still promoting them on social media and replying to email requests. But Devon's workaholic ways were on another level.

She checked her phone while Devon continued checking his emails. Cherisse had messaged after Reba tried to brush off her questions about the mysterious hand in the photo. She hadn't even noticed a portion of Devon was visible when she'd sent it. There was no way she was telling Cherisse who the hand belonged to—only because Devon wouldn't want her to. Reba didn't care either way, but the man was hung up on keeping their work relationship private.

She ignored Cherisse's string of emojis and focused on Devon, who was frowning at his screen. "I don't plan to watch you work all day, so are we doing this or what?"

Her own schedule was light while Cherisse was away, which was why she could easily fit in these sessions with Devon. She would gladly watch his fingers in motion like this, but there were far better uses for them.

"Right, yes, sorry. One sec." He responded to whoever was causing that sour look on his face, then got to his feet, raising his arms in a full stretch above his head, giving her a nice peek at his stomach and a very obvious dick print. *Oh, hello there.*

She remembered their last time in the kitchen when she had pushed her hand under his t-shirt and copped a feel of his warm skin.

Bad, bad Reba. No time for lusting right now.

Was it her fault he was wearing those soft-looking shorts that weren't hiding shit? No, it sure wasn't. That print looked like it would fit just right in so many places.

"Reba?"

"Hmm?" The elastic waistband she had caught a glimpse of was perfect for easy hand access. She loved those pants. Buttons made things a bit difficult at times. Elastic for the win.

"Reba," he said, a bit louder this time and a hell of a lot closer. He had moved towards her while she had been fully fantasising about dipping her hand into his shorts. Oops.

She dragged her eyes up to his face. "Yeah?"

He rotated his neck, looking tired as hell, perma-frown more pronounced than usual. "Let's go to the kitchen."

"Wait, hold up." She placed her hand on his arm to stop him. She reached up and pressed her thumb between his brows. "Wipe that frown away first. No negative energy allowed in my kitchen."

His hand reached up, circling around her wrist in an attempt to stop her thumb from rubbing at the spot. "Your kitchen?"

"While I'm in it teaching you, it's as good as mine, yeah."

He tugged her hand away from his face. "I'm tired. I don't need you touching me."

"Why? Are your stone-cold defences down or what?"

He didn't drop her hand, just kept up that loose grip around her wrist. Reba wasn't complaining. She liked being all up in his space. The fact that he was allowing it was unusual, though. "Never. Armour's intact and impenetra-ble." He sounded like he was trying so hard to convince himself.

"Well, that all sounds like bullshit to me. You're still holding my hand," she pointed out, noticing the mole at the tip of his nose for the first time. Huh. Well, wasn't that just cute and strategically placed for kissing?

"So I am."

What the hell was up with him? Either he was truly too tired—which was making him act out of character—or something else was going on that she didn't have a clue about.

He shook himself and finally released her wrist. "How was your shoot?"

"Ah." Had he been thinking about that all the time? He had asked about it during their conversation on Thursday, too. She grinned up at him. "You really want to talk about that now? We need to get to baking."

"I'm curious. How did it go? I can't help wanting to do a deep dive into things that just seem outside of logic to me."

So that was it. Devon was trying to understand the situation. Maybe she could tantalise him with some details. She still had so much work to do to get him to succumb. Reba wasn't a sore loser, generally, but in this, she would definitely pout if she failed.

Apart from the shoot being super professional and going smoothly, she had asked the photographer for some sexy single shots after the main shoot. She *could* share those if she felt so inclined.

"You can't make sense of everything," she said.

"But I can try."

"We can bake and talk. I know you can multitask." She didn't wait for his response, but he was clearly following her to the kitchen.

She noticed the cupcakes set up under a plastic food cover. They looked just like the photo he'd sent, a clear improvement from his first attempts. Of course, he wouldn't allow himself to be bested by some baked goods.

"Oooh! These look pretty." She removed the cover and inspected them.

He had decided on vanilla cupcakes with strawberry frosting. Each cake was topped off with a strawberry, a blueberry, and a sprig of mint leaf. Devon's overachieving ass had ensured a good presentation, but the taste would determine if he had listened to anything she had said previously.

"It's good." He sounded confident.

"I'll be the judge." She bit into the cupcake and chewed. Finally, the cake itself was moist and not too sweet, the frosting a perfect complement to the vanilla. "Okay, you pass. This is good. You've improved!" She raised her palm for a high five, and he complied without a single complaint.

She was *so* weakening his armour bit by bit. He may not want to admit that, but it was happening regardless.

She munched on another cupcake while instructing him to get out the ingredients. She had sent him the recipe they would be working on prior to today, so he'd had enough time to sort out everything they would need. Spritz cookies were her favourite to make since she could use the piping bag to get inventive with her shapes. A cookie stamp was easier in ensuring the shapes came out perfectly, but Reba preferred to use the bag. The consistency of the batter was more important in determining how well the process went than worrying about a symmetrical cookie shape. The unknown factor was half the fun.

"So the photos came out beautifully. The photographer was great, and Scott worked his magic." She watched Devon's more than capable hands unwrap the softened butter.

"What magic is that?"

"Not sure how much you know about his work, but he's a creative director and does makeup, so he made us all pretty and designed the entire set, chose the props for the whole thing. It was like a work of art, but not so overpowering that the models didn't stand out."

"Sounds interesting."

"For sure. I have some behind-the-scenes shots if you wanna see."

Devon reached for the mixer. "You've done this kind of thing before?"

Reba watched the ingredients come together into a fluffy mixture in the bowl. "Not like this, no. I've done some light modelling in the past for Catwalk when they existed. Why do I feel like I'm under a microscope here? You're trying to figure me out, aren't you?"

She felt his gaze on her, so she looked up and met those searching dark brown eyes. "It's what I do."

"Well, don't hot up your head about it. I'm not that complicated. Just different from what you're used to, I suppose."

He kept mixing and watching her with that intense gaze. He could keep trying to dissect her, but she wasn't all that complex. Most people expected that what she showed them was an act. That she could be moulded into something more manageable. If they didn't believe she was who she said she was, that wasn't her problem.

"You're definitely not like anyone I've ever met."

Reba nodded. "I know, so thanks."

Reba turned off the mixer—whoops, that had been running too long—dipped a finger in the batter and tasted it. "That's good. For once, just let things be. I'm not a problem to be solved." She dipped her finger in the batter again, bringing it up to his mouth this time. "Taste?"

"That's a bad idea. I do that, and then what? We carry on like I didn't have your finger in my mouth?"

"Bad ideas are some of the best ideas." She waved her finger around. "And yes, you don't need to make a production out of everything or over-analyse it. Sometimes you just wanna suck another person's finger into your mouth, and that's it."

He leaned forward, and she thought he was actually, for once, going to give in. Instead, he looked her right in the eye and asked, "But would that be it in this case?"

It could if they both decided, but Reba tried not to lie to herself or others if she could help it. If Devon did this, she wasn't leaving it at that. She was too revved up. She sucked her batter-covered finger into her mouth and licked away anything that remained on her lips.

"No, it wouldn't be it."

"Then I can't."

"Won't. There's a difference. You can do anything you want. You're in control of your reactions." She shrugged. "But you won't."

"You're like fucking kryptonite." He held up his hand before she could reply to *that*. "Don't. I didn't mean...just..." He scrubbed a hand over his face. "Not a word. I need sleep, and I need this to be done with."

"Okay, Superman. Even though *you* just said your armour was all sturdy and shit, but I'll leave it be for now." Reba pulled the mixing bowl over to her side, suppressing her smile. Oh, she was so winning this bet. "Put the star tip nozzle on the bag, and let's see if the batter is fine for piping."

For once, she wasn't so certain. Eyeballing it, the batter looked like it wouldn't give too much trouble when placed in the piping bag, but she had gotten too caught up in her back and forth with Devon. Now, it was anyone's guess if this would be the right consistency. Dammit. If she failed at this, Devon would definitely take note.

"You're not going to be on my ass about saying that?"

She shrugged as he scooped batter from the bowl and

placed it in the piping bag. "Nope. I've been called worse. Plus..." She grinned. "You just admitted you're affected by my presence, so that's gonna sustain me for the rest of the day."

The long sigh he was in the midst of releasing died away as she took his hand, showing him how to squeeze the bag to make the desired cookie shape.

"You can do different shapes and designs. Don't think about it too hard."

"I watched some videos, so I have an idea of the shape I want."

She made a zig-zag motion with the bag. Perfect, the batter was coming out easily. "Go wild, Superman. They don't all have to be a round shape. C'mon, you can do it. Just this once."

His hands tightened on hers as he tried to stop her from making a long-shaped cookie. "A circle is fine."

"Look, we can do those, but get creative with it too." She tried to yank the bag from him, but he was insisting. Were they really about to scrabble over some goddamn cookies because Devon couldn't just let go and not follow a plan? Hell no. She released the bag just as he moved to pull it from her, so of course, the thing went flying across the kitchen.

They both watched as the batter-filled bag hit the fridge then slid down to the floor.

Reba pursed her lips. "Can't you just follow my lead? It's what you signed up for."

"Technically, none of us signed anything, which thinking about it now, we probably should have." He pointed to the tray. "What is this shape even supposed to be?"

Living a fun-shine life was Reba's motto, but damn if

Devon wasn't testing even her usual cheerful demeanour. Men who didn't listen to her were super annoying. Definitely a top peeve.

Reba grabbed the front of his t-shirt and dragged his face down to hers. "Just listen to me for once, goddammit."

His nostrils flared, but the corner of his mouth twitched. "And if I don't?"

Reba narrowed her eyes. "Then you're going to lose the bake-off."

"Hmm." He looked down at the portion of his t-shirt she had bunched up in her hand. "You're wrinkling my shirt."

"Well, frankly, my dear, I don't give a fuck."

"That's not how that goes."

"I don't care!" she shouted, surprising them both. Wow, okay, he was getting her too riled up, which wasn't the vibe she was trying to bring today. At least not this kind of riled up. She'd gone from the lusting side of the Devon-o-meter to the "If you don't respect my authority, I will punch you" side.

Devon grinned. Reba blinked in shock. Did he just…? It wasn't one of those grimace-grins she had seen from him. This was a real, full-on smile. Oh shit, talk about her panties disintegrating.

"Ah," he drawled. "So this is how you feel, isn't it?"

"I don't know what the hell you mean." She was still too stunned to comprehend anything at the moment.

His smile should come with a danger sign attached. The incessant throbbing between her legs was both thrilling and sort of inconvenient at the moment. Her thighs were crying out for a delicious beard burn, and how was she going to get that when Devon didn't want to cooperate and ravish her?

"When you try to frustrate or tease me," he oh so eagerly admitted. "I get it now. It's more fun when I'm not on the receiving end of it."

She hadn't been subtle about what she was doing, but the nerve of him to call her out like this? Yeah, she had been trying to get him to inject some more fun into his life, but not at her expense. Leave it to Devon to still try to control things and do it his way. She was a little bit in awe if she was being honest with herself. Still annoying AF, though.

"Are you telling me you were being an ass on purpose?"

"I admit nothing."

She balled up more of his shirt because she would wrinkle the hell out of the thing for spite. How dare he try to turn her own plan against her? Oh no, no, no, that wouldn't do at all.

Devon might think he'd done something, but Reba would show him. "You think you can beat me at my own game? You just made the biggest mistake of your whole life. You will *never* win this game."

Her reputation was at stake here.

"I don't think you understand how competitive I can be. It's my job to find innovative ways to win."

"You tried something. I admire that. Truly." Reba yanked on his t-shirt hard. Devon might dominate at his job, but where Reba was concerned, he wasn't prepared—especially not for her to tug him like that. He stumbled forward, his face even closer to her now. "But one thing you're going to learn is I don't always play fair. Sorry, not sorry," she announced right before she leaned in and sucked on his bottom lip.

CHAPTER FOURTEEN
DEVON

HE'D MADE A MISTAKE, JUST AS REBA HAD SAID.

That couldn't be his hand coming up to cup the side of her face, to pull her closer instead of pushing her away like he was supposed to do.

He hadn't lied when he'd told her he was tired. Or that she was like kryptonite. Clearly, he *had* lied when he'd said his armour was intact. That shit was disintegrating with every flick of Reba's tongue against his.

The piping bag was somewhere on the floor behind him. He needed to pick that up. Get them back on track, yet his hand was tugging on her hair, telling her silently to tilt her head back so his fingers could reach up and trace her neck.

Reba's moan when he cupped her neck caused him to turn them, so her back was pressed against the counter with his front fully pressed to hers. She rubbed against him, and Devon's tongue delved deeper, drinking in the taste of the cookie batter. She'd gotten her wish after all, hadn't she?

He would have been better off just taking the batter off

her finger like she asked. This was too much. Hurricane Reba was in full force because God... He hadn't done this with anyone in so long. He felt fucking thirsty. Actually, he had never dry-humped anyone in this kitchen or any kitchen before, so this was...something. The most random thought of his mother telling him he needed to christen his new place by having that housewarming entered his mind, and clearly, this wasn't what she'd had in mind.

Neither had he.

Reba had struck again, and this time, Devon was allowing himself to give in. Just for a moment. They would end this soon, and then what?

Stop thinking, just enjoy.

The voice in his head sounded too much like Reba. He couldn't allow her in there while he was already letting this happen. Control. He needed it. Too bad it had fled to parts unknown.

Her hand crept into his shorts to cup his ass, drag him closer. There was nowhere else to go. They were as close as could be. Her nails dug into his flesh, and he broke off their never-ending kiss to stare down at her, trying desperately to catch his breath.

She licked her lips. "Guess my underwear question is answered. Boxer briefs. I approve."

He took several deep breaths, trying to clear away the lust that was fogging up his brain. A difficult task with Reba's hand still on him, squeezing, the both of them still pressed against each other like this. She could definitely feel how hard he was.

"Just stay like this. For a little while," she urged. That soft tone, so damn persuasive.

He almost allowed himself to be drawn in again, but he was no starry-eyed youth who would get lost in that devouring gaze. Who would nod wordlessly and let Reba lead them astray.

He drew back, inhaled deeply again. "I don't think so."

"Fine. Well, back up because your friend there is giving me ideas." She looked down to where his dick was tenting the front of his shorts. Damn. "Need a minute? Or five?"

"No."

Of course, he did. Walking around with his dick waving about would be rude. Except his need to regain control of something meant he refused to leave the kitchen to supposedly go compose himself. He could get right back to the cookies. He didn't need time to recover from any of this.

He moved away from Reba and retrieved the piping bag on the floor.

"At least you should be a little more loosened up now. Don't try to fight me on the cookies again."

He didn't look back at Reba. He couldn't, not yet. Not when the taste and feel of her was still so fresh. Temptation was right behind him with pastel pink hair and probably a knowing smirk. Devon had to be strong.

He looked down at the bag in his hand. The batter had remained inside. While he usually kept a clean kitchen, the thing had been lounging on the floor as he had lost his entire mind.

Think about something calming, he silently told himself. He forced himself to focus on some of his favourite structures. That always soothed him. Reminded him why he had chosen this profession. Images of a building that was shaped like a violin resting against a piano danced in his mind. The building was located in China, and Devon had yet to fulfil his dream of seeing it in person, but some day, he absolutely would.

A lot of his colleagues spoke about how romantic the

building concept was when he cared more about the aesthetic of it.

"We can still use this," Reba's voice floated over his shoulder. Too close. "None of it leaked out. I'll take it for my unconventional cookies if you want to use fresh batter."

"Do whatever you feel like." Caught up in trying to compose himself, his words came out harsher than intended. "I'll use a different bag," he added, an attempt to soften his words.

He turned to face Reba. Her brow rose. "Try that again," she said, tone as sweet as honey, and yet he knew she didn't appreciate his bluntness.

"Sorry. I meant that sounds fine."

"Hmm. If you're this cranky after kissing me, I might be losing my touch."

He handed her the piping bag, meeting her gaze head-on. Reba may have been like a devil silently taunting him with that raised brow and smirk, but Devon would prove they could make it through this without another slip-up.

"It's me, not you. You have definitely *not* lost your touch." Alright, he needed to get them back on track, not make this moment more awkward.

Reba was loving his discomfort. It was exactly what she had been trying to do from the beginning. He might have been a fool to kiss her back, but he wasn't one about this. She had told him she wanted to get him out of his comfort zone. Fucking kryptonite indeed.

She smiled oh so sweetly and gestured to the cookie tray. "Yes, I know. Let's get back to this, shall we?"

They had resumed working on the cookies—Reba making hers in extra-weird shapes while he stuck to those that he had seen online—when her phone rang. He had purposefully put on his music today so he wouldn't have to make it through another one of her playlists, so her phone had only been set up to film sporadically. She put down her piping bag to check the screen.

"I don't know this number, but it could be a potential client. Let me take this." She swiped to take the call. "Hello?"

Devon continued with his piping. It looked like they were going to get a lot of cookies out of this. Hopefully, they would be a success, and he could casually take some to work. He had been resisting Reba's call for him to aim to be a bit more personable to his co-workers—the karaoke notwithstanding—but while he had been working on his presentation last night and this morning, he had created a spreadsheet to determine just how risky her suggestions were.

He didn't actually have anything to lose by being more outgoing, he supposed. The numbers showed as much. It also showed he would need to expend time and effort. Those were what gave him pause. Did he have time to devote to this? Would the outcome be favourable? What if he did all this and still didn't get that Principal position? Then what?

Dax wasn't the only one he needed to impress. He may have built the company from the ground up, but he answered to the Board as well, and some of the members were the type that would want Devon to jump through hoops and kiss ass to prove he had earned a place as partner in the firm. Devon didn't kiss anyone's ass. He expected his abilities to speak for themselves.

Which was why the notion of the cookies didn't sit quite well with him, but he preferred to test out the theory, at least. Failure wasn't an option. Of course, plans got derailed all the time, but Devon wasn't ready to accept that he wouldn't achieve the next phase of his goal.

Would showing up to the office on Monday bearing cookies fast-track that plan? He wasn't sure. People were an unknown variable in this whole equation. He couldn't plug in the entire board or every single one of his co-workers in his risk software simply because he didn't know them that well outside of their work encounters and would be lacking key input data. Which, he supposed, was what Amanda had been talking about.

"So this is what we're doing? Calling from unknown numbers now?"

Devon jerked out of his musing at Reba's caustic tone. He'd never heard her sound like that, even when she had been angry at him. Her back was to him as she continued her phone conversation.

"Yeah, I enjoyed the free sushi. That doesn't mean I want to suck your dick again. How is it my problem you just now realised you screwed up?"

Devon cleared his throat to get her attention as perhaps, in the heat of the moment, she forgot where she was. She looked over at him.

"Maybe you'd like to take this in the other room?" he suggested.

She rolled her eyes. "Don't worry about who that was," she said back to whoever was on the line. "Have a good day. I'll be over here enjoying my deep-voiced, big-dicked companion." She ended the call, phone clutched in her hand. "This mother-effer, I swear."

That sounded like a situation that could escalate into some drama. "Everything alright?"

She placed her phone back on the counter. "Yes, great.

Absolutely fine. Just my ex regretting his life choices, I guess. What the fuck else is new?"

"Do you...want to talk about it?" He cringed as soon as the words left his mouth. He would prefer not to, but Reba looked ready to explode. It was an intriguing sight when he was used to her sunshine persona.

She shook her head. "I'll save you the hour-long tirade about how men are all assholes. I'm good."

"Thank God because I really didn't want to."

A laugh burst out of her, and he felt a sense of relief. "Then why did you even ask?"

"You just looked so..." He trailed off.

Reba was usually frank with him, to a fault. But if he told her she looked like she needed comfort, they would go right back to that moment with the kiss. She would tease him about the type of comfort he could provide. Maybe he should have just said it anyways, consequences be damned. He didn't like that look in her eyes. She would have forgotten all about this asshole ex of hers. Why he felt he needed to soothe her at all was odd. She could clearly deal with whoever this guy was. None of this made sense.

Exhaustion. That had to be the reason for these...feelings.

"It's my fault for dating losers. Or so my parents say." She picked up the piping bag. *"Why can't you just find a nice young man who isn't ashamed to introduce you to his family, huh? If you stopped being so flamboyant, you'd find a perfectly good man."*

"They've said that to you?"

"Well, the first part, yeah. I seem to somehow always find the ones who love what I do in the bedroom but suddenly want me to be a whole different person when it's time to get serious. Apparently, I'm the good time girl and not the one who people see for the long term." She shrugged like none of that mattered, but Devon hadn't gotten to where he was without being observant.

He might not be a people person, but that didn't mean he couldn't read others. Reba was bothered by this.

"Their loss." It sounded like empty platitudes, yet he felt compelled to say something, anything, to get her back to her usual self.

It bothered him, this mix of annoyance and sadness in her expression. He wasn't the best at showing what he felt —his sister called him out on his Virgo ways a lot, not that he believed astrology could rule who he was as a person— but that didn't mean he didn't feel things at all. Feelings were just inconvenient, and he preferred to keep his under wraps.

"So you say. You wouldn't date me. I bet you have a list of all the qualities you prefer in a partner, and I fit none of them."

He said nothing. Of course, he had a list; it was what he had used to compare what he wanted to Monica's traits to see how compatible they were. Was it so wrong to want to calculate the risk of a given situation? Monica's reaction had surprised him, leading him to not recognise the easy-going woman he had someday thought he'd marry.

She had basically told him he didn't get it and he didn't want to understand why she was upset. Perhaps she had been right. He was out of his depth with these things. "Is that a bad thing? The list, I mean."

She stared at him, hand still on the piping bag. "Oh my god. You really have a list? I was joking."

Well, this was awkward.

"Can I see it?"

"Absolutely not."

Nothing in this world would compel him to do that. He had learned from Monica's reaction. He and Reba weren't romantically involved—that kiss notwithstanding—but he still wasn't sharing that with her. He didn't want another lecture about how he shouldn't reduce others to a risk percentage.

"Come on. I'm curious. It would make me forget I want to send a bag of exploding glitter to my ex's house."

He flinched. "My god, you're the actual devil, aren't you?"

Exploding glitter. Just the thought of that all over his house was enough to make him break out in hives.

She flipped her pink ponytail over her shoulder. "The devil ain't got nothing on me. But don't worry, I'll be too busy enjoying free wine at this fancy thing I'm going to tonight to plot any glitter bombs. Oh, hey, actually, you should come with me."

"Why in the world would I want to do that?" He was trying to limit the time he spent with Reba. "I'm not in the mood for another one of your socialising plans."

"Oh, you'll want to attend this. A Sweethand client sent two tickets to some cocktail exhibit thing tonight. History of Buildings or something like that, at Stollmeyer's Castle. Cherisse is obviously not here, and I was only going for the free fancy shit, but you actually know about this stuff. Maybe you've even heard of the event?"

She was correct—the devil had nothing on Reba. Here she was, dangling his version of a juicy steak right in his face. Of course, he'd heard about this exhibit. The company's board were all invited, and Devon had been internally sulking about it all week. For once, there was something he actually cared to attend, and while he sometimes got perks as a Senior Manager, it was usually to some useless event he didn't give a shit about. Apparently, they were trying to keep the guests limited for this one, it being highly exclusive and all that. And here was Reba with two tickets.

"You have tickets to the Historical Society Gala? How in the hell?"

"The devil works hard, but I work harder." She winked. "So, is that a yes? I can debut Cassandra tonight. The dress code sounds fancy as heck. I think a red wig is just in order for this."

He could imagine Reba running wild through that exhibit doing God knows what. She might run into Dax. The two of them could end up plotting things, supposedly for his own good. He couldn't have that. He needed to keep an eye on her. Dax liked Reba, and he would be only too eager to go along with all her ridiculous notions. Besides, he would get to be immersed in the history of the region's architecture. He couldn't say no to this, and Reba damn well knew that.

"I mean, unless you already have tickets?"

"I don't," he ground out.

"Huh, really? Well, isn't that a shame? And here I come with an extra ticket. Must be fate."

"Fate as a concept doesn't sit right with me." The thought that no matter what he did, his entire life was already mapped out? No, thanks. There were things he couldn't control; didn't mean he didn't try.

Like right now, he wouldn't show Reba how his heart rate jacked up at the thought of this exhibit. For her, it was just a free cocktail party. For him, the chance to revel in information about historic sites around the Caribbean. He had an entire section of his life plan dedicated to visiting key structures around the world. Might seem lofty and expensive, but he was determined to make it happen someday. The exhibit was his kind of fun, and the last person he expected had the power to hand it to him.

"Of course, it doesn't. You want the ticket or not?"

"Yes, thank you."

"Let's get these in the oven, then." She waved at the cookie trays where he had finished piping his regular shapes. "I'm adding sprinkles to mine. You can even use a fork to add some more patterns to the batter if you wish."

"I suppose I should. Might make them more appealing to my co-workers."

Both Reba's brows jerked up. "Are you taking these to work?" She clapped her hands, eyes shining with glee.

"Yes, well, what you said might have some merit. Maybe."

Reba rubbed her hands together. "Oh, you should totally put them in cute packaging with a ribbon."

"Absolutely not. A plastic container is quite fine." He didn't want them to think this would be a habit. Then they would expect things from him. Frankly, he was tempted to simply leave the container in the kitchen with a note for everyone to take one. He didn't need to link himself to the cookies in any way.

"You need to at least make it look pretty. I'll help."

"You've helped quite enough, thank you."

She folded her arms. "You want this ticket or not?"

He should have known this would happen. "You truly are the devil," he muttered.

Reba grinned, shooting finger guns his way. "I never miss."

"No glitter," he warned. He wouldn't budge on that.

She did a little dance, and he forced himself to ignore the unnecessary booty pop she added at the end. Regret. He felt that strongly. He should have continued to ignore Reba and her silly messages.

Damn this bake-off.

Damn Cherisse for not being available.

And damn the small smile threatening to grace his mouth as he continued to watch Reba shake her ass around his kitchen.

CHAPTER FIFTEEN
REBA

REBA WAS ABOUT TO CHANNEL A SEXY BLACK JESSICA RABBIT AT this swanky event, and nobody would be ready. She'd been holding on to this dress for about a year now. It wasn't the type of attire you just strutted about in anywhere. It needed all eyes focused on it for it to really have served its purpose, which meant tonight was the night.

Trina had scoffed at her impulse purchase, claiming that she wouldn't find a single occasion that would warrant a dress like this—which was why she sent Trina a text when she was ready, smile turned up to maximum smug levels.

> **Reba:** *you were saying???*
> **Trina:** *where you going like that madam?* 👀
> **Reba:** *out* 😒
> **Trina:** *with Mr. Grouch?*
> **Reba:** 🫢 *enjoy your night.*
> **Trina:** *heffa you betta tell me!*
> **Reba:** *sorry, can't hear you over the sounds of me winning.*

Getting Devon to accompany her to this wasn't exactly a victory, but she was fine letting Trina think otherwise.

Reba went all out to achieve the look. She didn't do things in half measure, especially when she was prepared not only to have all eyes on her but to leave Devon speechless. She gave a satisfied smile when he opened his front door and didn't say a single word. His eyes made a thorough sweep of her from the top of her red wig all the way down her exposed leg to her shoes.

"You..." He visibly shook himself. "You won't blend in that."

"I only blend my makeup. You didn't see this coming?"

He had asked her to meet at his house where she would leave her car, and they'd take his. Something about having calculated that course of action as the most feasible time-wise, based on the event's location.

Reba didn't care much about arriving to any event on time. Making an entrance was her style. Being on time never achieved the desired effect. But she'd agreed to just roll with his insistence that they leave at precisely eight o'clock.

"I don't think anyone has ever seen you coming, Reba."

Oh, the unintended double entendre she could have fun with there. Instead, she chose to behave herself, just this once. She stepped back as he locked the door and led her down the driveway, his blazer slung over his arm. Reba took the opportunity to take a peek at his ass in those pants. The tailored black pants weren't winning any most creative fashion awards, but Devon's behind was working overtime there. She drank in the flex of his back muscles in his white shirt.

He opened the car door, looking back at her just when

she pressed her teeth into her bottom lip and whispered, "Damn."

Yeah, she got caught staring at him, but when had she ever cared about that? "You're not wrong about that," she replied to his earlier statement. "So you like it?" She placed her hands on her hips, letting Devon enjoy the visual.

They would look so good together. If only she could convince him to take a photo with her.

The intriguing tic in his jaw was working overtime as he stood waiting for her to get in the car. At this angle, he was definitely getting a perfect view of her cleavage. She had slathered her entire body in the free lotion she had gotten from the shoot, which left behind a subtle glittery glow. Devon might not like glitter, but he had to appreciate how her skin was popping tonight. She'd left her neck bare of any jewellery, the shimmer of her dress speaking for itself. Besides, she didn't want anything to interrupt the visual of all her brown skin on display.

"Yes."

Simple, yet oh so effective. She smiled and rummaged around in her bag until she found her phone.

"Can you get a pic of me? Your lighting out here is perfect."

He looked down at the phone she thrust into his hands while Reba posed so he could catch her at a side angle, her red hair spilling over one shoulder, the other left bare.

He took a single photo, ready to hand her back her phone.

"You need to get more than that. C'mon. Three, at least."

"Why do you need three when the first one is already perfect?" he said, deadpan as ever. Anyone else delivering that line, she would say they were flirting. Devon was dead serious. Not a single smile nor smirk in sight.

She hadn't been prepared for that compliment, so she drank it up like the thirsty praise ho she was. There was just something about a genuine compliment that got her hot and bothered, more so than physical touch sometimes. She was confident in what she had to offer, yet it never hurt to have someone verify that.

She prayed for his car seat because tonight, she had chosen to go commando. He better stop saying all those nice things if he didn't want her squirming in his car.

The photo in question was indeed perfect. His outdoor lights were bright enough to light the way, but they weren't as harsh as fluorescents. There was a warm quality to them that cast her in an ethereal glow.

"Fine. I can work with this."

She lingered in his driveway, taking some more selfies until Devon asked, "Can we go?"

"One sec. I need to get Cassandra in this light." She pouted into her camera, throwing in a wink at the end of her Boomerang because a static photo wasn't enough.

She spun to face Devon who was leaning against his car, waiting not so patiently. "Now we can go."

They arrived at the venue at the perfect time. Well, she supposed they did. Devon wasn't on her ass about being late, so she figured they had done just fine. The outside of Stollmeyer's Castle was familiar to Reba. She had driven around the Queen's Park Savannah enough times, and the castle wasn't something you missed. She had never been inside but was fully aware it was among their island's Magnificent Seven buildings.

Devon was looking up at the building, eyes roaming over the structure like he wanted to reach out and touch.

"When was this built?" she asked. Architecture wasn't something she cared deeply about, but she wanted to see Devon in nerd mode, specifically because she suspected it would make him ten times hotter.

There was just something pleasing about a person when they got all passionate about a particular subject.

"Between 1902 and 1904."

"Wow, so it's *old* old." She tilted her head up too before moving forward to rest her hands against the cool brick. "It really does look like a castle with that thingie on top there."

"The thingie is a turret. It was supposedly modelled after Balmoral Castle in Scotland."

"Ah. Should we go in?" She was looking forward to Devon gushing about buildings and shit, but that didn't mean she wanted to stand out here all night when there was wine and more people to admire her dress inside.

She took a quick selfie with the castle as the backdrop before signalling to Devon that they should proceed. Guests were walking about, drinks in hand, as they conversed in small groups about the photos and paintings of Caribbean historical buildings on display.

"Ooh, this one looks nice." She stopped in front of a photograph of a white house that looked like it had been lifted straight out of the past. She couldn't place the time period—not that she needed to because Devon had gone into lecture mode before she could catch a glimpse at the info card.

"Ambard's House," he said. "It's actually on this same street. Before White Hall. It's a little hidden by the trees, so you might miss it." Next to the photograph was a painting that was an exact replica. "Another of the Magnificent Seven. It's quite stunning in person, with its porthole

windows and iron cast elements. It's still a private residence to this day."

"It's really pretty." She didn't have the knowledge to
describe the style of the house, but it was undeniable that it
was beautifully constructed. "Have you ever worked on
anything like this?"

"Not really. Places like these wouldn't undergo any
major renovations since they're considered Grade 1 proper-
ties. Cultural heritage sites aren't supposed to be altered,
really. My firm also does more modern type designs. Of
course, if a client wants us to replicate or incorporate a
French style like this in a new building, that's something to
consider. But with us getting a lot of government
contracts, we tend to want to stick to a more modern look
and feel."

"Makes sense."

Reba spied a server moving around with what she
imagined was champagne and was about to get the
woman's attention when a familiar face popped up right in
front of hers.

Reba stepped back as Remi Daniels' head of luscious
curls filled her vision. "You do appear in interesting places,
don't you?"

"What're *you* doing here?" She hadn't anticipated
seeing anyone she knew, especially not Remi.

Remi waved her camera. "Island Bites business." She
turned to look at Devon, who was still busy staring at the
photos. "This doesn't seem like your scene."

"Free drinks and food? Why not?" Reba kept her tone
light. Devon would turn around and see Remi at any
moment. Or maybe he wouldn't even notice since he was in
his element, caught up in the photos and paintings.

Either way, he wouldn't want to have to explain why

they were here together. Not that the reason was all that complicated.

"Maybe so. Explain to me how this duo came about." Remi wasn't going any damn place until she got a reasonable explanation.

Reba couldn't fault her one bit. She would be wondering the same if she had run into Remi and Devon out somewhere. It just wouldn't compute. Devon didn't mingle with them, had always seemed so far removed from their little world. The age difference was a factor, especially since he gave off the vibe of being far older even when there were actually only a few years between them.

"First, tell me, did it hurt when you fell? This white jumpsuit is really something." Remi was already so tall, but the jumpsuit was giving gazelle vibes, especially since she was rocking some heels with it.

Remi huffed out a little laugh. "Don't try to flirt-distract me, ma'am, it won't work. Now, what's this all about? Since when you and Devon so good to be showing up places together?"

"A client gave two tickets as a thank you, but Cherisse is obviously not here. This is Devon's thing, you know, architecture and stuff, so here we are."

"Uh-huh." Remi didn't look satisfied with Reba's response. She reached past Reba to tap Devon on the shoulder. "Well, hi there."

He looked from Reba to Remi, then down at the camera in her hands. "Of course." He said it like he had expected something like this when Reba couldn't fathom how.

"Fancy seeing you two here. At an event. Together. Didn't have that on my bingo card, but here we are indeed." She smirked, waving her camera. "Photo to capture this momentous occasion?"

Devon's forehead creased. "No."

Reba could see the wheels in Remi's head turning, which meant she had to take front on this before Remi jumped to the wrong conclusion. "Hey, lemme just talk to you a sec. I need a drink too. You want anything?" she asked Devon.

"I'm good."

"Awesome." She linked arms with Remi, shot Devon a thumbs up, and dragged her over to one of the servers.

"Is something going on with you two?" Remi asked as soon as they were out of Devon's earshot. "As wild as that seems, I know people just fall at your feet. Even grumps like Devon may not be susceptible."

"If I didn't know you were pining over someone else, I'd totally kiss you for that compliment, but it's not what it looks like."

Remi shook her head. "Don't get me started on that, okay? We're focusing on you. You're both here looking sexy as shit. What is going on?"

Reba sipped from the glass she had taken off the tray. "Okay, look. He didn't want anyone to know, so don't tell Cherisse cuz then Keiran would know."

"This isn't making me think that nothing is going on."

"I'm helping him out with something baking-related, and he'd rather his family not know, for reasons. Which means you can take all the pics of me you want. Or him if he allows it, but not us together."

"You're helping him with baking? None of that is adding up. Like, why does he even need baking help?"

"Don't ask. Just take a cute pic of me with this drink and leave it be. Or we could talk about your lil' King-sized problem that you haven't provided us with an update on lately?"

Remi shot Reba a look that screamed, '*I think the fuck not.*' "Alright, I'll leave it for now. Won't say anything to Cherisse. She should be too busy getting a good workout with Keiran to care anyways."

Remi took her photo and sailed away to continue getting shots of the other guests. Devon's jaw was working overtime when she returned.

"Crisis averted. Remi won't mention us being here together. I still maintain you should mention this to your fam, so it doesn't come across as some weird secret you've been harbouring, but whatever floats your boat."

"This damn island is too small," he grumbled.

"I can go distract her some more with my ass and cleavage if you want. It's a sacrifice I'm willing to make." She grinned as Devon's expression turned sourer. "Hey, c'mon. She's not going to say anything. Don't get all grouchy now. You should go chat with another building enthusiast to feel better."

"You really think you can flirt your way through any situation, don't you?"

She tugged on his blazer, enjoying his little nostril flare. "Yes."

"Was I boring you earlier?" he asked out of the blue, probably to change the topic and bring them back to safer territory. "You said I should go find someone to talk to about this."

"Nah, but I can't appreciate what you're talking about as much as someone else who knows this stuff can."

"We came together. It would be rude to just leave you alone."

Reba patted his arm. "I'm fully an extrovert. I'll be fine."

"I won't. I don't think it's a good idea for us to be separated."

"This is your scene. You don't have to worry about conversation." She gave him a thumbs up. "You got this."

Reba thrived in situations like this. It was easy for her to befriend anyone. It didn't matter who they were. She would eventually have them eating out of her hands. This crowd, in particular, would be fun to tame. She'd noticed enough designer items worn by the guests to discern that she wasn't exactly fitting in. Fine by her.

She was aware of glances being thrown her way. If she broke off from Devon, it would give the curious ample time to circle and try to find out if she was anyone important. She could already imagine what story they were concocting about her. She was no stranger to gossip.

"You're not quite getting what I'm saying. I'm not worried about me in this situation."

Oh. She drained her wine glass, stashing it on the tray of another passing server. "You think *I'm* gonna cause havoc amongst the one percent? I see."

She hadn't done a single thing but show up in a fabulous dress, a show-stopping wig, and makeup that was perfection. Yet Devon was concerned that her mere presence would somehow ruin this for him. She couldn't help the laughter that burst from her. Devon's eyes reflected his surprise.

He had clearly thought she would be upset by his admission. She waved down another passing server, plucking a drink off the tray. "Be a darling and keep these coming, will you?" The man gaped at her but nodded before resuming his stroll around the room.

"Don't worry," she told Devon. "I won't embarrass you."

"That's not it. Dax is somewhere around here, and you two somehow hit it off. I..." He folded his arms, serious mode activated. She could pinch his cheek just to aggravate him but decided to let him continue. "Look, can I be frank?"

She gestured for him to go on. "Oh, don't let me stop you from speaking your truth."

"He likes you, and I don't think that's going to work in my favour. Can you promise you won't get caught up in some ridiculous scheme of his?"

She took another sip of her wine, enjoying the sweet taste on her tongue. She would need to try some of the finger food that had been floating around as well or take a trip over to the food table that offered something a bit more substantial. Keeping her wits about her tonight was crucial because Reba had every intention of scheming with Dax if that's what he wanted. It was too fun to resist.

She reached up to rub the collar of Devon's blazer between her fingertips. "He does, it won't, and I definitely will *not* be making any such promises." She patted his cheek, deciding not to resist after all. "It's easier to just give in, you know. Fun things happen when you do. Like in the kitchen."

Oh, he definitely didn't like to be reminded of that. He had given in to her kiss, which she could have counted as a success where the bet was concerned, but Reba didn't. Not until he initiated something himself. She wasn't going to let him forget it, though. He caught her wrist, trapping them in the same tableau from earlier. Why was that move so damn sexy? She took another sip of her drink to wet her suddenly parched throat.

"I'm not playing your games again. Not here."

She tugged at her hand. It didn't budge from his grasp. "You're the one holding me again like you want to play a game. Just FYI, I do enjoy a little rough play."

He dropped her hand like it was suddenly hot to the

touch, his chest rising and falling as if breathing was difficult. She supposed it was. If he was as affected as she was,
yeah, breathing was a bit of a challenge at the moment.

"It's okay to want things that don't fall in line with your
perfectly planned life."

He rubbed at his forehead for a few seconds before
moving his hand to refocus on her. "I agreed to come with
you because this isn't an opportunity that just anyone has.
This," he spread his arms wide to encompass the room, "is
what I like to do for fun. I don't want to be a pawn in your
seduction plan. Or whatever it is you're doing."

"I want you to have your fun, Devon. I really do. But I
want something more."

She pointed at the area that was set for the food. It was
time to fortify her stomach if she intended to try as much of
the fancy liquor as possible.

He looked confused. "Food?"

"Yes, but I want you to watch my ass as I walk away,
knowing that I'm not wearing a single thing under this
dress." She threw a wave over her shoulder and sashayed
away.

CHAPTER SIXTEEN
DEVON

HE GAVE HER EXACTLY WHAT SHE WANTED BY WATCHING HER WALK away, hips swaying in the tight red fabric.

He wasn't the only one watching. Eyes had been sliding her way from the moment they arrived, different pockets of people trying to figure out who she was. Reba was basking in it all. You didn't wear a dress like that and not expect attention.

She knew what she looked like with that red hair and dress. Knew the exact reaction she would get and was pleased about it all, none of which made sense to Devon. This level of attention wasn't something he ever felt the need to grasp for himself, but Reba was practically glowing. Had she used those damn products from her photoshoot? He didn't ask. The less he thought about that shoot, the better.

His main focus, besides trying to stay clear of Remi and her camera, was hoping there would be no unexpected moments with Reba and that dress. From the second he had opened his door and seen Reba on the other side, he had been constantly looking out for some sort of wardrobe malfunction.

Yes, that's why he had been stealing glances of her. His vigilance mode was on, primed and ready to stop any accident from happening. The dress looked like it was held up by a prayer and wishful thinking. There were no straps. Devon wasn't savvy enough to know about whatever type of contraption you would need to have on under a dress like that to ensure it stayed where it was supposed to.

Reba hadn't tugged up the bodice once, and now that she had declared she didn't have on a single thing under it, he wondered how the hell it was staying up. That was the only reason he was allowing himself to linger on the casually tossed statement. Not because his imagination was suddenly in overdrive, trying to force up an image of her out of that dress.

Was she glowing everywhere?

Fuck. He wasn't going there.

There didn't appear to be any wardrobe-related crisis on the horizon, yet he stood in the same spot, watching her over at the food table. She had already struck up a conversation with an older man, who looked positively hypnotised by her. The man wasn't even putting any food on his plate at this point, just nodding at her, mouth slightly open, eyes flicking down occasionally.

She didn't look like she needed rescuing, so he didn't charge over there like some fool to tell that guy to hurry the fuck up and get his food and go.

But he sort of wanted to, which felt strange. Devon wouldn't stand by if someone genuinely needed help, but he wasn't this guy who was easily bothered by another man breathing near the woman he...had no claim on and absolutely didn't want like that. This sudden bout of possessiveness was weird. Was he coming down with something? Or was he still mentally exhausted from earlier?

That made more sense than whatever emotion was compelling him to stroll over there.

Dealing with the current work situation and Reba all in the same day was bound to drive anyone to the brink. One of the architects on the team was throwing an entire fit because he and another co-worker were going through some relationship strife.

Workplace romance gone wrong was not an acceptable reason, in his opinion, to not be getting your shit done. He didn't give a damn. Vic and whoever the hell he was allegedly having this drama with needed to get it together, or Devon was going to suggest he be replaced for this project.

He didn't even know how to begin approaching Vic about this. It was awkward as hell, which was why Devon had not yet told him point-blank that maybe he shouldn't have gotten tangled up with a colleague to begin with.

He felt a slight headache coming on at the thought. It truly was all so unnecessary and exhausting. He refocused on Reba again. She was still handling this guy, as expected, just like she seemed to handle everything with her sunshine cheer. Seriously, the man looked like he was ready to drop to one knee and beg Reba to marry him.

"How the hell does she do that?" he muttered. If he could siphon off some of her natural charm for himself, he would be a shoo-in for this promotion, and maybe he would know how to sort all this drama out without jeopardising their project.

Reba didn't look like the type to kiss anyone's ass, but

she definitely knew how to straddle that line between making someone feel like the centre of her attention without it coming across as sucking up. Maybe he *should* let her teach him her ways.

A light touch on his shoulder forced him to look away, and as if he had summoned the demon himself with his thoughts of the potential promotion, he came face-to-face with one of the board members. The one who definitely liked him the least.

Solomon Spiers always wore this expression like everyone was beneath him, including Devon. He kept on dyeing his silver hair this weird shade of black that was so obviously too much; it made him look like he was desperately trying to cling to his youth. The young women he was rumoured to be constantly involved with were another bit of evidence towards that claim.

Devon didn't have time to get lost in office gossip, and yet, he kept hearing others chatter about it during the few tea breaks he allowed himself at work. The kitchen was the gossipers' hot spot, apparently. They were always huddled at a table talking in what they thought were hushed tones but were definitely not.

"Devon. What're you doing here? Did Dax work his magic and find you a ticket?" Solomon asked. "I know he'll move mountains for his golden boy."

Devon mentally counted to five slowly. "Dax had nothing to do with this. I just got lucky, and a...friend had an extra ticket."

Reba chose that precise moment to return, food in hand. Solomon's eyebrow hiked up, his eyes scanning Reba from head to toe. The urge to jab an elbow into the man's side so he would stop looking at Reba like that was strong. Devon kept his arm at his side.

"Well, don't you just have lovely friends?" Solomon stuck out his hand. "Pleasure to meet you."

Reba shook his hand, and Solomon held on for far longer than was polite. Devon cleared his throat, but Solomon looked too enamoured to care. Reba easily extracted her hand. "Hi. You're a colleague of Devon's?"

"Somewhat. I'm on the board of Dax Designs."

"Oh. Cool."

"Yes, cool indeed." Solomon smiled right into Reba's cleavage before actually looking at her face. "So how did you manage to get tickets for this event? Are you in the buildings business too? If so, prettiest builder I've ever seen."

The condescending tone grated against Devon's ears. Reba simply smiled. "I'm not, but I *do* know people." She left it at that, saying nothing more as she reached for the kebab on her plate.

"Ah yes, well. Of course, you do." Solomon watched Reba as she took a bite of whatever meat was on the wooden skewer.

Devon's hand curled into a fist at his side. It would be a bad idea to punch out a board member for staring at Reba's lips. He was swiftly getting on Devon's nerves, which meant it was best to remove himself from Solomon's space.

"Well, we should continue looking at the exhibit," he suggested.

"It was lovely meeting your friend." Solomon looked ready to reach for Reba's hand again, but she waved her kebab, showing that both hands were full.

Solomon dropped his hand and left.

"That's who you're trying to impress into a promotion?" Reba's nose wrinkled. "He gives off gross old man vibes."

"I don't want to have to impress him at all. He doesn't

even like me and expects that I'll suck up to him. I'd rather have the glitter bomb delivery, to be honest."

"Why doesn't he like you? He thinks you're gunning for his job or what?"

"I could care less about being on that board. Principal is my goal, and he doesn't want to see me there for some reason."

"Principal? That's like a top-level position?"

Devon nodded. "Yes, it's like a Partner of the firm. Dax has hinted at grooming me for one of those positions, but a few board members, Solomon especially, don't seem to agree with that. Apparently, I don't grovel enough for their liking."

"You're definitely not the grovelling type," Reba pointed out.

"You're right, but..." Was he actually going to say this? He sighed.

He'd been working his ass off all this time with great results. The route to Principal seemed to have some obstacles in the form of assholes like Solomon, which made things tricky. It meant all his good work wouldn't mean a damn if one of the people who had a say in his promotion simply didn't like him.

The bake-off was merely one tactic. Devon didn't believe in leaving anything to chance. He had to cover all his bases.

"But," he tried again. "Maybe I *do* need you to coach me on being more likeable, so these assholes will change their minds."

Reba paused with her last kebab halfway to her lips. "Well, this has to be my lucky night. You're admitting you need me for more than baking?"

"Let's not get too carried away. Thinking on this and calculating the probabilities of this situation going my way with just participating in the bake-off, I've concluded that you could be useful in other areas."

"That's a whole roundabout way of saying I was right." She finished off her kebab, flagged down one of the passing servers and snatched up a glass of wine, pointing at him to take one from the tray. "We need to toast to this!"

"We really don't." Reba wasn't paying his protests any mind. She balanced her glass on her plate and picked up another one, shoving it in his hand. He only took it to avoid the thing falling and causing a scene.

Reba grinned up at him. "Come on, say it. *'You were right, Reba.'*"

He ground his teeth together, refusing. Telling her she was correct all along meant admitting *he* was wrong. He didn't like that one bit.

She picked up her glass, waving it around, the golden liquid inside sloshing about. "Do iiit," she taunted.

"Fine. It's between us." He tapped his glass against hers and took a sip of wine. Just the right amount of sweet. He preferred red wine when he allowed himself to indulge, but this would do.

"Of course. Our little secret." She winked, tossing back the wine like juice. "Now, take me around and nerd out with me some more."

"I thought you wanted me to find someone who would be into this stuff to converse with." He hadn't seen Dax yet. He could strike up a conversation with any of the other guests who could be in his field or simply have an interest in architecture. He wasn't inclined to engage in small talk at the moment, though.

If it was up to him, he would wander around, drink everything in, and talk to no one. He didn't have a problem attending things like this alone. He had done so in the past after he'd imploded his relationship with Monica and his few friendships.

Reba placed the empty glass and plate on a nearby table, brown eyes gleaming. "I changed my mind. Tonight, you're all mine. We're going to learn a lot." She slid her fingertips along his cheek, running her hand along his beard. "So soft."

His hand twitched with the urge to grasp onto her wrist and stall her movements. He forced himself to remain unmoving. It was becoming a habit of his, capturing her wrist. The last time he hadn't wanted to let go, for some inane reason he couldn't imagine. The hand on his face felt...not unpleasant too.

Kryptonite.

Yeah, he needed a boost to his armour, stat, before Reba burrowed deep enough to do damage.

"You done?" he asked in the sternest voice he could manage without drawing any attention their way.

Reba remained unfazed as usual. She tapped his nose with her index finger, looking extremely pleased with herself. "Now I'm done. Let's go, new bestie." She twirled ahead of him, pausing once to look back. "I'm about to show you a whole new world."

Devon called up all the strength he could muster. He had faced down arrogant clients who thought they knew better than him. He had dealt with his father when he was being an entire fucker during the whole cheating scandal. Surely dealing with Reba would be easy.

"Don't gloat. It's unbecoming."

"Says you. I look good in any attitude." She smoothed her hands up the sides of her dress and gestured for him to follow her.

He ignored the tiny flare of something in his chest and pants. Yes, he could deal with her just fine.

CHAPTER SEVENTEEN

REBA

SHE DIDN'T REMEMBER FALLING ASLEEP. SO, WHEN THE LIGHT nudge came on her arm, she opened her eyes, totally disoriented, eyes sweeping from Devon to out the car window. She squinted at his driveway. When had they gotten here?

"Oh."

He took off his seatbelt. "You knocked out while I was talking about Ambard's House. Guess I bored you to sleep."

Reba shook her head, trying to shed the remnants of sleep, not that it worked. She felt too tired, not awake enough to drive back home. She pressed her head back against the seat, letting a long yawn escape.

"Think I need at least an hour more." She snuggled into the car seat.

"Hey, you can't just keep sleeping here."

She raised her palm. "Five more minutes, please. Can't drive yet. Sleepy." Her words were punctuated by another lengthy yawn.

She remembered begging Devon to show her Ambard's House after they had decided it was time to leave the exhibit. Or rather, he decided. Reba could have gone on until they were literally told to leave. Not that she was so immersed in the exhibit itself, but the people-watching was intriguing.

Even though Sweethand catered to a range of clients, she didn't usually rub shoulders with this group of people. It had been fun to recognise some familiar celebrities who she was certain only came to be seen and didn't give a damn about the photos and paintings on display—though she wasn't judging them. She would have done the same thing.

But Ambard's House had caught her eye. It looked like a pretty dollhouse in the photo, and she didn't want to miss the opportunity to see it up close. It was walking distance from Stollmeyer's, and because Devon was a giant nerd, he hadn't balked too much at her insisting.

She had peered over the wall at the house while Devon had talked about the structure. He'd continued talking about it while back in the car, she supposed. She had no idea when she had dozed off exactly.

Devon sighed. "Reba, I'll take you home if you like. You can get your car in the morning."

She cracked her eye open, tilted her head his way. "You're tired too."

"I'm fine," he said just as he released a jaw-cracking yawn. His annoyed expression was too funny to keep her laughter in. Devon liked control, but a yawn was going to bust out whenever it wanted to.

"See?" She took off her seatbelt. "Let's nap for an hour. Then I'll be good to drive."

"We're *not* taking a nap in my driveway."

She pressed her hands under her cheek. "Well, invite me in then. I have my baddess bag on standby. I can get a quick change of clothes to nap in. This dress is great but not made for sleeping. I'll set an alarm. Look at me having a plan and everything."

"What the *hell* is a baddess bag?"

"Various purposes, but in case I need a change of clothes for whatever reason. Also for pre- and post-sexy times," she said.

She had been accumulating things for this bag for years now. As much as she hated planning—when it didn't apply to Sweethand stuff—this was one of the things she had been consistent with.

"You have a bag in your car? For that?"

Reba grinned. "Of course. I got condoms, fresh undies, and casual clothes in there too. There's also granola bars. Some other stuff." One item, in particular, she didn't think he wanted to know about. Glittery and useful for when she was feeling extra adventurous.

Devon's brows raised.

"I need to refuel after vigorous activities." She winked. "And I don't stay long enough to get fed most times, so baddess bag. Some people think that's what I am, and I might as well own it."

"Smart to be prepared, I suppose," he grudgingly agreed. "It's a good plan, actually. I should probably keep a bag in my car too. Just for the change of clothes, I mean," he added as if she would judge him for having his own baddess bag.

She'd figured Devon didn't do spontaneous sex, but life did have a way of throwing curveballs. Reba made sure she restocked those condoms regularly, even if she wasn't using them all the time.

"I'm shocked you don't already. What do you do if you mess up your clothes?"

"I don't."

Of course, he would say that. God forbid Devon did something like accidentally have ketchup fall on his shirt, like the rest of the mere mortals around. "So, can I take a small nap before hitting the road? I can just stay on the couch."

"No need to sleep on the couch when I have a perfectly good guest room."

They exited the car, and Reba retrieved her bag. Devon kept eyeing it like something would spring forth from the inside. He probably thought she would get glitter on his stuff, but she assured him that the pink and blue sparkly mermaid scales didn't shed.

He showed her to the guest room, which was decorated simply with a bed, a built-in closet, and a chest of drawers off to the side. The colourful throw pillows on the bed gave her pause. They didn't mesh with the rest of his décor.

"My mother made those as a housewarming gift," he said as she picked up a bright orange one to inspect the design on the front.

That made sense. She couldn't imagine Devon picking this out on his own.

"Because God forbid you willingly allow a smidge of colour to enter your house."

He pointed at her. "I let you in, didn't I? I think that's enough."

Reba dropped her bag on the bed, grinning as Devon winced. He truly expected an explosion of glitter at any moment, didn't he? "Oh, he's got jokes, huh?"

"Anyways, bathroom's down the hall. There's towels there, just put it in the hamper when you're finished. I'm also setting an alarm for an hour just in case you sleep through yours."

"Wow, you really want me gone as soon as possible, hmm?"

He didn't respond—just kept staring at her bag. They stood in an awkward standoff for a few seconds before Reba decided to set things in motion. Tiredness was seeping back in, and while she wanted that nap more than anything right now, she also didn't want to pass out in this dress again.

"When did you start the bag?" he asked. She loved talking about her bag, usually, but not at the moment when she wanted to just rest. There was one guaranteed way to get Devon on his way.

"Hmm, can't recall. It's not that strange, is it? Perfectly normal things in here." She rummaged in the bag, smiling to herself. "Well, *these* aren't quite for everyday use," she said as nonchalantly as she could manage when dangling a pair of heart-shaped glittery handcuffs from her index finger.

Devon blinked. "You...cannot be serious."

"Oh, I assure you, I'm always serious about these."

"How can you just...?" He visibly shook himself, throat working as he swallowed. "You just let anyone use those? On you?"

"Not just anyone." Her plan had backfired. Devon was more interested than she thought. She had expected him to be put off and leave immediately.

She twirled the handcuffs, sleepy as hell but amused as his eyes followed the round and round motion. "So, unless you're going to help me see if these still fit, I need to get out of this." She pointed at her dress.

He jerked as if realising finally that he should be appalled by this. "Right, yes. Sure." He backed away towards the door. "Sleep well."

He shut the door, and she couldn't help the laugh that burst out of her as she went about removing her makeup and her wig before hopping into the shower. His face! She wasn't forgetting that in a hot minute. The water refreshed her somewhat, but not enough that she felt confident getting behind the wheel.

Exiting the bathroom after lotioning up and throwing on her favourite underwear, her comfy shorts, and one of her camisoles, she wondered which room was Devon's. Not that she was about to make some impromptu appearance in there. It was just her curiosity jumping out at the moment, making her wonder if he continued the same monochromatic décor from downstairs into his bedroom.

The fact that he had hidden away his mother's colourful cushions in the guest bedroom definitely made her think he didn't have much colour in his room either. Not that she was about to barge in and find out. That would be weird. She enjoyed teasing him a lot but waltzing into his bedroom uninvited would be crossing a line for sure. Besides, she actually didn't have seduction on her mind right now. She really did want a nap.

She took a sleepy barefaced selfie and posted it with a "goodnight luvs" caption before laying back on the comfy bed.

The alarm sounding in the distance came way too soon before it randomly shut off. Reba stretched, refusing to open her eyes. Her body still felt like she needed at least two more hours, but she had promised Devon she would be out of here in an hour.

She wondered if she could persuade him to just let her stay until morning. They did have another baking session, so it could make sense. She opened her eyes, nearly yelping as Devon's face came into view.

"What the hell, man?" As handsome as he was, she had *not* been prepared to see him now, this close.

He pulled back. "Sorry, this looks weird. I wasn't watching you sleep. I came to see if you were awake—my alarm went off —and you were moving around, so I dismissed your alarm." He blinked down at her, brow furrowed. "You look different."

She pulled herself up into a sitting position, legs crossed, rubbing her eyes. She looked him up and down. "Well, I'm sure you do as well when you're sleeping. More peaceful, less frowny, I'd assume."

"I've never seen you without any makeup on before. Your hair's covered. You look more innocent, I guess. Radiating less of a chaotic vibe."

She snorted and patted her silk headscarf. "Don't be fooled. My chaos energy is *very* much intact. Sleep simply recharges me." She stretched purposefully. Sleep may still have her in its lovely grasp, but Reba's flirt-o-meter was good to go at any time.

Devon's eyes followed her movements as she twisted and turned her body while she stretched. Her top and shorts were cotton, perfect for moulding to every line and curve of her body, no matter how she moved.

"Yeah, I just bet," he muttered. He remained standing over her, eyes roving her face like he couldn't get over seeing her like this. "You're still tired, aren't you? You don't hide it as well now."

She rolled her eyes. "You seriously need to work on your compliments game. You really just told me, to my face, that I look tired."

"But you do," he pointed out.

"Yes, well, you said an hour, but I'm still not fully recharged. So now what?"

"Stay."

The word surprised them both. Devon looked like he wanted to take it back immediately. Sometimes Reba could be altruistic and shit if she wanted, but she needed sleep more, and she was not about to tell him it was fine. If he wanted her to stay, she was damn well staying. The bed was super comfortable.

"Wow, do I really look so innocent without makeup that you just can't help but feel sorry for me?" Reba had no remorse about using that to her advantage.

She swung her legs over the side of the bed and looked up at Devon. She tugged on the ends of his t-shirt, swinging it back and forth, her knuckles almost touching his stomach but not quite.

"Yes." He looked down at her hands on his t-shirt. She expected him to scold her about wrinkling his clothes again, but he kept his gaze on the motion of the fabric, not telling her to stop.

"You should have never admitted that."

"It's good to know your weaknesses, so you can work on conquering them."

Oh, she liked night-time Devon. He seemed a lot freer with his words. "Devon, Devon, Devon. I'm not the type of weakness you get over."

His Adam's apple bobbed. "I refuse to accept that."

"Why are you fighting this so hard? Giving in doesn't mean failing."

"It's late. I should get back to sleep. You can catch a few more hours before you need to go."

"I don't see *you* leaving, though."

"You're still holding onto my shirt."

"But you could disentangle yourself at any time if you

wanted." She got to her feet, hands still playing with the hem of his t-shirt.

"My bathroom probably smells like you," he said suddenly.

She cocked her head. She had brought along her own body wash as well. His bathroom totally smelled like vanilla. She loved the scent when baking and showering. "It does."

He closed his eyes for a brief moment before reopening them to fix her with his dark stare again. "Why the fuck are you doing this to me?"

"What am I doing?" she asked oh so softly. "Tell me in exact detail."

His hand came up and gripped her shoulder. Reba felt his touch against her skin like a jolt. He played with the strap on her top, finger curled around it, as he tugged it up and down before releasing it to slide his hand up to cup her neck and squeeze ever so lightly.

Well, fuck. She felt that gentle grasp to her core.

"You can just pretend it was a dream tomorrow. If you want," she managed to say.

Girl, stop talking.

Now wasn't the time to scare him off. She was close to getting what she wanted. Trina's voice talking about the bet echoed in her brain, but she mentally swiped it away. Yes, she wanted to win—he hadn't said the words out loud, but his actions were telling her he definitely wanted her— but that wasn't the only reason why she would let this happen if Devon was willing to take it there and not leave her hanging.

His hand was now fully encasing her throat, driving her out of her mind because *holy hell,* that shit was hot. She thought it was safe to say he wanted to take it there. He was free to change his mind at any point throughout, didn't mean she wouldn't pout about it. She was horny and needed some goddamn relief.

"Just a dream, huh?"

"Yeah." She moaned as he pressed his thumb to her pulse. She tilted her head up, watching him as he continued to caress her neck.

"You like this?" he rasped out, eyes never leaving hers.

"Please, yes. Yup," she croaked out because shame? Pride? She didn't know them. Didn't carry those things around on the daily and definitely not in the bedroom.

"Ah, so you *can* listen when you want to?"

Shit. She was going to lose it. Could she come just from this alone? She didn't think so, but it didn't hurt in helping her along. Well, she had wanted to know how Devon did seduction, hadn't she? She'd been right about him using that voice to his advantage. This gravelly tone he had going on was making her want to wrestle him down to the sheets. Get this show on the road.

She wouldn't be able to take him. That wasn't her goal. She simply enjoyed playing around, having fun in all aspects of her life. Which was the perfect counterbalance to Devon, she realised. He would definitely take it seriously, which would work in her favour. All that intensity focused on her? Oh, yeah.

"I can be good when it's beneficial to me."

His hand moved up to her jaw. "It will be. Don't doubt that."

Fuck, okay, cocky Devon was on another level of hot. "Just kiss me already. All this foreplay is nice, but..." She bit her lip.

If he didn't get on with it, she was truly going to tackle him. He might think she looked all sweet and innocent now, but she was the same Reba. She would fight dirty.

"Patience will get you everything."

"Will it get you to actually kiss me cuz..." She trailed off when he leaned down, gripped her chin harder.

"Stop talking."

She licked her lips because if he wanted something, he was going to have to be a bit more proactive. "Make me," she taunted.

He obliged, taking her mouth in a hard kiss that spoke of all that lovely tension Devon had been holding back. She wanted him to release every bit of it. Reba leapt up, wrapping her arms and legs around him. Devon turned them so he could sit on the bed, which put Reba right in his lap, straddling him.

He deepened the kiss, feasting on her mouth, hands roaming down her sides to stop at her breasts. She arched into him as his thumbs rubbed over her nipples. Yes, finally, she had his hands right where she wanted them. He cupped her through the material of her top, covering her completely since she was working with a bit less than a handful. She rode him a little, causing his grip to tighten on her breasts.

He pulled back, breaking the kiss. "Can I take this off you?" he asked, hands still massaging her through the thin cotton.

"If I can take yours off too, sure." She needed to touch him. After what she had seen at the beach, Reba was eager to get her hands full. Of everything. "Pants too, if you're feeling up to it."

Penetration didn't have to happen. She would be okay with a good old dry humping session, but who would she be if she didn't at least ask to see Devon without a stitch of clothes on? Get a good look at what he was working with.

He leaned back, reaching down to pull his sleeveless t-shirt over his head and toss it on the bed at the same time she got rid of her top. She got off of him before he could get a feel, leaving his hand outstretched. Smile wide, she shimmied everything off, pants and panties, tossing them his way. He caught everything before it hit him in the face. She untied her scarf, freeing her hair.

He clutched the pants in his hands, eyes sweeping every inch of her as she took out her hairpins, slowly massaging her hair, so it came out of the neat wrap she had done to fall around her shoulders. She'd just have to redo it when this was over. She spun in a circle before resting her hand on her hip, brow cocked.

"Now you," she said, looking down at his pants where his dick was straining against the soft fabric.

He tossed her clothes off to the side, keeping his hot, hungry gaze on her as he rose to his feet. Reba drank in his chest, hand twitching as she wanted to desperately run her hands through the smattering of hair that dusted his glorious brown skin.

Good things come to those who are patient, no? Or so her mother liked to say. Reba wasn't so sure. And she was *definitely* out of patience. She was about to get exactly what she wanted, and she was not about to delay it. Not the way the throbbing between her legs kept intensifying.

She almost reached down there to get a head start. Would he like that? If she showed him what she wanted him to do?

She didn't get the chance to act or ask because Devon removed his shorts, and hello, good sir.

"Fuck. Me."

Devon took his dick in hand, giving it a leisurely stroke. "If that's what you want."

"Want, want, want," she chanted. "Taste, please?"

"You first." He gestured for her to get on the bed.

She didn't listen. She walked up to him, knocking his hand away so she could get all of his hard, hot length into her hands. "Such a gentleman, but..." She stroked him slowly, enjoying his slow swallow as he thrust into her hand.

"Me first, yes, but this way. This is what I want." She mouthed at his neck, biting into the skin gently.

"You said you'd be good," he hissed out.

She clucked her tongue before nibbling down his chest to lave at his nipple, her hand never ceasing her up and down motion on his dick. "This *is* me being good. Aren't I being such a good girl right now?"

She kissed her way down his chest, licking at his abdomen, head tilted up so she could see every change of expression.

"You're a fucking demon, aren't you?"

"Here to torment, yes, sir."

"Shit, don't call me that." He squeezed his eyes shut as she kissed his pelvic bone, so close to where she wanted to be.

"You're going to want to see this," she told him, eyes level with his bobbing dick now.

"I can't...it's been too long...I'll..."

"Come? That's the end goal, isn't it? And we know how much you love to achieve your goals," she crooned, licking him and enjoying the way he jerked on her tongue.

He opened his eyes, hand tunnelling into her hair, getting a firm grip. "Fucking hell, Reba. Get up here, now."

He tugged on her hair, but she kept going because she would get every single thing she wanted.

It was also way too much fun to disobey. She gave one last lick, tongue lapping up his salty taste just as he tugged on her hair again. She allowed him to drag her up to her feet for another searing kiss as he manoeuvred them over to the bed.

She lay back, grinning up at him, tongue flicking out to trace her lips, a reminder of how far he could have allowed her to go. Devon ran his fingers down her stomach over to her tattoo. His touch lingered over each petal of the hibiscus. Hmm, he seemed to like it. How interesting. She didn't get to ask before his fingers got to her clit. He rubbed at her, watching her hips as they moved in time with his fingers.

"Now who's torturing who?" she groaned out. "I don't want to be presumptuous, but you might want to get the condoms from my bag now. Don't think we want to waste precious time looking."

He reached into the bag at the side of the bed while she drank in the flex of muscle in his ass and thighs. She would be getting a bite out of that at some point. He placed the packet next to her and didn't bother resuming what he'd been doing with his fingers. Instead, he dipped his head and went right for it.

She bucked up at the swipe of his tongue. Oh, shit. She wrapped her legs around his head. It was too much. She would come, and then what? She wanted to come on his dick. Now. She tapped at his shoulder, but this mofo was paying her back for earlier because he wasn't letting up.

"Yeah, just...shit, Devon! Stop, stop, stop. Need it now!"

He looked up, and God help her, his mouth was so...glisten-y. "Mmmm?"

She narrowed her eyes, chest heaving. "Get that condom on now. Pretty please?"

He finally did as she asked, and Reba didn't wait; she wrapped her legs around his waist, urging him forward. Then he was inside and moving, and she was just...yeah, that was her teeth in his shoulder. Sorry, not sorry because shit, he felt good.

Devon moved his hips like a man on a mission. He didn't do failure, so of course, he was trying his best to get her to come. Wouldn't take much. His fingers and mouth on her had almost gotten her there earlier.

"More?" he grunted.

"More. Everything. Give me everything," she gasped out. "Please."

"I enjoy when you say please."

"Hey, I'm always polite."

"Hmm."

She rolled her hips. "Shut up and just fuck me."

He listened. Thank you, Jesus.

"Hang on," he said.

Reba was too blissed out to know what the hell he was saying until he rolled them, placing her on top.

"Whoa, okay. Hi," she said, blinking down at him.

He gripped her ass, urging her to keep moving. She obliged, adding some bounce so he would have a nice view of her tits in motion. His hands came up to grip them and squeeze. Success.

She twisted her hips, pulling a long moan from him, and before she knew it, she was coming. He wasn't too far behind, his grip on her tightening as he surged up one more time. Reba fell forward, a smirk on her lips.

"Now I'm even sleepier."

His hand stroking her hair surprised the hell out of her, but she didn't move, just lay on top of him.

"I need to get rid of the condom."

She rolled to her side, watching him through lowered lids. "Yeah, do that."

She lay on her back, breathing in and out slowly. She should get her clothes on or something. Go pee and try to sleep. Unless Devon expected her to leave now. Yeah, she was going nowhere. She was too relaxed; her limbs felt extra heavy.

She could wait for Devon to return, suss out where his head was at, but nah. He would just have to deal with her in his guest room—she was going nowhere for now. Maybe a little rest, and they could have round two. Then she could try to go home.

She smiled to herself as she drifted off to sleep.

CHAPTER EIGHTEEN
DEVON

DEVON WOKE UP TO THE ENTICING SCENT OF VANILLA AND AN empty bed. He was definitely not in his bedroom. The bright pillow lying next to his head clued him in.

The guest room.

Reba.

Everything they had done last night.

He jolted up, looking around. Her bag wasn't on the floor. Had she just left?

A small noise downstairs made him jump up and throw on his t-shirt. Luckily, he had on his shorts—less time wasted. Every second counted when the woman you'd just had amazing sex with was probably trying to sneak the fuck out.

He rubbed at his eyes. He didn't even know what time it was, having left his phone in his room. He hadn't planned on having sex with Reba when he'd come to check on her. That was supposed to have been a short visit to make sure she was awake and ready to be on her way.

How the hell had they gotten here? There was usually a method to these things, at least for him.

It wasn't that Reba, in her bright clothes and makeup, was easy to resist. He had been silently struggling from the moment he had agreed to let her help him. But Reba looking soft and drowsy, dark brown eyes unframed by any shiny eyeshadow, was somehow much more dangerous. She had looked so vulnerable, like a peaceful angel dozing on the bed.

A lie, clearly. The Reba of last night was hell-bent on wrecking him and his life just as much as her colourful persona.

He debated whether he should take a second to brush his teeth or not. Even though time was ticking, his habits were too ingrained for him not to at least dash some toothpaste in his mouth and swish some water around before rinsing. He briskly made his way down the hall to the stairs, ready to walk down, when he caught sight of her at the door, bag slung over her shoulder, her shorts and top from last night nowhere to be seen. He supposed the sunny yellow dress had also been in her bag of never-ending supplies.

So she'd had time to shower—the fresh vanilla scent made him believe that to be true—and get ready to leave without saying a word to him. It definitely irked him.

"So, you're just running out like this?" he called down. She froze, hand on the doorknob. He stomped down the stairs. "Seriously?"

She turned around. Her eyelids shone with bronze; her lips were slick with a deeper maroon colour. So the makeup was back on. She had time for all of that and yet hadn't been about to leave him a note or anything.

He shouldn't be this worked up about it, yet the casual sweep she took up and down his body threw fuel on the fire already simmering in his chest. Dangerous Reba was back, and Devon needed his guard way up.

Her tongue peeked out the corner of her mouth. *Do not look at her mouth, you fool.*

"I'm not running. I'm very casually walking out."

He looked her right in the eyes. "Is this what you do? Fuck and run? You don't even..."

She held up a finger, cutting him off. "One, we just established I'm not running. Do you see these shoes?" She kicked out her leg, showing off her pale-coloured heels. "Two, let's be real here. I'm making the morning-after situation less awkward." She shrugged. "That's all."

"Who says it needs to be awkward? You didn't give us a chance to find out, did you?"

She cocked her head to the side, gaze contemplative. "If you wanted me to stay and cuddle, you can just say so. Are you actually upset with me about this?" She seemed confused.

Hell, so was he. This was what he had wanted hours ago before sex had happened. She was doing them a favour by ensuring there didn't have to be a weird, tense moment when he woke up and she was here. And yet, he wasn't used to his bed partner just disappearing, leaving nothing behind except that damn intoxicating vanilla scent.

"It's been two years."

"What?"

"I haven't been with anyone intimately in two years."

"Oh?" Her brow crinkled. She still didn't get it.

Neither did he. Making an attempt to explain was difficult and made him want to cringe, yet he made an effort. "I just didn't expect you to be gone. No note. Nothing. It's not what I'm used to. Maybe I'm old-fashioned or whatever, but the first woman I have sex with in the last two years, and she dashes out like the house is burning down? Makes a man feel a way, you know?"

Reba wrinkled her nose. "Note? I don't do notes. Do people still write notes? I would've sent you a text or something later." She patted her stomach. "I need food too, and I don't think you would have appreciated me raiding your fridge, so leaving felt like the best idea. I didn't mean to make you feel bad or anything."

"Yes, note writing is still a thing. Even in 2018."

Her mouth twitched. "Are you saying you'd write notes to your boo? How sweet." She grinned. "So there's a romantic beneath all that, huh? Colour me surprised."

"Look, we're getting off-track. I would've liked the courtesy of you not just leaving after, well, everything."

"After we fucked," she said matter-of-factly.

Yeah, that.

She'd dozed off when he returned from throwing away the condom. He'd pulled on his pants, but when he moved to cover her with the blanket, she tried to tug him down next to her. He had told himself it was best he left and went back to his own room, and yet he had gotten in next to her anyways.

"Just for a while," she'd mumbled.

Just for a while had turned into hours with them snuggled up against each other. His body had stirred to life again, but he'd ignored it. They both needed the rest. He hadn't woken up until now. And when he did, he'd found her gone from the bed.

"We're supposed to be baking today too. It makes sense to stay. It's week three already. Four more weeks seems like a lot, but it isn't. Not if I want to actually be able to do this cube."

That was much better, he thought, than him acting hurt

about her leaving. It was best he stayed on a more reasonable point. She didn't have to leave when they already had a standing baking appointment. He could also make them breakfast, which would shave down any time she might take to go looking for something to eat.

"So, that's what you're really upset about, then? Because you think I'm backing out on our deal?"

He nodded because what else was he supposed to say? That he missed the feel of her warm body against him? Fuck no.

She reached for the door handle. "I'll come back later. I promise, but I need to go."

"Why do you need to go? I thought you'd want to stick around to gloat. You got what you wanted, after all."

She spun around. "Now I know you're not implying this was all one-sided. You definitely wanted this."

"No, that's not what I'm saying, but let's not pretend you haven't been trying to get me out of my comfort zone since we started this."

"So what? Stop framing this like I'm the bad guy or something since I'm supposedly ditching you. You expected me to be clingy the morning after? Because that's what you're used to?" She laughed. "Newsflash, buddy, I assessed the situation and figured this was the best course of action. I thought you'd appreciate that? The fact that you're arguing against it *is* pretty unexpected." She poked him in the chest. "And don't give me this bullshit about our baking deal because the level of emotion you're pushing out here, it's not adding up, sweetie. If you want to go back to bed and tussle, just say so. I can spare a minute or two."

He closed the space between them. "A minute or two? You know that won't be it."

Reba shrugged. "Quickies are a thing, you know. And dresses offer easy access."

"How convenient. Is that why you leave one in your bag?" He dipped his hand under her dress, trailing up her thigh to the edge of her panties.

She bit her lip, finger dropping from his chest to curl around the strap of her bag. "Three compelling reasons why I should stay. Go."

"I can feed you."

"Your dick?"

He rubbed at her with the pad of his index finger. "No."

She pouted. "Then bye. Although..." She pressed her head back against the door when he pushed a finger inside. "This isn't so bad. Nothing like a good fingering to start the weekend right."

"How can you just say things like that?" he asked, enjoying the clasp of her against his finger. Everything was going off the rails—his usual morning routine shot to hell —but he wasn't going to stop unless she wanted to.

"Life's too short to not say what you're thinking. Mmm, like right now, I really want to come all over your face."

"Fuck, Reba, just..."

They both jumped as the doorbell rang. *Who the fuck?* Reba shook her head and ground down on his finger one more time before muttering a curse under her breath.

"Yeah, if that isn't a sign," she added. He pulled his finger away, wiping it under his t-shirt. "Yeah, I really should just go." She turned away.

"Wait, don't..."

She opened the door, barely giving him a moment to step away and compose himself, bringing them face-to-face with his mother. Finger raised as if preparing to ring his doorbell again, she looked just as shocked as Devon felt. Ah, shit.

"Is that why you haven't been answering your phone? If I knew you had company, I wouldn't have come over." His mother looked from Reba to him, eyes landing on Reba's bag.

The situation looked exactly like whatever his mother was thinking.

"What are you doing here?" He had just been fingering a woman at his front door—he really didn't have the capacity to be polite, even to his mother. Not with all the blood in his body currently in his dick.

"You've been ignoring my calls and emails. I figured you'd be true to your routine and be at home, so I decided to stop by."

"Hi, Ms. King," Reba jumped in, giving a small wave. "I work with Cherisse."

"Yes, I remember. Didn't know you and my son were close, though."

"We're not," Devon said, not looking at Reba's face to see her reaction to that. Technically, he wasn't wrong. They may have been as physically close as two people could be last night, but not in the way his mother was implying.

Or maybe sex was exactly what his mother was referring to. Dammit, Reba's chaos was already affecting his perfectly ordered life. He quickly assessed his options. The more they all stood around his front door, the more awkward this got.

"Reba is assisting me with a baking thing." As much as it pained him to finally admit it, given the situation, this was the best course of action. Throw his mother off the scent.

He felt Reba's stare on the side of his face. He still didn't look at her.

"Oh? Reba looks like she's leaving, though."

"Well, actually, I just got here and realised I left something in my car, so I was heading back to get it. Didn't even have a chance to put my bag down."

He looked at her then. What was she playing at? She wouldn't actually drive away, would she? Leave him to explain to his mother why Reba had left when she'd just said she had gotten here.

"I'll be right back," Reba said.

Devon stepped aside so his mother could move past him. It also gave him a few seconds to calm himself down. He closed the door behind Reba and took two deep breaths before facing his mother.

"Baking thing, huh?" she asked, draping herself over the lone armchair.

He scrubbed a hand down his face. "I just woke up, so before you get into me about that, I need to refresh myself."

"What happened to your alarm?"

"Forgot to set it. Reba woke me up when she got here."

His mother crossed her legs and gave him a look that said she wasn't exactly buying any of this. "That's very unlike you, but then again, so is you having a baking thing you need help with. That you didn't bother to ask *me* for help."

"We'll discuss it later." More like never. He had only revealed this so she wouldn't question Reba's presence.

While she still looked a bit sceptical, dropping their baking sessions into the mix was less awkward than sex talk. He made his way upstairs, brushed his teeth properly this time, jumped in the shower, and took a quick bath, willing his erection to calm the fuck down. At least this bathroom smelled as it should, with its regular Febreze scent. Not a trace of vanilla to be found. Something that made sense when everything else was currently in shambles.

He had been about to fingerfuck Reba at his door, for God's sake. What had gotten into him?

He would need to change the guest room sheets too. Later. After everyone was gone and he could focus without Reba or his mother around. Jesus, how was this his life right now? What happened to his quiet work weekends?

Reba happened when you invited her in.

All because of that ridiculous call-out at work. He shouldn't have fallen for it.

He shook his head and retrieved his phone from where he'd left it on his nightstand. Sure enough, he had a couple of missed calls and texts from his mother. The messages were only about one thing: her insisting he have the damn housewarming/blessing.

Now that she was here, she wouldn't leave until he agreed to the damn thing. Maybe he did need a priest to come exorcise Reba's lingering energy after they were done with these baking sessions. But he couldn't say that now, could he?

Enough stalling, he had to get back downstairs. Leaving Reba and his mother in the same room was asking for trouble. Who knew what Reba would say?

He found them chatting about the potential party. A safe-ish topic, thank God.

"He emerges. So fresh and so clean," Reba said from the larger couch, which meant he had to sit next to her. It would look strange if he remained standing.

He chose the spot farthest away from her, on the other end of the couch. That's what normal Devon would do. His mother would expect that. He respected personal space, and besides, he and Reba had a professional relationship. But even with the space between them, she was too radiant in that yellow dress. His eyes kept landing on the little bows that kept her straps up.

If his mother hadn't shown up, he could have easily tugged on one of those dangling strings and bared everything to his hungry gaze.

Do you really want to be thinking these thoughts with your mother right there?

Shit, he was a mess.

"So your mom was telling me about this housewarming idea. Sounds like fun."

Devon turned away from Reba and narrowed his eyes at his mother. "I haven't agreed to any party."

She shrugged. "Not officially, but I promise you won't have to do anything. I'll sort out the food and clean up after. I'll even play host. Just give me your guest list."

"Why is any of this necessary?"

"Blessing your new space is important, and why not make it a celebration? Owning a home is an amazing thing."

It was and had been on his list of goals for some time. Yet, he didn't want a bunch of people all up in his space. Even if his mother was taking charge of everything, which meant he could hide out in his room.

"It'll be a good chance to test out your baking skills, too," Reba piped up.

He glared in her direction. "I'm already doing that with the cookies on Monday."

"Cookies?" his mother asked. "I can't believe you're actually baking. What is all this for? And no offense to Reba, but why didn't you come to me?"

Devon sighed. This was why he didn't want to talk about any of this. The questions. The teasing. He wasn't in the mood.

His mother crossed her arms. "And I hope she isn't doing this for free? I've raised you all to not sell yourselves short, and I hope you wouldn't do the same to someone else."

"Can we just not?" Devon rubbed his forehead. "Of course, I'm paying her."

"He's been very good to me, Ms. King. No worries." That goddamn teasing tone would be the death of him.

He kept his gaze on his mother, who was waiting patiently for him to give in. Devon didn't give up that easily, but his mother was tenacious.

"Fine." He raised his palm before his mother could get too excited. "No co-workers. No neighbours. Just family. A small gathering. Get your priest to do his thing, and when I'm ready to shut it all down, I don't want to hear anything about me being a party pooper."

"You should invite at least some neighbours. And your friends," his mother added. "Don't think I don't realise you've been neglecting them. Working towards something is great, but don't alienate the people who care about you while on your path to greatness. I can work with next week Saturday for the party. It's Independence weekend, after all. Give me the names and emails, I'll send out e-vites on your behalf. Maxi will help me with the graphics and stuff. You can let me know what foods and drinks you want."

The neighbours were easier than the friends part. If he reached out to the friends he hadn't spoken to in almost a year, would they even want to hear from him?

"Make sure Reba's on that list too," his mother added. "She can help with your baking efforts."

Reba grinned. "I wouldn't miss a party for anything. I can help with the set-up too. And with Keiran on vacation, we'll need a DJ. I know a guy."

"Excellent. Keep her around. It's important to know people with the right connections. Plus, she's fun. I hope some of that rubs off on you." His mother winked, and Devon realised Reba had gotten yet another person to fall under her spell.

Reba beamed over at his mother, obviously delighted with this entire turn of events. Was there a single person she couldn't win over? He had thought he was stronger than this. Obviously not, since he was currently wondering how soon his mother would leave so they could pick up where they left off. Those damn strings on her dress kept appearing in his sightline.

His mother's phone rang. She pulled it out of her bag and smiled down at the screen before getting to her feet. "Excuse me a sec," she said before moving into the kitchen.

Reba smoothed her dress over her legs. It didn't quite cover her thighs, and Devon's eyes flickered over the tiny scar above her right knee.

"Why're you pushing to help with this party? You know a guy? A DJ isn't necessary."

"Every party needs a DJ."

"We can hook up my phone to some speakers."

Reba shook her head. "Lord, you are hopeless."

"Are you punishing me because I wanted you to stay?"

"If you think this is punishment, then I have truly failed at making you come into the fun light." She scooted over as she turned her body to face him, knees knocking into his.

"Parties are not my thing. Plus, I like my personal space to remain free of people."

"I'm people, and yet here I am. All up close and personal."

"That...wasn't supposed to happen."

Reba tapped his leg before moving back on the couch, putting space between them again. "The best things aren't always planned. Anyhoo, off our current topic, but are you inviting those friends your mom mentioned?"

"I don't know." He wasn't sure how to approach it. He could tell his mother he'd tried and leave it at that, but Devon didn't like lying unnecessarily. "I've sort of neglected them for work. Why would they want to hear from me?"

"Reach out. Just be genuine. Let them know you fucked up, and if they say no, well, you tried."

"You think it's that easy?"

"I'm not saying it is, but don't you think their friendship is worth fighting for?"

These friends had actually put up with his no-fun-having ass, as Reba liked to call him. They had been fine with all of that until he had basically made them collateral damage and disposable on his path to his achievements.

He had fucked up, and it was up to him to make it right. "I'll try."

"Good. Invite them out to something as an icebreaker."

"That's a good idea," his mother joined in as she came back into the room. "We're taking Leah to the amusement park at the Queen's Park Savannah tonight. I remember one of your friends has kids, no?"

"Ohh, yes! "Reba said, clapping her hands. "If they have kids, they'll have a buffer in case things get awkward between you two."

His mother took up her handbag, slipping her phone back in the pocket. "You should come too, Reba. Let's just make a fun night of it. We can get a head start on discussing party plans."

No. No goddamn way. Reba and his family all together at some weird attempt at a friend reunion? "This sounds like a terrible idea."

"It's unconventional, sure, but hey, you gotta think outside the box."

His mother was nodding along with Reba, and Devon sighed. Why the hell was everything being turned on its head? He was quickly losing control of his well-ordered life.

"None of this matters anyway if I get a negative response from Jeremy." He'd decided if he was going to target anyone, Jeremy might be the most receptive. "It's Sunday, so he may be spending time with his family."

He might also not want to hear from Devon at all. Jeremy was the one he had been closest to, and while he had reached out to Devon the most after communication had sort of tapered off, even he had eventually stopped messaging and calling Devon to ask him to hang out. There were only so many times someone would keep that up after countless rejections. Jeremy did have a wife and children, so in theory, Reba's idea about the family as a buffer wasn't so far off if things went downhill. Neither he nor Jeremy would be alone if they realised there was no resuscitating their dying friendship.

He hadn't allowed himself to think about anything other than work, and now, as he pondered on the possibility of rekindling their friendship, Devon realised it would be sad if they couldn't.

He and Jeremy had gone to the same secondary school. They had kept up their friendship when Devon had gone to the Caribbean School of Architecture at the University of

Technology in Jamaica, and Jeremy had remained in Trinidad to study at the University of the West Indies.

It truly was his fault that he'd pulled away when he'd gotten the Senior Project Manager position. It was demanding, and Devon had made his choice to focus solely on that and then, hopefully, levelling up to Principal.

"You won't," Reba said, voice oozing confidence.

"Alright, I'll leave you to your baking," his mother said. "Let's arrange for later. Devon, call Jeremy, and we'll see you all tonight." His mother breezed out of the house before he could protest more.

"So, who's ready to bake a cake?" Reba twirled, her dress flaring around her, exposing her thighs even more. "Can't wait to see all you've learned."

He was supposed to be baking on his own, with her just standing by, taking notes and filming him for the prep entries. How he was supposed to do any of that while acting as if nothing had happened between them and that he wasn't nervous about speaking to Jeremy was beyond him.

The already daunting task became impossible with Reba up under him, observing his every move, filling his senses with her scent. She recorded him as he went through the motions of making the cake, capturing his less than stellar moments. He had nearly fumbled the flour all over the counter and floor, catching the measuring cup before it completely slipped from his hand. Reba had given him a raised brow but hadn't said a word.

When he almost absentmindedly used the salt instead of sugar, she gripped his wrist.

"Whoa, hold up. I love salty food, but I'm not sure about the salty-sweet effect for this cake."

He calmly replaced the salt and picked up the sugar to measure the correct amount. "It's fine. I'm good."

"You're two scoops short of making a mess." She cocked her head at him. "Am I distracting you that much?"

"No." *Yes.* Absolutely yes. All he could think of was what she would do if he swiped a bit of batter on his finger and offered it to her, a copy of her move from the last time.

"Hey, you want to ravish me in your kitchen. It's normal. I mean, I'd want to have my way with me too."

"There's nothing normal about any of this," he shot back.

She shrugged like she didn't care. It was his problem to fix, so why *should* she? He was the one who couldn't seem to get his head right enough to get this cake done. It was harder now that he knew the sounds she made when he twisted his hips just right while thrusting. Reba didn't hold back, felt no qualms about being loud with her pleasure.

"Let's just focus."

"Okay, you first." She gestured at the bowl where he had been trying to add the ingredients.

Nothing about this should be hard. In theory, it was just a larger version of the cupcakes, wasn't it? Sure, she had tried to up the level a bit by choosing a two-layer marble cake—which meant he had more work to put in to get it right. If he couldn't get to the batter without screwing shit up, the rest would be a disaster. He wouldn't let a simple cake thwart him.

"If you can't get this right, how you gonna do the Rubik's Cube?" she asked in a playful tone. "That requires a lot of focus. I know your analytical brain can do the math, but it takes more than that."

Her teasing tone did nothing to improve his tenuous

mood. "We still don't know if *you* can make the cake. So how can you teach me?" he shot back.

"Still underestimating me, I see. Finish getting the first batch of batter right, hmm? We have plans tonight after all and can't spend all day on this, as much as I enjoy seeing you struggle through wanting me."

He scowled at her but went back to the batter. He hated that she was right. He *was* struggling, and he did want her. Again.

The idea of that priest coming to exorcise her from his house, and life, was looking more appealing by the minute.

CHAPTER NINETEEN
REBA

THE FIRST THING THAT DREW REBA'S EYE AS THEY ENTERED THE Savannah was the big colourful Ferris wheel. The wheel spokes were lit up in interchanging colours and looked so pretty against the night sky she couldn't help but snap a couple of photos for her Instagram. There were already a few people riding it, a mix of excited squeals and some fearful shouts echoing around the area. She was definitely going on it before they left.

Chatter, cheer, and chaos. She was totally in her element.

She also wasn't leaving until she'd won one of those giant stuffed animals. She was terrible at those games, her coordination off. Didn't mean she couldn't convince someone else to win for her. A tall, scowly someone who had rocked her whole world last night.

She glanced at Devon, who was looking around as if he would rather be anywhere else. His mother, sister, and niece were busy chatting about what they wanted to try first. The crowd could definitely overwhelm someone who didn't enjoy these sort of things.

Devon might not be into this entire scene, but Reba was no amateur. He'd be having fun by the end of the night.

"You see him?" she asked.

"Not yet." He checked his phone. "He said he's by the bumper cars. I suppose I should go over there and see. It's a bit crowded, so I can't really tell."

Devon had spoken to Jeremy while his cake was in the oven. After he had managed the marble effect without any other potential disasters, he had left the kitchen to have that conversation. Reba would have liked to be a nosy fly on the wall, but she understood that Devon wouldn't feel comfortable having this talk with her around.

Whatever had been broken between the two friends wasn't her problem to meddle with. She'd merely offered some simple advice: be truthful about messing up.

He hadn't elaborated when he'd returned, but obviously, it had gone in his favour with Jeremy agreeing to meet to chat.

"It's so noisy. This might have been a bad idea after all," he lamented, frowning up at the wheel.

"It's great!" Reba pointed at the carousel. "Definitely going on that. And the wheel. Oh, look at that one."

They all looked up at the contraption that was rising high up in the air. The people who were strapped in looked sort of dazed and a bit terrified. Reba could see why as the ride started swinging from side to side and the screaming began. The riders were literally clutching onto the safety bars for dear life. Oh yeah, she was trying that one for sure.

"Feel like having your entire soul leave your body?" she asked, eyes fixed on the swinging ride.

"Not a chance in hell," Devon muttered. "I see him. I'll be back."

Reba shrugged and followed the other Kings to the

carousel. As they went round and round, she clutched onto the horse she had chosen, trying to capture a video to post without getting dizzy. She caught glimpses of Devon talking with a guy who was about his height but with a broader build as the spinning ride slowed down. She couldn't tell how it was going from here, but at least some sort of progress was being made.

She couldn't survive without her friends. She'd met Cherisse and Remi later on, having known Trina and Ayo from secondary school days, but their friendship was no less important. They all kept her sane most of the time. She didn't know how Devon was going about this no-friends life. But then again, she wasn't hyper-focused on following through on some rigid goals timeline. She was happy where she was for the moment. One day at a time was fine for her.

They got off the carousel, and Maxi's adorable daughter pointed at the children's rollercoaster.

"Sure, sweetie," Maxi said, beaming down at Leah.

"Can the pretty lady with the pink hair come too?" Leah asked, pointing at Reba.

Well, this child had her heart forever. "I don't think adults can fit on there, hon." The rollercoaster was a mini version of the real thing, and Reba was definitely not going to be allowed in those seats. "But we can play one of those games to win a stuffed animal after? And you can call me Auntie Reba if you want."

"Okay, Auntie Reba," Leah said as her grandmother took her hand to lead her over to the rollercoaster.

"You're raising the sweetest child." It had to be said. Children tended to be honest, and Reba would take any compliment she got from a tiny human.

"Thanks." Maxi smiled as she looked over to where Leah and Ms. King were waiting in the line to go on the ride. "She used to call Cherisse the pretty cake lady before she and Keiran were a thing. Now it's Auntie Cherry."

"Too cute."

It was also funny that both Leah and Reba were unexpectedly dressed alike, sort of. Leah wore a long denim jumper over a pink t-shirt. Reba had chosen a short pink jumper that showed a lot of thigh but covered her ass—it was a family outing, after all—thrown over a white crop top. Her jumper had tiny rainbows on the back pockets. She'd finished off the whole look with her rainbow Converse sneakers.

Devon hadn't said a word about what she was wearing, which meant he had *thoughts* about it. She knew enough about him now to know when he was saying a lot by not saying anything. That quiet, searching gaze of his spoke volumes. She'd changed out her usual simple nose ring for a tiny heart-shaped stud.

She looked cute. That was never in question. The real mystery was whether he would acknowledge it at all. Probably not with his family around.

"I wonder how that's going?" Maxi interrupted, pointing to a spot a little way off from the bumper cars.

The crowd had died down some since most of the people who had been waiting were now happily ramming into each other's cars. She could see Devon and Jeremy clearly now. Devon's body language was sending all sorts of 'I don't want to do this' messages. He kept folding and unfolding his arms and fidgeting. But they kept up their conversation, Jeremy nodding along to whatever Devon was saying.

"No one's tussling on the ground, so that's something."

"My brother doesn't really do physical altercations. He

doesn't need to. He just gives you this look. Makes you question your whole existence."

"Oh, really? I'd like to see that. Bet he looks so hot and intimidating." Maxi's brow raised, and Reba considered retracting, but that would create more questions. She shrugged instead. "Your brother *is* hot. I'm not tryna make this awkward, but facts are facts."

Maxi laughed. "Reba, I'm used to you just saying whatever by now, so it's fine. But mummy *did* tell me you were over there this morning. With him. Baking?"

"That's exactly what happened. Baking." And so much more, but talking about having sex with her brother would be weird, even for Reba. "Is there something you're trying to ask me, though? Because I feel like you are."

Maxi pursed her lip. "Well, I mean, you do look kind of cute together. Just saying."

"It's a working relationship," she echoed Devon's words. "Now, if you wanna talk about the relationship you and Remi have, which is *not* all business."

"I don't...um...we talk? So we're sort of friends now? That's...yeah. Friends." Maxi fumbled out.

Reba patted her shoulder. "Girl, that was weak as hell."

Maxi covered her face and shook her head before looking back at Reba. "It's complicated. That's all I'm willing to say at the moment."

"Just fuck and have fun."

"That's your life motto?"

"Eh..." She rocked her hand back and forth. "Loosely."

They both laughed, and mission success. Maxi might still have questions about her and Devon, but she was too flustered now to keep asking. Adorable.

"Hey, I see some cotton candy over there. Should we...?"

She didn't get to finish her sentence before Devon appeared, eyes focused on both of them.

"Ferris wheel?"

"What?" She blinked up at him.

"You wanted to go, didn't you?"

"Well, yes, but—" She looked over at Maxi, who was watching her brother like he had grown another head all of a sudden.

She waved them off. "Go ahead. I'm going to check on mummy and Leah."

He took her hand and led her over to the line.

"What are you doing? How'd the talk go?"

"We're doing what everyone else is. Going on rides. Great. He'll come to the party."

"Okaaaaaay." None of that explained why he was holding onto her hand for dear life as they were ushered forward. He only released her when they were led to a seat and buckled in. He didn't look at her, just stared straight ahead, that damn Adam's apple bobbing.

The wheel started moving, and Reba enjoyed that initial dip in her stomach. She loved peering down as they went higher and higher. The night sky was especially gorgeous, and everything looked so tiny from up here.

"Shit," Devon uttered.

She looked over at him, and shit indeed. He looked so tense, ready to jump off the ride, one hand gripping the railing, the other in his lap curled into a tight ball.

"You okay?"

"Yes. Fine."

"Hey." She tapped his arm. "Look at me a sec."

He didn't move. "I said I'm fine."

"Devon King, you better look at me right now."

"Or what?" he asked, gaze still locked forward, hand still tightly furled in his lap.

"Ferris wheels are pretty romantic spots, you know." When in doubt, flirt it out.

She didn't know what was up with him when he had practically dragged her onto the ride—had actually held her hand in public for everyone to see, just as she had finished telling Maxi their relationship was all about business—but she would suss out the problem. She dropped her hand to his thigh, squeezed lightly. "Ever had a handjob on a ride?"

His head jerked over to her at last, and *whoa*, alright, that explained it. His dark gaze looked a little wild, too wide, a hint of panic reflected there. He was trying to hide that shit, but his body was giving him away.

"Why in the world did you come up here if you're afraid?" she asked, a touch curious and exasperated.

"I'm not. I just have a healthy distrust of this." He waved his hands around just as the wheel gave a small lurch. "Fuck." His hand gripped onto hers that was still on his thigh. "I wasn't thinking. Just saw you and Maxi talking and..."

Ah, so things were sliding into place now. He'd rather go on something he considered a death trap than face the possibility that Reba might blurt something out to his sister.

"Are you telling me you came on this thing, which you hate, just so Maxi and I wouldn't talk?"

"I'm sure my mother mentioned everything to her already."

"Yes, we spoke about that briefly."

"What else?" He started kneading her hand gently. Did he realise he was doing that?

"Nothing much, really. I didn't ask, but Remi probably also told her about seeing us at that exhibit. Maxi said we look cute together."

He frowned. "I like to keep my personal stuff private."

"And it still is. I didn't tell your sis that we had sex. You rushing up and holding my hand like that might raise some questions, though."

"But what about your friends?"

"Not yet." Trina would be especially thrilled to hear that sex had happened, even though she had bet against Reba being able to charm Devon. Reba wasn't counting the sex as part of this. It would feel squicky.

"I don't like this. This is what I wanted to avoid."

"What *do* you like, Devon? Except that thing I do with my tongue," she smirked. He wasn't as relaxed as she was, but he had loosened up some since she'd distracted him from where they were.

He peered down as the wheel kept moving. "This is really fucking high up. How can you enjoy any of it?"

"It's a thrill. Haven't you ever just wanted to do something that has your heart screaming a little? And look how pretty it is from up here." She gestured around, trying to get him to look anywhere but down.

"It's..." He looked around. "This was a mistake."

"I need to take a pic." She slowly reached for her phone with her free hand, sliding it out from the small crossbody bag she had strapped across her body, and took a quick photo of herself. She could have released her other hand to take a proper photo, but Devon seemed to be deriving some sort of calm from her touch.

"I got you, okay?" she told him when she'd finished, giving his hand a squeeze to reassure him.

"You don't if this wheel unhinges from the bolts and takes on a life of its own."

She poked his side. "What am I gonna do with you, hmm? The wheel's going nowhere."

The wheel chose that exact moment to stop, to let the first set of people off, she presumed. Devon's entire body locked up. She felt it in the flex of his hand. They were still a couple of seats up from the ground, which meant the moving and stopping was going to happen a few more times before it was their turn to hop off.

She reached out to grab his chin and turn his face her way. "We're almost there. Talk to me. You haven't told me how cute I look tonight."

"I don't need to tell you something you're already aware of." He reached up to remove her hand from his chin. His other hand stayed clutching hers. "But if you need the words..."

"I do. I like hearing it."

"This whole look is cute. And yet, somehow sexy at the same time? I don't know how you do that. It drives me out of my mind."

Well, well. She leaned in as much as she could, given the small space of the seat. "Good. You should be on your toes a couple times in your life. Gets the heart pumping. What else? Tell me more."

His eyes dropped down to her mouth. "My heart's already getting a workout from this damn contraption. What's that colour called?"

"Heart Breaker."

"Yeah, I can see how that's fitting."

"Why? Do you think I'll break your heart?"

"Have to have one to break."

"Please," she scoffed. "You're a softie who writes love letters."

He closed his eyes, lightly thunking his head back against the seat. "It's cruel to use that against me while up here."

"Hey, I'm just stating a fact. Not making fun, and *you* chose to come on this."

"I wasn't thinking clearly." He opened his eyes, turned his head in her direction. "This isn't how I plan to die."

"If your last sight gets to be my face, you'll go a lucky man. Me being the last person you had sex with? Super bonus."

That made his lips twitch, and Reba felt something warm bloom in her chest. A sense of accomplishment, probably. She was definitely winning at this game big time.

"You probably think I sound like a big baby, complaining about a ride even kids get on easily." The tiny smile he'd allowed slipped away.

"Uh-uh, don't put words in my mouth at all. I'm thinking no such thing. You think I don't get afraid too?"

"What are you afraid of, then?"

Reba was okay being open about most things, but the first things on the tip of her tongue would ruin the mood.

That people will never take me seriously.

That no one will want me for anything other than a good time.

Who am I without all this colour to distract?

Eww, okay, no. Saying any of that didn't sound cute or fun.

"Monochrome," she replied flippantly.

"Taking shots at a man's décor while he's trapped on a wheel of hell. Nice." Teasing. He was actually teasing her in his own way. It also didn't go unnoticed that he was looking at her lips again.

Heart Breaker was a fave because it had some serious staying power. She could fully ravage Devon in this seat, and the lipstick would go nowhere. She wondered if he wanted to test that theory? He did enjoy logic-ing things to death. She could make it fun, at least.

The wheel started up again, and he kept staring at her. She flicked her tongue out, licking her bottom lip. His eyes followed the motion. The next time they stopped, she took matters into her own hands, literally, releasing his hand so she could cup his cheeks before leaning in, giving him time to object. They weren't as high up as before; someone on the ground might be able to identify them. He didn't remove her hand this time, so she planted a soft kiss on his mouth.

He wrapped his hand in her ponytail as if trying to anchor himself. She sipped at his lips, enjoying the tentative flick of his tongue against hers.

"We're almost at the bottom," she warned against his mouth.

"Right, my family could see. Anyone could see." He didn't pull back. Did he expect *her* to be the voice of reason? He should know her better than that by now.

"They might already have. I'll just tell them I was trying to calm you down."

His hand was still wrapped around her hair, face still close to hers as their breaths mingled. She patted his chest. "Win me something from one of those stalls. Please," she added as their seat got to the bottom.

"We'll see." He gave her hand one last squeeze as the attendant came over to help them out, and God, if they weren't where they were, Reba would have dragged him to her and kissed him like she truly wanted to. Hard and dirty.

It didn't get easier to not think about hauling Devon off into some dark corner when he did exactly what she wanted—win her a huge plush unicorn. He hadn't taken his intense gaze off any of the clowns he had to shoot down. Reba had stood by watching, barely hanging on to her composure by a thread. There was just something so attractive about his focus and determination.

She was extremely horny for his competence. She couldn't help her squeal when he got them all and pointed at the unicorn after he'd asked her which one she wanted.

"It suits you," he told her as she pressed her face into the soft fabric.

His friend Jeremy, who she'd been introduced to briefly after they'd come off the Ferris wheel, had accompanied them to the stalls to try his hand at winning as well. He released a small snort, sharing a loaded look with Devon. Now, what was that about? The men didn't enlighten her.

Had he shared what they'd done with Jeremy? That seemed unlikely, given how he'd reacted to her merely chatting with Maxi. He and Jeremy had just gotten back on a good footing. That friendship was shaky as shit. He wouldn't have told Jeremy, and yet that sly grin said something was definitely up.

Mindful of his family next to them as they tried to play one of the games to win some toys, she kept her tone casual as she asked, "Why, cuz I'm a unicorn?"

"You very well might be."

She had so many questions to that. Did he mean because he'd never met anyone like her? Or was he referring to how she affected him? Or both? She needed the words, even though, as she'd told Maxi, it was all just about business. She couldn't help her curiosity, wanted to know what made a man like him tick. She knew she was definitely one of the things, given everything that had gone down last night, but there was so much that was still a mystery.

"Devon likes winning," Jeremy said, mouth curved up in a small smile. "As long as I've known this guy, he refuses to lose at anything, but like I also told him, it's okay to fail sometimes." He gestured over to his wife and children. "I failed at resisting her so many times. And I'm glad for that."

Reba liked this guy. He was obviously teasing Devon, who rolled his eyes and looked at another game. "Do you want another one?"

She shook her unicorn. "I'm good for now." She tugged on Devon's arm. "But before you go off to win again, I need to show you something I saw over there. Something I think you'll like."

She mustered up as much wide-eyed innocence as she could and gestured for him to follow her. She caught Jeremy's grin and barely resisted winking back at him. The other Kings were so busy trying to win more games they didn't notice. Devon, none the wiser, followed her all the way behind one of the tents.

"What do you want to show me?"

She hooked her arm around the unicorn, securing it at her side and ensuring it was out of her way. She hooked her other arm around Devon's neck and brought him down so she could really see his reaction.

"You didn't really bring me over here for this," he said in disbelief.

"Mmm, yes." She sucked on his bottom lip, basking in the way he closed his eyes and wrapped his arm around her waist despite his exasperated sigh. He could act all put off about this as much as he wanted, but he had to be as wound up as she was. "I need to thank you properly for my gift."

"The gift you told me to win for you."

"Grateful all the same. I'll be quick. Promise."

He tugged her closer, embracing the unicorn too, which made her giggle even as he tasted her, angling his head to slant his mouth over hers.

"I should have worn a jumper dress instead," she murmured against him, rubbing her thighs together.

His hand dipped into the open sides of her jumper and rubbed at her exposed skin. At least she'd had the foresight to wear a crop top. It was a little chilly back here without the body heat from the crowd, but she didn't mind. Devon was warming her right up as their tongues tangled, mimicking what she wished they could do. He tasted tangy like the tamarind ball he had munched on earlier. It mingled with the sugary aftertaste from the cotton candy she'd been sharing with Leah and Maxi. Spun sugar and tamarind would be an unusual taste otherwise, but it didn't matter now, not when the wet heat of him was driving her completely wild.

His hand slipped up her waist and cupped her breast through her top. He slowly broke the kiss but didn't stop touching her, looking down into her face with eyes ablaze. "We should get back."

She sighed as her nipple plumped up beneath his touch. "I guess." She rubbed her thumb over his bottom lip. "Lucky for you, Heart Breaker doesn't transfer. To be continued."

They returned as casually as they'd left, Maxi, Leah, and his mother none the wiser about their exit. They were still busy cheering each other on as Maxi tried to knock over all the bottles.

"Saw the thing you needed to see?" Jeremy asked.

"Yes." Devon left it at that, and Reba didn't bother to say a word.

Jeremy's gummy smile said enough for all of them. Oh yeah, this guy was a keeper. She hoped Devon didn't screw up their tentative friendship again. She wouldn't mind hanging out with him another time. He seemed cool. Might be useful for some embarrassing stories about Devon when he was younger. She wondered how he and Devon had become friends in the first place.

Her phone buzzed with a message from the group chat. Trina had claimed she would drop by at some point to hang out. Ayo was busy with some family thing.

> **Trina:** *I here girl, where you???*
> **Reba:** *over by the stall games. I'm the cutie in pink* 😊
> **Trina:** *like that's helpful. What tall and sexy wearing? My hot guy radar is better* 👀
> **Reba:** *you know what? you a whole mess yes. I'm holding a big ass unicorn. You can't miss me.*
> **Trina:** *so why you can't tell me what he wearing???*
> **Reba:** *cuz it's regular jeans and a t-shirt. My hair is pink. I'm dressed in pink. I have a giant unicorn. I'm a walking neon sign basically.*

There was nothing regular about Devon's jeans. Not when they fit his legs and ass like that. The t-shirt was a little snug too. Trina hadn't lied. She could find a specific hot man in a crowd, but Reba was suddenly antsy about Trina joining the fray.

She could tell Trina she had basically already won, but she was hesitant for some reason. Which didn't make sense, considering she loved winning.

Her phone buzzed with another message.

Trina: *I see that cute ass so I found you. And I don't mean yours. Damn what regular about them jeans??? If I didn't have a man...*

Reba rolled her eyes as Trina strolled up. Trina wasn't getting rid of Aaron anytime soon. Those two couldn't seem to quit each other, even through all their ups and downs.

"Told you my radar never fails."

This time. she hoped her friend's "I know you had sex" senses were shorted out because she didn't want the mood to turn awkward. Teasing Devon had become her favourite pastime, but if all went well, maybe she could convince Devon to take her back to his place to help ease her little horny problem. She didn't need Trina ruining her potential sexy plans. She loved her, but tact wasn't something Trina understood or gave a damn about.

If Devon thought Reba just said whatever she thought, then he could be in for a rude awakening with Trina, who was currently blatantly checking Devon's ass out. Reba had felt that ass with her bare hands, so she got it, but damn, Trina needed to tone it down.

Reba hooked her arm, drawing Trina to stand in front of the men. Yeah, she needed Trina to semi-behave so she could get that dick later.

Priorities and all that.

CHAPTER TWENTY
DEVON

THE COOKIES IN HIS HANDS FELT LIKE A BRIGHT BEACON TELLING everyone to look directly at him as he walked into the office at his usual time on Monday. Even though he had them in a nondescript brown handle bag, he was sure everyone would know something was off.

Devon didn't usually break patterns, was strict about certain things. He came in before eight, wore his usual suit, came in with his leather bag, and didn't usually have anything extra on him. In his mind, Corinne was eyeing that bag with curiosity when she called out her typical cheerful, "Morning!"

But that was just his sleep-deprived brain messing with him. No one was looking at him funny as he made his way to the kitchen to quietly drop the cookies off. The kitchen was thankfully empty, but he needed to move quickly. He removed the simple plastic container from the bag. Reba hadn't had time to fancy it up as she'd wanted to. Fine by him—no glitter to get on his hands.

The note he'd placed on top was self-explanatory:

BUTTER COOKIES. PLEASE TAKE ONE.

He would silently listen out for comments from his co-workers later. A huge yawn escaped as he pondered if to leave the cookies near the fridge. Most people liked to put their lunch in there and would easily see the container when they came in.

He'd hoped his cold shower would make him a bit more alert this morning, but that didn't seem to be the case. He'd gotten home after the amusement park with grand plans to shower and go right to bed. Instead, he'd found himself thoroughly cleaning out the guest room since he hadn't managed it after the baking session or before he needed to leave to meet his family and Reba.

He couldn't allow another moment to go by without ridding the room of her scent and presence somehow. She'd wanted to come home with him after to finish what they'd started behind that tent. Her intentions had been quite clear. The heated looks. The accidental, seemingly casual touches. The not at all subtle emojis he'd discovered when he'd checked his phone while waiting at the food stall. The amount of tongue emojis followed by water droplets and eggplants were excessive and explicit. But he'd needed to clear his head, had acted as if her message had gotten lost in translation.

Her friend Trina had also been watching like a hawk, narrowed eyes moving between them, curious and specula-tive. So Reba had been honest. She hadn't told her friends about the sex because this woman had been on high alert trying to decode whatever was going on between them.

Going home alone had seemed like the best idea. Except, right then—and now, if he was being honest—his mind had been foggy with thoughts of Reba.

He'd even found her panties under the bed in a crumpled heap, but not her shorts, the thing a goddamn reminder of everything they had done on that bed. Clearly, Reba had missed it in her haste to leave. He'd texted her right away about it even though it had been late. She hadn't replied until much later this morning.

> **Devon:** *I found your underwear under the bed.*
> **Reba:** *oh. Morning* 😊 *Must have missed that. They're my lucky pair. I'll let you know when I can come get them* 😴
> **Devon:** *Ok*

Short and to the point. He refused to think about her lying in her bed, looking all soft and sexy as she replied to him. He'd tossed his phone on the bed and begun his morning routine—which now included quickly washing her underwear and letting it dry.

If he was smart, he would meet her in a public place to make the exchange. He didn't think even Reba would try to have sex with him atop a café table in the middle of the day. But the thought of handing over her underwear in a space like that had him overthinking all the potential awkward possibilities. Reba, being her unpredictable self, could pull the thing out from the totally normal bag he would put it in and start waving it around. He could at least control and minimise what would happen in the safety of his own home.

"Are those cookies?"

The query startled him. Devon stepped away from the counter. "Looks like it."

Sharlene, one of the other Project Managers' interns,

came over to peer into the container, lunch bowl in hand. "Huh, no name on it."

"Guess it's for anyone to take. There's a note." Devon walked out of the kitchen before she could start asking him more questions.

His plan was to quietly smuggle in some pieces of the marble cake tomorrow. It meant he'd have to be earlier than Sharlene so she wouldn't find him near it again. It wouldn't take much for her to wonder if he had baked the treats. He was supposed to be incognito with this endeavour.

The encounter made him wonder if he should abandon the cake drop-off. It had turned out fine after his initial stumbles. Reba had given him a gold star sticker and everything. That she had suddenly pulled the sticker pack out of her bag, peeled one off, and planted it on his chest had surprised him. She'd taken too long rubbing the damn sticker in place, claiming she was simply ensuring that it stayed on. Her smirk had suggested otherwise.

He'd been trying to get her to stay before his mother had come along but had soon realised this thing pulsing through his veins urging him to fuck her in his kitchen was not conducive to having a peaceful time, so he hadn't pushed it further. If he gave Reba an inch, she would take a whole dirty mile.

Back at his desk, he pulled up the proposal they would be showing the client next week, the first week in September. The resort and spa they were pitching would be in line with the eco-friendly slant the client was set on. The proposal took the location into consideration, ensuring that the building would work in conjunction with the nature that surrounded it. Like the perfect Sanctuary. In fact, that was the project code name Devon had come up with.

He was excited about this one and might have been putting in more hours than was feasible to come up with the best presentation. The resort would include all the luxuries guests could expect from such a place with the calming effects of the flora and fauna. The structure would fully look like it had sprung up right in the midst of the greenery itself. At least that was Devon's plan. Now, if only he could sort out this ridiculous situation with Vic. They were so close to making this perfect.

With Reba in his space, he hadn't been able to focus on his approach there. It would be awkward, and Devon didn't want to deal with this shit.

Not now when he was getting random flashes of smooth brown skin and Reba's voice in his ear as she...

Okay, *no*. He could not do this here.

He might not want to deal with Vic, but he had to set up a meeting regardless. Vic's personal shit couldn't jeopardise this project. Devon had wanted to replace him immediately, but he had to at least talk to the man since he had been working on this from the beginning. Handing it over to someone else to take over at this late stage didn't sit right with him.

He sent off an email letting Vic know they needed to meet ASAP. This was the first step, and Dax would be looking at how he dealt with the situation. He was the Project Lead, after all. Even if he needed to liaise with HR on this, he couldn't ignore it outright.

His phone buzzed as he was going over the proposed design they had so far.

Keiran: *So what's this I hear about you taking baking lessons??? Is this why you wanted to talk to Cherisse before we left???*

Devon sighed. Keiran resurfacing from his combined work/vacation mode was not what he needed right now. Maxi had obviously told him. He didn't bother to respond, leaving Keiran on read.

His phone buzzed again, and he considered tossing it in his drawer, but he knew some of his co-workers who were working on other projects off-site primarily used What-sApp to communicate, which meant he couldn't completely ignore his phone.

It wasn't the work chat. It was Keiran, *again*. He'd sent a photo this time.

Keiran: *this you bro???? wut really going on here??*

Younger siblings were so damn annoying.

The photo was taken from last night at the park. Devon hadn't willingly posed for any, but Maxi had still caught him in one, in the background of her selfie. Hell, there were probably more. He was just standing there in the back, not looking at the camera at all. It was way worse than that. He was looking at Reba, and...ugh, was he actually smiling? In the shot, she was looking up at him with a smirk. She had probably been saying something outrageous at the time. Who the hell knew? He couldn't recall.

Parts of last night were a blur, while others were so vividly clear in his head. He had actually ridden a Ferris wheel. Willingly. Reba hadn't made fun of him when she'd realised he'd rather be anywhere else. In fact, she had tried to soothe him in her own way. Her way being flirting, but he'd appreciated it. He should have probably told her so.

He stared at the photo again. Seriously, what had she been saying to make him smile like that?

Devon: *I went to have a chat with Jeremy.*
Keiran: *Your friend Jeremy who you been blanking for months now? At an amusement park? That's weird but ok, but I not talking 'bout that tho. Are you smiling???? At Reba?*

He'd attached a gif that looked like a shocked Pikachu.

Keiran: *this whole thing is...weird. Maxi said Reba's helping with whatever this baking thing is but* 🙂

He wondered if it was too late to trade in his siblings for something that was of more use to him. Like a lifetime supply of frequent flier miles or something. He could travel to the countries on his bucket list, see their innovative buildings. Who needed a brother and sister anyways? Being an only child sounded great.

Devon: *I do smile. Sometimes*
Keiran: *Not like that.*
Devon: *Is there a purpose to this? I'm working.*
Keiran: *me too actually. Just for a bit cuz Cherisse's already giving me the look lol. But seriously I'm just playing with you.*
Keiran: *Unless there's something you wanna talk about. I'm a good listener. I like Reba. She's cool. Fun. All the things you aren't. if some of that rubs off on you well...*
Devon: *No thanks.*
Keiran: *fine. be boring. on another note. This house-warming thing? I'm invited or what?*
Devon: *Are you even going to be here? I thought you weren't.*

Keiran: *well we get in that same afternoon actually. Might be tired or might decide to storm your big bashment :P but who doing the music? Can't have the people listening to a stale setlist.*
Devon: *There's no bashment. It's really mummy's party so do what you want. I don't know details. She and Reba are planning it.*

He didn't intend to get involved. Once his mother ensured his house was clean after, he didn't care if Keiran wanted to show up. He planned to shut himself in his bedroom as much as he could. He was still fixing up the space he would use as his office, so he couldn't actually work in it yet.

He'd make a brief appearance, then hopefully, everyone would be too caught up in the party vibes to wonder where he'd gone off to. At least that was his plan. Maxi and Keiran would try to corner him and ask questions. He just wanted everyone to stay out of his goddamn business, so the less visible he made himself on Saturday, the better.

He hadn't lied when he'd said Reba was like a unicorn. He was out of his element here. He didn't know what any of this was. Could barely articulate it to himself, far less to anyone else. It wasn't that he couldn't take picong from his family, he just didn't want his personal business out there.

And things with Reba were very personal now. He wasn't sure where they should go from here. She seemed quite fine continuing as they'd been, with a side of steamy sex thrown in.

He...wasn't so sure. Another thing throwing him off. Yes, it had been two years since he had been intimate with a woman, but it didn't make sense that Reba was the first to break his drought. They didn't have a single thing in common.

His brain was forcing him to try to make sense of this again. She had told him that wouldn't work—he couldn't dissect her. But her effect on him wasn't something he could just let happen without at least trying to pick it apart.

He'd told her about that list he had, and she was right. She didn't fit a single one of the things he was looking for in a partner. Whatever was going on here was truly baffling.

Keiran: oh. She's planning it with mummy? How interesting...

He ignored Keiran's reply and went back to the presentation. At least this was something he could control. Putting in the work, ensuring the best proposal for them to win the bid—even with Vic's mess trying to derail the entire thing. That wouldn't happen on his watch.

Lunch rolled around, and instead of pushing through on his work, he called Jeremy. He'd left his desk and gone up to the roof. His office felt suffocating all of a sudden. He'd gotten a good deal done, yet thoughts of *her* kept creeping in. He needed air.

The talk with Jeremy at the amusement park had been a bit stilted at first, but Devon had been honest about his fuck-up. Jeremy had always been a straight talker, so making excuses wasn't going to fly with him. He had screwed up their friendship, and even though he'd acted as if he didn't need anyone because his work came first, he'd missed the guy.

The man knew him better than anyone. Devon didn't like to overshare in general, but Jeremy was a good listener the few rare times he did open up. He'd been there when his relationship with Monica had imploded, had tried to talk Devon through what had gone wrong. Jeremy had also seen The Reba Effect in full action and had figured something was amiss. He didn't ask outright, and Devon hadn't offered any details. He hadn't shot down any of Jeremy's questioning looks, though—just ignored them while Reba and her friend Trina had been chatty.

"I'm in trouble, I think," Devon said the minute Jeremy answered.

"Does trouble have pink hair and the devil's grin?" Jeremy's teasing tone was as annoying as he remembered.

He looked out at the city down below. The surrounding buildings ranged from older structures that could use some sprucing up to food places that offered various options to the workforce that occupied offices, such as the one that housed Dax Designs. A variety of architecture that spoke of a mixing of the past with more modern looks.

"Yes," he replied.

"I knew it. You didn't want to say anything, but I've never seen you like that, man."

Devon walked over to the small garden someone had set up in a corner of the roof, a little way off from the tables and chairs where people who worked in the building liked to come for lunch. He couldn't identify the flowers that grew out here, but an effort had been made to add some colour to the roof. When he had first started at the company, the space had been simple, with a few tables and chairs for anyone who needed a breather away from the cold offices. Now it had been transformed into a more relaxed spot.

Not that he came up here a lot to eat lunch. He was fine doing so by his desk before diving back into work.

"Like how?"

"That woman's got you under her spell. You really went on a Ferris wheel? I'm not gonna lie, I'm surprised. She's not your usual type at all, but I approve."

Why did everyone seem to think he and Reba would be good together? Sex was one thing—he couldn't deny their chemistry there—but they were so different. "You don't even know her."

"Maybe, but any woman that's got you a mess like this gets a thumbs up from me."

"I'm not a mess."

"It's your version of a mess, but a mess all the same," Jeremy pointed out.

"I'm rethinking this newly reformed friendship," he deadpanned.

Jeremy laughed. "*You* called me."

Yes, he had. "She doesn't fit anything on my list. I haven't tried the risk analysis yet, but..."

"Not that damn list again. Bro, just delete that thing. And these damn analysis spreadsheets? They might work for career goals and whatnot, but with people? It can get tricky and messy real fast. Looking for certain things in a partner is fine, but you need to be open to the possibility of meeting someone that just rings your bell, even if they're not what you were looking for. Look at me and Darcelle."

"Darcy's too good for you." Jeremy's wife was almost as tall as the both of them and a total sweetheart who could still kick anyone's ass if they crossed her.

Devon had witnessed Jeremy falling hard. It had been baffling yet hilarious at the time.

"Yeah, you don't think I know that? It's why I'm grateful every day she chose me."

Devon looked back out at the hills around the capital

city of Port of Spain. "I just want to stop this distraction. It can't be that hard. Once this baking thing is over…"

"You are so hopeless, I swear. Forget the list. Just enjoy whatever this is."

He couldn't just do away with his system entirely. His lists were a big part of his life. For Jeremy to tell him to discard this specific one? He didn't know. Monica had gotten pissed off at the very existence of it, while Reba had been curious.

"You have this imaginary supposedly perfect woman built up in your mind, based on a past that doesn't even exist anymore. You realise that, right?"

The question threw him. Was that what he'd been doing? True, the woman who had been the mould for the list criteria wasn't in his life anymore. Hadn't been for years. She'd suddenly chosen a path that didn't make it easy for them to continue a relationship.

"You need to look back on that time with clear eyes. Perfect doesn't exist, and honestly, you two weren't even all that suited."

"What do you mean?" He and Joya had been the perfect couple. No fights or disagreements. Their goals had been aligned—well, until she had gotten an opportunity she couldn't pass up that took her outside of the Caribbean.

"You were too alike."

"Yes, that was the good thing about it."

Jeremy laughed. "No, man. It wasn't. You were both so focused on everything being fine and perfect with no room for flaws that you put unnecessary pressure on each other. Why do you think she was glad to get that opportunity in Italy or wherever she went?"

"Spain," he corrected automatically. "That's not true. We were good together."

"Nah, she held back a lot. Not wanting to shake things up, cause drama or whatever."

Joya had looked thrilled about the internship she'd gotten. In fact, he hadn't even known she'd applied for it, her reason being if she hadn't gotten it, she didn't want to have everyone around feel disappointed too. But thinking back on it now, he wasn't so sure if she'd been a hundred percent honest with him about that. Had she felt like she couldn't be?

"Did she say something to you?" Devon asked.

"Not in so many words, but if you really listened, it had been heavily implied."

"Well, shit."

"Haven't I been saying I'm the smarter one for years? You can keep being the pretty one."

Jeremy had been running with that joke since they'd become friends. It was ridiculous, but Devon let him be.

"Listen, I'll let you go because I know that analytical brain of yours is working overtime with this newfound insight. You're right, I don't know Reba, but what I do know is you shouldn't overthink this to death, okay?"

"I'll try." It was the best he could do.

"I'll leave you with this one bit of advice. Shaking things up isn't all bad. The drama you're so afraid of dealing with might actually do you some good. I'm off."

He stayed on the roof a few minutes after Jeremy's call. He had always wondered why Jeremy hadn't seemed so keen on him and Joya. He'd simply chalked it up to his friend not wanting to get heavily involved in his relationship.

He'd thought they'd been well-suited, but had he simply been imposing his ideal on their entire relationship? That was a sobering thought. He had tried to keep in touch with her when she'd left, but after some time, they'd drifted apart. Then there was Monica, who he'd thought wanted the same things as him.

She'd basically screamed in his face about his list. He cringed at the memory. He'd thought that had been a clear sign that she wasn't truly for him, but was Jeremy right?

Something to actually give some thought to, but not now. No matter what Jeremy said, he had to get his work done before delving deeply into analysing anything else.

His life was shaken up enough by a devil with pink hair.

CHAPTER TWENTY-ONE
REBA

[Monday, 2:35 p.m.]

Reba: hey can I come for my stuff later? 😊
Devon: Not a good time. Sorry
Reba: hmm so when then? During the party on Saturday?

[Monday, 5:00 p.m.]

Reba: helloooo you leaving me on read???
Devon: Not during the party. That wouldn't be ideal.
Reba: why not?

[Tuesday, 8:15 a.m.]

Reba: Devon King, you left me on read again. Don't forget I know where you live...

[Wednesday, 7:45 a.m.]

Reba: *ok I got side tracked with something so my panties when? It's my lucky pair. As you can see I did get lucky in them so...*

[Wednesday, 5:00 p.m.]

Reba: *now you're just being rude. are you still at your office?*
Devon: *Yes*
Reba: *hmm so you do remember how to type? Alright, ok. You brought this on yourself...*

THE BUILDING THAT HOUSED DAX DESIGNS STILL HUMMED WITH life when she walked in, takeout boxes in hand. Five-thirty wasn't that late for everyone to be cleared out yet, and it *was* still light out. The guard was more than happy to direct her to Devon's floor again, even though she remembered where she was going. Even the receptionist seemed to recognise her when she got up to his floor. Reba supposed it was the pink hair that made her unforgettable.

Today, she had it worn in a plait wound around her head like a crown. Queen mode had been activated the moment she realised that Devon was ignoring her. It was best to take matters into her own hands.

"He still busy? I brought him some dinner," she told the smiling woman.

"Well, thank God cuz I don't think he's left that office in hours."

As much as she'd prefer her presence to be a surprise,

the receptionist wouldn't just allow Reba to breeze right in. She told the bubbly woman her name and waited as she called.

"Yes, a Ms. Johnson is here to see you. She came to drop something off? Okay, yes, fine." She hung up, giving Reba a sheepish smile. "He doesn't seem like he wants to be bothered, but he's fine if you just go in and drop off the food at least."

She had no intention of *just* dropping anything off, but she couldn't tell this smiling woman that. "Thanks."

She approached his office, knocked, and waited. He looked extremely flustered when he opened the door, tie loose, top button of his shirt undone, eyes narrowed as they swept over her.

"I don't like surprise visits to my office, as you already know." He looked down at the bag in her hand.

"Well, I hope you like Chinese. You've been ignoring me," she said, sashaying past him into his office. "But kind soul that I am, I brought food because I figured surely this man is probably wrapped up in his work and so weak from hunger that he simply didn't have the energy to reply to me."

She placed the food on a corner of his desk and turned to face him.

He approached her as if she were a wild animal that could strike any moment. It almost made her laugh. At least his instincts were spot-on. Devon was about to learn a simple lesson. He'd ignored her, which was slightly dangerous for him because it had forced her to go into full-on revenge mode, the best way she knew how. He liked her in dresses, so she had chosen tonight's carefully. White this time, it was long enough that it reached to her calves, but she'd left some of the buttons at the front undone, just enough that it would show a lot of thigh depending on how she was positioned. The capped sleeves cupped the rounded curves of her shoulders, leaving enough bare skin for him to drink in.

"I told you I was busy."

"Hmm, you said. I would think you'd be eager to return my underwear, but if you wanted my panties as a keepsake, all you had to do was say so. I would've brought another one just for you. You can't keep these."

His jaw clenched. She'd suspected after he hadn't given in to her obvious messages Sunday night that he would pull this, try to distance himself, which fine, she didn't want to impose on him totally. He had work, she got that, but the panties really were her lucky underwear. It wouldn't have taken much for him to have her swing by and collect them. She wouldn't have even pulled any of this if he hadn't done an about-turn and locked her off.

She executed a smooth jump up onto his desk, tugging her dress up so when she crossed her leg, he got an eyeful. Oh yeah, he'd received her message loud and clear.

His eyes went so round. "Shit, you're not..."

She shrugged. "Well, if you'd kept your promise and given me what's mine, we wouldn't be here with me bare-assed on your work desk."

She bounced her leg, her skirt settled high on her thighs. He didn't have to wonder for one second whether she was wearing anything under her dress because she had shown him very clearly that she wasn't.

"Okay, look, you can leave now. I'll give you what's yours."

"Yes, you will, but however will you make this up to me?"

"Reba." He stepped closer, clearly unsure of his next

move. "You can't expect me to just drop everything..." He sounded exasperated. Good.

She uncrossed one leg, pressing her shoe into his stomach, halting his movement. His hand reached down to grip her ankle like he couldn't help himself.

She pushed the tip of her foot into his shirt, and his grip on her ankle tightened. She wasn't wearing a bra with this dress either; her nipples were surely poking through the top. She didn't look away from him to confirm. All she wondered was whether Devon wanted to undo the rest of her buttons and bare her breasts to his hungry gaze.

He probably wouldn't do that here in his office, but she could fantasise about it.

"I can see you overthinking all the possible scenarios." She slowly dragged her foot down to his crotch, rubbing gently. "Maybe this'll help move those along. Just pick one. I'm sure I'll enjoy whatever you choose."

"Fucking kryptonite," he swore. "Devil in the fucking flesh."

"Yup. You might want to lock that door."

He didn't move. If he wanted to go bravely, it was fine by her; it heightened the excitement. He squeezed her ankle. "You can't always get what you want. Demanding shit on your terms."

"Who's demanding? You have something that belongs to me. I don't think it's wrong to come collect."

"You know damn well what you're doing. This game of yours...it's been a long fucking few workdays, okay?" He scrubbed his hand down his face.

He did look rumpled. His version of it, anyway. Still too put together in her mind. She could imagine he thought his facial hair was bordering on scruffy when it still looked perfectly coiffed to her. The right length to cause delicious friction along her skin.

"Sounds terrible. Truly. Wouldn't some food and a little fucking help?"

"God, you are just so..."

"Amazing? Beautiful? Fabulous?"

His hand glided up her calf to her thigh. "All of the above. That doesn't give you the right to just do whatever you want. Although, I appreciate the food. Haven't eaten really since breakfast."

She dropped her foot and spread her thighs. "You need to take better care of yourself, so eat." She didn't only mean the Chinese food. "Doesn't that feel nice?"

It felt great to her. Especially when his hand remained on her, squeezing her flesh, kneading at her skin.

She bit her lip as his hand pushed her skirt up. "Higher," she instructed. He moved up to where the crease of her leg met her pelvis. Oh, he'd definitely gone too far up. "Lower."

Lower would mean dipping into her wetness. She squirmed as his thumb brushed over her lips, her hips moving, begging for more. Deeper. He rubbed at her folds, not yet breaching her but close, so close.

Her back arched, and Reba was fully splayed on his desk. The picture they would make if someone walked in right now. Nothing they said could cover up what would be obvious, especially when he moved into the V of her legs, and she spread them wider. His erection was prominent, pushing against the material of his pants, and *God,* she was so wet. There was no doubt she'd leave behind a spot on the front of his pants if she just rubbed up against him. But fuck if she cared. He nudged at her bare flesh, and she pushed forward, tried to ride him through the fabric.

"Yes, like that," she moaned out, not a care for decorum.

Why should she give a damn? This wasn't her office, and it wasn't her co-workers who could catch them like this.

He leaned down, mouth to her ear. "Keep your voice down."

"You're well aware how loud I can be. This *is* me keeping it down." She ground against his fingers while trying to tug him closer with her leg. Devon groaned in response. "I want to feel more of you. Take off your pants."

"No."

"But why?" she whined. Even now, he was resisting her? She was supposed to be getting her way, but he wasn't cooperating.

He pulled back and rubbed his fingers against her again, slowly slipping one inside, pumping in and out. "You'll take it the way I give it to you, and you'll love it." He pressed another finger into her, and she groaned, fucking herself on his fingers.

Okay, maybe having it exactly her way wasn't important in this moment. She was out here getting fingerfucked on Devon's desk, so she'd still won, hadn't she? Proved her point that he could try to ignore her all he wanted, but it wouldn't be a lasting occurrence.

It wasn't long before Reba was coming apart around his fingers. He removed them, trailing his wet fingers across her lips. He didn't have to say a word. She opened for him and sucked them inside. She swirled her tongue, eyes fixed on him, as her hands moved down to the front of his pants. She grasped him through the fabric, never letting up on the suction on his fingers.

His expression bordered on pain, eyes scrunched as she enjoyed the shape and feel of him in her hand. "Okay, enough." He pulled away from her, fingers slipping out of her mouth, not allowing her to get him off.

She could pout about it some more, but if he wanted to deny himself, then he would be the one to suffer. "Fine. If you like to torture yourself." She slid off his desk.

He had mentioned he didn't usually bring a change of clothes, so coming in his pants might not be the best idea. He took several long inhales before moving around his desk to sit in his chair, using the wipes on his desk to clean his fingers, eyes dazed as if he couldn't believe he'd allowed himself to do that.

She slid into the chair across from him. "Feel better?"

"No."

"That's because you won't let me ride you in that nice chair of yours."

"I had to talk to a team member about not letting his private shit interfere with work," he said suddenly. "I hated every minute of it. After the meeting, he looked me dead in the eye and said, 'She's worth every bit of this shit.'" He shook his head. "I don't get it. How could jeopardising your career be worth any of that?"

He'd gone from fingerbanging her to talking about work. Reba should feel some kind of way, but he'd never really spoken about his job with her. Not like this. Maybe it was his way of calming that erection down. She didn't know, but she listened. "Everyone has different priorities."

"No, he's being selfish. His actions are affecting the project and the team as a whole. I don't care what you do in your private life, but there's got to be a line somewhere."

"So that's what's been keeping you busy?"

"Yes. While trying to ensure our presentation gets done. We meet with the client next week."

"I don't care that you're busy. Well, I still maintain you need a better work/play balance because right now, you've got none, but you didn't have to give me a whole brush-off. Maybe I *was* a little hasty in my actions," she muttered.

"Really? You're admitting that?" He leaned forward, fingers steepled. "Do you understand now why waking up to you gone felt the same way? Like a brush-off?"

Not this again. And why the hell was she admitting to not thinking things through before she acted? It was the exact thing her parents had been harping on about for years. She ignored them because she didn't think her spontaneous nature was some fatal flaw. The orgasm had scrambled her brain, apparently. She was talking nonsense.

"Forget I said that."

"Oh, no. No way in hell am I letting this slide."

"You just fingerfucked my brains out. I can't be held accountable for anything I say in this current moment."

His smug grin was not what she needed right now. This wasn't how this was supposed to go. He reached for the takeout container, opening one to take a sniff. The delicious scent of Chinese-style chicken and fried rice filled the office.

"Where'd you get the food?"

"Valpark Chinese Restaurant."

"Good choice. We can eat now if you like."

She folded her arms. Orgasm or not, she decided to not let him off the hook after all. "You didn't even want me here, to begin with. What are you up to?"

"Nothing. You barged in here. May as well keep me company."

"*You* said we would leave so I could get my panties," she pointed out.

"I can't be held responsible for what I say when you walk in here in that dress."

Oh, he thought he was so cute. "Touché, but grab the

food and let's go, then. I think you'd prefer the quiet of your home after this."

She could see he was contemplating defying her, staying right there. But after a quick staring match—that he was obviously going to lose—he slowly began packing up his stuff. Reba knew he was trying to make her impatient. She wouldn't lose her cool, though. She'd been telling him all along that he wouldn't win, even if he tried her own tactics on her. Even if she wanted to have that body all to herself. She felt more than relaxed now and would take her panties when they got to his house and go.

The receptionist was also packing up her stuff when they exited. She looked at the bag of food hanging from Reba's wrist.

"Leaving early," she noted. "Good. He needs someone to drag him out of here at a reasonable hour."

"Corinne. Can we keep the lectures to a minimum for tonight?" He had made an attempt to look more put-together before they'd left the office and buttoned up his shirt. Reba had the strongest urge to undo every single button.

Corinne continued to ignore Devon and prattle on about him taking better care of himself.

"I already have one mother. All of this isn't necessary," he grumbled.

"Well, stop acting like a child that can barely take care of themselves, and I'll shut up," she said, smiling at him as she finished up packing everything.

Reba didn't bother to cover up her laugh. Devon, getting scolded right in front of her? Her night was officially made.

"I'll do my best to make sure he doesn't overdo it," Reba promised.

Devon kept waiting on Corinne, even though he was obviously irritated by her chatter. The floor was a bit quieter now, and Reba appreciated that he wanted to make sure Corinne didn't have to leave alone.

Devon stared at the elevator buttons the entire ride down, sighing every time Corinne launched into another thing that Devon should do to take better care of himself.

"I like her," Reba said when they had escorted Corinne to her car, watching her drive off.

"Two peas in a fricking pod, the both of you. You'll follow me?" he asked as soon as Corinne disappeared in her Mazda.

"Yup."

The drive gave Reba some time to decide on her next course of action. She'd bought the food, and she would eat it before she left. What happened after that was up in the air.

He watched her as she exited her car after parking behind him in his driveway.

"You came to my office with nothing on under there," he said as if he still couldn't believe it.

It made her smile. "Well, when I get my undies back, that'll change, won't it? I'm assuming you washed them."

"Of course."

"Then good." She gestured up his front walk. "After you."

He let them in the house. She settled onto the couch, placing the food on the table so she could take out the container. She'd ordered the same thing for both of them, hoping that he would actually be alright with it. Chicken and rice seemed like something most people would enjoy, so she had gone with that. She inhaled the delicious food smells. She'd get a head start on the meal while he retrieved her property.

She felt his eyes on her as she opened the container. "What?"

He shook his head. "Nothing."

"Speak your mind."

"You're not going to wait for me to eat?"

She reached for the disposable fork in the pack and proceeded to open it. "Nope. The more time you waste here, the longer you'll have to stand there and watch me eat."

"You're truly unbelievable."

"Thank you," she said, mouth full of fried rice. Oh yeah, this was good.

He shook his head again and headed upstairs. He returned quickly with her precious panties in a small brown bag and placed it next to her on the couch, then took up his container and sat in the chair opposite her.

She broke off a piece of chicken, ensuring to get some of the best part, the skin, and brought it to her mouth. "No need to go so far away."

"I think I need to keep my eye on you."

"Aww, you don't have to be afraid of me."

"You showed up at my office with nothing on under that dress," he reminded her as if she would forget.

"I wasn't wearing underwear at the exhibit, either. You didn't seem to mind then."

"Not the same thing. My office is not for any of that."

"Hmm, and yet..." Reba licked the taste of the chicken off her fingers, watching Devon as he watched her, reminding him of exactly how much his office was supposedly not for such activities.

He shifted in his seat, the food container nearly tipping

off his lap. He grabbed onto it before the entire thing ended up on the floor.

"I've never done anything like that at work before."

"Really? Office sex is *so* fun."

"We didn't even lock the damn door. I can't believe I did that."

"The best part is the possibility of getting caught. Anyone could have walked in while your fingers were in me."

He spooned some rice into his mouth, chewing slowly before getting to his feet. "We need something to wash this down."

Her eyes went right to the dick tenting the front of his pants. "Just water for me," she replied. Mr. Calm was still in need of some relief. She chuckled as he went to the kitchen, food still in his hand. She would see how long he held on to that control.

He returned with a chilled glass of water and a beer for himself. "I should have asked if you wanted this room temp."

"It's fine."

He took his seat, the hand that wasn't holding the food container brushing the front of his pants like he wanted to adjust himself.

She took up the cool glass, waving it at his crotch. "Don't hold back on my account. I love a good show."

He froze, hand dropping away to rest next to him. He placed the food on the small coffee table and leaned forward, elbows resting on his knees, fingers intertwined. "Is that so?" His voice was pure gravel at this point. It made her pause with the fork halfway to her mouth.

Yeah, she felt that tone buzz down the entire length of her body and settle right between her legs. She hoped he was going to follow through with everything that tone implied.

"Let me ask you this. Is there no limit to the outrageous things you say or do?"

She tapped the fork against her lips. "What do you think?"

"I think you enjoy playing with people. Seeing how you can push their buttons until they just give up and give in. I don't get the need for it, but I suppose I respect it."

She stuck her fork into her rice. "You respect it? That's a damn lie. You find it annoying."

"Yes, but I'm still in awe of whatever this skill is. That's not a lie."

"Wait, what?" Where the hell was all this coming from? Devon was stone-cold sober and telling her he respected her skill with charming people? That couldn't be right.

"Your powers of persuasion are...unlike anything I've ever seen. You implied that I could masturbate right here, right now, and I..."

"You?" she prompted. Was he actually going to say what she thought he was? Because holy shit, maybe she was more powerful than she'd ever thought.

He cleared his throat. "Have this urge to do just that. It doesn't make any sense."

"But will you?" She set her food aside and pulled the table forward until there was enough space in front of Devon for her to walk around and drop down to her knees. She leaned back on her heels. "Will you?" she asked again.

He swallowed. "I've never done that before."

"That's okay," she assured him in case he felt embarrassed about it or whatever. Reba liked to tease him about being boring, but she didn't want him to think she was judging him for not having explored certain things sexually.

"Do whatever you like. This isn't about me. It's for you. Let go a little. You've earned it, given the week you've had."

"You're right. I really wanted to go off on Vic."

"I don't know that guy, but fuck him. Focus."

He leaned back into the chair, legs spread. Oh yeah, now they were getting somewhere. Reba didn't appreciate manspreading generally—at least when they were encroaching on others' spaces—but this... Jesus Christ. The picture he made was glorious. If only he would allow her to capture it, she could use this for her own private time whenever she was feeling a bit frisky. But she would have to take a mental snapshot instead. He would never go for that suggestion.

He unbuckled his belt, and Reba bit down on her lip, clutching at her dress because that was *so* hot. The slow slide of his belt from the loops, the way he coiled up the brown leather before resting it on the couch.

She swept the open sides of her dress off her thighs and made herself more comfortable when Devon undid his button and slid the zipper down. She thought he would pull his pants all the way down, but he didn't. Instead, he reached in, and... God, it was difficult not to reach under her dress at the exact moment he palmed his dick in one hand.

"You're so quiet," he murmured, hand stroking up and down.

"I'm taking this all in. I don't want to miss a single thing."

And she didn't. Not the way his strokes started slowly then sped up. Not the way he never took his gaze off of her, eyes moving over her body like an actual caress. And she definitely didn't miss the pure pleasure on his face as a chorus of fucks dropped from his lips.

Reba liked to think she was a helpful person in general,

so she pushed up her capped sleeves so they would be secure on her shoulder then unbuttoned her dress the rest of the way, giving him a peek of her bare skin as his hips moved in time with his strokes. She could help a guy out.

"You can come on me if you want," she offered. She was generous like that.

"Fuck, Reba." His head fell back against the couch, hands jerking faster now. He came with a loud groan, spurting all over his poor white shirt.

Head tilted back, chest rising and falling with his deep breaths, she rose from the floor, walking up to lean over him until he looked her right in the eyes—well, for a few seconds until they dropped to where her dress gaped open.

She patted his chest. "You did good. How do you feel now?"

"Better."

"Good." She stepped back, leaving her dress hanging open. "Now, do you want to finish this food and I leave or..."

"I'll take the or."

"You sure you up to it?" she teased. "You look a bit wiped there."

He zipped his pants up partially, so they didn't fall down when he stood. He traced a line across her collar bone with the tip of his finger. "You'll find that when I really put my mind to something, I can get the work done."

"Mmm, I like the sound of that." She swept her hands out. "After you."

If he was certain he could go again, she would trust him to know his own body. Besides, getting him ready again was half the fun.

CHAPTER TWENTY-TWO
SEPTEMBER
DEVON

THE SOUNDS OF LAUGHTER AND INCESSANT CHATTER WERE FOREIGN to Devon this early on a Saturday morning. Or any morning, for that matter. The voices drifted up to his room each time one of his early morning guests stepped into the backyard.

Of course, his routine had gotten shaken up since he and Reba had started this baking journey, but the multiple voices were definitely *not* the norm. He'd sequestered himself in his room to go over the Sanctuary presentation while his mother, Reba, Maxi, and Leah were busy downstairs sorting all the stuff they had bought for the housewarming.

He and Reba should have been working on baking, but all of that went on the back burner, thanks to his mother. They had arrived at seven in the morning with an armload of bags that contained party stuff. He'd let them in and left them to their own devices.

Reba had given him a secret smirk before he turned away. "I have something to show you later," she'd said.

Devon couldn't imagine what the something could be, but he was mindful of his family around. He tried to act like he hadn't seen Reba Wednesday night or Thursday morning. Like they hadn't had sex at all. Difficult, considering she looked effortlessly sexy in pink shorts and a t-shirt that declared: *I Know I'm A Handful, But That's Why You Have Two Hands.*

It reminded him of exactly what he had done with his hands. In his office, on his couch, in his bed.

He hadn't thought much of the fact that they had gone to his room this time and not the guest bedroom. Although, waking up to Reba curled up in his bed when his alarm had gone off at four *had* been a shock. She'd stayed.

Don't overthink this to death. It doesn't mean anything, not to her. Not like that. She was probably just too tired to get up. You wore her out, after all.

His brain had gone into overdrive while he'd done his morning workout. Usually, he'd go for a run around the neighbourhood, but he hadn't wanted to leave Reba alone or wake her up just yet. If she was still sleeping the closer it got for him to leave for work, he'd have no choice, but it had been quite something to look down at her sleeping form. She'd looked peaceful and unlike the wrecking ball that had smashed into his life almost a month ago.

She'd come downstairs eventually while he had been making breakfast in his shirt, his belt around her waist turning it into a dress.

"I left my bag in the car, and my dress is a balled-up mess somewhere," she'd explained.

He'd only had enough energy in him to offer to get the bag for her if she watched the eggs cooking on the stove. Otherwise, he would have peeled the damn shirt off, and they'd be going at it again, right there in the kitchen.

Even now, as he rearranged slides on the presentation, his mind flashed back to how she had looked in his shirt, makeup a little smudged, eyes drowsy, her lids lowered as she watched for his reaction. Reba did everything with a purpose. It might have been practical for her to wear the shirt instead of coming down naked, but he was certain she knew exactly what she was doing.

"Focus on the now, you fool," he muttered.

He had spoken to Dax about Vic and decided that it was best to put someone else on the project. Vic was too volatile to trust with being a part of the team who would walk the client through the proposal in the coming week. He hadn't liked being pulled off of Sanctuary, but Devon had to think about what was best while Vic sorted out his life.

Chelsea, who he had put on the project now, had stared at him wide-eyed when he'd told her on Thursday that she was taking over for Vic and should spend the long weekend —Friday being their Independence holiday—getting familiar with the presentation as she would be handling that part. It was a lot to put on someone in a junior position, but Devon suspected she had been picking up Vic's slack for some time. It was also a moment for her to shine.

Oddly enough, his morning-after-sex chat with Reba had helped him reach his conclusion about Vic. She had showered and changed into a casual outfit from her bag, surprising him by asking about the Vic drama while they ate.

"So, do you feel clearer on what you want to do now?"

"Are you asking me if us having sex helped?"

She smiled around a forkful of her eggs. "Yeah."

"I don't know. It's a potential shit show in the making," he'd admitted.

"So, stuff isn't going as planned. Such is life. If you *must* make a plan," she made a face at that, "then at least be open to changing it when presented with new information."

Her words had given him real pause, made him realise that while Vic was good at what he did—when he wasn't bringing his personal drama into the office—he wasn't the only one who could do this.

Devon was nervous about these changes, but if Dax hadn't trusted him with new responsibilities and challenges, he wouldn't have moved up the organisation like this. They would do a run-through on Monday, and either Chelsea would prove her mettle or Devon would have to do the entire thing himself. He was prepared to, but Dax kept reminding him in not so subtle ways that a good manager knew how to delegate and utilise the skills of their team.

A knock on his bedroom door startled him. What now? He eased himself up from his chair and opened the door to Reba.

"Hi," Reba smiled up at him, a black plastic bag in her hand.

"Did my mother see you?"

Reba rolled her eyes. "I'm not some amateur. I asked her where your room was because I had a special baked delivery. She wouldn't think I already knew my way."

"Special baked delivery? It's not one of those brownies, is it? Is that on the menu?"

He hadn't taken any interest in the preparations, and there would be no children there tonight—one of the few things he had insisted on. Maxi's babysitter would be watching Leah, so it wasn't too farfetched to think Reba was bringing her brownies into the mix.

"Um, no, you're making the desserts, remember? Or did you forget?"

Right, she had mentioned he should use the party as another anonymous tasting moment.

"You forgot," she answered for him. "Let me in, please. I promise this is just an innocent baking-related visit."

He didn't care so much about Reba in his room a few days ago, but in the bright light of day, with his family downstairs, he hesitated. She claimed her visit was innocent, but he could never be sure with her.

Don't put it all on her. You're the one who keeps giving in.

That jolted him to action. He could, and would, control himself. He stepped back to let her in. She sat on the edge of his bed while he turned his chair from his desk, so it faced her—his small way of putting space between them. Otherwise, he might do something reckless.

She handed him the bag, waiting for him to take it. "Now, I remember someone questioning my skills not that long ago, and I thought how to say 'fuck you' in the nicest way possible."

"I don't understand." Reba kept his head spinning in all directions.

"Because I had plans to see the fireworks show with my fam on Friday night, I thought Friday morning was ideal for a little baking challenge." She gestured at the bag. "Open it."

He had stayed clear of any Independence night activities. The fireworks show in the Savannah was a crowded affair, even more so than the amusement park, and he'd wanted no part of it. He'd been invited by his family, but Devon had declined, preferring to use his holiday to work.

He opened the bag and pulled out the clear container. He looked at what was inside, then back at her. "Did you really make this?"

"Because I knew your ass would be sceptical." She held out her phone, showing him the paused video on the screen.

She pressed play, and Devon watched in awe at the time-lapsed version of Reba making the mini version of the Rubik's Cube cake he held in his hand.

"You actually did it."

"Of course, I did. I even had to do math; my brain still hurts." She wrinkled her nose. "There's a fork in the bag. Go ahead and try it."

He opened the container to stare at the perfectly edible cube before reaching for the fork. It looked exactly like the real thing. He looked up at her. "It looks too perfect to eat."

"You better eat it. Talking 'bout it looks too perfect. Do you know what went into making this? And it's a mini; the bigger cake's gonna take way more work. Need me to entice you? It's vanilla cake with a black chocolate ganache for the grid lines. I used a ruler and everything to make sure I was precise." She narrowed her eyes at him. "Eat the damn thing."

Devon nearly laughed as she huffed at him. He didn't think she'd appreciate it, so he dug into the cake, taking his first bite. It was delicious.

"It's good," he said, unable to resist teasing a bit after all. It was a foreign thing for him, this need to give as good as he got. Usually, he didn't care to reciprocate, but her reactions were sort of endearing. That pout, especially. "Perhaps several mini versions would be more of a hit than one large version?"

"Nah, it's easier to do this once with one big cake. It'll still showcase the difficulty level. We can work on the minis first, so you get the basic steps down, if you want, then move up to the bigger version."

That sounded logical. As impulsive as Reba was, when it came to baking, she clearly knew her shit, even if her methods were unorthodox and she refused to follow a recipe.

"I'm sorry I doubted you."

"Thank you. I'll admit, I didn't know if I was going to just give up halfway, but look at those perfectly sexy lines. *I* did that."

"You did."

Devon was this close to saying to hell with everything and pulling her in for a kiss because, oddly, he was proud of her. She had made him eat his words, proven him wrong. Usually not something he enjoyed, but the way she was smiling made him want to smile back too.

Is that what happened after having sex with someone following his two-year dry spell? He didn't know what to do with this rush of feelings. He rubbed at his chest, his heartbeat knocking against his palm.

"You okay over there, Superman? I know my hand sweet and all, but..." She cocked her head. "You're looking a bit shell-shocked over there."

"I'm good, really." He dropped his hand to his lap.

"Hmm, I'm not so sure. Look, I know I play around a lot, but you *can* talk to me."

"No, I'm good."

Talk to her? Not likely. Jeremy had advised him not to overthink, but easier said than done. He itched to rip apart every single interaction he'd had with Reba to come to some sort of understanding of how they had gotten here.

Here being this odd space where he wanted to keep having sex with her but also perhaps something else, too... something more. Fuck, he hadn't meant to think that. Even the thought felt too loud. Obviously, Reba wasn't a mind reader, but it felt dangerous to even think it.

"Then why are you looking at me like that?

Shit, what the hell was his face doing? "I don't...what?"

"It's the cube, isn't it? Of course, math would turn you on."

He didn't dispel her theory. The perfect lines of the cube were causing him to look at Reba in a new light. He was used to math in his daily life; it was an inescapable part of his work—that he actually enjoyed—but not so much for her.

The playful moment turned charged. Aware of where he was, he didn't do anything, didn't move to take her hand or pull her forward like he wanted to, but she got the message. Her tongue swiped out over her bottom lip, followed by her teeth pressing into the plump flesh that was painted a peachy colour today.

The sudden knock on his door made them both jump. Reba bit her lip, looking like she was trying to hold a laugh in.

"Hey, we need Reba back, so if you two are done?" Maxi called out loudly.

He sighed at Maxi's playful tone, although her interruption had been perfectly timed because where his mind had been about to go was startling. To more what-ifs, which could have turned into action when he had firmly told himself they would do nothing as long as his family was still here.

Reba got to her feet. "Hold that thought. I know you'd prefer to stay up here the whole time, but don't be a total stranger tonight, okay? I've picked out the perfect outfit." She tossed a wink before going to join Maxi.

～

REBA'S EXIT LEFT HIM IN A RESTLESS MOOD, WHICH MEANT HE threw himself into working on the presentation, going through the slides with Chelsea, who had video-called him to chat until his stomach rumbling had forced him downstairs.

His mother had graciously brought over some oil down for them. Leah wasn't fond of the dish as she found it looked too mushy to taste good, so she had her own chicken and fries to munch on.

He took a look at the set-up as he scooped up a spoonful of salted meat and provisions, basking in the flavourful taste of the coconut milk. Everything looked fine to him, nothing too over-the-top, and most of it confined to the backyard so there wouldn't be a bunch of people trampling throughout his house. They would be allowed through the kitchen to get to the downstairs half-bath.

Of course, the priest would be allowed in so he could bless the entire property before the party itself got underway, but otherwise, Devon was fine with how they had planned out everything. Nothing too fancy, a couple of tables and chairs set up, twinkle lights thrown in for some ambiance, or so his mother claimed. Didn't matter to him. They'd also created a section for the DJ and food. He could work with this.

"Well, is it to your liking?" Maxi asked.

"It's fine."

"Ah, yes, love to hear something is fine after we spent all morning on it. Truly."

"Your sarcasm isn't needed. I didn't say it looked bad."

"Would you call your work fine and think it's something of worth?" Maxi shot back, hand on her hips. Reba and his mother watched on, amused. "It's supposed to be whimsical and cute but make guests still feel fine with brukkin' out. I told Reba's DJ friend to make sure we have some songs to wine low to on their setlist."

"Whimsical isn't my style, but I'm sure the guests will love it."

"Really sorry for whoever you con into marrying you. I swear you're the worst."

"Now, now, children." Ms. King looked between them. "You'll make Reba think we always get on like this,"

"Oh no, don't worry about me. This is making my afternoon." Reba grinned and waved between Devon and Maxi. "Please, do carry on. My sis and I never argue. She takes all the fun out of it. Just shakes her head at me and walks away. God forbid she ever look anything other than perfect. This is refreshing."

"We're *not* arguing." Devon didn't do confrontations if he could avoid it. He knew Maxi wasn't really angry—he'd seen her truly upset before, and this wasn't even close—more like annoyed with his reaction. But they should be well aware he wasn't going to gush about how amazing the set-up was. It was fine and functional.

"No, we're not, but come nah, man, at least give us a little praise for our hard work."

"Yeah, Uncle Devon. Can you say it looks pretty?" Leah piped up, munching on a fry as she smiled over at him ever so sweetly.

Great, now he had a child trying to guilt him, unwittingly. Leah wasn't yet aware that it was difficult for him to refuse her anything. God save him when she got older and realised that. If she turned out anything like Reba, they were all doomed.

He stole a glance at Reba, who was grinning at him.

"Okay, fine, I'm sorry," he said to Maxi. "Thanks for doing this. It looks pretty nice. Is that a props table?" He hadn't noticed the other table at his first glance, set up with what looked like various items guests could use to take photos. That was definitely a feather boa on the top there.

"Yep, all Reba's idea." His mother smiled in Reba's direction. "Isn't it a lovely addition?"

He supposed. He wouldn't be making use of it.

"Auntie Reba said she would bring over the stuff so I can use it too sometime. Cuz I'm not allowed here tonight." Leah rolled her eyes, and everyone laughed.

"We'll have our own photo sesh. I'll ask Auntie Remi to take our pics, so it's all cool and professional, but still fun. No fussy adults around."

"You're an adult," Devon pointed out.

"But I'm not fussy, so."

"Yeah! Auntie Reba is cool!" Leah looked at Maxi. "Mummy, can I have hair like Auntie Reba for my photos?"

"Um..."

"Hair chalk is an option. It washes right out, but only if your mom says it's okay," Reba told Leah, who was already bouncing in her chair as if it was all a done deal.

Devon didn't know how to feel about Reba bonding with Leah. His niece had obviously taken to her because she was a fun adult, but he couldn't fathom what sort of influence she would have here. No one needed a mini Reba running around. One was enough to upend his carefully put-together life.

"We'll see," Maxi said, not committing to anything.

His mother looked at her watch. "Well, we're pretty much all done. I just have to go prep the cutters and main dishes at home. We'll come back before the start to set up everything in the kitchen. Keiran and Cherisse are coming in soon, too. Her mom is picking them up. You and Reba even have some time for another baking session before the party."

"Well, so we do. Devon is making the dessert for tonight, so we better get on that, huh? I'll keep him in check." Reba grinned even wider. He worked extra hard not to show a single reaction that would make his mother look at them funny. "After we finish eating."

His mother clapped her hands. "Excellent. Devon, come show me where to stash these boxes out of sight. We'll need them when the time comes to pack up everything."

He helped her take them into his office. It was the best place to put them.

"Reba is such a lovely young woman, isn't she? She was so helpful with this," his mother practically gushed.

"Hmm. That's good," he said noncommittally.

"She's so good with Leah, too. I'm sure she'll make a great mom someday, don't you think?"

Devon paused, box in hand. He should have known this was why she wanted him alone. "Yes, I'm sure she would. If that's something she wanted." He had no clue. They'd never discussed it. Had no reason to.

"You and her seem to get along quite well. I'd say you two have even become friends, yeah?"

"Yes, we get on just fine. I don't know about friends. She's been helping me with the baking just as I told you."

"I know, but you're spending *a lot* of time together. That can make two people friendlier, you know. And she's sweet. You can't tell me you don't enjoy her company, at least."

He stacked the same size boxes together, refusing to be lured into this trap his mother was clearly setting. "Do we have to do this now?"

She leaned against the wall of his office, arms folded. He

didn't have any furniture in it yet. He really should get on that before the space became a default storage room.

"Yes. You two look interesting together. I didn't think of this combination since you're so different, but I see it now. Is there any interest there? Romantically, I mean."

So they *were* getting right to it. "It's a business relationship."

"So you said, but are you sure there's nothing there?"

There was a fire raging between them that made him want to touch her at the most inappropriate times, but he would not say that to his mother. "I'm...this is a working relationship. Just like I said."

She raised her hands. "Okay, alright. Understood. But are you open to finding someone right now?"

"Maybe. Can we just focus on the task at hand?"

"Sure, honey."

He didn't know why he'd said maybe. He didn't want her to take that as a sign for her to start throwing every single woman she could find his way. He didn't need—or want—his mother's help in that area.

He didn't tend to rely on this idea of a gut feeling. He analysed a situation to determine possible outcomes, but right now, his stomach was churning. His mother continued smiling even though he had shot down her hopes about Reba. What was she up to?

He hoped he was wrong, and she wasn't planning something. He just wanted to survive this damn party and figure out what the hell was going on with this odd feeling in his chest whenever he looked at Reba.

CHAPTER TWENTY-THREE

REBA

"Boy, if you don't stop trying to hassle this DJ…"

"But he playing shit. You hear how he bring in that song after the Bunji? What was *that*?"

"Keiran Matthew King."

"Yes, my love?"

Reba giggled at their antics. "Is that really your middle name?"

"It isn't. In fact, I get a new one every two weeks."

Cherisse made a face, and Keiran looked so whipped. They really were too cute. The party had been going for about an hour now, and already Keiran was trying to take over from the DJ she had asked for a favour.

Granted, he was right about those transitions, but Reba thought Flex was just a little nervous. He would get in the groove soon. Either way, she was happy to have Cherisse back. Boss lady was glowing. Not just from her newly acquired tan, but she and Keiran looked so damn happy.

It made her all warm and fuzzy inside. Provided a nice little distraction, too. Otherwise, she would be looking out for another King who had gone MIA as soon as she had arrived.

Devon had taken one look at her, said a brief hello, then just turned and walked back into the house. She would be offended had it not been for the way he had frozen and swept her from head to toe before speed walking away. He'd only seen the front of her—she was dying for him to see the back. Because there was none to speak of.

The black bodysuit dipped all the way down to her waist in the back, meeting the top of her glittery gold miniskirt.

"Where's Devon?" Keiran asked, looking around for his brother too. "He really about to disappear at his own party?"

Reba nodded. "Yeah. He did say it's really your mom's party."

"Hmm, I shouldn't be surprised, but he could come tell that DJ to let me take over. Since it's his house, he has authority."

Cherisse rolled her eyes. "We're not staying here long. I'm tired."

"Yeah, I did that, didn't I?" He wiggled his brows, and Cherisse poked him in the arm.

"Glad you two had fun and good weather too." They had definitely gotten lucky, considering they were into the rainy/hurricane season. "You should try some dessert. Devon made them."

"Oh, really? You two are really doing this baking thing, huh?"

"Yup."

"That all?"

Cherisse perked up at Keiran's question, eyes brimming with questions too.

Reba pressed her hand to her chest. "Mr. King, are you asking if I seduced your brother? Whyever would you think such a thing of me?"

"That's not a no, is it?" Cherisse piped up, brow raised.

Damn, they were going to tag-team her? "Well, you see, it's not even like that at..."

"Reba."

His voice behind her felt like a whole hand skimming down her bare back. Oh yeah, he'd definitely gotten a glimpse of her bare skin now since she was facing Keiran and Cherisse.

"Well, there he is. Where you been hiding? I need to ask you about this DJ. He need to..."

"I'm here for Reba," Devon cut Keiran off.

The crotch of her bodysuit had to be damp because what was Devon on with that voice right now?

She turned around, her skirt swirling around her thighs. He wasn't looking at Cherisse or Keiran, his full attention on her. Oh. "Yes? How can I help you, Mr. King?"

"I need to talk to you about these desserts. I think something's wrong with them."

"You sure? We taste-tested them before. They were okay."

"No."

"Um, okay. We'll be right back," she told Keiran and Cherisse.

If she didn't know any better, she would say Devon was pulling the same move she had at the amusement park, but why would he?

She followed him into the kitchen. "What's wrong with the dessert?"

"Nothing. Just follow me, please."

She kept walking beside him. "You've been hiding from me."

He opened a door and led her into a room that looked like it was still under construction. No furniture in it. Some boxes on the ground. "I...couldn't stop my reaction to you," he admitted. "I needed a moment to myself."

"Wow. Did you jack off in this moment to yourself?"

He was dressed in a casual shirt with a few of the top buttons undone—enough for her to enjoy a nice view of his throat—and dark jeans. It would be easy to picture him in his bathroom, unzipping to take himself out of his jeans. He didn't look like someone who'd found release and could relax, though. In fact, he looked more tense than she'd ever seen him.

"No. Why are you shocked? Men must react to you all the time."

"Not just men, but you're good at hiding your reactions. Usually. I wouldn't expect that from you." She looked around the unfinished space. "Why are we in here?"

"Because." He turned to her. "Just because. I'm losing my fucking mind over here. You came to a house party in a little glitter skirt that could blow up at any moment if there was a strong breeze and...the back."

"Yes." She smirked. "I was hoping you'd see the back."

"There's no fucking back on this top."

"It's a bodysuit, actually." She twirled. "So you like it, then?"

"Yes." He walked into her, forcing her to back up against the wall. "I can't fucking breathe right around you. This isn't normal for me. I don't..."

"Lose control? How long were you looking at me before you decided to come over? Keiran and Cherisse are probably thinking all sorts of stuff now."

"A while. Two years and I was fine. Then you just show up, and...I don't know. Broke something open in me, I think."

"Well, two years is a while, I suppose. The longest I've gone without sex is maybe a couple months?" Since her ill-fated attempt at a relationship. She searched for his reaction to that. She knew a lot of men would have a heap of opinions about her sex life. She didn't give a damn. She enjoyed sex. If they couldn't handle that, well, fuck them.

"I made do until—"

"A sexy tornado entered your life? It's okay, you'll survive with limited collateral damage." She arched into the wall, baring her neck, inviting him to touch. He seemed to like that part of her a lot. "That poor priest has no idea what's about to go down in this house after he blessed it. Actually, *I* don't even know what's about to happen. Tell me."

"I just wanted to touch you, that's all."

He did just that, cupping her neck as she'd wanted. He released her and twirled his index finger, signalling for her to turn around. She obeyed, gladly. He didn't waste any time skimming his fingers down her bare back.

She looked over her shoulder. "Just touching?"

"Yes. We can discuss anything further after the party."

She wanted to pout at that, but the fact that he had sought her out in front of his brother and Cherisse and brought her in here was progress in her mind. He had to have considered how that might look to anyone watching. Devon didn't do things without thinking it through like she did, so what had made him decide he didn't care and do this anyway?

Was he so turned on that his usual control was nowhere

to be found? Reba found it fascinating and exhilarating to think she had done that.

"What the hell has gotten into you?" She breathed out as his hands travelled down to her waist.

"You. Kryptonite, remember."

"Yes, yes, I know, but...shit. I like this Devon. A lot."

He made his way over her ass, squeezing before giving her a pat and removing his hand. "I'll need a minute before I can go back out there."

She turned around, watching as he took several deep breaths. "What are you going to tell your brother when he asks about this?"

"Not a damn thing. There was a momentary dessert crisis that was solved."

"None of that makes sense, but go ask him about the DJ. That'll distract him."

"The DJ?"

"He's trying to take over because he thinks Flex is shitty." She spread her arms wide. "I don't even know what to say about that."

"Alright. I'll try that."

"Save me a dance," she said before he moved towards the door. "I need to work off some of this pent-up energy you created here."

He gave her a small smile before shutting the door behind him. She would wait a bit before walking out, give herself some time to savour what had just happened. It felt like she had hallucinated the entire moment.

She smiled as her phone chirped from her pocket.

Ayo: Trina keeps pestering meeee. Insisting you're hiding something from her??
Reba: Trina needs to chill

Ayo: *how's the party? How did he react to your outfit?*
Reba: *as expected* 😉

Which was an entire lie. Nothing Devon had done had been expected. She had gotten the reaction she wanted, but everything he'd done and said? She was shocked, thrown off by the intensity. Devon was definitely not someone who did anything in half-measures. He was an overachiever who didn't like failure, and wasn't she just reaping the benefits of that? Her heart was racing again, just thinking about how he almost had her ready to come with just a trail of his finger down her back.

Right now, she could definitely tell Trina she had won that bet. He still hadn't outright said, "I want you." But did it even matter at this point? His actions screamed it. Her phone chirped with a reply from Ayo.

Ayo: *so does that mean you won the bet?*

She didn't respond. She needed to get back out there and get a drink. Her throat was too dry, and she had to channel this energy somewhere else before she locked herself in his bathroom and got herself off.

She opened the door, mind full of all the delicious things she could do to Devon once they got some alone time. She was busy picturing herself going down on him when she ran right into Cherisse.

"Oh, hey."

"Hey, I came inside to look for a quiet place to return a call." She waved the phone in her hand. "What're you doing in here?"

"Nothing."

"Nothing? You're just chillin' inside? Thought you'd be

in the kitchen. Everything okay with the dessert emergency?"

"Yup. All good. Great."

Cherisse pursed her lips. "I saw Devon heading back out. He looked a little...how should I say this? Pleased with himself."

Reba pressed her lips together. She didn't have to tell Cherisse everything about her personal life, even though their relationship went far beyond just that of employer and employee. But God, she wanted to.

"You know that man doesn't like to fail at anything," she said. "I guess he was glad we got the dessert situation sorted."

"I suppose. But do you care to explain why you're in here?"

"Nothing to explain. I'm... I just needed to...um." Dammit, she was fully blanking on an excuse that would make any kind of sense. Fucking Devon and his sexy ass self, making her brain fuzzy.

Cherisse laughed. "Right, so is this what we're really doing? Are the three of us really about to get into this King business? I can*not* believe this."

"Whoa, hold on. I'm not getting into anything like that. Not the way you're thinking." She and Devon were having sex, sure, but this other stuff Cherisse was saying was not it.

"So you weren't in here fooling around with Devon, is what you're telling me?"

Reba sighed in defeat. She'd put up a good fight, hadn't she? "Okay, look, I didn't say *that,* but you're implying this is a situation similar to you and Remi. It's not. Nobody's trying to get boo'd up here. It's all about the fun."

"Hmm, where have I heard this before? Oh yeah, right, from myself."

"Cherry, come on. I tried that relationship shit, wasn't for me. And Devon surely don't want me like that."

"You don't know that."

"Yeah, I do. He has a plan for his perfect partner, and I'm pretty sure I'm not it."

"And how do you feel about that supposed plan?"

She shrugged. "I think it's silly to have a plan like that at all in general. But it doesn't matter to me personally. I've got no real stake in this. It's sexy fun."

"Hmm," Cherisse said again. "Alright, missy."

"You don't think a man like Devon would want to change me too? Look, I get it. You're in love and all that jazz, so you want that for everybody, but I'm good, thanks. Go make your call. I'm heading back out."

She headed straight for the drinks table. Wine sounded great after that mini-interrogation. Why did everyone think she and Devon could be something? *Should* be something?

It was a party. She didn't want to have serious thoughts about anything except what fun the end of the night would hold for her and Devon. But as she downed one glass of wine way too quickly and got another refill, she looked around until she saw him at a table with his family. He was standing as if trying to make an excuse to leave and go hide out in his room, but his mother's constant chatter didn't give him the right moment.

He looked around as if plotting his escape, and they locked eyes. Even from here, she could tell he definitely wanted her to save him. She was about to do just that when Dax stepped in front of her, blocking Devon from her view.

"Hello again."

"Oh, hey."

"How's our boy doing with the baking?"

"Did you have any of the dessert yet?" she asked him instead.

Devon had chosen to try brownies tonight. The cutters had already been passed around, and guests were happily munching on geera chicken, meatballs, and samosas—both veggie and chicken. Ms. King hadn't been so sure about putting out the dessert so early since she had her system—appetisers, then the main dish, followed by dessert and corn soup later in the night to sober up anyone who needed it—but Reba had convinced her to switch it up a bit and have some of the brownies out early.

She couldn't get accurate feedback too late in the night when the guests were too tipsy to care if the brownies tasted good or not. Anything would taste amazing after a few drinks. The tray currently held crumbs. Devon's dessert was a hit.

"I swiped one before it was all gone. Was surprised it was out so early."

"Then I believe you answered your own question." She smiled as his eyes grew wide.

"He made those?"

"Yup."

"Without help?"

"What sort of teacher would I be if I didn't let my student soar on his own? I think you'll love his entry for the contest." She winked.

"Care to share a hint?"

Reba wagged her finger at him. "No spoiling the surprise. It's on theme, that's all you need to know."

"I knew you would be a good influence on him."

"I don't know about *good*, but he'll at least not be allergic to fun once I'm done with him."

She looked past Dax to where Devon and his mother were now talking a little away from the table, a big frown on his face. He looked displeased. Reba wondered what was going on there. Arms folded, he wasn't trying to hide that he was not happy about whatever his mother was saying.

"I hope this isn't too forward," Dax continued, snagging her attention again. "But I'm having a late birthday thing. It'll be a while after my main party and the bake-off since I have to wait for some people to fly in. I'd love for you to join us. It's a private event on a yacht. Just for a few close friends of mine. I've been trying to convince Devon to come, but you know how he is."

"Boat party? Oh, I'm so there, whether Devon wants to go or not."

He laughed at that. "You're more than welcome either way."

"Sweet, but I'm pretty convincing. I'll persuade him."

"Excellent. Well, I won't keep you any longer."

By the time Dax left her to go chat up someone else, Devon was gone. Had he finally made his escape upstairs? She made her rounds, barely holding in her cackle when she saw Keiran at the DJ table, Flex beside him looking annoyed as hell. She was going to get an earful after this, but she didn't care. All she could think about was stealing a moment with Devon. Even though he had assured her they would have their own little private session after the party, Reba couldn't help seeking him out inside.

She was almost at the top of the stairs when she heard Devon's voice.

"I don't know what to do about this."

"It doesn't have to be a big deal." She recognised Jeremy's voice. He had shown up as promised. What were they talking about up here? She should turn around and leave them be, but curiosity got the better of her. "How do you feel about it? What're you thinking?"

"I don't know what to think. Why the hell would she invite Joya here?"

"I don't claim to know her reasoning, but I'll assume when you told her you're not interested in Reba like that, it meant it was okay to switch those matchmaking gears. And Joya being back here after all this time? She must think it's a sign or something."

Reba's hand curled around the railing. Well, alright, then. She had just said the exact thing to Cherisse, hadn't she? Devon wasn't into her like that, so why did hearing those words feel so...weird? And who the hell was this Joya person his mother had supposedly invited?

"We haven't spoken in ages." Devon sighed. "Things ended, and we tried to stay in touch, but obviously, we didn't. This isn't ideal. I don't want any sort of scene to be made."

"Look, man, what's there to even consider here? You and Reba have something going on, right? Joya doesn't matter. Talk to her or not, but she shouldn't be a factor in anything. What did I say when we last spoke? I keep telling you. Joya and that list need to remain in the past."

"Reba and I are *doing* something. Having something is different." He sighed again. "This a whole train wreck waiting to happen, isn't it?"

"But what do you want? Do you want her?"

"I don't *want* to want her. Is that what you want to hear? I even did a risk analysis, and she landed in the red zone."

"You did a what?"

"I plugged in most of her qualities and personality

traits, and obviously, she's a high risk. It's all very inconvenient and..."

Welp, she had heard enough. She tiptoed back down the stairs. Reba had known he would feel this way. The entire conversation had gone as expected, with the exception of some random ex suddenly being tossed into the mix. But then again, this woman didn't sound like some random at all. Jeremy had mentioned her and the list in the same breath. Did that mean she was the basis for Devon's perfect partner criteria? And what the fuck was up with him doing some analysis to determine how much of a risk she was to him?

He should be happy to even breathe the same air as her. Her head felt like it was spinning with all this. Or maybe she should have eaten more before guzzling that wine.

Should she tell him she had overheard his conversation? Tell him he didn't have to overthink anything? She couldn't compete with some woman who had been the basis for every relationship that had come after, so why would she stand in his way? They could reconnect or whatever. She didn't care. She could go be risky and sexy somewhere else.

Yeah, the sex was amazing, but this was never going anywhere. No matter what anyone said about them looking cute. No matter what annoying fluttering took up residence in her body. It was the same thing all over. She was good to fuck, but when it came down to anything real, she would never be the first choice.

Which, fine. She and Devon wouldn't work for anything other than a good time in bed, anyway.

You seem really worked up about it for someone who don't care.

"Yeah, we not doing this," she muttered.

She swept into the kitchen, annoyed at that damn voice

and herself. She was letting Cherisse get into her head. None of this mattered. Damn wine. She needed to get something to eat. Then, she would sort out what to do when Devon came back down.

"Oh, it's you."

The voice made her stop in her tracks. She hadn't even noticed the woman in the kitchen when she'd stormed in. She didn't recognise her, but she liked her casual partywear of white jeans, nude heels, and a black top. Her hair was pulled back in a slick ponytail. She looked cute and classy.

Reba squinted. Her head was getting a little fuzzy, but she was certain she had never met this woman. "Uh, do I know you?"

"Oh no, sorry, you don't. I saw you with Devon earlier. Do you know where he is? I've been looking, but it would be weird to just walk into the house like this." She gave a small laugh. "We haven't spoken in ages. I love your hair, by the way."

"And you are?" she asked, already knowing—because as far as signs went, this one was a whole ass siren going off in her face—but needing it said. She wasn't about to be rude to this woman, but what were the chances after over-hearing that conversation?

"I'm Joya."

"Right, yes. Of course."

"Um, so do you know where he is by chance?"

"He's inside. I'm sure he'll come out eventually." She spied a bottle with a label that said *Pommerac Wine*.

Don't you even think about it...

"Shush."

Joya's smile slipped. "I'm sorry?"

"That wasn't directed at you."

Adding homemade wine on top of the Moscato she had

consumed was a terrible idea, but wasn't that her thing? Bad ideas and not thinking shit through? Like jumping into sex with Devon, which had been a sexy good time but had definitely had an expiry date. She hadn't expected it to be this soon, though.

Joya was eyeing her like she wanted to back away. She didn't blame her—great instincts on that one. Reba was feeling a bit feral all of a sudden. It wouldn't be fair to lash out at this very nice woman who had probably just innocently come to this party to reconnect with an old sweetheart.

She giggled at that, thinking of Devon as a sweetheart. He was, even though he would never refer to himself like that. He would scrunch up his face if she ever called him that, but he was. Writing love notes and shit. Cute. Joya herself probably had a stash from Devon.

She grabbed up the bottle. It was time to get out of here. The alcohol was buzzing through her way too quickly. "Well, nice meeting you, Joya, and good luck." She saluted her with the bottle.

Confusion continued to crease Joya's forehead, but Reba was done here. Time to get her drink on and make more poor life choices.

By the time the main course came out, Devon had still not emerged from the house, but Joya had. Cherisse's yawning had convinced Keiran it was time to leave, which left Reba to her own devices pretty much. Which was *fine*. This was her thing, making small talk and chatting up people even when she didn't know them. She avoided Ms. King, preferring to tease Flex since he had control of his music now with Keiran's absence.

But as she begged off dancing with another guy, who she assumed was one of Devon's neighbours, she took another cup of the way too strong homemade wine. Damn, this shit was lethal but delicious. Like her. Devon should be so damn lucky to have her.

It was funny that he had finally said it out loud but then proceeded to say he didn't want to want her. All in the same breath. Talk about irony.

Alright, time to pack it in. She was done. Tired of dancing and faking fun. Over it. Her sexy plans for the night were fizzling before her eyes. She couldn't see how they would get to it when she couldn't stop looking at Joya interact with Ms. King. Maxi kept eyeing Joya as if she couldn't believe she was here. Her mother had apparently kept this little surprise to herself.

At around eleven, she texted Devon because why not make even better choices when tipsy?

Reba: *hiding out again? You owe me a dance.*
Reba: *or maybe you'd rather dance with Joya? She's cute. But I'm cute too, see?*

Before she could think better of it, she attached one of the pics from the glow photoshoot. It was a little risqué, but he could see all that he would be missing. A few seconds passed before it occurred to her she shouldn't have sent that because it made it sound like she cared. Fuck. She tried to delete the damn thing, but sluggish reflexes— fricking wine was lethal—meant the tick turned blue before she could do anything. Okay, it was really time to bounce.

She squinted at her phone, looking for the number she needed. She wasn't going to be driving herself home.

"Hey, I need a favour, pretty please, with a hot guy on the top," she begged when Scott answered. Calling Trina or

Ayo was not an option. Too many questions would be asked, and she wanted to answer none of them.

"What's up, gorgeous? You okay? You sound a little off."

"Come get me? I'll send the address, need a rescue ASAP."

"You okay?" he asked again because Scott was a sweetheart.

She laughed even though she didn't feel like it. "Honestly? I don't think so. Also, a little high on homemade wine. Please save me before I do something rash. Well, more rash. Rash*er*? Whatever. Moscato and that wine was *not* my best idea, let me tell you."

"Okay, be there in a few. Hang on, alright?"

She would try. Her hand hovered over her phone. She was tempted to send an SOS to Ayo because her mind was fuzzy and whirling all over the place with the sudden attack of what felt like jealousy, but it totally couldn't be that, could it? She didn't do that. Devon was just another hook-up. The weird flipping feeling in her stomach was because she had overdone it on the drinking. Yup. Totally made sense.

Yeah, now wasn't the time for her to try to make rational decisions or message anyone. She placed her phone on her bag. At least no one was approaching her over here as she waited, but all that could change so quickly.

Devon's housing development was in the Trincity area, not that far away from where Scott lived in Tunapuna, but the Independence long weekend meant people were out and about. That could delay him some. It was probably best she wait out front for him. Less chance of her making a fool of herself in front of Devon's family or other guests.

She casually tried to disappear to the front of the building to wait for Scott, was so close to reaching the driveway when she heard her name being called. Damn, she was getting some shitty luck tonight.

She didn't stop, just kept walking as if she hadn't heard him.

"Where're you going?" Devon asked, falling in step with her.

"Home."

"What? Just like that?"

"Yes."

"Wait, hold on." Hand light on her shoulder, she stopped to look at him.

"You send me some strange text, then you're leaving? How the hell do you even know who Joya is?"

"Because my hearing is superb. She seems nice, not given to doing random weird stuff. Just your type, right?" Okay, she needed to stop. "Doesn't matter. I'm tired and ready to leave, so bye."

"I can drive you home."

"Not necessary. I called a ride already. You're free to do whatever without worrying about me." She waved towards the backyard, where Flex was pumping out some vintage calypso music for the older guests. "I'm cool. We're cool. So, do your thing."

"Reba, *what* is going on?"

She didn't want to get into this. Mainly because she didn't know why she was *being* like this. The wine coursing through her system didn't help, either. It was better for both of them that she went home, slept this off, and...yeah, she'd figure out the rest in the morning.

She patted his chest. "It's okay. You don't have to be all torn up about any of this. You can have the one that got away. You're free. We bake, get you the win, then you can ride off into the sunset with little Ms. Perfect."

Devon frowned down at her. "I don't understand."

"Well, you and me both, buddy!" She shook her head. "I think I had too much to drink." She definitely had gone overboard, which ordinarily she wouldn't care about. She was the life of the party when tipsy, but somehow she had turned into this passive-aggressive, slightly sulky version of herself.

A horn honked behind her, and thank you, Jesus, she could get the hell out of here before she embarrassed herself further. Talk about being messy in the most un-fun way possible.

"Scott's here. I'll text you about my car. Bye."

"Reba..."

"Nope, can't talk. Must go."

She slid into Scott's car, refusing to look back at Devon.

"You good?" Scott asked.

She didn't look at him either. "I just want to go home before I get even messier." She glanced his way. Scott was looking his effortlessly naturally gorgeous self, as usual, dark brown skin popping in the bit of glow the streetlight provided. Unfair. "Why are you always so damn pretty no matter what time of day it is?"

Scott shrugged. "The Trim genes are pretty magical, but let's focus a bit. Devon King?" he asked, brow raised. "That's a handsome ass mess you got there."

"Can we go, please?" He was trying to cheer her up by teasing. She appreciated the effort, but the longer they stayed here, the more afraid she was that she would do something ridiculous like cry, which eww, no. She was too cute to be doing any of that.

"Alright, I got you. You know that."

"Thanks." She peeked out the window, and the damn

man was still standing there looking like a whole confused sexy meal with that frown.

She looked away, closing her eyes as she pressed her head back against the seat. She breathed a small sigh of relief when Scott drove off. She didn't want to think about anything she had said or done tonight.

All of that noise was a problem for future Reba.

CHAPTER TWENTY-FOUR
DEVON

"I WANT TO DO SOMETHING IMPULSIVE, BUT I NEED TO KNOW IF IT would be a bad idea."

The silence on the other end of the phone grated on Devon's already extended nerves. It had taken everything in him to admit that, get the words out. He expected laughter or something, at the very least.

"Are you there? Hello?" he prompted.

"Um, *who* is this?"

"You know damn well it's me, Keiran."

"I'm not sure cuz the brother I know wouldn't be calling me at six on a Sunday morning for advice. But then again, you *are* calling me to ask if you should do something impulsive. Which defeats the entire purpose of being impulsive." Keiran chuckled. "Yeah, it's definitely you, isn't it?"

Devon had known this would be a mistake, but he didn't know who else to ask. His rekindled friendship with Jeremy was too new to call him this early on a Sunday, even though they'd had that chat last night. So his next best option after the weirdness of the party had been Keiran.

He really needed to work on fixing the few other friendships he had abandoned because his siblings weren't the ideal audience for this. By their very nature, they were inclined to tease him mercilessly, but he needed someone to either talk him out of this or tell him it was fine. Imprudent decisions weren't his forte.

In fact, the longer Keiran's laugh went on—seriously, didn't he need to breathe at some point?—the more he wanted to tell him to forget it and end the call. Yet Reba's face and body language from last night haunted him. The party had ended around midnight, an hour after Reba had left. He had texted to ask if she had gotten home safely. He'd gotten no reply, the message left unread. It was only when they had finished cleaning up—he'd found himself helping out even though his mother tried to shoo him away —that he discovered Reba's bag and phone.

Her car was still parked outside. She had to come by at some point for it—they were also supposed to bake today —but a wild thought had wormed its way into his head. She would want her phone right away, wouldn't she? He could drop off her stuff and just take her back to the house to get her car. They would get a chance to talk about why the hell she had left like that.

The unannounced visit wouldn't give her much time to dodge him. It was essentially what she had done with her unexpected visit to his office. In spite of his misgivings, he was determined. Last night's conversation had been playing over and over in his head as they'd cleaned up while he politely told his mother off for inviting Joya like that. He had tried to piece the events together from when he had left Reba in his home office. Given what she'd said before leaving, it was safe to assume she had overheard him talking to Jeremy. Parts of their conversation, anyway.

God, what a mess.

"Would it be weird to just show up at somebody's house?" he repeated to Keiran. "I have something that belongs to them. Their phone, actually, so I can't call them. I don't know her home number."

"Her?"

Shit. He was slipping. "Irrelevant. I just need to know if..."

"It isn't Joya, is it?"

"*No.*" Their chat last night had been brief, a moment to clear up the awkwardness his mother had created. He didn't think they'd be seeing each other after that.

She had explained she'd only given in to his mother's invitation because she wanted to catch up with him after all this time and running into his mother at the grocery had been some sort of weird kismet. His mother had definitely "tried a ting" and failed. Joya was talking to someone back in Spain, exploring the potential for more. She had just returned to Trinidad for a family event. All things she had not told his mother since she hadn't considered her invitation had an ulterior motive behind it.

She'd laughed off the entire thing, urging him to do the same. He couldn't because of Reba's reaction, which had surprised him.

"Just go drop off the thing and stop thinking so hard," Keiran told him, big yawn following his words.

"It's probably too early to go right now."

"I think she—who you refuse to name, but we both know that I know who you mean—might like that you did something a little unexpected. But your choice at the end of the day. I'm out."

Keiran hung up. He didn't allow himself the time to pick this idea apart. Twenty minutes later, he was in front of Reba's house. He used the doorbell, wondering who would answer. The one time he had been here to pick her up for the karaoke with his co-workers, she had hustled him away before he could say a thing to her parents. He braced to be faced with an annoyed Reba.

The woman who answered the door definitely had her face, but the black hair with blunt bangs and the khaki-coloured dress were so not her style he wondered for a second whether this was the sister he had heard about. Until she opened her mouth.

"What the hell are you doing here?" She squinted at him. "And this damn sunlight out here is doing too much."

Well, it was definitely her, and she wasn't happy to see him. "Your hair is black."

"Yes, how observant of you." She folded her arms.

He blinked at her. "I didn't know you owned hair in that colour or clothes in that shade."

"Well, you see, I woke up, hungover, to my mother telling me we have to go to church for somebody's child's christening and if I could please not come with my usual flair?"

"Oh, that makes sense."

"Does it? Because I'm happy to stay home and sleep, but she's insisting. So the church wig and dress came out. And all these people we'll see at the church are coming back to the house for post-christening breakfast. Why am I even telling you any of this?" she muttered. "You're at my house for no reason that I can think of."

He couldn't stop staring at the wig. "It's not you," he said. "I mean, it's a nice wig, but..."

"Why are you here?" she cut him off.

Right, he needed to stay on track. "I brought your phone and bag, but I need to talk to you first. Before I hand them over."

"Wow, blackmail this early? How rude. I really am a bad influence on you, aren't I? I'm sure that's another point you can add on that analysis of yours."

Well, that confirmed she had heard that part of the conversation. "May I come in?"

"No."

"No? I suppose that's fine, but can we talk before you leave?"

"Is that your karaoke friend?" a voice called out behind Reba. A head popped up over her shoulder. "Hi there, friend. Sorry for my rude daughter. Reba, why you have the man standing out here? Come in, come in. You didn't tell me your friend was visiting today? You ate yet? Tall man like you could probably eat some more even if you did, eh?"

"No, he's *not* staying. We have to get to church."

"Well, you have a guest, so you can stay." She looked back at Devon. "It must be important for him to be here so early. So please, do come in."

Devon looked from Reba's unamused face to her mother's cheerful one. The decision was easy, regardless of the consequences. "I'd love to come in. Thank you."

Reba's mother tugged her away from the door. "Don't mind her. She's had too much to drink at some party."

"My party, actually. I brought her stuff for her. And to take her to get her car."

"All of a sudden, it's your party?" Reba huffed.

"Oh, aren't you a gentleman? They don't make them like this anymore, you know. Especially not them lil' boys she like to talk to up the road. I'm Yvonne, by the way."

"Devon." He bit the inside of his cheek to stop the smile that wanted to form at Reba's rolled eyes.

Yvonne ushered him into the living room, where an older man was busy tucking his shirt into his pants. A younger woman stood next to him. Reba's father and sister, he assumed.

"Everyone, this is Reba's friend, Devon," Yvonne announced. "He's taking her to get her car at his house. I'll let Rhonda know something came up. Reba can give you something to eat. We have plenty, so don't worry about taking something. Better to do so before the hungry masses get here after the mass."

"I'm good, really." He needed Reba to be amenable. Asking her to dish out food for him wasn't going to do that.

"Damn right he's good. Plus, if he's hungry, he got two good working hands." She pointed down a hallway. "I'm going to change real quick. We can just go get my car one time." She held out her hand.

Her family didn't look like they would leave until she came out; they were making no movement towards the door, so he handed her the phone and bag. He didn't think she would lock herself in her room and leave him out here with an audience, but he really couldn't be sure of what she would do, could he?

"Don't mind her," Yvonne said, leading him over to the table where the food was set up buffet-style. "She's been like that since I woke her up. So, what do you do, Devon? If you don't mind me asking."

He looked at the spread. He had already eaten a quick, simple breakfast before heading out—wholegrain toast with peanut butter and banana slices—but his eyes landed on the tomato choka in a clear dish with some sada roti on a plate beside it. There were several other sides to go with the sada, plus puffs and pastries, both savoury and sweet. Everything had neat labels, so there would be no guessing what each item was. Devon appreciated the organisation of the table. He hated having to figure out what something was at a buffet, which opened up the eater to potential food allergies and just plain eating something they didn't like.

"I'm a Senior Project Manager at an architectural firm. Dax Designs."

"Oh, that sounds important. I bet you play a major role." She picked up a disposable plate from the stack on the table. "Tell me what you prefer. I'll fix you up, don't worry. You good with a little of everything?"

"That's not necessary, I can dish it out myself."

She didn't hand him the plate. "It's fine. You're a guest. No trouble at all," Yvonne assured him. "Reba rarely brings her friends over, so this is my pleasure, truly. You'd think she was ashamed of us or something."

"Just let her do it."

He looked up as Reba walked over, looking much more like herself with her pink hair freed, pink sweatpants, and a grey crop top with a big pink heart in the middle. She was still looking at him as if she didn't want him here. It was oddly unnerving. He had gotten used to her over-the-top bubbly demeanour; he wasn't certain how to react to her hard stare.

Of course, she had shown him small glimpses during the times he annoyed her. Nothing compared to this level, though.

She took his arm and led him over to the gallery area, away from her father and sister, who hadn't joined in the conversation with her mother but had quietly been listening.

"I suppose I should be grateful for you showing up." Reba dropped his hand and pressed her back to the ledge so she could face him, arms folded. "I get to escape this whole church affair. Even though my mother is going to hassle me about you when I get home."

"Why would she do that?"

"I told you. You're perfect boyfriend material in their eyes. Stable and shit."

"Is that bad? You make it sound terrible."

"Yes, when they think if I date someone like you, I'll calm down. Be less *this*." She tugged on the ends of her hair. "Be more like my sister, who I love dearly, but I'm *not* her. Never gonna be her."

"You sort of looked like her with that black wig," he said, hoping to lighten the mood. Instead, Reba didn't even crack a smile.

"You'd like if I was like that, wouldn't you? Less of the chaos agent that I am."

"I like you the way you are," he said.

It had taken him some time to realize that. Her all-over-the-place energy had definitely collided with his subdued nature, and according to his risk analysis, she definitely fell into that red zone. It didn't matter; he couldn't deny the crackle between them.

She narrowed her eyes. "No, you don't."

"Yes, I do."

She stared at him, saying nothing. The longer it went on, the more uncomfortable it became—simply because he wanted to kiss away that frown—but Devon didn't shift his gaze. He wanted her to know he was serious.

Yvonne came over to hand him the plate, shattering the tense moment. "Enjoy." She turned to Reba. "You didn't have to change. You looked fine."

"She looks more herself like this." The words fell from his mouth without much thought.

Reba shot him a look. "Okay, let's go." She grabbed onto his t-shirt and literally dragged him outside. Her grip on his shirt turned into her pressing a palm against his chest to stop his forward motion towards his car. "What was all of that back there? *'I like you the way you are.'*" She pitched her voice lower to mimic his words.

"Stating facts is all." He reached for her wrist, but she pulled her hand away from his chest before he could touch her.

"No, that's bullshit. Last night was all, 'I don't want to want her.' Now, it's all, 'I like you the way you are?'" She scoffed. "I know *I* play games, but not like this. I don't care if you think I'm a huge risky inconvenience in your life, but don't suddenly lie to me now."

"You didn't hear everything I said last night, did you? Just that part?"

The part she had heard wasn't that great. But he hadn't lied. He didn't want to want her. Reba had come in like a whirlwind, and he hadn't known how to deal with that. The sudden appearance of Joya had added to his already confused state.

In spite of that, and before he had talked to Joya, he had told Jeremy one thing he had known was a fact, even though the analysis had revealed that everything about Reba was risk incarnate. He was fascinated by her and found himself thinking about how she would approach a given situation. That had made him uneasy. He had his routines and didn't like to deviate from them, but Reba had shown him it wasn't necessarily a bad thing.

Jeremy, being the damn clairvoyant he was, had asked the hard question. "What else? When you see her or think of her randomly?"

"I think my heart tries out for the Olympics or something." It had been the first thing that had popped into his head, the heart in question doing exactly as he'd said.

Jeremy looked super smug at that. "Well, there you go.

There's your answer, bro. Fuck your lists and red zone risks or whatever."

He couldn't just get rid of his lists, but his reliance on them where people were concerned might need some rethinking.

"I heard enough," Reba said and started walking towards his car. "Let's just go."

"I told him I can't stop thinking about you. About how my heart feels like it wants to jump right out of my fucking chest. I may not want to feel what I do, but it's there. It feels weird to admit, but there it is."

She stopped and turned back to face him. "You want the idea of who I *could* be if you mould me just the way you want. Into the perfect little candidate. I'm not some checkbox on a list."

That damn list would truly haunt him forever. "I was wrong, okay? That list hasn't done me any favours, and it's useless because here you are."

"Yes, here I am. Everything you like to fuck but don't actually want. Which I told you is cool. Just be honest with yourself and me. My sister's single, just FYI."

"Reba."

She tugged on the door handle. "Can you open the car, please? And what the hell was that whole thing about me looking more myself? I don't need you defending me."

"Maybe not, but it doesn't hurt to have someone in your corner."

She rolled her eyes, waiting on him to press the button on his key fob to disarm his alarm. He disengaged the locks and walked around to the driver's side. She wasn't going to believe a word he said, which was fine. Words were a little trickier for him, but he would convince her she was wrong. Devon was a man of action.

What exactly do you want to convince her of? Do you even know?

"You enjoy having sex with me." That wasn't the best way to make his point, but it was easier than saying, *'I think I like like you,'* which would make him sound like some awkward teenager.

She snorted when he drove away from her house. "You want me to stroke your ego now, is that it? I'm still too hungover for this."

"No, I..." He was making an absolute mess of this. "I know you think I was trying to dissect you like something under a microscope, and I'm sorry. I'm not good at this. I need to analyse things I don't understand, and that can come across in a weird way. My spreadsheets help me with that."

"Perhaps, but I'm a real live person! Not a problem to be solved. Plus, I still have zero idea what you're going on about."

"The sex has been amazing. If I haven't said that, just know that it has been. I just happened to realise it isn't all I want." He tapped his fingers against the wheel. She was still saying nothing. He glanced at her. Her entire body was turned his way, mouth slightly open, just blinking at him.

He had to refocus on the road, but her stare burned into the side of his face. Or that could be his body's reaction to what he had dropped in the broad light of day like that. Sharing things like this made his entire body lock up like it was covering him in the necessary armour to protect the soft insides he had just exposed with those words.

"Joya and I aren't rekindling anything," he ventured on. "I just want to make that clear first. I know you thought otherwise. We talked briefly last night. I told my mother I didn't appreciate her trying to make this a thing."

"She seems nice."

"Yeah. We don't really know each other like that anymore, though."

"Hmm. Joya not being in the equation doesn't make a difference, does it? I'm not one of your proposals that you tweak until it's just right. You put me in a whole risk thingie."

"I know that. I'm not trying to. I just...it's what I do, but I shouldn't have done that to you."

She reached over and fiddled with his radio until some R&B blared out. He didn't have a clue who was singing, but he recognised the genre. He also knew she was trying to change the topic by distracting him with the sudden blare of the music. Reba was good at that, distracting him, but Devon wasn't going to be swayed today.

He lowered the volume, and she sat back. "Well, here's something you *don't* know. Trina bet that I could get you to fall for my charms. Get you to actually say you want me. What do you have to say to that?"

He stopped at the light that was one street away from the turn-off to his neighbourhood, which gave him ample time to look at her again. She was gazing at him expectantly, waiting for his reaction to her surprising words. With all the random things Reba had done since they'd met, he hadn't anticipated that.

This was another thing she was tossing in his path to distract from his confession. "Was sex part of it?"

She bit her lip, looked down at her nails. "I'm tempted to say it was, but no. That just kind of happened on its own."

"Okay."

She looked up. "That's it? Okay?"

"Yes, I'm not really surprised by this."

She raised a brow. "You're not?"

"Reba, it was obvious you were pushing my buttons from the start. I figured that was just all you, which I do know is true, but I didn't know someone had also bet you to do it. You were going to win, either way, it seems. I thought it would be easy to just ignore you, but clearly not, and I think I'm fine with that. More than fine, actually." He blew out a breath and shook his head. So this was what it felt like to talk about his feelings. Unpleasant but strangely freeing. Who knew?

"Why aren't you upset about this?" she demanded.

"Why do you want me to be?" he shot back.

That one struck a nerve. She turned away to look out the window. "Just drive."

He didn't bother her again until they got to his house. She jumped out of the car, ready to head over to hers, but she wasn't running away that easily.

"We're supposed to bake today. We have two weekends left. Don't tell me you're about to leave me hanging?"

"I'm in no mood for this."

"Let me make you one of my hangover cures."

"Have you ever been hungover in your life? I wouldn't think you'd allow yourself to lose control like that."

He didn't make it a habit. The one time he had gotten so drunk, the experience had made him never want to lose control like that ever again. Hell, it had definitely been what had pushed him to grab onto control the way he did. He brushed a wayward strand of her hair away from her face, letting his finger trace over her ear as he tucked it behind. He didn't smile at the way she bit her lip, but he wanted to. Badly. Reba might be the master at flirting, but Devon had his ways. He was just less in your face about it.

"The one time was enough," he admitted. "But as you

know very well, certain factors do contribute to me having a slippery hold on control sometimes. Please. Let me take care of you. You can even nap for a bit while I get the baking stuff organised. I have an idea, but I'll need to go to the grocery for some food colouring."

"I don't... You just want to watch me sleep again, you weirdo."

The laughter burst out of him unexpectedly. "You *do* look like an angel when you're sleeping. It's hard not to look at you. The difference is startling."

"I'm no angel," she tossed out before walking up to his door. "Come on, then."

He had won this round. She wasn't getting into her car and driving away. Everyone liked to get on his ass for his rigorous plans, and while he was beginning to understand a little of why they went so hard at him over that, he wasn't about to do a complete 180. He had also come to learn the damn tight feeling in his chest wasn't some weird heart-burn, but the realisation that he was maybe ready to allow a little chaos into his life if she would have him.

CHAPTER TWENTY-FIVE
REBA

IT WAS THE ODDEST THING TO BE "TAKEN CARE OF" BY DEVON.

She hadn't seen this part of Devon before, so when he told her to just relax on the couch, she didn't argue anymore, too curious. She would indeed be taking that nap when he left to get the extra items he needed to try his own Rubik's Cube cake. He had insisted he was ready, especially with the bake-off two weeks away. She was too exhausted to go back and forth with him over that or the ridiculous things he'd said in the car.

There was just no way he was serious about any of it. Devon didn't want her for more than sex. He couldn't. Why would he when he had told her over and over, in different ways, that she was a problem for his well-preserved control? High-risk, just as he'd told Jeremy.

Yet that tiny, winged thing had taken a place in her stomach again. It was flopping all over the damn place as she watched him retreat to the kitchen to prepare whatever this hangover concoction was. She had thought that damn annoying fluttering was some sort of weird side effect of mixing the white wine and the homemade one.

And now the ever predictable Devon was deviating from his script with this shit. She was too used to men trying their sweet talk on her to keep the sex going but balking at the idea that they could introduce her to their precious family just the way she was. Devon didn't come across as a lyrics man, too serious to go that route, but what was she supposed to think? That he had suddenly had a whole ass epiphany about her?

It didn't make sense.

Sex with Devon was more than great. After her mini-meltdown last night, she had been ready to throw that all away because she thought he wanted to see what he could do with Joya.

Because you didn't want to get hurt first.

Now that Joya wasn't even an issue, Reba was still thinking if she shouldn't just jettison the entire sex situation.

Why? Because you feel the same as he does, but you're a damn coward?

Nope. No, fuck that noise. That last thought had driven her to lay back on the couch and check her phone. Anything to not have to deal with her subconscious wilding out like this. She and Devon as anything other than fuck buddies was a joke. Not because she didn't think she was a catch. She was. He'd be damn lucky to have her, but the mere fact was that he couldn't seriously want her for a real relationship.

He could say all the right things, but did he mean them? Not that it mattered anyway. She didn't *want* him to mean them.

On her phone, there was a message from Scott checking up on her and an entire trail of a one-sided conversation from Trina. She replied to Scott first, letting him know she'd be okay and thanking him for the rescue.

Trina's monologue she'd deal with later. After that nap. She needed a clearer head for that one because she was going to get her ass reamed for supposedly leaving her on read. She set the phone to the side and had almost dozed off when Devon came back out with something in a glass. The colour was the dark green of spinach, which he had probably added in there. Reba did *not* do her veggies in liquid form.

"Oh, *hell* no."

He didn't budge. "It looks less than pleasing, but I assure you it will work."

She wrinkled her nose. "What's in it?"

"Some kale, apples, cucumber, celery, lemon, and a bit of ginger."

She gagged because it brought back too many childhood memories of her mother trying to force her to take some bush remedy to strengthen her immune system. "I'd rather just suffer, thanks."

He placed the glass on the table near her. "My mother swears by it, and the one time I did have to take it, I was fine after. With some food in my stomach as well."

"That shit looks nasty. Probably tastes like the lawn outside. When did you even have to take this?" She couldn't picture him drunk at all. She wondered if he was trying to trick her into drinking some nasty ass thing he had never actually taken himself.

"I'll admit, it's been some time. Years, actually, but I'll never forget the moment. Or this drink because I never wanted to feel like that again. Or have to drink this, to be honest."

"Tell me the story, and I'll consider taking a taste." She

pushed up into a sitting position. As much as the couch was comfortable, she didn't want him hovering over her like this. Too many ways for her mind to go into the gutter when she had just told herself she wasn't going to keep having sex with him. Especially if he had supposedly caught feelings.

"I had just gotten accepted into the program I wanted to do at UWI, Mona campus. My friends thought a party was a good idea. I resisted naturally."

"Naturally," she echoed. She could picture a young, too serious Devon balking at the idea of such a celebration.

He picked up the glass of death and held it out, waiting for her to take it before he went on. "They managed to convince me, saying I just had to show up. It was at someone's house, so I figured a safe space, you know. Nothing much could go down there that I wouldn't be able to handle. Somehow they got into daring me to drink all sorts of shit. Telling me if I was so much in control, I could handle it."

She sniffed at the drink. "Ah, yes, good old peer pressure."

"The challenge aspect appealed, so I did it. Went way overboard, then had to be literally carted home because I couldn't even make it to the car on my own. Felt like shit next morning, and my mother made me this."

She took a tentative sip. The apple and lemon were working overtime to mask the taste, so it wasn't too horrible. Not great, but she wasn't going to throw it all back up. "Is that why you lean into your lists and routines like that?"

"Yeah." He nodded. "That scared me. I didn't ever want to feel like that again. Letting go felt like I'd regret it immensely."

"I can see how that could scar a person. Letting go

doesn't always have to be scary like that, though."

"I'm beginning to see that."

She drank more of the hangover concoction purely to avoid that look in his eyes. It was...soft. She didn't know how else to describe it. He had looked at her in a myriad of ways—frustration, disbelief, lust—but never like this. Her stomach acted up again. Jesus, maybe she needed a purge or something.

"You should get to the grocery soon. I'll nap while you're gone, so we can get cracking when you're back."

"Try to eat something too. It helps. If you haven't eaten breakfast, you can have what your mother packed for me."

"Okay." There wasn't anything else for her to say.

The crackle between them this time felt different. Not the burning sexual tension that had been sparking before and after they'd had sex. This was something else, something sweeter, gentler, scarier because *where the hell had this come from*?

He cleared his throat. "I'll go."

"Yeah, go do that."

"You can use the guest bed if you want."

"What about your bed?" She might be feeling ready to pass out, but she could still push his buttons, given that he had caught her unawares with all this "care." She needed to balance things out again.

He nudged the glass in her hand, urging her to drink more. "You've already been there, so it's not a problem. Just no eating or drinking in the bed, please."

Damn, he wasn't even going to get a little ruffled about it? Fine. She liked his bed. It was comfy. She might as well take advantage of all this attention he was giving her. Even if it intensified that damn thing battering away at her insides.

He took up his wallet and keys and left her on the couch, contemplating what the hell was really going on. She wanted to take that nap but needed someone to run all of this by. As much as Trina was going to give her hell for this, she wouldn't mince her words, and she would be brutally honest. Besides, it was time to collect her winnings, wasn't it?

She drank the rest of the green juice, ate some of the food off of Devon's plate, then made her way to his bed to message Trina.

> *Reba:* can I call you?
> *Trina:* oh so she's alive???? And wanting to call me? What's going on with you??
> *Reba:* just tell me if I can call you before I pass out in this comfy ass bed.
> *Trina:* who's bed?

Reba didn't bother to reply to that. It was easier to call, even though she usually resisted that.

"Now tell me that man kidnapped you and kept you in his bed, and that's why you ignored all my messages. It's the only reason I'll accept," Trina said as soon as the call connected.

"Well, I'm in his bed now, but that wasn't it."

"Explain."

"I left my phone at his house after the party. I only got it back a little while ago. When he brought it to my house."

"Hmm, okay. Doesn't explain why you're in his bed now. Hold on, you not calling me while he's sexing you up, are you? Because that's wild even for you."

Reba laughed. "Negative. He's not here. Went to get some stuff for baking."

"So what? You just playing Goldilocks and sleeping in the man bed just so?"

"He's..." She wrinkled her nose. "Taking care of me, apparently. I'm hungover as shit, so he made some green thing for me to drink. It's a little weird."

"Just tell me this. You won that damn bet, didn't you? You're not slick at all."

"Yes, fine. I did."

"So why you didn't say so?"

"Um..."

Trina's snort was so loud in her ear. "You had sex," she stated. "You are *so* predictable."

"What? Me? You take that back. I'm not predictable." That was plain ass rude. Trina knew her better than that.

"Not in the usual way folks think someone could be. But when you want to avoid something, you find all how to distract. Turn up the sexy. In my case, you plain avoided me. In Devon's case, he wants something more, doesn't he? After all the sexy fun, now you're calling me in a panic."

"I do not panic. I called to confirm I won."

"Yeah, sure. You can't lie to me, missy. I'm right about him, aren't I?"

Reba hated when Trina was right about anything. She gloated so annoyingly. "Okay, fine, yes, he said some wacky things that cannot be true."

"How you know?"

"Because..."

Trina sucked her teeth. "You don't even have a legit reason. He strikes me as the type to not play around. So if he said something, he meant it. Does he seem duplicitous to you? Plus, he not like them little boys you like to play around with then get vex when they show you exactly who you thought they were."

"Wait, what the hell? That's not..."

"Hold on, not done," Trina interrupted. "You go for the exact opposite of the men your parents suggest. A bunch of fuck boys, which okay, have your fun, but when they show you who they are, of course, it still hurts. I get that, but your parents might be onto something. You need someone to balance off your chaos, not accelerate that shit."

"You think I need to be less of me?" Well, damn. If her best friend even thought that way...

"Oh no, that's not what I'm saying at all. I love your chaotic fun-shine ass. You complete me and all that, but..."

"But?" Reba prompted.

"You need someone with a little more maturity to keep you grounded. And *you* can help him add that spice to his life. Sounds like a win-win to me."

"Do you really think a man like that won't get tired of me after the novelty wears off?" Why was she even asking this? She wasn't considering her and Devon as a thing. That would be way too farfetched, right?

"Give him a chance and find out. Aren't you Ms. Risk-Taker?"

Sure, she thrived on living her life that way, yet this felt *too* risky. She really wanted that nap now. "I need to go sleep off this shit."

"Yeah, go do that. We'll talk later."

She was sure they would. Trina was going to tell Ayo all about this, no doubt. Then she'd have both of them breathing down her neck about what she wanted to do.

Not her problem right now because sleep was calling. With a head full of thoughts and a stomach taken over by nerves, she curled up on Devon's sheets and willed sleep to come.

CHAPTER TWENTY-SIX

DEVON

THE GROCERY RUN TOOK SLIGHTLY LONGER THAN ANTICIPATED. HE had planned to be in and out in no time as he knew exactly what he was there for with no detours in mind, except he had seen those foil balloons for various occasions near the cashier. There was no reason for him to be standing in front of the selection for so long, contemplating if he should get Reba one.

She would be surprised, sure, but in her current state of annoyance at him, would it have the desired effect or the opposite? He did want to cheer her up, but would a cheap-looking *Get Well Soon* balloon do that? In spite of his hesitation, he checked the price then grabbed the first one before he could question his decision to death.

He didn't need to do this, but he wanted to, regardless of if she threw it back in his face. Actions and all that. Some foil balloon wasn't going to have her falling into his arms agreeing to date him, but he still felt compelled to get it.

As he pulled into the driveway and stepped out of the car, the balloon bobbing about slightly, he came face-to-face with his neighbour, who was out watering his plants.

Mr. Garrett was an older man with a wife and four noisy grandchildren who sometimes visited. Watering can in hand, his eyes dipped down to the balloon in Devon's hand, then back up.

"Well, morning, neighbour."

Devon was definitely not about to be caught in any small talk. Mr. Garrett was retired and spent most of his days in his gallery, people-watching. He would have noticed Reba's car out front, might have even seen her arrive this morning.

Devon waved and kept it moving, stepping inside. He was certain they all gossiped about him at their monthly community meetings, especially since he had never attended a single one, always begging off because of work. They had certainly gotten more fodder since he had started baking with Reba, and probably after last night too.

He deposited the things for baking into the kitchen and went upstairs with the balloon. She was still asleep, curled up on her side, looking exactly like the angelic being he had claimed she mimicked when she slept. He hadn't lied. Sleep transformed Reba completely.

Her hair was a light pink wave across his pillow, darker at her roots where the colour was growing out. Her top had rucked up a bit to expose more of her stomach, his eyes drawn to her navel ring, a bunch of dangling stars this time.

He snapped himself out of it and clutched the balloon tighter in his grip. "Reba." He shook her shoulder lightly.

She rolled over and shook her head. "I was having a nice dream." Her eyes remained closed, no attempt to get up.

"You can rest a bit more if you like. I can set things up in the kitchen."

"Just give me a sec," she mumbled. "You're paying me, so I should be instructing."

"I brought you something," he said.

She opened her eyes a fraction and squinted up at him. She blinked as if trying to clear away the sleep. "Is that a balloon?"

Of course, she was confused. "Uh, yes. Here."

She sat up, face still scrunched up. Her arms rose above her head in a full stretch before she reached for the balloon. "Why?" she asked, twirling the balloon around.

He shrugged. "Just because."

"You don't do things just because. Is this a bribery balloon or something?"

"Why would I be trying to bribe you?"

"I don't know. This is just unexpected."

So maybe the balloon hadn't been a good idea after all. "If you don't want it, I can get rid of it."

"No, no, it's fine. I just—" She looked at the balloon, then back up at him. "Thanks."

He truly wanted to know what was going on inside her head. "You're welcome. Come down when you're ready, okay?"

"Uh, okay."

She looked more awake when she joined him in the kitchen, watching him arrange the ingredients. He glanced at the recipe on his laptop screen. He had every intention of following the instructional video. Reba didn't say anything, simply watching him.

"Thanks for the balloon. Weird but cute. Just like me." Her elbows were on the counter, face cupped in her hands as she watched him.

"I wouldn't say you're weird, just overly chipper with a penchant for chaos."

"I like that. Might put it on a business card."

"You're in a better mood, I see."

"Well, napping isn't just for babies. I feel refreshed."

"Great." He needed to get started. There were way more steps to this than baking cupcakes or cookies. He had to ensure the four square cakes he baked were the correct height. Cut each cake into three log-like lengths so he could spread black ganache icing in between. Stack them up so they looked like one cube and cover it with more ganache.

"Are you making a mini or going for the big one?"

"Big one." Just as she had suggested when she'd made the small version. The mini wouldn't help him if it was the larger size he would be tackling at the bake-off in two weeks. "What you said made sense."

"Say that again, so I can get out my phone and hit record." Her mouth curved into a small smile, and he returned it with a big one of his own. It felt strange to just let one loose like that, but he couldn't stop himself.

"Oh."

"What?"

"When you smile like that..." She trailed off and cleared her throat. "Better get started. You'll need to chill your cube cake once it's covered in ganache before moving on to the fondant squares."

He kept his triumphant grin to himself. He wouldn't hassle her to finish her sentence, but maybe he needed to break out a smile more often. She had looked literally stunned for a moment there.

Looking around, he realised he had forgotten one thing. "I need to get my set squares and rulers to make sure the fondant covering for the cake is a precise cube. And dye the fondant the colour of the squares."

"Wow, you really studied this recipe, didn't you?"

"Well, yeah. It's a lot." He could visualise each step he had to take to get to the end, and it wasn't an exaggeration to say it was a lot. He would need to time himself as well to ensure he could finish within the time allotted to each participant of the bake-off.

This wasn't going to be easy. Devon did love a challenge. It was a little harder with Reba hovering, offering advice, but that was what he had signed up for. The change in their relationship did add a different level of tension, especially with his confession. Didn't matter; he worked well under pressure. Usually.

Reba watched intently when it was time for him to ensure the baked cakes were the right height for the cube. She had moved from standing across from him offering advice to right up under him, peering down as he sliced off bits of the cake squares to ensure it was the perfect cube shape.

"Now why is this shit hot?" she muttered. He paused and swung his head her way. She stepped back. "What?"

"You know I heard that, right?"

"So?" she challenged. "You're not the only one that can state supposed facts."

"Well, why didn't you say it directly to me?"

She waved at the knife in his hand. "Because I don't need you getting any more outrageous ideas, and we're not having sex again. You need to pick up the pace with this. You'll be judged on how well you finish during the time."

He sliced the edge off one cake after measuring. "Oh? When did we decide on no sex?"

"*We* didn't. I did. You're obviously confusing things. I get it, my pussy is magical, but it's best we revert to business, no pleasure if you can't mix it up with other things."

He immediately got hard hearing her talk like that. She wasn't even trying to rile him up, but it didn't matter; she didn't have to try. And maybe she was correct. After two years of no intimacy with anyone, the sex could be escalating his feelings, but he didn't think this was a matter of Reba not reciprocating them. She didn't believe he felt what he did. If she didn't care, none of that would matter.

"Alright, no sex is fine."

"Why?" Exasperation coloured her tone. "Why are you being so agreeable?"

"I'm quite fine with continuing to have sex with you, but this isn't a one-sided thing. You don't want to, so I respect that."

Her brow creased. "But you don't even know why I'm saying no."

"'I don't want to anymore' is a valid reason," he pointed out. He was curious, of course, but he didn't need to badger her about it. Besides, he would show her they could work beyond sex. "Now, I've stacked the pieces. It'll look more like a cube when we spread the ganache."

She didn't say anything, so he went about putting the ganache they'd prepared in between the yellow cake then over the entire thing until it looked like a perfect black cube. He went over the edges again to ensure it was smooth.

Reba filmed him, even though he wouldn't upload this to maintain the element of surprise. The video would be useful for him to review after, see where he needed to shave off some time or do better technique-wise.

When they put the cake in the fridge for the ganache to harden a bit before the next step, he thought about going over his presentation again. They were showcasing to the client this coming week. He felt ready. He would drill with Chelsea tomorrow again to be certain.

"I have a bit of work to do while we wait. The presentation I mentioned. Is that okay?"

"Show me."

"What?"

"Run it through for me. I'm not the client, but I can pretend I am. It could help to have someone not connected to this in any way give you feedback."

It all sounded harmless enough. Reba sat back on the couch as Devon picked up the clicker to change the slides on his laptop. She didn't interrupt as he went through the entire presentation, just nodded as he spoke.

When he came to the end, he looked at her expectantly.

"So, you want me to be honest?"

"Always." He meant that. It wouldn't do him any good to sugar coat things. They hadn't been like that since they'd started this baking journey. Regardless of what came after it, he wanted her to tell him as it was.

"I'm not an expert by any means."

"Reba, I value your feedback. Please, tell me."

"I can't speak on the actual architect stuff, but I think you need to add a bit more personal touch? Why should the client choose you over anyone else who comes with a probably equally good proposal? You touched on how Dax Designs values the eco-friendly side of things; well, I think you need to give more examples. Anyone can just say that, but are you all really living it?"

"Huh." He rubbed at his jaw. They had included a small portion of that, but Devon had been way more focused on their expertise in the business and actual design than leaning heavily into their mandate to ensure eco-friendly buildings. "You're right."

Reba shrugged. "Despite what a lot of people think, I'm not just a pretty face, you know." She said it nonchalantly, but Devon saw behind her casual response. Somewhere along her life, someone had used her looks to cut her down.

"I never thought you were just that. You're a nuisance to my equilibrium, too."

She rolled her eyes. "You sweet talker, you."

"Better at letters, remember?"

"Yeah, yeah, whatever. How much sweet-talking can you do in a letter anyhow?"

He closed off the presentation and came to stand in front of her. "You doubt my skills?"

She looked up at him, challenge in her eyes. "Lil' bit."

"Hmm." He leaned down, gaze levelled with hers. "A wise woman once said, 'I'm irresistible, and you will fall under my spell.' I may not be at your level, but I know my strengths, and I play to them."

She got to her feet, forcing him to step back. "We should check the cake now."

He pressed his hand lightly to the curve where her shoulder and neck met, felt her pulse pounding under his fingers. "Yes, let's," he said, dropping a kiss on her forehead before walking off to the kitchen because she wasn't the only one who knew how to shake things up.

"What the fuck, man!"

Her loud sputtering behind him made him smile so wide he was certain anyone who knew him well and saw him now would wonder what had gotten into him.

He rubbed at his chest, heart racing again. He hadn't felt anything like this in so long and was determined to hold onto it even as the hurricane herself was determined to spin off in another direction.

CHAPTER TWENTY-SEVEN
REBA

"FUCKING HELL, NOT ANOTHER ONE."

"Pardon?"

Reba looked up from her phone, having completely forgotten she wasn't alone. Cherisse's expression remained neutral, but the man standing next to her was looking at her as if she had lost her whole mind.

Maybe she had, cussing like that at a client meeting. But really, it was Devon's fault.

"Fudge is what I said. You asked what we could do differently. Most people never consider the delight of fudge as a dessert. It's different and local. Your foreign visitors would literally eat it up. What about an entire section of just local sweets?" she asked, pulling that save out of her ass.

Mr. Carlton nodded, rubbing his beard. "Hmm, I wouldn't have considered it either, but it sounds good. Is that something you can do?" He turned to Cherisse.

"Of course." She gestured for Mr. Carlton to continue the walk through the venue.

He would be throwing a party to wine and dine some

international clients and had reached out to them to do the desserts. Reba blew out a breath. God, she could have almost cost them that job if she had been any louder.

Damn Devon King's entire existence. The man had sent her another cat meme. The folder she had set up just for that purpose on her phone was thriving, but the why of it all was making her lose her mind.

She looked down at the message again. The meme was a reply to her text telling him good luck. He had that presentation today. She hadn't expected a response in the first place, let alone a bunch of cat memes, which he was basically spamming their chat with now.

This man really didn't do anything halfway, did he? It was sort of cute.

They wrapped up with Mr. Carlton and Reba drove them back to Cherisse's apartment, where they found Remi staring intently at her laptop.

Remi didn't look away from the screen. "How was the meeting?"

"Great." Cherisse hovered over Remi's shoulder, looking at her screen. "Reba cussed in front of the client but made a quick save, so all good."

Reba's face heated. "Now why did you need to bring that up? I don't have a good excuse. Just saw something on my phone that surprised me. Sorry."

"It's cool," Cherisse assured her. "He's fully on board with the local sweets idea. This is why I keep you around. I've never thought of adding that to our menu. I can experiment with different flavours of fudge."

"Sounds fun." It did. She had missed Cherisse when she'd been gone, but now, they could resume all their usual work shenanigans.

Remi perked up. "Fudge?"

"Yes, you get to taste-test." Cherisse rubbed her hands together and turned to Reba. "I know you still have to help Devon with that bake-off, but I can't wait to fully steal you back. I have some plans in the works. More on that in due time. Speaking of Devon..."

Oh, Cherisse wasn't being slick at all. "Nothing to talk about there."

Remi turned away from her laptop to look at them. "I still want to hear more about the fudge, but yes, do tell me more about Mr. King. Have things progressed since I saw you two looking like a sexy power couple at that exhibit?"

"Excuse me? What exhibit?" Cherisse asked.

"Uh..." Right, she had never told Cherisse about that. She shot Remi a look. She shrugged, the "I don't give a shit" message coming through loud and clear. "That was also nothing."

"Hmm. You sure?" Cherisse's eyes narrowed. "Keiran told me Devon called him for advice this morning. On whether he should make an unannounced stop at your house on Sunday. That sounds like a whole lotta something to me. Care to share what that was about? What happened after we left the party?"

Devon hadn't shared that. Huh. So even in an attempted moment of spontaneity, the man had still needed to run it by someone. That shouldn't be so endearing, and yet Reba smiled at the picture Devon had probably made while talking to Keiran. She dropped down onto the couch. Better to get comfortable since an interrogation was coming. Remi had already given up on her work and turned her chair around.

"He just returned my phone and bag. That's it."

"But didn't you have to return to get your car?" Cherisse

insisted. "After you left with Scott. You would've gotten your stuff anyhow."

She loved this group of people, truly she did, but Scott could have also kept that little tidbit to himself. She hadn't gone into details with him, but it had been obvious that Devon was the reason she was fleeing the party.

"What exactly did Scott say?"

"Keiran just brought up he was at the party, and Scott casually mentioned he took you home cuz you weren't feeling a hundred percent up to driving."

"You know what? Fine. Devon took me back to get my car, fed me, made me some hangover drink. I took a nap, and we baked after. That's it. He also sent me a couple of cat memes today. Happy now?"

We also had the hottest sex ever, and he randomly kissed me on the forehead on Sunday, too, like a weirdo, but it was oddly sweet.

She didn't say that. She was still trying to process what the hell had gotten into him. She'd tracked his every move after that kiss. He hadn't said a thing as they'd removed the perfect cube-shaped cake from the fridge and proceeded to roll out the black fondant squares they were putting around the cake so they could stick the different coloured squares too. Those were made of fondant as well. Reba had thrown him several sidelong glances as they'd cut out the smaller squares. Devon didn't even look at her, just continued to work, diligently measuring and drawing the grid lines, so they knew precisely where to place each square.

She had focused on his hands, mind wandering back to the moment he had touched her neck right before he had pressed his lips to her forehead. That had been a mistake. The oven wasn't even on, yet the kitchen had felt heated.

Devon had clearly retained a grasp on the control that

had previously been in shambles while *she* was unravelling bit by bit. The urge to swipe the whole cake off the table and beg him to have her right on top of the counter had gotten so strong. The only thing bringing her back to reality had been the sting of her teeth digging into her bottom lip.

"Well, that's sweet," Remi said, dragging her back to the present.

"He was being a decent human being. Do I need to give him a medal for that?" she asked a little sharply.

Cherisse and Remi exchanged glances, doing that silent communication thing. Annoying soulmate behaviour, which Reba usually found adorable as hell, but not today. Not when she was being asked to explain herself when she didn't even know how to verbalise what was going on.

"Okay, so you don't like being wooed, is that it?" Cherisse asked gently, making her feel like an ass for her harsh tone.

This was no different than how she had teased Cherisse about Keiran or Remi about Maxi. Yet, coupled with Trina's words, she couldn't help feeling like everyone thought they knew how she should feel better than her. It scraped at that one insecurity she had, the one she didn't look at too closely, preferring to slap some glitter on it to make everything nice and shiny.

The one where she thought her family was right. That maybe all she was *was* simply a colourful plaster she had put on.

Instead, she decided to focus on what Cherisse had said. "Being wooed?"

"Yeah. You *do* know that's what he's doing, right?"

"I...no."

"Does Devon even like cat memes?"

"He ignored them all when I sent a few months ago. I don't think he gets them."

"But who loves them? You do," Cherisse pointed out.

"So what? Lots of people do. That doesn't mean anything."

"What else has he been doing?" Remi piped up.

Forehead kiss forehead kiss forehead kiss

Her mind wouldn't let her forget that, apparently. He had also done something else that she had been ignoring, but should she mention it? She bit into her lip to stop from blurting it out. It still felt like it wasn't real.

"Oh, he definitely did something else." Remi pointed at Reba's mouth. "Tell number one. Lip-biting."

"I do *not* have a tell," Reba insisted.

"Just spit it out. If it's nothing, then it shouldn't matter."

"Fine. He left me something in my bag. I found it randomly. I don't even know what it's supposed to mean. It doesn't rhyme, but I suppose it could be a poem? I don't know."

"Show us," Cherisse said.

She pulled the mystery note from her bag. She had found it after getting home on Sunday. Had read it so many times because the shock still hadn't quite worn off. It had been going round and round in her head since then.

Lightning strikes. Embrace it with open arms. The beautiful chaos.

Cherisse looked up from the piece of paper. "Did he write this himself? Are these his actual words?"

"I dunno."

Remi leaned over to read it too. "Girl, you didn't ask? This man is definitely on a wooing mission."

She hadn't mentioned it at all. Had acted as if she hadn't gotten it, and he wasn't asking either.

Cherisse was watching her closely. "You don't want to be wooed?"

"He's probably not serious anyhow, so it doesn't matter."

Remi shook her head and turned her chair back around to face the laptop. "Devon King? Not serious about something? Say that again, and really listen to yourself."

Reba sighed. "Look, fine, if it'll get you off my back. He told me he wants more than sex. Which, uh, surprise, we've been having. Until now, I guess, cuz I said we wouldn't be doing that anymore. It's clearly clouding his judgement. What am I supposed to do with this supposed 'more' that he claims he wants? Let's say, hypothetically, I *did* feel something that isn't just sexy feelings. But I don't want to?"

"Been there," Cherisse said.

"Still there," Remi joined in.

Reba got to her feet, needing to direct all this pent-up energy and frustration elsewhere. "Him and me don't make sense outside the bedroom. Relationships aren't even my thing!"

"You've tried like once," Remi informed dryly.

"Sex is my expertise. I'm good at it. It's been proven, over and over, that I'm *not* girlfriend material. I'm not..." She bit her lip, turned away. Tried to swallow past the sudden thickness in her throat.

"Oh, honey," Cherisse said behind her.

"I'm fine. I'm *fine*."

"No, I don't think so." Cherisse's hands came around her, enveloping her in a hug. "I'm sorry those fools made you feel like that. Fuck those assholes."

"With a rusty rake," Remi added, joining in on the hug fest by placing her arms around Reba's front.

Reba let them surround her with their love and mushiness for a few seconds, breathing in and out to ensure she wasn't actually going to cry.

She tapped at Remi's arm. "As much as I'm loving this sexy sandwich, can you just...step back a sec? Both of you, please?"

They gave her much-needed space, Remi going back to her chair and Cherisse sinking into the couch. Reba looked back and forth between them.

She swallowed past the lump in her throat. "Trina sort of told me the same thing about Devon. He doesn't play around, and I get that, but this is a lot to process."

"So process it. At your pace, even if we've been on your ass about it. Just really think about it without letting every experience before colour what could be. Trust me, I know how a shitty past can mess you up."

She trusted Cherisse. Knew she, Remi, Trina, and Ayo had good intentions. At the end of the day, she was the only one who could decide how to proceed. If Devon was truly showing her he was serious, maybe it was time to pay more attention.

"Now, I need you to take me somewhere," Cherisse said, slinging an arm around Reba's shoulder. "It's a Sweethand-based surprise, actually."

"Ooh, yes!" Remi clapped.

Reba looked between their smiling faces. "What's going on? You two keeping secrets?"

"Yesss. Send me pics of her face!" Remi went back to her work as Reba tried to figure out what Cherisse was up to.

Whatever it was would be a good distraction from this entire Devon mess.

Boss lady wasn't breaking, though, no matter how hard Reba tried. Cherisse's lips were sealed as she gave Reba directions to wherever the hell they were going. The drive gave her some time to think about what they had told her.

She had made a half-hearted attempt at being in a serious relationship. When that backfired, she had gone back to what she knew, was familiar with. Fun flings with guys that her parents would definitely never approve of. Damn, had she been sabotaging her happiness all this time?

"Turn in here," Cherisse instructed.

Reba looked through her window as she pulled up into the parking area. They were in front of a small building with papered-over windows, a Sold sign placed on the front door.

"Um, Cherry? Is this what I think it is?" Reba asked calmly, even as she wanted to squeal.

Cherisse took her hand and led her to the door. "Come on. See inside first before you go off." Her wide grin was definitely saying what Reba had guessed.

The inside was empty, but Reba's mind was already churning with the possibilities.

"So," Cherisse spun in a circle, "we're in Sweethand's new location. No more doing this out of my apartment, thank you, Jesus."

Reba finally allowed herself to scream and hug Cherisse. This had been one of Cherisse's dreams for a long time. "Oh my god, it's really happening! Are you gonna have dining in? I can already see some cute tables and chairs set up right in this corner."

"Definitely. Maybe we can get Devon to help with the

interior layout. I don't know if that's a thing he does, but..."
She grinned, and Reba rolled her eyes.

"You ask him. It's your place." Reba twirled around.
"This is amazing."

"It is, but there's more."

Reba stopped twirling. "More?"

"Oh, yeah. I couldn't have gotten here without you, you
know that, right? I want to offer you the Manager position."

"I'm sorry, *what?*" Reba choked out. She couldn't have
heard right. "But I...I don't have a degree or anything.
That's a big position."

"Reba, do you really think I give a damn about some
piece of paper? The moment we met, I knew we were going
to be baking up some magic."

"You literally walked up to me and said, 'I need you.' I
thought you were hitting on me."

Cherisse laughed. "Yeah, I did come on a little strongly
then, but when I saw what you had done at that small gathering, I hunted down the host and badgered them until
they pointed you out."

"You mean the whole scene I caused wasn't the reason
you hired me?" Reba had gotten into it with the host that
day too. The fact that Cherisse had wanted her to help with
Sweethand even then still blew her mind to this day.

"I mean, I did admire your fire then." Cherisse chuckled.
"I know this is a big responsibility, but I couldn't offer it to
anyone but you first. If you prefer to stay in your current
position, that's fine too. I'd totally get it, but you've been
there with me throughout all of this, and you deserve to go
to the next level with me by my side, so think about it?"

"I..." She was legitimately at a loss for words. Her
parents had always accused her of not being ambitious
enough, of not wanting to aim for more than an assistant.

Reba was truly content with where she was. Cherisse seeing potential in her as a manager for an actual Sweethand location was so unexpected and yet gratifying that she thought Reba was capable of this. She didn't want to let Cherisse down, but this was huge.

"I'll think about. When are you anticipating the opening?"

"I think we're safer if we aim for early next year. It's already September."

"I'll definitely have an answer way before then."

"Don't stress too much, okay? Whatever you choose, I'm happy with. If you pass on the new position, I'll definitely need you to help me choose and sit in on interviews."

"Deal!"

"Now, what do you say about some lunch to celebrate? My treat."

"Oh, no, no, boss lady. I got you. You've done so much.

"Alright, you don't have to twist my arm. Rent in this place ain't cheap!"

Reba snorted. She took photos of the empty space so she could compare it to when they had everything up and running. And maybe she would show it to Devon too, get his opinion on it. Just because he was in the business. Not because she was going to use it as an excuse to talk to him.

Not at all.

CHAPTER TWENTY-EIGHT
DEVON

SHE WANTS ME. SHE WANTS ME NOT.

The mantra went around and around in his head as Devon attacked the punching bag. Sweat dripped everywhere, but he wasn't ready to stop yet.

She left you on read. Maybe that was too many cat memes, even for her?

More jabs at the bag as the new set of repetitive statements made a nice little home in his brain. He had thought she would appreciate the memes. One for every time he had ignored the ones she had sent him months before. Maybe he should have spread them out?

Yeah, you really didn't think that through logically. So unlike you.

He gave the bag one last punch before just deciding he'd had enough working out for the night. His mind was not going to be put at ease. He *could* just call her instead of trying to, once again, analyse the situation to death.

He took off the boxing gloves and placed them on the table so he could take a swig from his water bottle. His mind might be racing, but he hoped this would at least make his body tired enough to get some good rest tonight. Maybe he would be too tired to dream about Reba again.

He blew out a breath, swiping his arm across his face. He needed to shower after he cooled off a bit. He checked his phone again. Nothing. For the millionth time since Sunday, he wondered if she had even found his note.

It had been a weird impulsive move to scribble the words and tuck it into her bag, hoping it would be a nice surprise. She had said she'd never gotten any letters like that, so he had wanted her to experience it. Perhaps she didn't understand his words? She had to know it was from him.

The doorbell going off startled him. He didn't usually get visitors at 7 p.m. on a work night. His mother and siblings knew better than to just show up when chances that he could still be at work would be high.

With the Sanctuary presentation over with, there were several more projects in various stages to focus on. This time he had needed to work off some steam, so he'd come home at a reasonable hour.

He opened the door, more than surprised to see Reba standing there.

"Hi." Her eyes travelled down the front of his soaked t-shirt and shorts. "Did I interrupt?"

"No. I was done. Come in." He stepped aside to let her pass. "I was just thinking about you, actually. Wondering if I overloaded you with cat memes."

"Well, the memes were a lot, but I saved them all." She flicked her orange nails at the ends of her hair that brushed her chin.

"Your hair's different, again."

"Oh, yeah. I took out the extensions. This is my actual

length. I need to touch up the pink, though; these roots are out of control."

As much as he was intrigued by this new look, he was more interested in why she had shown up. She sat on the couch, legs crossed, waiting for him to do the same.

"Can I take a quick shower, then we can talk about why you're here?" He didn't usually sit on his furniture when sweaty.

Reba took her time to slide her gaze down his chest, sucking in her bottom lip then releasing it. "As much as I'm enjoying the workout aftermath of that t-shirt clinging to your chest, do what you gotta do."

So flirty Reba was back. He couldn't tell if that was good or not. Whether she was using it as a diversion tactic or it was genuine.

You're trying not to overthink everything, remember?

He pulled himself away from that stare, taking the steps two at a time. His shower was quick. Tossing on another t-shirt and shorts after he towelled off, he forced himself not to create scenarios of how he thought this was going to go. He couldn't possibly guess what was going on in Reba's head.

She was taking a selfie when he came back downstairs. She looked up at him. "Do you want to take one with me?"

He sat next to her. "Is this some kind of test?"

"Maybe I'd just like to see how your face looks next to my face."

"I think that we already know we look good together. That was never in question."

"Okay, fine, maybe I did want to see how you'd react. You say you want to be with me?" She pointed to the photo on her phone. "This is who I am. I love selfies. Love social media. I love sharing parts of my life with people that follow me on there. Not every part, obviously, but you get my point. I'm a social person."

"Are you saying to be in a relationship with you, selfies are mandatory?"

"Of course not. I'm just pushing your buttons because it's fun." She reached into her bag and pulled out a familiar piece of paper. It looked wrinkled—like it had been folded and unfolded a few times. "What does this mean? Why did you give this to me?"

So she had read it. Explaining his thought process to others was never something he enjoyed. They either didn't get it or thought it was odd. "Sometimes I have to write things down to process the jumble of things I'm experiencing." *Emotions. They're called emotions, buddy.* "This is what came out in that moment."

"Beautiful chaos? Is that how you see me?"

"Yes."

"It's pretty. Kind of." She folded back the piece of paper. "I should have told you thank you immediately. It's better than how a lot of people see me."

"Their loss."

Reba took a deep breath, all playfulness vanishing as she put the paper back into her bag. "So, Cherisse offered me a manager role for the new Sweethand location that'll be opening next year."

"That's amazing." She didn't look as thrilled as he'd expected, her frown at odds with the good news. "It *is* amazing, isn't it?"

"Definitely. I just don't know if I want the promotion."

"Why wouldn't you?"

"I'm not qualified for that? I don't have a degree. My experience is hands-on and not manager level at all."

Devon frowned. Did she really think she wasn't worthy

of this role? "Other than Cherisse, I assume you're the person that knows everything about Sweethand. Don't you handle the social accounts? Plus, didn't you tell me you basically ran those executives' lives at your previous jobs? Why wouldn't that qualify you for a manager position?"

"I, well...when you say it like that. There're so many expectations that come with a title like that. What if I suck at it? I can't let Cherisse down. I should stick with what I know I excel at."

"A list would come in handy here." He grinned at the face she made. He was only partially joking. His lists might have backfired where relationships were concerned, but otherwise, they worked quite well in helping him parse out his thoughts. "A pros and cons list."

"I *can* try that, I suppose."

He leaned back. "See, we make a good team. Look at us learning from each other."

"Yeah, that." Her sober expression didn't change. If anything, it got more serious. "I need to think about that, too. You, me...us? It doesn't have to be awkward, these last baking sessions, while I figure some shit out. It's just to fine-tune the process. The baking process, I mean, not..." She gestured between them.

"I understood you, don't worry. Will you come to Dax's birthday party with me still, or is that asking too much?"

"The yacht thing?"

"Oh, he told you about that? But no, I meant the public event for everyone. The boat is private. I don't know that I can do either without you there. I'm not good at these things, as you saw."

"It's the perfect chance to practice without me."

"Ah, so that's a no, then? But you'll be there for the bake-off?"

"I can guarantee the contest appearance, yes."

"Okay."

Reba got to her feet. "I should go then."

"If you must."

He led her to the door. She paused before turning back to him. "I've never been wooed before," she said softly. "It's not so bad. I just...maybe I'll make a pros and cons list for you too."

"Well, it would serve me right, wouldn't it?"

That earned him a small smile. "See you this weekend." She planted a quick kiss on his cheek, looking shocked after as if she hadn't planned to do that. "Uh, yeah, sorry, you hate surprises."

He reached for her wrist and brought her hand up to press against his chest. "Feel that? I think I'm not doing so bad on those kinds of surprises."

She stepped back. "Okay, cool. I'm going now."

"Bye, Reba."

He watched her walk down the driveway and get into her car. He shook his head as he closed the door. The throbbing in his chest was really inconvenient, but what could he do? Love didn't really give a shit, and...*fuck*.

Had he just really thought that?

No, it was too soon for all of that, wasn't it? And yet, he had been ignoring all the signs. It had been so long since he'd had to even consider such an emotion. Clearly, he was rusty.

He rubbed at his chest. Where had he left his phone? Shit. He found it on the table, sent a quick message to Jeremey.

Devon: *I think I'm in trouble*
Jeremy: *What's going on?*

Devon: Did you know I was in love woth Reba?

Jeremy: a typo. Ok you are definitely in crisis.

Devon: with* fuck just tell me Jeremy!

Jeremy: um yes, it was sort of obvious to me. You just realised this?

Devon: YES

Jeremy: ok now we got caps. This shit is serious. Take a couple deep breaths. You said you wanted to be with her. How could you not connect the two?

Devon: I DON'T KNOW

Jeremy: bro you are seriously a mess of a person without me.

Devon: Yes I am. I won't ever take you for granted again. She doesn't know how she feels. What do I do?

Jeremy: give her time and DON'T try to control the situation cuz you can't. just get some rest. I need to go seduce wifey since te kiddies are asleep. Bowchickawowow

Devon: the*

Jeremy: correct my typos all you want. You're the hopeless fool falling in love so...good night!

Devon sat down hard on the couch. Of course, Jeremy was right. He couldn't force the situation in the direction he wanted. Reba needed time; he would accept that. He simply wouldn't think about what would happen if she did an analysis on him and found she didn't want him after all.

～

DEVON TRIED TO GO LIGHT ON THE WOOING FOR THE REST OF their sessions. He didn't want Reba to think he was going against her wishes, not giving her time to think, but he couldn't help how he acted. When he felt like this...*love love love love*...he couldn't help but show it with little actions.

He felt like his eyes were full of hearts when she started swaying to one of the songs he had on by a favourite singer, Etta James.

"I don't know who this is, but loving the vibe," Reba said, dancing with an imaginary partner while he poured the batter in the square pans. He was getting no help from Reba this time because it would be all on him on bake-off day.

He slid the pans in the oven, closing the oven door just in time to catch her hand to twirl her into him.

"Uh, hi?"

"Hi." She didn't pull out of his gentle hold and placed her hand on his shoulder, keeping the other clasped in his as they swayed.

"This is wooing," she accused even as she danced with him.

"Is it? Two bodies moving in sync does not wooing make."

"Don't try to logic at me right now."

"I'm not trying to sway you. Well, sway your mind. I'm not, I just love this song."

"Hmm."

"Wooing would be me doing this." He tightened his hold on her waist, drew her in closer. He watched as her lips parted ever so lightly.

"Yeah?" she breathed. "Then what?"

"Then this." He squeezed her waist before removing his hand to cup her chin, tilt her head up. "But it's not wooing so..."

"Right. Nothing to see here. You should sort out the ganache and fondant."

"Of course." He stepped away from her, shaking himself out of the spell he had fallen under. He hadn't meant to do that, but he definitely would have kissed her if she hadn't put a stop to it.

The next day wasn't any better. Reba giving him a pep talk about what to expect for next week. Making him binge-watch various baking shows to help him get into the mindset when all he could think about was how good she smelled. That damn vanilla scent and how much he wanted to beg her to come to this damn party he didn't want to go to.

Since it was their last session, he had organised dinner for them while they watched the shows. Reba had looked at him suspiciously, obviously thinking he was trying to pull a fast one like the dancing from the previous day.

He wasn't, not really. It was all just to thank her ahead of the competition next week.

"You cooked for me? You didn't have to do this. You paid me. That was thanks enough."

"I know. I can't help wanting to do things for someone I l—" He coughed. "Like and have come to care about."

Either Reba hadn't caught on to his almost giant mistake, or she was ignoring it.

"We should've gone out to celebrate or something. This feels too cozy, if you get what I mean."

He got it. It felt couple-y, which was exactly what he preferred, but he asked, "Do you want to go somewhere?"

"Have you ever been to a food rave?"

"I have no idea what that is."

"Great!" She jumped up. "It's this amazing thing that combines food and music. Just good vibes. You in?"

That sounded loud and crowded, yet he stood up. It could be another test, or she could genuinely just want him to go with her. She was thinking things through, yet she had asked him to come with her. So he said yes.

And found himself pressed up against her on a Sunday night as she jumped up and down to the live band that was belting out some rock song he didn't know. Reba was singing loudly, pure joy on her face. Devon swore his heart grew two more sizes. God, he was in big trouble here.

When the band finished their set, and he could hear again, he pulled her into a little corner. "Why did you ask me to come here...with you?"

Reba had swapped out her shorts for a miniskirt she had in her baddess bag and tied the front of her t-shirt, turning the casual attire into something a whole lot sexier. "I just wanted you to see this, you know? I'm sorry if I'm sending mixed signals."

"No, don't be sorry. This is something."

"You hate it."

"Not at all. It's a little loud, but I enjoy the concept. Really."

"Good! You're the first person I thought to share this with, if that means anything."

It meant everything to him, though he didn't say that part out loud. She might not have made up her mind, but her words were somewhat telling. Maybe they had that one thing in common. Truths didn't hit them right away; they snuck up on them.

He was a patient man. Even if the outcome didn't work in his favour, he could still wait. He took her outstretched hand and followed her back into the crowd.

CHAPTER TWENTY-NINE
REBA

THE DAY OF THE BAKE-OFF BROUGHT RAIN, AND REBA WAS CLOSE to using that as an excuse not to go. She should have been up and ready to head to the venue since it was all the way down Chaguaramas, but the weather made her want to stay under the covers.

If she was a little more honest with herself, it wasn't just the weather making her want to stay right where she was. She had been thinking. Had even made a list for the manager position just like Devon had suggested. She had been joking when she'd said she would do one for them, and yet the devil perched on her shoulder had her doing just that.

She had stuck the two lists in her notebook last night, which, come to think of it, didn't seem to be on her nightstand. She wasn't sure where she had left the book, actually. Even so, the one for her and Devon was burning a hole into her brain because the *con* side was far longer than the *pro,* but was she going to be a whole wimp and allow that to stop her? When had she ever run from anything that was deemed too risky?

Ugh, this was why she didn't do relationships. Too much work.

She rolled out of bed, grabbing her phone to check her messages.

Devon: *Will I see you there?*

Of course, her eyes would fall on that one first. He had been the last person she had talked to last night. She had coached him through the social interactions at Dax's party. It had been funny, and it had also given her some satisfaction that he had come to her for help. She could have gone to the party with him but hadn't wanted the added pressure from his boss, who apparently adored her.

Sometimes being this loveable was truly a curse.

She had felt a bit guilty after he had come with her to the food rave, but she hadn't lied. She had wanted him to open his eyes to things he might not consider fun otherwise. He had been stiff at first, gradually loosening up as the night wore on. Not too much, though. But she couldn't allow them to give in to that intensity that sizzled between them. Thinking did not include having sex.

As hard as it had been to say goodbye at the end of the rave, she had done it.

So now what? Why was she hesitating to get dressed and on the road? She had promised she would be there to cheer him on, so she really ought to get moving.

She got her ass in the shower, taking her time with her body scrubs even when she didn't have the luxury of all of that, given the time and the rain, but she would always show up looking her best.

Her mother eyed her as she came down dressed in

jeans, sneakers, and a t-shirt, her Sailor Moon hoodie thrown over her arm, her concession to the weather.

"Going somewhere?" her mother asked.

"Yeah."

"In this rain?"

"I promised someone."

"That someone your karaoke friend?"

"Yes, if you must know." Her mother kept looking at her as if she expected her to say more. "What?"

"I found your list."

Oh, shit. Dammit. Had she left her things downstairs? Wait, her mother had said *list*. Singular. Which one had she found?

"Oh?"

"Are you going to accept that manager offer?"

Her heart rate piped down a bit. "I don't know. Where did you find it?"

"It was on the ground by the couch. Looks like it fell out of your notebook. I don't know the details, but what's to think about here? Why wouldn't you take a managerial role?"

None of them got it. How could they? They never made an effort to understand her. To get that just because she enjoyed her current role didn't make her unambitious. What was so wrong being content with what she did? She hadn't decided to turn down the role yet, but the fact that her mother thought it should be a done deal was aggravating.

"Who doesn't want to advance in life?" her mother continued.

"Some people are born for those roles, and some are just not. They thrive in other ways."

"You don't even try, Reba. You're really fine just being an assistant for life?"

"If that's what I choose, then yes! I'm not ever going to be a carbon copy of Jinelle. Isn't one perfect daughter enough for you?"

Her mother folded her arms, a sure sign Reba would be stuck in this lecture forever. "That's not what we're trying to do. I want the best for all my children."

"And what if being a PA is the best for me? Why can't you just listen, for once?"

"Alright, fine. And what about Devon? You won't even give him a chance because of a list of cons you've built up? All of which aren't even really cons."

"Of course, you saw the other list, too." It was such an amateur move for her to leave that laying around. She had been more wrapped up in her thoughts than expected.

"He's a good catch. Why won't you give him a chance?"

"You! You're the reason I'm afraid to," she blurted out. "Because every time I think about it, I feel like I'm proving you all right. That I need to be with someone like him to fix me. So I can be seen as an actual person and not the colourful façade everyone thinks I've created. I do like him, maybe more than that. I do want to give him a chance, but every single moment I think about that, I hear your voice. Telling me that no one will really want me the way I am."

Her mother's eyes grew wide with shock. "Honey, I never meant to make you feel like that. I just thought I was helping you. This is a lot to take in."

"And this is why I'm a mess where relationships are concerned." She shook her head. "Why I can't even believe that he wants me just as I am. And he does. I had my doubts, but he's shown me. I don't need to be some watered-down image of myself because *you* think that would help me in life. Respectfully, screw all of that."

"Well, honestly, I..."

Reba held up her hand. "I don't have time for whatever guilt trip you're about to throw down. I love you all, but frankly, your parenting needs work. And I got places to be and a man to lock down."

Her phone rang. She turned her back as her mother continued trying to talk to her. She needed an umbrella to get out of here.

"Where are you?" Cherisse shouted in her ear as she answered the call.

"I'm on my way. How's it going?"

"Not great, actually. I think he's actually flustered, which is bizarre cuz it's Devon. He's never flustered."

"Oh, shit. Okay, I'm coming." She tossed on her hoodie, tucked her phone away into the pocket, and grabbed an umbrella from near the door.

"Reba," her mother said as she opened the door.

"I really don't have time."

"I know, but we'll talk when you get home?"

"Maybe." She dashed out, the grips on her sneakers making sure she wouldn't go skating on the wet driveway. She stuck her wireless headphones in and called Cherisse back.

"Play-by-play of what's happening?" she asked as she exited her area.

"He got this look on his face when he took the pans out. I don't know if the cakes fell or not. A bit hard to tell from this angle."

"Oh no, that's no bueno." The cakes were the base of the entire cube. If shit went south with that, things were already downhill. It didn't make sense that he'd have an issue there, though. "It's gonna take me an hour with this rain."

"The crew and I are holding it down until you get here, but I think he's gonna need a big Reba hug after this."

"Who's there?" Reba hadn't asked if everyone was going, but she assumed so.

"Ms. King, Maxi, Leah, Keiran, Jeremy, and me."

"He's not going to like bombing this in front of you all."

"Nope."

Reba didn't want to think she was the reason he had lost focus somewhere. It could just be a stroke of bad luck. But would he think so? Not that it would be fair of him to blame her, but she did feel bad for not being there at the start of it like she'd promised.

This wasn't the best way to start something, but she hoped he would understand.

CHAPTER THIRTY
DEVON

"Uh, it doesn't look so bad?"

The camera flash brought Devon out of his daze. He looked at Maxi, who didn't even look contrite. "Oops, sorry, didn't realise my flash was on. Just wanted to immortalise this. Even if it looks like a science project gone wrong."

"It's really not *that* bad," Keiran said again.

Devon appreciated the attempt, but there was no way to soften the blow. The cake really did look a mess. All his careful plans had gone down the drain the moment he realised Reba hadn't replied to his message or shown up. Even so, his lack of focus was all on him.

Dax had still come over and given him a hug after the results were announced. "It didn't go as planned, but the fact you participated and put real work in is noted. Trust me."

"Just wasn't my day. I'll show you a photo and video of what it was supposed to look like. I actually did succeed at it before today." Devon showed him the perfect cube, and Dax looked back at what he had actually made.

"Oh, damn. What went wrong?"

"I got in my own head. That's all."

"Is it edible?" Maxi asked.

He hadn't even cut into it when he'd seen how not-perfect the cube had turned out. "Knock yourself out if you want to find out."

"Not now, Evan!"

The voice rang out, and Devon looked up to see Reba running towards him, a baffled Evan behind her.

"He tried to make small talk with me," she huffed out. "As if I give a damn about him. I'm sorry...oh, wow." She looked down at the cake. "That is not great."

Devon couldn't help it. He laughed. There was nothing really funny about any of this, and yet he couldn't stop himself. Even in this situation, Reba could still make him smile.

"Oh dear, is he having a breakdown now?" some lady off to the side asked.

"He's fine. It's the best sound I've ever heard." Reba laid a hand on his arm. "Uh. You are okay, right?"

"Yes. You're here."

"I am." She took his hands in hers. "I'm *so* sorry I broke my promise. Forgive me."

"I lost."

She glanced at the cake again. "I figured as much."

"Evan won." The man had annoyingly been celebrating since. The fact that Reba had blown him off had given him immense pleasure.

"Meh. Evan's a jerk. You're way better-looking than him. I don't know what his relationship status is, but you definitely have a better-looking girlfriend, so."

Devon blinked at her. "What?"

She looked around at the others who were also staring, listening intently. "Let's talk."

She led him away from the main baking area. Or the disaster zone, as he was now going to dub the place.

"You called yourself my girlfriend," he said.

"Yeah, if you'll have me after I didn't even show up when you needed me. As you already know, I'm unpredictable. A lil' messy sometimes, but I will be a social buffer for you, and I'll tell Evan off if you want me to. In the nicest possible way, so he won't even notice he's being dissed."

"Are you sure?"

"No, I'm not sure. I have no real experience with this relationship thing, and yeah, I'm a red zone risk factor, baby. Maybe I should get a t-shirt made? I will definitely fuck up, probably, but I'm a risk-taker, remember? And maybe you're learning to take some calculated risks too?"

He pushed her hoodie off her head. "That has to be the worst speech ever."

"But you are into it and me, right?"

"Yes."

"So, can you kiss me now? Because it's been a while."

He ducked his head and took her mouth. It had felt like forever indeed.

"Devon, just one favour."

"Hmm?" he murmured against her lips.

"Please don't tell anyone you hired me for baking lessons because that cake is a monstrosity for real. I don't want people linking me to that."

He huffed out a laugh, and she grinned back. "Okay, deal."

Reba tugged on his t-shirt. "Now, let's leave so I can give you some cheer-up sex."

"Let's. I feel really down at the moment."

"Good Lord, I've created a monster."

EPILOGUE

THE MOONLIGHT FROM THE YACHT WAS MORE BEAUTIFUL THAN anything Devon had ever seen. Actually, that wasn't true. While the silvery light on the dark water was a sight, Reba standing at the railing looking out was more breathtaking.

They had slipped away from the main party to get some alone time, as well as to give Devon a reprieve from Dax's invitees. His level of people skills was reaching its limit. He didn't know how Reba did it.

Even after experiencing her in her element, he couldn't fathom why she enjoyed this, especially now that it was obvious they were a couple. Dax's guests couldn't stop asking invasive questions about how they met and how long they'd been together. One noisy woman had even brought up engagement talk, which, after only two weeks of officially being something, was absolutely not on the table.

He fiddled with the piece of paper in his hand, figuring it was now or never.

"Here." He handed her the letter.

"Another one?"

"I told you I can be spontaneous in my own way. Just read it."

"Oh my God. Another romantic letter? Why are you so sweet?"

Devon looked around. There were maybe three other people roaming around, not paying them any mind. "Can we use our inside voices, please?"

Reba grinned, looking beyond pleased. God, she was stunning with the moonlight washing her in its glow. He had never stood a chance of resisting her.

"You know I don't have one of those. This is the cutest shit ever. Don't think I'll get used to this."

"I swear if you keep making a big deal about it, I'll throw it into the sea."

Reba clutched the letter to her chest. "Uh-uh, no way. Not before I read it. But I *do* have a little bone to pick with you before I read this." She pouted. "You let me miss your birthday, mister."

He wondered who had spilled the beans to Reba. He'd gotten the usual messages from his family and co-workers, but it had been just another workday for him. "Uh, I'm not big on birthdays. So I didn't say anything."

"But I would've wanted to celebrate you properly. I give the best birthday lap dances." Reba grinned.

Devon could picture it so clearly. "Maybe a late birthday gift wouldn't be so bad."

Reba winked. "Can be arranged. Now, let's get back to this, shall we?" She unfolded the paper, eyes moving quickly over the words.

He had agonised over this one as he had the first and the others that followed, not wanting to create a pattern but purposefully choosing moments she wouldn't expect it. He knew she appreciated it more then. He might not be able to say the words out loud yet, but he hoped the short letter was enough.

"The first time I saw you, I knew you'd be a problem for me," she read. "I didn't quite know just how much. I resisted every step along the way but...you're a force. There was no way I wasn't going to fall under your spell. I will try my best to convince you every day that I want all that you are. Even when we're driving each other to possible murder. Just always remember that you are and will always be my beautiful chaos."

She looked up at him, smile wide. "This is the corniest thing I've ever read, and I love it."

"Really?"

"Oh, yeah. Did I tell you I'm getting a t-shirt made with 'beautiful chaos' on it too? I love that. Like I told you, no one's ever described me like that before." She stepped up to him. "I know you don't really do PDA, but would it be okay if I kissed you now?"

They were off in their little corner of the yacht. "Yes."

She wrapped her arms around his neck. "I might be okay with this romantic shit after all."

"Don't expect declarations on a yacht all the time."

Reba pouted. "Fine. Kiss me, Superman."

And he did, long and slow and sweet. Reba, of course, turned it into something hotter.

"Did I mention I'm not wearing anything under this dress?"

"God, you'll be the ruin of me," he groaned.

"Oh yeah, that's my goal, really."

"We're stuck on here until we return to land," Devon pointed out. Now was the worst time for her to do this.

Reba waggled her brows. "Have you ever had sex on a boat?"

"No."

Her smile grew wider. "Well, stick with me, kid. I'll open you up to a whole new world."

Her words were a buzz over his skin, making him both scared and aroused. He took her hand and kissed her knuckles.

"Baby steps, please. Don't kill me this soon into our relationship."

She pouted. "Fine. Suffer while you think about my bare ass under this dress."

He gripped the railing but couldn't help the smile. Oh yeah, he was in for a wild ride.

BONUS

Keep reading to check out some of Devon's favourite
things...lists! 😊

Devon's (old) Criteria for the Perfect Partner

- Ambitious
- Does not enjoy/create drama
- Loyalty
- Knows where they want to be in 5 to 10 years
- Honesty
- Integrity
- Level of maturity suitable for an adult
- Not messy – figuratively and literally
- Ready for commitment
- Wants children

Devon's Criteria for the Perfect Partner (revised by Reba "the sexiest woman I, Devon King, have ever met" Johnson)

- Pink hair (or whatever colour I choose on a given day)
- Rainbow wardrobe
- Loud (inside voice does not exist???)
- Spontaneity babyyy!!
- Opinionated
- Loves glitter
- Fun-shine spirit!
- Plans?? Lists?? I don't know her
- Bess baker
- Cute tattoo and piercings. He literally can't stop looking at it / tracing it with his fingers / playing with my navel ring?? Bro my eyes are up here!!!
- Children? YES. The world needs an army of cute mini me's. Well, maybe just two. 😊

Reba's Pros & Cons List – Subject: Devon King
Cons

- Doesn't know the meaning of the word fun
- Too many lists!
- Needs to be more spontaneous
- Needs to let go more. You couldn't control a thing?? Ok, but did you die???
- So grumpy...which...kinda cute, I guess, but smiling? Doesn't seem to know how?
- A bit old-fashioned
- Too much work, not enough play

Pros

- Hopeless romantic / Wooing skills are good, it's cute

- Sweet but pretends he isn't. You can't fool me tho!
- Takes care of me
- Top level pipe-laying skills / Good kisser. 😊
- Likes and respects me for me.
- So sexy?? Like in sweatpants. It's too much I just wanna...*signal lost*

ACKNOWLEDGMENTS

These acknowledgement were supposed to start very differently. But in the midst of getting ready to edit this book again, last year, I lost my mom. Unexpected, and most days I'm still in a state of disbelief. She read my first book and enjoyed it. I never thought she would because she didn't really read fiction. I was actually nervous for her to read (because I mean the sex scenes??? LOL) but she loved it! So I worked towards making this the best book it could be, with her in mind.

I don't want this to get too sad so I also truly have to thank BTS for getting me through some rough times in 2021, including my mom's passing, and inspiring a specific scene in the book that involves glittery handcuffs. If you know, you know lol! Their music and content have really been a source of joy since the end of 2020.

To Jen, you are always THE BEST cheerleader and supporter. I appreciate you so much. If you didn't know that before I hope you do now.

To Silvana (thebookvoyagers as most may know her on Twitter) thank you for always being a bright spot in this community and for your support of me and my books. I am so so grateful to you and I hope Romancelandia knows how lucky they are to have you!

To my agent, Lauren, thank you as always for choosing to work with me. I still remember screaming when I got that email how many years ago hehe. Looking forward to cranking out more books together!

Shout out to Leni Kauffman for again doing the damn thing with this cover! Your talent is out of this world, no exaggeration. Like, do you see Reba's hair on the cover??? DAMN

Kai, you always make the editing experience so fun. Your comments need to be framed I swear! 😊

Look out for more fun with the Island Bites crew 😉

N. ♥

Do you love contemporary romance?

Want the chance to hear news about your favourite authors (and the chance to win free books)?

Kristen Ashley
Ashley Herring Blake
Meg Cabot
Olivia Dade
Rosie Danan
J. Daniels
Farah Heron
Talia Hibbert
Sarah Hogle
Helena Hunting
Abby Jimenez
Elle Kennedy
Christina Lauren
Alisha Rai
Sally Thorne
Lacie Waldon
Denise Williams
Meryl Wilsner
Samantha Young

Then visit the Piatkus website
www.yourswithlove.co.uk

And follow us on Facebook and Instagram
www.facebook.com/yourswithlovex | @yourswithlovex

PIATKUS